P——— for
Cry———

"Suzannah's happy ending is a we——————————————tional fiction will appreciate. ————————————————————*Weekly*

"Twists and dances like a bouncing bronco, but beneath the humor beats a strong foundation of heart."

—Jacquelyn Mitchard, *New York Times* bestselling author of *The Midnight Twins*

"*Crybaby Ranch* follows the up-and-down and all-around adventures of a brave woman who's willing to ask questions we've all asked ourselves. The writing is vivid and will hold you through to the end—bringing home fresh answers to old questions about strength and weakness."

—Clyde Edgerton, author of *The Bible Salesman*

"A more winning heroine than Suzannah...would be hard to imagine. From page one, we are in love with this wry, insightful, funny survivor of the Sandwich Generation, squeezed between her mother's Alzheimer's and her husband's detachment. In reflections both luminous and humorous, she charts her way to love and independence." —Sarah Bird, author of *How Perfect Is That*

"Women and men are suddenly revealed in *Crybaby Ranch*, an illuminating arc-of-life writing that unfolds in a rich detail of simple and complex feelings."

—Craig Johnson, author of *The Cold Dish* and *Death Without Company*

"Like a cliff diver, Tina Welling's fiction flies, tucks, and slices into the dark depths of her characters. She writes with insight, humor, and complete control. If they ever make compassion an Olympic sport, Tina will have a room full of gold." —Tim Sandlin, author of *Jimi Hendrix Turns Eighty*

Also by Tina Welling
Crybaby Ranch

TINA WELLING

NAL
ACCENT

NAL Accent
Published by New American Library, a division of
Penguin Group (USA) Inc., 375 Hudson Street,
New York, New York 10014, USA
Penguin Group (Canada), 90 Eglinton Avenue East, Suite 700, Toronto,
Ontario M4P 2Y3, Canada (a division of Pearson Penguin Canada Inc.)
Penguin Books Ltd., 80 Strand, London WC2R 0RL, England
Penguin Ireland, 25 St. Stephen's Green, Dublin 2,
Ireland (a division of Penguin Books Ltd.)
Penguin Group (Australia), 250 Camberwell Road, Camberwell, Victoria 3124,
Australia (a division of Pearson Australia Group Pty. Ltd.)
Penguin Books India Pvt. Ltd., 11 Community Centre, Panchsheel Park,
New Delhi - 110 017, India
Penguin Group (NZ), 67 Apollo Drive, Rosedale, North Shore 0632,
New Zealand (a division of Pearson New Zealand Ltd.)
Penguin Books (South Africa) (Pty.) Ltd., 24 Sturdee Avenue,
Rosebank, Johannesburg 2196, South Africa

Penguin Books Ltd., Registered Offices:
80 Strand, London WC2R 0RL, England

First published by NAL Accent, an imprint of New American Library,
a division of Penguin Group (USA) Inc.

First Printing, March 2009
10   9   8   7   6   5   4   3   2   1

 REGISTERED TRADEMARK—MARCA REGISTRADA

LIBRARY OF CONGRESS CATALOGING-IN-PUBLICATION DATA:

Welling, Tina.
Fairy tale blues/Tina Welling.
p. cm.
ISBN 978-0-451-22594-8
1. Married women—Fiction. 2. Marriage—Fiction. 3. Self-actualization (Psychology)—
Fiction. 4. Domestic fiction. I. Title.
PS3623.E4677F35 2009
813'.6—dc22   2008044959

Set in Adobe Garamond
Designed by Alissa Amell

Printed in the United States of America

For John Buhler,
who gave me the best line in this book.
And now I give it back to him.

Acknowledgments

It adds a special pleasure to the creative process for a writer to have readers in mind as they work. I had very special readers in mind when I wrote this novel: my sister and brother and their mates. Both in-laws and outlaws take openhearted pleasure in my work. It's only fair that they take something, because I take so much from them: their stories, funny lines, and unique perspectives and experiences. Thank you, Gayle Caston, Tom Welling, Debbie Welling and Bob Caston.

My sons and daughters-in-law contributed to this project, and I am grateful to them: Trevor Buhler, Amy Buhler, Toby Buhler, Amber Buhler.

I feel profoundly privileged to have John Travis as my teacher. Going on meditation retreats in Jackson Hole and in India with him has enhanced my life with meaning and joy. The fictional retreat leader in the novel is a mere shadow of him.

Ellen Edwards is a perceptive editor with a strong sense of ethics, a clear vision of story and mastery over language. I feel immensely fortunate to work with her. Thank you, Ellen.

My husband, John Buhler, offers support in every way from his heartfelt happiness over my pleasure in the writing life to creating delicious ragouts and pasta sauces for our dinners together. And always he is my first reader.

My gratitude goes to Susan Marsh and Patti Sherlock, two exceptional writers, who offered steady support as readers of my manuscript—a considerable gift. Gratitude also to my agent, Charlotte Sheedy, for her expertise over the years. Through the professional assistance of Rebecca Vinter and Meredith Kaffel, my writing life is smoothed and eased. Susan Wasson, Judy Johnson, Eric Boss and Judy Boss, thank you once again for your generous spirits.

For financial support my thanks goes to Pursue Balance, a nonprofit organization in Jackson Hole, Wyoming, that offers Growth Grants to individuals who are pursuing personal or environmental balance through adventure, study, the arts. I also offer thanks to the Wyoming Arts Council for personal support and statewide support of writers.

An enormous part of my pleasure in this work is the weaving of chance remarks, stories or shared events that find their way into my creative process. In this project I thank Coulter Buhler, Libby Vallee, MacKenzie Caston and Elaine Mansfield. Inspiration and support for my subject came from two books in particular: *Medea's Folly* by Tanya Wilkinson (PageMill Press, 1998) and *The Light Inside the Dark* by John Tarrant (HarperCollins, 1998).

One

Annie

It seemed longer than just twelve hours ago that I walked out on my husband during our anniversary dinner. This morning after a shower, I smoothed lotion supplied by the hotel over my body, nose to toes. Not that my skin needed it in the humid warmth of Florida like it did back home in the dry cold of Wyoming, but this old habit grounded me. And besides the clothes I had been wearing, old habits were all I'd brought along.

We were celebrating at the Granary, a restaurant high atop Gros Ventre Butte, the lights of Jackson Hole glittering below. Surely Jess had caught on by now that I wasn't returning, yet I still pictured him sitting where I'd left him, watching champagne bubbles spiral up his glass.

Before Jess left for work yesterday morning, I had sneaked a gift bag filled with his favorite chocolate-covered raisins into his backpack with a mushy card and the time and place of our dinner reservation. Last night, once we had ordered our champagne at the Granary, Jess slid a package across the table to me. I recognized the gift wrapping from the goldsmith's on the town square. I read his note written on the back of our store's business card.

I love you for a hundred raisins.

I dissolved into a teary laugh at his silly note, and a surge of love for Jess flooded my heart. My fingers tugged on the ribbon to loosen the bow. I paused and looked into his eyes, aware of the difficulty I'd been experiencing with him lately. Yet aware, too, that we had shared a deep and resilient love during our twenty-six years together. Though Jess' note exposed the fact that he had likely shopped for his gift after being prompted by my gift to him that morning, I instantly forgave him.

I read the note again, out loud this time. "I love you for a hundred raisins."

My voice softened into a whisper near the end. I reached across the table with both hands and looped the ribbon around my husband's shoulders. "I love you, too," I said.

He held one of my hands and grinned at how touched I was by his card. When Jess directed his attention my way, he knew just how to reach me, and he could always make me laugh. For the past two and a half years, though, his attention had often felt tucked away, unavailable to me. To be fair, since our sons, Cam and Saddler, had left for college, I may have expected more in the way of intimacy from Jess than I had before the house became ours alone. Perhaps starting tonight things would improve. Inside of me, a party balloon floated with hope.

"Go ahead, open it up," Jess said, releasing my hand and leaning forward to watch.

I unwrapped the package. Inside glimmered blue topaz ear studs. Topaz was my birthstone and blue my favorite color.

I looked up, eyebrows lifted, my smile still in place, assuming he was teasing me. Jess smiled back at me, looking open and at ease.

"To match your beautiful eyes, AnnieLaurie," he said. They were the same words he had said last Valentine's Day when he presented me with this exact gift. A pair of topaz ear studs, same starry blue. Which at that moment I was wearing. In fact, hadn't removed since he'd given them to me eleven months before.

It all came rushing in. How Jess lived in perpetual unawareness, like a second grader who came to school wide-eyed that he was late, wearing unmatched socks, having forgotten his lunch. Jess walked through his life and our marriage with this same benign look of happy innocence. Yet until now I had never been conscious of this as a source of our trouble. Or felt quite so angry.

I could barely breathe. I felt as if a geyser churned in my chest, and at any moment it would explode noisily into scalding tears.

"I'm going to the restroom," I said when I could speak. I grabbed my purse and the satiny gift box. I passed the waiter bringing our bottle of champagne down the wide staircase from the lounge above. The Granary was built on the side of the butte, full of windows full of Tetons, though on this January evening I only saw myself reflected in the window glass, long rippling velvet skirt and silky shirt, standing at the banister.

Some women say they could live through anything but the loss of a child. But, for me, just as unbearable would be the loss of my mate. I stood on the steps, watching my husband follow the beads of champagne as they spilled into the glasses. I was forty-six years old, married to Jess for more than half my life. And I felt then as if I had lost him just as surely as if he hadn't shown up for our anniversary dinner at all.

Jess didn't look toward the staircase, though by then the waiter was glancing my way, as were a few other diners, so I continued up the steps. In the coatroom I wrapped my handwoven scarf around my neck, removed my coat from the hanger, found my fringed leather gloves and stepped out into the whipping snow to the car.

The switchbacks down the butte were iced and treacherous, and I gripped the steering wheel and negotiated the steep, curving road in four-wheel drive. This road always made me uneasy, but this January night my thoughts scared me more. I was heading for the airport.

I caught a shuttle to Denver, then another flight to Orlando, rented a car and headed straight for the Atlantic Ocean, a place where I'd always found comfort. I arrived a couple hours before dawn. Now wrapped in a hotel towel, I stood before the sliding-glass doors that led to a balcony overlooking the beach, undecided about what to do next. I barely noticed my lack of sleep; instead, I felt stunned by a sense of loss. I realized that I had been working hard on a marriage in which my partner worked very little. Resentment, built from years of keeping this fact from myself, finally toppled like a many-storied building, burying me beneath it. For two hours I had been tossing and turning in a hotel bed far from home, as if trying to wriggle out from under the rubble.

Now I realized it would take more than a few sleepless nights to tidy up this mess. Yet I didn't have any notion of what it would take. All I knew was that once my marriage had been a romance full of laughter, sweetness and spirit, and that Jess and I had met every tough time with the determination to work it out, while couples around us broke apart, switched partners, sued each other for custody of kids, cutting horses and golden retrievers.

I checked the clock beside the bed—seven a.m.—and subtracted two hours for Mountain Time. I should phone Jess, report my whereabouts.

I didn't look forward to the call. Jess' first response would be to construct a story to excuse his actions; his second would be to diminish the issue. This time, I'd refuse to get entangled in his defenses. For once—despite how unreasonable it was to flee three thousand miles without notice—I had taken action and not just talked about my trouble while following Jess around the house, trying to hold his attention.

As I hovered near the phone, I pictured Jess' expression when I opened the earrings and I realized the guy was so intent on shedding responsibility that he turned innocence into a vice. He wore it like a mask, peering at the world through a pair of blue eyes as clear and faultless as those topaz stones he had given me.

See? Already distance on my marriage was offering insight.

Two

Jess

I will never forget looking up the staircase at the Granary in time to glimpse the vanishing hem of AnnieLaurie's black velvet skirt. Why the hell was she going to the restroom? That girl had a bladder the size of a rain barrel. Her mother had taught her to never use the public restrooms at school, and so she had trained herself at age five to wait all day until she got home to use her own bathroom. Something else rang off-key that night. A kind of déjà vu floated around while I watched her open the box holding the earrings.

After she went upstairs, I sat there and sat there until our waiter approached and said, "Sir." I looked at him with a kind of wariness. As if he were going to tell me something more upsetting than that the chef was out of food for the night. Something about Annie. But what could go wrong in a ladies' restroom, I encouraged myself, besides falling into the toilet?

"Sir, would you like to order now, since the lady has left?"

"The lady left? What lady?" I asked stupidly.

The waiter gestured to AnnieLaurie's glass of champagne, tiredly sending up a bubble now and then.

"What do you mean she left?"

"She took her coat . . . and drove away." The guy looked miserable. "They told me upstairs."

"In my car? Our car?"

"A Tahoe."

I knew it. During that long wait I had stared out the window, my mind deliberately blank. I mean, my brain had removed its own batteries. Now I spoke to the waiter in a voice I'd use asking a doctor, *It's cancer, isn't it?* I said, "Black and red?"

"Yes, sir."

I yanked the ribbon Annie had placed around my shoulders, wadded it up and tossed it across the table beside the torn wrapping paper from the gift I'd given her.

As it turned out Davy, who worked in our store years ago, now managed the bar upstairs. He offered to drive me home in half an hour. While I waited, I finished the bottle of champagne. Figured I'd go home and face the music with a bit of a buzz. I pictured Annie sitting on the sofa with her well-ordered grievance laid like a snare, waiting for me to place one word in the noose. It'd be a full hour before I could get Annie giggling over the problem and carry her off to bed.

While Davy drove and described his day of skiing—"I'm not kidding, Jess, powder to the armpits."—I worked up a good anger about the wasted ninety-five-dollar bottle of champagne. Somewhere in the back of my mind, Annie's probable response bubbled to the surface: That the money wasn't as wasted as I was. Hell, I'd be better off apologizing right away, I decided. But all the while I knew this night was not usual. Neither of us was the dramatic type. We didn't slam doors or yell or throw pots of oatmeal at the walls. And we never just up and left the other guy.

Davy dropped me off in the driveway. My heart beat so fast I detoxed on the doorstep. Sober as the sun, I opened the door and found an empty house.

When Annie didn't turn up by midnight, I called my friend Judge Eddy and urged him to discreetly ask questions at the police station about any road accidents, avalanches, a woman hurt.

I finished throwing up the champagne about three in the morning. At five she phoned.

Three

Annie

He picked up the phone on the first ring. "Jess," I said.

"AnnieLaurie. God, are you okay? Where are you?"

"Florida."

"Florida." He said it like a foreign word, as if trying to wring meaning out of incomprehensible sounds. He even pronounced it *Flor-da,* leaving out a syllable.

I didn't know how to explain myself, so I jumped in with the obvious. "I'm going to spend the day here."

"The day?"

"Well, maybe longer. You know, take some time."

"No, I don't know. What the hell are you doing?"

I had no idea what I was doing. Leaving like this was the most impulsive act of my life. Then the perfect answer came to me. Last year, at the store, we'd hired a professor from an East Coast university who was taking the winter off in Jackson Hole to rest and do research.

I said, "I'm taking a sabbatical."

"A teaching sabbatical?" Jess sounded completely puzzled.

"A marriage sabbatical."

"Shit, what does that mean?"

"A semester or two off. You know . . . some time."

"Annie, why?" Anger crept into his voice; he sounded defensive already. "What the hell? Didn't you like the earrings?"

Jess thought he was making a joke. "Nice as the ones you gave me last Valentine's Day."

Silence.

"Really? Oh. Annie, gee," he said boyishly. I heard him sigh; then he gathered momentum. "But look, it's not like I got my girlfriends mixed up. I got my earrings mixed up. We can solve this. You don't just walk out on me in a restaurant while I wait and wait and the champagne goes flat and people stare."

How embarrassing. I hadn't thought of that. Then I came to myself. This was often how our arguments turned. I slipped easily out of my own feelings and sank deeply into his.

"Well, AnnieLaurie?"

I held my silence.

"Please come home, Annie. We'll talk."

My favorite thing—talk—and he knew it. However, it really meant: I talked, and Jess sat with his jaw muscles clenched, his eyes staring into the distance.

The image settled something for me. I could not take that look one more time without doing something a lot more drastic than going on a temporary leave of absence. If I didn't deal with the feelings I'd been experiencing in my marriage now, my miseries would continue to mount.

"I'm not coming home. Maybe in a few months." Suddenly I felt as though there was much catching up to do, as if I had missed a lot of classes and needed to hand in makeup work. I had been accusing Jess of not dealing with our problems, but now I suspected that was true of me. I had pushed my dissatisfactions aside while doing my work and Jess' at the store, wearing myself down to ensure that I would be too tired to do anything more than numb out each evening on the sofa, too weary even to fight for control of the TV remote.

I would take a sabbatical, rest and do research.

"No more talk, Jess."

"Look, I'll fly down. We'll work this out. I love you. I'm sorry about the earrings. I just . . . forgot."

"You didn't forget, Jess. I've worn those earrings for almost a year. Every day, all day. You don't look at me anymore."

"Oh, now it's that I don't *look* at you. Usually it's that I don't listen to you. What next, Annie, I don't *smell* you?"

"I need a rest from being your wife, Jess. Don't come down; give me the time I need. Maybe a few months will do it. I'll be fine. My family is close."

"A few months is too long. Besides, even your sister, Daisy, would notice your presence among her piles of crap after that long and wonder why you're still around."

"I'm not at Daisy's." Leave it to Jess to get smart-alecky when he lost the reins. "I'm in a hotel. I'll let you know when I want to see you. And I will want to, Jess." My voice had begun to shake. I hung up.

I looked around the hotel room, then sat on the edge of the bed on bunched up sheets, where I'd tried to rest those couple hours before dawn. I opened my mouth to inhale a big breath, and a wail rose from my chest that sounded so alien I nearly checked behind me to find the source. A sob wrenched my body, doubling me in half. I curled onto the bed and muffled my face in the pillow. I bawled loud and hoarse, sounding like a bison calf lost in the sage-brush. I bawled until my throat ached and my stomach muscles were sore from the heaving.

I sat up and reached for tissues on the bedside table. Blew my nose and saw that the early-morning sky was brightening. The rosy carpet almost matched the line of clouds lifting the sun into place. Crying made me more miserable, as if the baptism of tears gave confirmation to my sorrow. Even so, I lay down on the bed again and let the pillow absorb more whimpers.

I must have dozed off a bit. When I opened my eyes, my palms immediately pressed against my chest, and I wondered what awful injury I'd sustained. Undigested grief, as if a bonfire, smoldered there. More like a "bonefire," as it was called centuries back, a fire of bones burned inside me.

I got up from the bed, blew my nose again, tightened my towel across my chest, walked outside and sat on the end of a chaise longue, which barely fit on the small balcony. I pressed my face between the twisted wrought-iron posts of the railing like a toddler peering through crib bars. My skin felt numb; my thoughts refused to follow my eyes' gaze outward. I tried to appreciate the softness of the morning air, the lulling expanse of rocking water.

My good spirits had always burbled naturally like a spring out of the ground, for no good reason other than the pleasure of its own flow. In Wyoming ranchers ran their trucks over and over such spontaneous springs to flatten them out. That was how I felt now, flattened out. I wanted to blame Jess, but I was the one who had laid myself out on that path. My mantra for our years together: if Jess and the boys are happy, then so am I. I waited for a hint of what any of them wanted, then worked to get it for them. Jess wanted a happy marriage, healthy kids, a successful ski shop, a comfortable home, friends over for candlelit dinners. I wanted those things, too, and we loved each other. That should make for a good lifetime partnership, shouldn't it?

Yet I had allowed him to float behind me, his hand weighing down my shoulder as I pumped upstream, swimming toward those goals we had both agreed on—that happy marriage, those healthy kids, the successful ski shop, the comfortable home, the friends. I felt mad that he had allowed me to do all the work, and resented his passive innocence when I complained and he responded that no one asked me to do it all.

"So take a day off, Annie. I'll cover the store."

I took him up on that once and Jess slept in the following morning, hadn't even set his alarm clock after making his noble offer.

But what was the use of recalling all these bits and pieces? It was the big picture I needed. A process involving time and distance.

Four

Jess

What did she want from me? I didn't know what she wanted.

She wanted too much, for one thing. Talk, talk, talk. Second sentence and my eyes began to drift about the room, my mind followed, and next I was leafing through an L. L. Bean catalog. And AnnieLaurie was furious.

"You don't listen to me."

Well, no.

Once, she was predictable. I didn't need to listen. Once, she just needed to vent anger or rant out a decision. I'd know she was finished when she'd say, "Oh, that's what I'll do." I could even get away with saying, "What will you do?" and, I'm not kidding, she never accused me of not listening, even though I'd followed the whole plot of a *Hill Street Blues* rerun. She just welcomed the chance to repeat it.

Now, if I didn't listen to her the first time—pounce.

As if any human could change an old habit overnight.

In a way, AnnieLaurie changed overnight.

One morning about five years ago, I woke up first, leaned on my elbow and watched her sleep. Slowly her eyelids lifted and she caught me. She recognized right away it wasn't a sexual invitation.

She said, "What?"

I said, "I don't know who you are anymore."

She said, "You're right; you don't."

Well, I didn't want to talk about it. I got up and showered.

Five

Annie

Still wrapped in a towel, sitting on the cramped balcony, I realized I had no appropriate clothing to wear in order to leave this place. Heavy velvet skirt and cowboy boots might startle people in the tropics. Before solving that problem, I wanted to get the hard phone calls over.

First, my dad. My sons, both cranking up for their spring semesters at the University of Wyoming, could wait until I felt steadier; they weren't likely to hear anything from Jess. If either of them phoned home, Jess would downplay my leaving or fail to mention it at all. Later he'd reach into his grab bag for a story about his omission—he forgot, misunderstood, intended to do it later. Jess didn't like being connected to bad news. I was reminded again that I had been in this marriage alone much of the time, and the thought raised fresh tears.

I tamped my grief, left the balcony and dialed Dad's number.

"Hi, Daddy."

"Annie L, hi. What's up, sweetheart?" Never one to talk on the phone, he was probably watching the morning news on TV and anxious to get back to it. I worried for a moment about alarming Dad with my own news, but not much alarmed my father. He had kept himself at arm's length from emotions—his or anyone else's—since Mom's illness and death four years ago, and prior to that, he had let Mom do the emotions for both of them. So I stated the facts: I had left Jess and was now in Florida, just up the coast a hundred miles.

"Left Jess where?"

"In Wyoming."

Dad took a moment before answering; I felt him gathering his thoughts or pulling himself away from the TV. "Well, honey, there's always somebody worse off than you. They found a Cuban gal all alone on a raft bumping off the edge of Bathtub Reef last night."

I began to cry. "Is she all right?"

"She'll live."

"That poor woman." I hiccuped on a jagged draw of breath. "She made that whole long trip all by herself." I sniffed. "She probably had to leave everything she loved . . . her home, her friends, her . . . " I couldn't finish. I was struck by the sudden realization that I'd also left my dogs.

"Well, Judas Priest, I was just telling you. Don't get so damn sloppy over things."

After promising I would feel better soon, I hung up the phone and sought out tissues in the bathroom. I had emptied the bedside box, and I now plucked the final wad from the bathroom box and would soon be resorting to toilet paper.

Before calling my sister, Daisy, I donned my long velvet skirt and, hoping to be the first and only customer, slipped down the back stairs to the hotel lobby shop. There I quickly grabbed a pair of pale linen Bermuda shorts size ten, the matching jacket, two tank tops from a shelf of tropical bird colors, all embroidered "left chest," as we called it in the resort business, with HIBISCUS ON THE BEACH, and a pair of flimsy sandals with a striped cloth thong. Toothbrush, toothpaste, deodorant. No underwear in sight, and I wasn't going to ask the woman who had flipped the CLOSED sign to OPEN, then set out the morning newspapers and was now filling her register drawer with money from a bank bag. I'd washed out my panties last night but they hadn't completely dried in this humid air; the waistband was a damp ring around my hips.

The saleswoman pinned on her name tag, CARA. She smiled at me, then glanced briefly at my long velvet skirt, then pretended that she hadn't and smiled even more kindly, which was generous of her. Either that or I didn't strike her as attractive enough to be someone's overnight date or hotel call girl. Or if I was, my pinkish eyes suggested it hadn't been a good experience for me.

"See the great blue heron on the beach? Been out there for about an hour now." She gestured toward the opened glass doors, toward the same beach I had been staring at since six a.m. Never saw a thing. But I saw the heron now. The light shimmered off her blue-gray feathers as she picked her dainty way into the shallow waves. The saleswoman, perhaps in her midsixties, with eyes that suggested she'd lived through some difficult nights herself, tallied up my purchases and said, "She's fishing for breakfast."

"She's beautiful." I had flown to the ocean last night as an injured child to its mother, then refused her balm these past few hours. All at once my ears opened to the sound of waves and my nose received the salty scent of the beach. I felt anxious to get out of these wintery clothes and feel the soft air on my skin.

I dipped into my evening bag for a credit card, noting the inappropriate glitter of the purse's black beads in the morning sunshine. Wouldn't take an FBI agent to guess I was on the lam for one reason or another. I lifted my eyes in dismay to the gentle lady behind the cash register.

"How about a tote to match those sandals?" she asked.

"I'll look like a tourist."

She said, "That would be good, wouldn't it?"

Making progress. I now wore shorts and sandals, had ordered room-service breakfast, blotches on my face had spread from a concentration around my eyes to a fade across my cheeks. So I looked less like a sobbing woman whose lover had left some money on the hotel dresser with wishes for a nice life and more like a tourist who had sat in the sun too long. This process could reverse when I called Daisy.

I loved my sister. Right along with Jess and our sons, Cam and Saddler, came Daisy. Do not take these people away from me— except for this temporary respite from Jess, please. Prayers over, I dialed.

"Daisy."

"I already heard," she said. "I'll come get you. Dad called but didn't know where you were, the idiot."

I stalled. Said I needed to hang out a couple days in the hotel; then I would drive right down. Said I could hardly wait to see her. Which was true, though I knew I could not afford to fall completely apart right now, which I feared I would do once I felt her arms around me. It was as if I struggled to keep from drowning in a steep-sided cauldron, rapidly filling with tears. Better swim around in it first, until I grew strong enough to pull myself over its edge and out into the world. Then I could use Daisy's solid good spirits, her relaxed, unconcerned approach to life, to motherhood, business, marriage and, God knows, housekeeping.

She excused herself to speak to her daughters. "I don't need to boil water for your instant oatmeal right now. Just turn the faucet on and let me talk to Aunt Annie."

"They're barely four and they're fixing their own breakfast?"

"They're as particular as their father. He won't even *try* instant oatmeal. The twins want me to make theirs with *boiling* water."

"But that's what the directions say."

"Oh, that's where they got the idea. Haven't started school yet, but the little squirts are reading everything. Drives me nuts."

When ventilating the woes of our marriages, Daisy and I talked in general terms, as if we shouldn't betray our mates by discussing them in a personal way. We said things like "When a husband talks to me in an irritable voice in public, I think the disrespect is tripled," as if we each married a harem of husbands and didn't wish to actually identify which one of them was guilty of misbehavior.

So Daisy said now, "This guy you left just went one step too far, didn't he?"

"He did. Of course, what he thinks right now is that I am taking it one step too far."

Daisy excused herself again to speak to her daughters. "You two shouldn't eat breakfast wearing Sunday-school gloves. Oh well, never mind." She said quietly to me, "You should see this. Libby lost one of her 'glubs,' as she calls them, and has substituted a white sock on one hand."

I surprised myself with the sound of laughter. It felt good.

Six

Jess

To latch on to a little thing like a duplicate gift, Annie had to be *looking* for an excuse to get on a plane out of here. Maybe she didn't need me anymore. Our sons were grown-up; she could run a business on her own and had claimed often that that was what she was doing anyway. She might stay in Florida, take over one of her dad's stores down there, not come back.

For three days now my head had spun around these thoughts until I couldn't stand my own company anymore. I shoved my feet into Sorel Pacs, grabbed a heavy jacket, gloves, pulled a wool knit hat onto my head and traipsed through snow on our unshoveled walkway to the street, our three dogs romping behind me. Supposedly this was my day off; at least our store manager, Hadley, convinced me to stay home. But rattling around the house by myself was worse than being pestered by customers all day long. I headed for the bike path that trailed Flat Creek. The day was gray with heavy, snow-filled clouds that kept the temperature from dropping too low, which by Jackson Hole standards meant below zero. Still, who wouldn't want to be in Florida instead of Wyoming in early January? Not the valley's best time.

The dogs and I walked to the end of the street, climbed over a five-foot snowbank the plows had created and stepped onto the pathway, groomed on one side for cross-country skiers, groomed on the other for walkers and skate skiers. Before leaving the house, I'd stashed a few tennis balls in my pockets for the dogs to chase and dig out of snowdrifts. I pulled the balls out of my pocket and gave them each a long throw.

I didn't know why I'd bought those stupid earrings a second time. Just wandering around the goldsmith's, and one of the saleswomen suggested something with a birthstone, and next thing I knew she had wrapped the package and I was off to snowshoe 25-Short on a nice winter day, duty done.

That was no way to buy Annie a special gift, and I should have just said right away on the phone that I was sorry. Really sorry and please come home. But I argued with her first. I don't know why I did that. Too damn mad, for one thing.

Nothing felt right with her gone. Like it wasn't real, but a play I was acting in, saying my lines without meaning. Even my body felt removed, as if I was wearing metal armor a couple sizes too big, and I didn't know how to work it. If I bruised myself rounding the corner of my desk at the store once more I was taking an ax to it. Meals were lonesome and sleep felt rowdy with pointless dreams.

I didn't know how to start my days or end them. The middle was easy. I wandered around the store, taking care of customers on autopilot. Anything more complex than matching a pair of skis to the proper bindings, I shoved off onto Hadley. She took care of the employees and their endless problems, smiled at the customers when I failed to, pointed me to the office and closed the door behind me when I stood comatose before the cash register, trying to recall what to do with the money in my hand.

Three dogs with tennis balls in their mouths, icy with frozen saliva and snow, pranced at my knees ready for another toss. One by one I let the balls drop into my open palm and gave them hearty throws. Then walked on. The creek was piled with frozen blocks of ice, great shelves reached out from both shores, and now, standing on the pathway bridge, I saw icy blades grow upward from the creek floor, appearing like stalagmites.

The trouble started back when our older son, Saddler, left for college two and a half years ago, and intensified a year later when his brother followed him. It threw me back to my own college years and felt almost as if that was the last time I'd had a chance to look up and direct my life. I had to stop and think what choices I'd made since then. Marrying Annie was the best one. After that, I don't remember making any choices; one thing just triggered another—business, house, kids. But I loved my life, every damn thing about it, except that I had meant to get ahead on my design ideas. No, the trouble started earlier, five years back when Annie began to veer off, doing stuff on her own. I had always worried about what that would lead to, and now I guess I knew.

I kept looking for some distraction from this loneliness. Memories worked like drugs; while I was under the influence of them, I was happy, but once they passed I felt worse, hungover, heart heavy. Still, they beckoned to me all day long.

Shortly after that morning in bed when I told AnnieLaurie that I didn't know who she was anymore, the whole family went down to Florida. AnnieLaurie, me, the boys. End of ski season, which coincided with our sons' spring break from high school, so we closed the store and took off. Instead of staying at Daisy's litter box or their folks' page out of *House Beautiful,* I rented a place of our own out on Hutchinson Island. We spent the days just lying on the sand, except for Annie, who kept her cell phone in her beach bag and confirmed store orders for the summer season coming up.

The boys and I played ball, swam out far enough to scare Annie, lost interest in that and lay around reading. Cam, our younger son, was into odd stuff, New-Aging it up with some book about astral projections and auras—had us concentrating on clouds to make them disappear. They disappeared, too. Somehow. But it was boring work, and once Cam wandered off with Saddler, I picked up his book, fanned the pages and spotted the name Anwar Sadat. Started reading. Turned out this author claimed Sadat was a "walk-in." A what? I had to read backward to discover this meant advanced spirits who have moved into the bodies of people already on earth. You recognized them by sudden, inexplicable changes in personality. Of course, you had to rule out schizophrenia first.

Some mean guy, Anwar Sadat, until one day he woke up on the dirty floor of an Egyptian prison . . . and became a peacemaker.

I checked on AnnieLaurie. She was talking to Ouray Sports about our summer tees and sweats, making decisions right and left, not looking at me for a clue to what she should buy. When did this happen? Once she couldn't decide between white and off-white without covering the mouthpiece on the phone and begging me to choose.

Maybe AnnieLaurie was a walk-in.

I sat up, dangled the book between my sunburned knees and looked out over the ocean. The sun was still low enough to backlight the larger waves; I saw fish swimming in the swells. So many things were different about her lately. She used to be uneasy alone. Now she loved her solitude. Once we did everything together; she wanted that, even though sometimes I just dragged along behind her, like when we were attending buying shows for the store.

When did she begin taking little trips alone? Yellowstone for four days this past winter, stayed in the Snow Lodge, skied around Old Faithful, ate all her meals by herself, even candlelit dinners.

I was sure she was alone. Annie was the kind of woman who confessed erotic dreams. She would never sneak behind my back.

That settled it then, I joked to myself—she was a walk-in.

I volunteered to jog toward Stuart Beach to pick up our halibut submarines and bring them back for lunch. Time to think.

Stuck some money in my pocket and went down close to the surf on the hard sand and jogged up toward the lighthouse at the House of Refuge. Used to be Annie would bounce off some idea for a trip, and when I'd squelch it, she dropped it. Now it was almost as if she hoped to go alone and asked just to be polite. And all this time I thought I had control of when and where we traveled. That was my job: planned trips, got reservations, laid maps all over the countertops at the store and asked our customers for advice. When we arrived someplace strange, I knew where to go for the best food and wine, the most interesting sights and the best museums and shopping.

Last fall I said to her, "I told the Quinns we'd go to Santa Fe for a long weekend next month."

This kind of tactic used to start a tirade about how I never tell her stuff. But she shrugged off one of my biggest crimes: making promises to other people on her behalf without checking in with her. All she said was, "First I heard of that. Maybe another time." What the hell was happening if I couldn't make her angry anymore?

Making her angry was my leverage. She got so wrapped up in trying to get me to understand how serious my transgression was that we never got around to actually addressing the transgression itself. In fact, it never seemed to occur to her that she could refuse doing whatever I'd set up. Once, that woman could not say no—period.

Now she could say no to me, and she could say no to the Quinns. Old friends, the Quinns. Annie and Gina were especially tight. I stopped to pick up a piece of beach glass, green, probably once an old Coke bottle. Since recycling I rarely found beach glass. Now I just found globs of oil from tanker spills. I put the glass in my pocket and took off at a trot; I'd make it a present to Annie.

Annie and I always talked about how hard it was to find a couple with both a man and a woman we liked. Usually one of them was a jerk; usually it was the man. But the Quinns were both great. They weren't mad about the Santa Fe deal falling through. We had enough history together to help us forgive one another most anything rough that came up.

I was thinking especially about the year Gina and Jim gave us a puppy for Christmas; then Jim ran over it backing out of the drive-way that same evening. Annie and I didn't know which to hold a grudge over: surprising us with a puppy we didn't want or killing it right when we started to warm up to the little tyke. So we just said, *Hell, let's forget the whole deal.*

That Santa Fe trip never happened. Neither did the expected tirade. And Annie didn't seem one bit worried about what the Quinns thought. She never asked a thing about it. Like that was a problem I'd created and I could fix. She had drawn some line in the sandbox, clear only to her, that defined her territory from mine, where once there was only *our* territory.

When I got to Stuart Beach, I ordered the halibut subs at the snack hut, then waited for them at a picnic table on the deck. Squirrels popped in and out of the garbage cans, gathering French fries and bread crusts. I watched, fascinated by their tiny, adept paws as they sat eating on top of the picnic table next to me. And while I watched, one of the little stinkers squatted and peed right on the table. As Jim Quinn would say, Note to self: never eat on the snack hut picnic tables. I removed my elbows from the tabletop. The cook called my number. I picked up the family's lunch and started back down the beach.

Anyway, thinking about it, I saw that held the first clues that if Annie was a walk-in, some advanced being from out of this world, I could be in trouble.

Then again, I thought, I could be in worse trouble if Annie wasn't a walk-in. She might just lose patience one of these days and . . . be a walk-out.

But I hadn't really believed that at the time.

Seven

Annie

*Y*esterday I found an apartment above a retired couple's garage only four and a half blocks from the beach. Pretty fast work, considering that was my third day in Hibiscus. Spent the first day benumbed on the hotel balcony, the next one walking the beach and on the third day I found this place and wired the bank for rent money. That action was the result of deciding a few things. One, that I was definitely going to carry through on my plan to take a sabbatical from my marriage. Two, that I wanted to settle here in Hibiscus, near my family but not with them. And three, that I needed to set myself up here before driving down to see Daisy.

This morning I hit the flea market and secondhand stores to furnish my new place. I planned to pack it with stuff, just stuff, as if having things to organize and dust would root me here. A place to be, with things to do. Already, piles of old, chipped pots and vases, splintery birdhouses and amateur paintings of bougainvillea and sea grape on gesso board lined the edges of the bare floors and covered the kitchen counters.

I was lowering an incomplete set of blue-and-white dishes into sudsy dishwater when I heard voices at the bottom of my outside staircase. I didn't know the neighborhood sounds yet and all morning kept running to my windows to check out why my landlord's puppy barked or which passing neighbor called a greeting to some other neighbor gardening. These particular voices were climbing right up my steps.

I toweled my hands dry as I walked out to my screened porch.

My landlord, Shank, nodded a greeting to me. "Here she is," he called over his shoulder. He set a suitcase down on the landing.

From the yard below his wife, Lucille, urged someone up the steps.

The top of a head appeared first, covered by a Teague Family Sports cap. The only clue I needed.

"Daddy."

"Hi, sweetheart."

I tucked the paper towel in my pocket and unlatched the screen door. "What are you doing here?"

"Thanks," he called to Shank, who was on his way back down the stairs. Dad turned to me. "Should I have tipped that colored fellow?"

"Of course not. He owns the place." Leave it to my father to assume anyone dark-skinned doing him a favor was a bellhop. I stepped to the railing and waved to Lucille down below, while checking to be sure Shank had not been in earshot of my father's remark. Then I hugged Dad.

"I'm surprised to see you." Dad felt firm in my arms, still muscular and lean at seventy-five. He had always loved athletics, been good at almost all sports throughout his life, but these days he kept mostly to golf.

"You didn't sound so good on the phone. Thought I'd come up for the weekend."

I'd phoned to give him my new address. This time Dad had related a newspaper article about a man arrested for having three wives. "I know I cried again, but, Dad, you tell the most depressing stories."

"You cried pretty darn hard. You think Jess has some extra wives?"

"Of course not. Is that why you're here?"

"No, no. I came to help you find some furniture."

"I just felt sorry for that man's wives." It choked me up again to think of the three of them, each blaming herself for her husband's lack of attention—which was what I had done for the past few years—while all along the husband was committing polygamy. Sometime back, while waiting in the dentist's office, I checked out a woman's magazine quiz titled "Is He Having an Affair?" Though I knew Jess was faithful and always had been, he flunked the test, exhibiting all the symptoms of detachment from the relationship.

I reached my arms around my father again. "Oh, Dad, it's wonderful of you to come like this." I got a bit teary, but held myself in.

Dad thumped me on the back, as if trying to dislodge something caught in my throat. His kind of affection you needed all your strength to endure. The few times I fell sick as a child, I had to brace myself to receive his sympathy. Thump, thump. "You know your mother and I love you," he would say.

Bruised shoulder blades will forever stir my emotions.

Dad pointed. "Looky there, you can see a bit of ocean. See that sparkle between the rooftops?"

"I know. I'm looking forward to seeing the sunrise over there." I'd just moved out of the hotel today, and even though I didn't have a bed yet, I planned to spend the night camping on the floor. That may have to change now; camping was not one of Dad's activities; he only considered it a sport if it involved pursuing a ball, which Daisy had told him years ago was a Labrador retriever's perspective and not a good approach to business.

I lifted Dad's suitcase to carry it into the screened porch. Bottles clinked. I paused at the sound, wondering if he'd become a secret drinker. Since Mom's death, Dad seemed at a loss about how to conduct life on his own.

"Careful, careful." He reached urgently to grab his leather bag from me. "You better give me that."

"What's in there?"

Dad unzipped a side pocket, and three cobalt bottles of Milk of Magnesia tipped out.

"Three? For just a weekend?"

"That's because I knew you'd be knocking them around in there. This way at least one bottle might survive."

"Are you sick?" Then I remembered. My dad was overly involved with his regularity, his own and any pet's of his. Once we had a black standard poodle named Clem, who had learned to squat if he wanted praise or attention from my dad. I hoped to avoid an intestinal update, so directed Dad into my new apartment and told him, "I don't have any beds yet."

"You said on the phone that there are two bedrooms; getting beds in them is the easy part." He stuck the bottles in three different pockets of his pants, lifted the suitcase himself and followed me into the apartment.

"Where the hell did all this junk come from? It's not that colored gal's, is it?" My father held tight to his suitcase, waiting for my answer.

"It's my stuff." I wanted to reprimand both his use of "colored" and "gal" in referring to a black woman easily as mature in years as he was, but Dad didn't take censure well.

"Thought you up and left without a stick." He set his suitcase beside the door and picked up a Mexican pot, its once gaudy colors now faded.

"I found some garage sales and a flea market. Florida is full of secondhand stuff."

"That's because everybody dies in Florida." He set the pot back down and started for the sink to wash his hands. "Stick around long, you'll start dying like the rest of us." He dried his hands on a paper towel I handed him. "This isn't too hygienic, you know, bringing in stuff from a bunch of dead people. We got homosexuals down here. They die and infect things."

"Dad, gay men don't infect things, even if they do have AIDS." I advised myself to back off. My dad had been known to stop speaking to people for similar retorts. Even family. As teenagers Daisy and I got the silent treatment for offering opinions absorbed from the world beyond his realm. I needed my father just now. I picked up his suitcase and carried it to the smaller bedroom behind the kitchen, as if I could secure his company by holding hostage to his belongings. "I know you're just worried about me, Dad."

"Actually, I'm more worried about myself. Getting old, you know. I could pick up something from all this garbage that'd hurry things along."

"Wouldn't want that," I said under my breath, suddenly quite annoyed with him while at the same time relieved not to be alone for a while.

Dad followed me into the bedroom.

"By golly, this looks nice." He peeked out the window. "I'll be comfortable here."

The room was bare as a blown egg. Perhaps he was also advising himself to back off, also relieved not to be alone for a while.

I said, "We'll have to get mattresses delivered today and pick up some pillows and sheets."

"Let's go shopping then, but none of that used junk. Can't stand to breathe inside those musty places. With your K-Marts and your Targets you don't need to pay more than five bucks for anything brand-new these days. Lamps, pots and pans—all five dollars."

Mom had played hell keeping Dad out of those places. He had often brought home large plastic bags filled with his bargains from discount stores, bragging how little he'd paid. I was probably heading for the same situation.

You looked forward to seeing your parents when you'd been separated a while. Thought you had so much to tell them and share about your life. Then, about twelve minutes into the reunion, you remembered how damn irritating they were and why you moved away in the first place.

Back in the kitchen, Dad screwed up his face. "You don't know what you're getting into, honey, buying other people's problems. Let me take care of furnishing this place." He rinsed his hands again. "Once at K-Mart I got your mother a beautiful chair for her dressing table. The back of it, see, was wire, bent kind of heartlike." His wet hands described the shape in the air as I gathered my tote bag and keys. "And sparkly, like gold. Then this heart-shaped cushion on it. Pink, I think it was. You know what she did?"

I handed him another paper towel. "Jump with joy?"

"Made me take it back. Said it was a cheap piece of crap."

He finished the story as we headed down the outside stairs. I held the side-yard gate open for Dad while blocking Shank and Lucille's puppy with my foot to prevent her escape.

"She said it wouldn't last a year."

"Well, this will be perfect then." I bent over the fence from the sidewalk side and rubbed the puppy's ears, missing my own dogs. "I won't be needing this furniture as long as a year."

Even though Mom had died, I still got a spark of pleasure from taking Dad's side against her—the daughterly "I can be a better wife to Daddy than Mommy can" routine. Daisy and I laughed about this now, but right after Mom died we carried a lot of guilt over our behavior. We also learned quickly what a pill Dad really was and wished we'd sympathized more with Mom.

First, Dad and I looked for a store to buy mattresses and bed frames. While he drove Dad talked about how much he always liked this little beach town and how he wished Hibiscus were big enough to warrant opening an extension of the business. Teague Family Sports started in Cincinnati. He sold that store, moved to Florida and opened a store in Miami, then moved up the coast with the population growth to a second store in Fort Lauderdale, a third in West Palm Beach and a fourth in Stuart, where he and

Daisy and her family lived now. The fifth store was added when Jess and I moved to Jackson Hole.

"You saying you'll go back to Jess before your furniture wears out?"

"I just need to deal with some things, find some rules."

"Rules?"

"I mean . . . rules. Like how to be close without being trampled."

"You make Jess sound like a Brahma bull. He's a damn nice guy."

"That's part of the problem." True, but I shouldn't confuse Dad with trying to tackle that right now. I was too confused myself. How could I feel this miserable over such a nice guy? Like the gift of blue topaz ear studs, many of Jess' actions held both stars and nettles. While I nursed the sting of the nettles, Jess expected me to glow over the stars. I was invariably the troublemaker for pointing out the problem, while he steadfastly showcased the gift. "Hey, don't I get any credit at all for getting you a present?" he'd asked before I ended my call to him the morning I had arrived here.

I sighed. "I love him, Dad. Jess loves me. I just have to learn how I can live with him happily." Dad craned his neck to read store names on both sides of the street. I stared straight ahead out the windshield. Day four of my marriage sabbatical, and I felt less sad and more angry, which seemed to empower me to relax into my decision to spend the next few months on my own. I'd had a great time this morning shopping for household items. Unless sharing a college dorm room with Gina counted, I had never lived on my own. And though I chose Hibiscus by default—the beach town closest to the airport—it was a sweet place, and I was beginning to like it. I sat quietly, assessing this rising sense of excitement about my new life.

Dad said, "Well, I don't know why everybody thinks marriage has to be happy all the time. People get on each other's nerves, and that's just a fact."

This was Dad's way of feeling out the problem. Trouble was his antennae tuned in only two channels—extreme or inconsequential. Which meant that I often experienced trouble discussing things with him. From his perspective either I left Jess because he was a polygamist or I was being too sensitive and should shape up and ship back home. No middle ground. Maybe all Dad wanted to hear was that a happy ending was coming up.

"We'll work this out," I assured him. Not exactly the truth. *I'll* work it out. Jess would *wait* it out.

I said, "Just need a few simple rules. Then I'll go home."

A few? I'd settle for one good rule, anything to firm up the shores of this container called marriage. Any rule that allowed an adult human to live with a love partner while maintaining a sense of self. Because that was my problem.

About five years ago restlessness with my marriage stirred up the realization that I hadn't intended to work full-time at our store or to center my social life around family. Somehow I had ignored my own interests to the point that I no longer knew what they were. The boys were in high school with lives of their own, and the store was firmly on track and thriving. Resentment toward Jess cooked as he filled his days entertaining customers and sales reps on the ski slopes and hiking trails, defending his actions as his contribution to our business partnership. I tried to discover who that person was who lay smoldering beneath the daily demands that were doubled by his absence. I bought a journal. When I looked back, that seemed my first act of insurrection, because the examination of my life through writing led to changes that started out small, but had now ended with me in Florida buying a new bed.

Immediately upon my purchasing the journal, the sad realization had arisen that I had nothing to write in it. Somewhere along the way I had become estranged from myself. For the prior two decades if my thoughts and emotions hadn't complied with the company line, I disengaged my energy from them. I had only so much energy after all, being a mother and managing the store. Jess helped, both at home and with the business, but saw himself as my assistant, not my partner. And he did have energy left over. He hiked, fished, skied, met his buddies for beer at the pub, messed around with his designs in his garage.

Almost as if I were mothering myself, I began to tend to my life. I started with my body, eating only when hungry, instead of looking at my watch or appointment calendar to see if I had time for lunch. I stopped answering my cell phone during bathroom breaks, which used to end with me hurrying to get back to my desk. I reported in my journal how my body felt and what I noticed about my surroundings through my senses: smells, tastes, sounds, textures. Soon personal feelings nudged into my consciousness, rising timidly at first, like a beaver noses out of water, body submerged, beady eyes darting around for predators.

I wrote those feelings down. I began to value the time I spent with my journal, and that prompted me to suggest a new schedule to Jess in which he opened up the store in the mornings and I closed it in the evenings, giving me an hour or two before my busy day began to be with myself, writing in my journal or walking alone with my dogs. That moved into enjoying my own company on long day hikes and drives into the national parks that surround Jackson Hole. On the first occasion that Jess put down my suggestion for a weekend outing, I dared myself to go alone. I drove through Yellowstone up to Paradise Valley, Montana, to Chico, a famous old hotel, with hot springs and a four-star restaurant. Once I moved past a sense of estrangement over being alone, I opened into a sense of pure liberation. Instead of watching the faces of Jess or the boys to see if the outing was a success or figure out how I could make it so, I experienced the full sensual awareness of being me on the earth, hiking in the mountains, swimming in the hot springs and dining alone with fabulous food and wine, while eavesdropping on a conversation between movie actor Dennis Quaid and writer Thomas McGuane, both of whom I knew lived nearby.

Without those little trips I could never have gotten on that plane and flown to Florida for a marriage sabbatical. Never.

Still, in order to return home, I needed rules.

"Did you and Mom have any rules?"

"I didn't. Maybe your mom did." Dad smirked my way.

I was supposed to laugh. Ha, ha, men will be men. That was true at my house. Jess went about his life. I mopped up after him. Made the return phone calls, met his promises to others, wiped up his spilled coffee, apologized when he was late . . .

Must work on the bitterness.

Before leaving Wyoming I was often filled with such overpowering rancor that it burned holes in my chest, probably fried my cells.

What I wanted to figure out while on my marriage sabbatical was how to let Jess live his life without letting it inhibit my own. But there I went, putting Jess first, me second—my life as a by-product of his. Let me start again: what I wanted was to figure out how I could live my life, allowing Jess to live his life, with both of us enjoying that . . . and each other.

Big order.

I could wear out several sets of cheap furniture solving that puzzle.

At a stoplight Dad glanced over, lifted his eyes pointedly to the top of my head in his old way of acknowledging that I wasn't wearing a store cap and reached into his backseat. "What color?"

"That's okay; I don't need a cap." I sounded like I did as a teenager, balking at advertising the family business on my head—a must in our household. I noticed a comfort in my regressive behavior.

"One of our new citrus colors." With his eyes on the light and one hand on the steering wheel, Dad rummaged blindly with the other hand in a box behind my seat.

I felt at home sitting beside my dad as he drove his big creamy Eldorado. For three days I had ached with strangeness here in my self-imposed new life.

"Here you go." He sailed a tangerine-colored hat onto my lap. "I sent a box load of these to Jess before I left this morning, just so he'd know I wasn't taking sides between you two."

I stuffed the cap into my tote and thought, Citrus-colored caps in a ski resort—that would go over big in January. But I didn't say anything. I tried to picture Jess at the store without me there. Selling ski goggles and powder cords, neck gaiters and polar fleece vests. Listening to people come in the door and remark on Cat Crap, the goggle lens defogger we sold, which some people bought just for the name. Jess and I often mimicked our customers as a form of relief from the repetition of doing business in a resort town where most of our customers were brand-new to the area, often from densely populated cities in the East, often so overstimulated by the vastness of the land, the enormity of mountains and the variety of the wildlife that upon arrival they were too overwhelmed to find their way out of the store. Jess and I stood in front of the postcard rack, as tall as I was, and said, "Do you have any postcards?" We stood in front of the local candy we sold and said, "Huckleberry bonbons. Hmm. What's a huckleberry?" We heard these remarks dozens of times a week. "Where is the hole in Jackson Hole?" Pointing to a plush toy moose: "This elk is so cute, I just have to buy it."

Dad broke into my thoughts. "That's quite a pup your neighbors got." He scanned around the radio. "Didn't we used to own one of them wild-haired terriers when you were a kid?"

"Not wild-haired. *Wire-haired.* Yep. Smokey. Shank and Lucille's puppy is a mix though. Part Lhasa apso, part unknown. They said there was one more left in the litter. I should get it; I could use the company when you leave."

"Sending me off already?"

"I just feel much better with you here, so I'm thinking ahead."

"And thinking I can just as easily be replaced with a mutt," he said, finding his station at last. He looked happy. Dad thrived on having a mission. Today's mission was setting me up with furniture.

He began to hum along with Peter Gabriel singing "Biko." I smiled, knowing Dad didn't realize who Biko was, and that if he did know he was an African freedom fighter, he'd probably change the channel. I decided to keep the information to myself for now.

"Cats are better," Dad interrupted his humming. "They keep the rats out of the palmettos. Or bring them in," he added with a chuckle. "When we first moved down here, we had some bankers for dinner. Hoped to get a good loan for our first store. You probably don't remember this, but our cat Auggie dragged a big rat in the house through his cat door. The rat got loose, and Auggie chased that thing around our guests' feet. What a night. Never got that loan." Dad slowed for another stoplight and turned up the radio to join in along with the final chorus, " 'Biko. Biko-oo-oo-oooo, Biko.' "

My parents had sold the Cincinnati store as soon as I graduated from high school and left for college. They moved to Miami to open a ski shop. Right—I always had to repeat to friends—ski shop, Miami. Then I'd have to explain how my father had learned Miami had the largest ski club in the United States, but nowhere to buy gear for their trips. Now Teague Family Sports sold everything from skis to snorkels.

"I tell you," my dad summed up when the song was over, "you think you've come to paradise, flying down here to Florida, but you've just come to a bunch of rats and dying people." He wheeled into a U-turn, then pulled into the parking lot of Beds & More.

Dad loved Florida. He was just contrary. Sometimes when he talked, he canceled out much of what he said in the first half of his sentence with the last half. Also he was negative. My mother used to call him the "crepe hanger," said he'd missed his calling and his century, that hanging the black crepe over the windows and mirrors when someone died could have been his perfect career.

I said, "Florida is great; you're just lonesome. You need to meet someone." I got out of the car and waited for Dad to lock up. The Eldorado locked automatically, but Dad never trusted it and walked around the car testing all four doors each time. "The last few days I've seen women your age walking the beach that look wonderful with their bare feet and tanned legs."

"Were they short? Guatemalans, probably."

Eight

Jess

"Morning, Jess." Hadley turned to hang her jacket on a peg beside the office door. She glanced over her shoulder to me while stuffing her gloves in the pockets. "You look better today. Hear from Annie?" Of us all, Hadley dressed the best. While I often worked in my ski bibs, ready to shoot out the door for a couple runs, and Annie traipsed around in her socks, Hadley wore nice wool skirts, dress boots, sweaters and often a matching jacket or vest. Not even Jackson Hole bankers dressed that well. And the employee pool in this valley was a mess by city standards. Though every one of the kids was clean with shiny hair, that hair was rarely combed and they all looked like they'd slept on somebody's sofa in their clothes the night before. Which was probably true and the reason we had showers installed in our employee restrooms. The cost of living in this valley was exorbitant. Kids—again by Jackson Hole standards that meant anywhere from teens through late thirties—often lived out of a duffel bag and slept where they could. They worked only to spend money on ski gear and season passes.

"She phoned last night." I grinned and stapled a packing slip to its matching invoice, slit open another envelope and unfolded the bill. "Her dad, Skip, is visiting her."

Hadley, a bit older than me, maybe fifty-three or so, had worked with Annie and me almost since the beginning over twenty years ago. She knew the whole family, was witness to our marriage, watched the boys grow up, had met our visiting relatives. She kept her personal life to herself pretty much, but Annie and I, working here together with our boys around all the time, couldn't have hidden much even if we'd wanted to.

She said, "How is Skip?"

"I give AnnieLaurie two and a half weeks, three on the outside, before the guy drives her right over the Mississippi and back into my arms. Which is to say: the Skipper hasn't changed one bit."

Hadley laughed. Some of that laughter I imagined was relief to see me in a good mood for a change.

My father-in-law was a great guy; he had a good heart despite his mouth, but don't make me spend two days in a row with him or even sit me next to him at dinner. Down the table some, I thought he was witty and smart, and when he picked up the tab for the whole family—our group and Daisy's—I thought he was damn generous.

But up close, if his foot wasn't in his mouth, it was bobbing enough to make the silverware jingle. His brain moved faster than anybody else's tongue, so he was way ahead of whoever had the conversational ball and invariably clipped off their story with a one-liner that made even the target of his joke—and there was always a target—laugh hard.

Though he was funny as hell sometimes, I just ended up feeling invisible after a while. I found I wanted to run out the restaurant door and jump into the Indian River in hopes that a shark had wandered through the Intercoastal Waterway and desperately needed sustenance just then.

"Things are nuts out there this morning," Hadley said. "When it quiets down, I'm popping over to the Ski Corps offices and see if they have some job applicants they can spare. We need more help." When she saw my face, she added, "Temporarily." It was one thing to have Annie gone today; it was another to plan for her to be gone tomorrow. And the day after that.

Hadley left the office, shutting the door behind her. I stopped going through the mail and stared at Annie's desk. While I hoped the Skipper got on her nerves real quick, I liked that he had driven up to Hibiscus to visit her. She was crazy about him. Daisy, too. He was the big family patriarch right down the line. And I wondered sometimes how I had gotten into this line. But I loved the Skipper's daughter. I flipped through the recent packing slips and matched another to its invoice. The unpaid bill pile was growing.

The family's sports-gear business had grabbed me unexpectedly hard, too, just as it had the Skipper. "Hard by the nuts," as he said. The aspect of business as play or play as business lured me in. AnnieLaurie could take it or leave it—same with Daisy and her husband. So I was the only guy the Skipper knew who got the big bang out of Teague Family Sports that he did. Hell, he never relented trying to get me to change my name to Teague.

"McFall, McFall. What kind of name is that, Jess? Sounds defeatist. McFall, McFailure. Hell, Jess, I'd change the name of the store in a heartbeat if you just had a decent name."

Ha. He wouldn't change the name if a heartbeat depended on it.

I didn't care about that—just let me go to the store every day and have it be my job to test our new ski line in the snow during the winter and our new hiking gear on the trails during the summer. Most of our return customers were people I'd made friends with over the years. I was good with the customer end. Annie stayed here in the office; she was good with the business end. She often suggested that TFS, which was the shortened name we used for the Jackson Hole store, didn't need a social director as much as it needed someone who made the orders, kept up with inventory, dealt with the help and on and on—don't get her started. She liked to dismiss the importance of customer relations as well as my work with sales reps and preferred to think that we'd get our discounts whether I took them out heli-skiing or not. I didn't know how she thought I'd get to my work now that she had taken off and left the whole damn shebang for me to deal with.

The phone began ringing, two lines at once, and I figured I'd better grab them since Hadley said we were especially busy out front and short-handed to boot. Besides my having to pay the invoices, which was Annie's job, new catalogs were piling up unread, which was my job. I would page through them, circle the gear we should order, the T-shirt and cap designs; then Annie ordered the appropriate amounts of them. Give me a latte, my desk by the window loaded with a stack of catalogs and I'd call it a good morning's work. Then lunch, gear up and guide a rep or old customer down a ski trail and I'd call it a good afternoon's work. Now loaded down with Annie's stuff, who knew when I'd get to my own?

I wrangled phone calls for the next hour, intermittently slashing open mail, then got the bright idea of shifting the unpaid invoices cluttering my desk onto Hadley's desk. Since she was hiring someone for the floor out front, she'd have a little more time for office duty. Because enough was enough. I took a break, kicked back on my desk chair and watched the early-morning skiers tack downhill outside my window. The day was a dazzle of crisp light, blue sky with icy cloud shavings. It had snowed four inches overnight, but early this morning temperatures had spiraled down into the single digits below zero, too cold to snow.

I wouldn't get to mess around in the garage with my inventions, either. When Annie up and left, I was working on a kind of fleece ski hat—earflaps, visor—all with a goggle lens attached. This deal would revolutionize the industry.

My garage and our cars had no carnal knowledge of each other. From the beginning the space was mine alone to fool around in. I insulated it, heated it and put in a raised floor and good windows. I had an old treadle sewing machine in there and bolts of fleece, which were mostly in scraps on the floor right now. It was a two-car garage, so I could spread out. I had projects started all over the place. And none finished, Annie liked to point out when she came across a bill from Malden Mills for more fleece. But I planned to move in a big way on this hat-goggle deal. This one was going to travel the distance.

I watched a snowboarder careen downhill at top speed, wobble on a curve. I sat up straight, then leaped to my feet. The tumble was a fierce one, on and on downhill. I was afraid he'd never stop. And when he did, I was afraid he'd never live through the beating he'd gotten. I was too far away to help, of course, but my hand was already dialing ski patrol. I reached them, put in the report; and while I watched, they were on it. Patrollers zoomed over from the next slope in a snowmobile, a stretcher dragging behind it. I saw the boarder gesturing with his arms to the patrollers before they loaded him. A reassuring sign. I sat back in my chair and watched the rescue.

Annie said it was the solitude and creativity that counted with my time in the garage. Or she would say Creativity. Capital C. Lately, this seemed to be Annie's thing—the importance of creative energy. Which she claimed she had none of in her job running the store.

That was what started things changing with her. She began to mess up the dining room table with projects—yarn, fabrics, and then got into collages. But one day she just shoved them away and didn't seem too encouraged to go on with that work. It was a relief when she got that crap out of the dining room.

Creativity. She sure got creative with our marriage. Who the hell ever heard of taking a sabbatical from a marriage?

Nobody, that's who.

Nine

Annie

My dad helped in two important ways: he came to visit and he left.

His departure allowed me to claim my new apartment as much as his arrival did. I was so relieved to have the place to myself once I waved him off, I walked up my outside steps with a new sense of belonging. Before opening the door I stood on the top landing and admired the glitter of ocean between the rooftops, the grassy backyard and the shaded side yard where my landlords, Shank and Lucille, stood holding hands outside their screened Florida room, heads tipped toward their puppy, laughing at her antics with a rag doll. Both of them were retired, in their seventies, and I imagined they enjoyed long days and evenings together, and I marveled at that. How come he didn't get on her nerves? I would have trouble hanging around the house all day with Jess, week after week. Although we enjoyed each other's company, had lively conversations, lots of fun and even worked companionably in the store, it often felt like too much by the weekend. My landlords seemed to manage just fine. Sunday afternoon and they were shoulder to shoulder, holding hands. They felt my eyes on them, looked up and waved. I waved back, thinking, Boy, do I have a lot of work to do on my marriage. I opened my door and went inside.

I had my dad to thank for furnishing the place, even though I hadn't succeeded at steering him away from the cheap and tacky items that so pleased him. I stood before my biggest failure: a boxy wood glider, upholstered in chartreuse.

"I'm telling you, this damn Florida sun fades everything," Dad had said. "A couple hours sitting by a window and this outfit will be light as a grapefruit."

I began to slide the glider directly toward the nearest window, then changed my mind and made an abrupt turn toward the guest room. Let Dad live with this monster when he visited.

The most draining thing since leaving Jess was my indecisiveness. There seemed no real reason for doing one thing over another. Though I had been forced into making decisions about my marriage sabbatical, the process had been little more than just accepting what came my way.

Once, this state of indecision described my daily life. I used to check in with Jess about every little thing. But that changed about five years ago. I leaned up from pushing the glider and stared out the guest room window.

It began when I came across an old box of broken Crayolas from when the boys were little. I was about to toss them out, but instead found paper, sat down right there beside a window on the dusty subflooring of the storage room and drew abstract shapes and filled them in. I discovered the sweet oblivion that occurred when doing something you enjoyed for no reason other than the pleasure of it. The colors, all that light, I felt as if I had fallen in love with the sun.

Early-summer heat had accumulated in the uninsulated storage room built above our attached garage, so I opened the window. A wasp flew searchingly up and down the outside of the screen. I had always thought them unattractive, but I saw then that the wasp's body glistened with vitality. The hum of its wings seemed to be the sound of the cosmos. All that I saw from the second-story window hummed along with the wasp—the pines on Snow King Mountain, the aspens below in my yard, the chittering white-crowned sparrows bathing in dust beneath the black current bush, the lupine blossoms, my salad garden. And I was included; I hummed. My senses sharpened; I smelled the warmed metal screening, felt the afternoon air nuzzle my face and heard the distinctive call of a red-tailed hawk.

I had been writing in my journal for a few months by then, bit by bit opening to an awareness of myself and my experience outside of my roles as employer, wife, mother. In that moment I felt part of nature's exchange—the breathing in, the breathing out, the taking and the giving of the earth—what we called life.

I was filled with a sense of well-being, purpose and celebration. As if I were suddenly in on it all. As if every musician, entrepreneur, artist, inventor, dancer, actor and adventurer was related to me, was someone I understood and who would accept me as one of them. I was a magician, one minute cleaning out an old toy chest, the next producing luminosity.

I looked at the box of crayons in my hand, and I felt as though I held the secret of the universe: create. Create anything and be part of the great gushing fountain that waters aliveness.

That afternoon I began to want something for myself, just for myself, when all of my married life and motherhood I had only wanted things for others—Jess and our sons. And after coloring another sheet of paper, I decided that what I wanted was time and materials to work with and a place undisturbed in which to do it.

I sat there on the floor before the open window and realized I didn't have artistic talent; I couldn't draw, never could, not even bunnies for our children when they used to ask. How could I be creative, work around that lack of skill? I didn't want to involve Jess, the acknowledged artist in the family, with this question. I wanted to figure it out on my own, already sensing that I needed to keep this tender new passion close to myself. Since it was color I loved, I decided perhaps I could sew a patchwork coverlet and embroider colorful designs on it like one I had stored in a trunk that my great-grandmother had created. I found the coverlet and studied it.

That night after dinner, I followed through on my plan and covered the dining room table with my first project. In the storage room I'd found a pair of torn velvet pants of mine, several outdated silk neckties and old brocade draperies. I cut odd shapes out of the fabrics and began to sew them together, practically getting high on the color combinations. A late-evening dash to K-Mart for embroidery threads, and I was off.

"What's up?" Jess asked, passing through the dining room from watching TV with the boys.

"I'm making a crazy quilt."

"Good name—it looks pretty crazy to me."

The next morning I couldn't bear to leave my project and toted it to the shop to work on in free moments, which that day I began to create in my busy schedule. Doing something pleasurable just for me cleared the way for the real me to just pop right out and assert itself all over the place. In less than a year, this discovery of independent pleasure turned into a growing confidence that spread into all the areas of my life. I swear, I walked differently, I talked differently; everything I did was done with intention and wakefulness. It felt as if a dark veil, muting sights and sounds, feelings and thoughts, had lifted from me. I was alive, living through my own awareness, rather than the eyes of my family, and I was enjoying it. This new sense of self flowed into my work at the store, and while my resentment built over how much time Jess took off to ski and hike, I welcomed taking on more responsibility and began consulting Jess less. In the evenings and on weekends, I sat at the dining room table and created useful items for the house, gifts for friends when my projects turned out well, and donations to the secondhand store when they failed. It didn't matter where my projects ended up; I just wanted to create them, pass them on, create more.

And then I stopped. I created nothing else. I cleaned off the dining room table. I tried not to let myself miss it. I thought things would get better between Jess and me if I let it go. He was the creative one. I had known that from the beginning. The store was just to hold us until he got either famous or rich, or both. And here I was, bit by bit, borrowing his school art supplies, stashed away in his workroom these past decades, and using them myself. At first he had helped me, but then he began to take offense at my pastime, starting with complaints, ending with a full-out confrontation for which he'd dragged in our sons.

I returned Jess' art supplies to storage.

Yet it was too late for me to change back into the indecisive, dependent woman I once was. The confidence stayed; the wakefulness became a restlessness that I directed toward the store. And an uncomfortable severity edged my usually soft nature. I took charge of the store, the house, our social life, whatever crossed my path. And Jess backed off, more and more.

I left the chartreuse upholstered glider in the guest room and went into my bedroom and hung up clothes I'd bought this weekend. Dad had pestered me impatiently to hurry up, while slowing the process by pulling out his glasses and checking the price tags on items I'd selected, complaining about the markup. "They don't keystone clothing, you know. Hell, the profit on this stuff must be quadruple the cost, maybe more." He was such a nuisance that I only grabbed a couple changes of clothing. "This rag isn't worth sixty bucks. There was perfectly good stuff at K-Mart for you to wear."

I hung a blue cotton skirt in my closet beside a couple of matching tees and went into the front room to find a container to hold my underwear, since I had no dresser drawers. I rummaged around in my findings and discovered a big straw shoulder bag that I'd imagined holding a plant on the screened porch. I cleaned it out and hung it from the hook on the closet door and stuffed my panties and bras inside.

I put some lunch together now and took it out to the porch. I brought along a short stack of the secondhand books that I had bought at the flea market before Dad arrived—two old Somerset Maugham novels I thought I'd reread and a couple of Florida history books. But instead I ignored them and while I ate watched the blue-gray triangle of ocean against the pale sky.

In the beginning, when we were first married, I let Jess be in charge of our life together. He was older, more experienced and so good at reading me that I was barely aware he made all the decisions.

We said our wedding vows in a Cincinnati church full of my family's old friends, and after we'd said them, we looked at each other there before the altar and laughed right out loud with the joy and audacity of it.

That night Jess and I sat in the hotel lounge before going to the honeymoon suite he had reserved for us.

I said to him, "Love doesn't exist until it's put into action. Until then, the emotion is mere sentimentalism." Twenty years old. I felt wise, with a jump start on life. I said, "Really, Jess, let's not ever forget that." I lifted my glass of 7-Up for a sip. I wasn't old enough to order alcohol in Ohio, unless you counted 3.2 beer.

Jess, at twenty-four, clinked my glass with his bottle of six-percent beer. "Drink up and let's go put love into action right now." He kissed me on the neck to soften his wedding-night bawdiness, and I laughed.

This memory reminded me of what I had stuck in my purse to help celebrate our anniversary. A small leather-bound notebook. I took my empty plate into the kitchen and went to my bedroom to find my beaded bag.

Once locked into our honeymoon suite, Jess pulled his tie out of his pocket where he'd stuck it shortly after we'd raced through rice to our getaway car. I expected him to toss the tie on the coffee table, setting between the sofa and marble fireplace, and I slipped out of my heels, wiggling my toes into the lush jewel-patterned carpet. Jess surprised me by tucking his tie under his collar and knotting it with careful deliberation, checking that the ends lay flat against his shirt. He adjusted his collar, gave his neck the customary stretch, then bent his knees to watch his reflection in the darkened hotel window while he smoothed back his brown, almost black hair with his pocket comb. He pulled the drapes closed across the window, then turned to me.

"You," he said.

"Me?" I asked, as if chosen out of a lineup and about to produce an alibi. I had stood mesmerized by his preparations, wondering wildly if he were heading out on a date with someone else.

"You." He offered me his hand and guided me into the bedroom. He flung the double-sheeted duvet back, exposing a white expanse, like a blank canvas for us to paint ourselves across. Jess set me down, lifted my legs onto the bed, and stretched me out on the sheet.

From the inside breast pocket of his new going-away suit, Jess removed a pen and a small leather-bound notebook and laid them both—notebook open, pen uncapped—on the hotel's bedside table.

I began to laugh nervously, as if Jess were focusing a camera on me for porno shots. I felt pink with pleasure though. "What are you . . . ?"

"*Shh,*" he whispered. Picked up his notebook and wrote while reading his words out loud. "Surprises excite her."

"Jess," I laughed.

He set down his notebook and lifted my foot, running his forefinger up the center sole. Then he reported that action in the notebook and added my response, "Toes curl, lips part."

Jess filled pages of the small notebook. He had already intuited me as a person who needed to be reached through my mind.

Once given entrance, mixing science and sensuousness, he tunneled straight to my heart. When, hours later, Jess and I lay exhausted with sensation, he wrote his final entries, closed the book and handed it to me along with the pen—a Mont Blanc, as sleek and beautiful as a Rolls-Royce—his wedding gifts to me.

I opened the notebook now and read.

> *Tongue on back of knees: breath catches.*
> *Inside thighs: eyelids lower slowly, stay closed.*

I had easily become caught up in this game. One we had never played before or since, though we cherished the book and read it together on anniversaries. Always our language was locked into that quick jotting style. Jess could whisper to me, "Wet kisses on nostrils: tongue touches bottom teeth," and I was a goner.

I turned to his final jottings.

> *Inside labia darkens to rose.*
> *Tongue on clitoris: turns hard as a pebble.*
> *Breast: stay away from nipples till orgasm.*

I smiled, eyes watering. No one on this earth knew me the way Jess did. No one ever would. Jess knew me the way a gardener knew a plant raised from seed, witnessing the first emerging tendril, the unfolding of each waxy leaf. Jess watched me as I grew from a college sophomore into a woman, then his wife and the mother of our sons. He had loved me well. Beneath his recent preoccupation I knew that he still did.

I used to tease Jess that now all I needed to do was hand the book to any guy for a fun night. But there was never any guy other than Jess, not before we'd met or since. Women who have had sex with only one man all their lives are throwbacks, anachronisms, as rare as witches.

I sighed deeply and, feeling restless, stepped outside on my landing to check the sky. Shank and Lucille's puppy whimpered up at me from the bottom step. "Come on up, Mitzi." I patted my thighs. "You can visit." But she got altitude sickness on the third step, so I went down, sat on the bottom step and lifted her onto my lap. At home my dogs rarely left my side. A black Lab and two golden retrievers. They even lay outside the bathroom door, with one paw slid beneath the door so I'd not be lonesome. I ached now, I was so lonesome.

All three were named after mountains Jess and I had hiked in Jackson Hole: Leidy, Bannon and Ranger. The three dogs leaped into the car with Jess or me and spent their day at our store, gathering ear rubs. They rode to the bank with us, where every drive-in teller in our valley passed out Milk-Bones; and they accompanied us to dinner parties at friends' homes, where the three of them rested with the other guests' dogs around the dining table.

In Wyoming everybody owned a dog, usually a big one. Down here I'd spotted seagulls bigger than most Florida dogs. Tiny teacup poodles, Yorkies and frilly shih tzus that would serve as mere canapes for the coyotes back home.

Now I buried my face in Mitzi's soft puppy fur and wished she were my dog so I had the right to drop tears onto her sweet neck. She squirmed off my lap and I walked back upstairs.

I replaced the notebook in my beaded bag and tucked both away. Jess had dedicated our entire wedding night to knowing me intimately. I had dedicated the next two and a half decades to knowing Jess intimately. And though I wallowed in his attentions the night of our wedding and felt comforted by his gathered knowledge of me, Jess always felt uneasy by my gathered knowledge of him, as if I were stealing something I'd use as leverage against him in the future.

Most particularly he guarded the story of his mother's death. I knew many of the details, had heard them from his family members after our engagement, but never heard the story from Jess himself, who claimed he didn't remember it and was too young for the loss of his mother to carry much meaning. This protective characteristic of his threaded its way throughout our relationship, emerging in the most inconsequential aspects of the two of us getting to know each other. Always I had to tactfully press through his humorous diversions with my questions.

The next morning of our honeymoon we showered and got dressed together in the hotel room.

"Jess, you put your underwear on inside out."

"I always do."

"You do?"

After a few minutes of dodging my question with jokes, pretending he misunderstood or didn't hear me, he finally disclosed, "It's got to do with the angle of the dangle." He loosened up and made up a tune to go with that catchy phrase and swirled me around the hotel room, both of us in our underpants, singing.

"Our song," I said, " 'The Angle of the Dangle.' "

Eventually, I got the explanation that his penis naturally lay to the right when flaccid and it fell into the opening of the fly on Jockeys—unless he turned them inside out.

"Of course, guys with *small* penises don't have that problem."

"A little propaganda for the new bride?"

By then, of course, I'd been charmed out of analyzing his odd furtiveness—a pattern that continued on both his end and mine. Over the years I was a willing accomplice to his hiding behind humor, content to be entertained while he succeeded in avoiding topics that probed his inner life. I had assumed his reluctance to acknowledge emotional events from the past or address those of the present would lessen in time. Instead, unresolved issues mounted.

Still, love and humor graced the beginning of our life together and never abandoned us. But as if Jess knew his quality of deep attention would be an uncommon event in our life together, he'd produced an artifact to document the occasion: the leather notebook.

As I passed the guest room after putting the notebook away, the ugly glider hulked like a grumpy intruder, reminding me of Dad during his more negative moods, so I closed the door on it. Then back in the living room I was stopped by how Dad had pushed all the K-Mart furniture against the walls like in a doctor's waiting room—a doctor not doing too well. He had even fanned out his sports magazines on the glass-covered coffee table. "There, Annie L. Didn't know your pa was a decorator, did you?"

I nudged the black tubular framed love seat four feet out from the wall behind it; I let the matching coffee table stay in front of it, scooped up Dad's magazines, moved the lamp table to sit beside the "Full-Swivel Looks-like-Leather Chair with Ottoman." I removed the sign that belted out in bold print SAVE $60 RED-TAG SALE, which Dad couldn't bear to toss out, as it documented his best bargain. I angled the chair away from the wall, adjacent to the sofa. Stood back to look. Bookcases behind sofa, potted palms beside them, lamps lit and I'd call it home.

I dusted my used books and placed them on my new shelves, stacked a few beneath a small lamp on the snack counter, leaned some on a windowsill, set those I wanted to read right away on the floor in a tall pile beside the sofa. I hung two gaudy flower paintings, unframed, beside the TV—Dad's gift to himself, couldn't miss golf tournaments. Nailed three roughly built birdhouses on the other side of the TV. All garish attempts at beginning creativity, which was what excited me about them: that push within the soul that insisted we create something, however crude.

Dad had argued for a dining set that would have topped his savings on the swivel chair—he was clearly in a contest with himself over that—but I held out for a long worktable instead. I would eat at the snack counter that separated the cooking area or, like I did for lunch, out on the porch where we'd set up a grill and outdoor dining set. I had no real notion of what kind of projects I'd be doing on this worktable, but it was time to resume that discarded part of my life. No more cleaning my projects up every night, like I once did at home.

From my garage-sale loot I found a mug inscribed EVERGLADES beneath a picture of an ibis standing in weedy water. I set that on my new worktable and stuck a pen in it that I'd gotten at the Hibiscus Inn.

A start.

I scraped old wax off a pair of wrought-iron candlesticks, then washed a pink depression glass candy dish that I would fill with gumdrops and a milk white bowl that I would fill with oranges—Honeybells, those tiny sweet tangelos that only ripen in Florida during the last couple weeks of January.

I sat on a bar stool at the counter to make a grocery list, bounced back up for the pen. I needed everything. Dad and I had eaten all meals out this weekend—his decision, based wholly on my secondhand dishes. I stared at my pen thinking, then wrote: *Candles, gum-drops, Honeybells.*

I checked an old tin windup clock ticking on one of the bookshelves and discovered it was four thirty. Abruptly my stomach tightened. Sunday evening, one hour before dark, all alone, strange place, no food. Then I regained my balance, added charcoal and chicken breasts to my list and grabbed the car keys. I paused to look around my apartment first. This conglomeration of the shiny and recently purchased, the faded and used was my new home. An emotionally plump sense of well-being rose, almost a giddiness.

I was going to be all right.

Ten

Jess

Who the hell hired Lizette?

I looked out the doorway of my office and watched her—short jean skirt, black tights and cowboy boots. How does she walk on ice with those things or keep her cute ass warm with that short skirt on this twenty-six-below-zero morning?

By moving, I decided after watching her a few minutes. She fluttered like a bird. And that huge man's sweater that swung just two inches above her hemline with the immense arms that stretched like wings from her sides maybe helped to keep her warm, too. She unpacked a box of tropical-colored Teague Family Sports caps sent by the Skipper. Lizette. Her name fitted perfectly. She was pretty and feminine. She reminded me of AnnieLaurie at that age. Twenties—early, maybe mid-. She was goddamn pretty.

She lined caps along her left arm so she could carry a bunch at a time. Half a dozen fell. Why didn't she just drag the box over to the shelf? It wasn't heavy. She picked up the caps, stuck some between her knees, a couple on her own head and held one in her teeth, while she lined them up on her arm again. This was painful, like watching Lucy Ricardo without the hope of a TV contract. She had long blondish curls half piled on top her of head, half winding around her neck. I was ready to bet her personality matched her hair: all the hell over the place, but cute.

She couldn't hear me sitting back here at my desk, though I

laughed right out loud. The line of caps on her arm started sway-
ing, and Lizette lost the ones between her knees when she leaped
forward to maintain the right balance. I heard a muffled yelp
through the cap in her teeth. She was fun to watch.

Dangerous to watch.

Annie, damn you, leaving me alone like this. I felt vulnerable.
I grabbed my sheepskin jacket and plowed out the back door. The
air slammed my face with such fierce cold, I was afraid my eyeballs
would lock up. I headed for espresso, hatless head bent to push
against the steel pilings we call winter air out here. In weather like
this, I wished I was one of those guys with a lot of body hair.

Men don't leave their wives for younger women for the sake of
upright breasts and stomachs with no stretch marks. It's because we
want back the companions we married. I wanted Annie how she
used to be: fun, loving, accepting of me. And she hadn't shown any
relationship to that person for five years. She used to think I was
great; now she knew too much about me and had opinions about
all of it.

I pressed open the door and felt my body suddenly relax in the
instant warmth of the small, steamy café.

"Hi, Jess. Where's your hat and gloves?"

"Same place I left my brains, Bethany. How you doing?"

"Pretty good. Same old, same old?"

I paused before agreeing to my usual. "Give me something new.
Something . . . I don't know . . . that will make me act smarter,
look younger and feel richer."

"Ever try chai?"

"No. I'll give it a shot—no pun intended."

"It's tea. No shot necessary."

I carried a mug of what looked like my same-as-usual latte, but
smelled spicier, over to the window counter and raised a hip to a
stool. From here I could watch the idiots who skied in these subzero temperatures, which was either because they paid for their ski

package, by damn, and refused to waste the money or because they were plain local locos who lived only for the slopes. The red tram rolled overhead, carrying skiers toward Rendezvous peak, where at least inversion boosted the temperature up twenty degrees.

In another couple hours I'd have to go home to one more day without Annie. I should be used to a house without a woman since my mother died when I was a little kid. Gran Genie stepped in for a couple years and then Aunt Tula, but by the time I was eight years old, it was just me and my dad. Dad's idea of home cooking was a thing he called "McFall Food," a manly frying pan full of browned hamburger and onions with canned gravy mixed in. A jar of applesauce opened, a can of peas warmed and he'd call me for dinner. By the time I was eleven, I began to ask Aunt Tula to show me how to cook pork chops, make meat loaf and beef stew. When I was fourteen I baked a cherry pie to surprise Dad on Father's Day. From then on, he figured I was the official cook.

Annie and I always shared the cooking, housecleaning, yard work, tackling it together without too much of a plan. If I noticed she'd thawed chicken breasts, I'd start peeling potatoes; if she was weeding the strawberry patch, I'd mow the lawn. I loved how we worked together. But now it was just me in the kitchen, and maybe there was more of a plan than I thought, because I would decide to cook something for dinner, then find there were no groceries. Which matched the fact that I had no appetite anyway.

Housekeeping was easier; somehow it didn't take any emotion to vacuum and dust, like it did to fix dinner. You saw a dusty table-top, you swiped it with a cloth; the trash can got full, you carried it to the garbage can. It was all pretty straightforward. Cooking . . . took love. And I couldn't gather enough of it on my own to even get a grocery list together.

So the house was clean and tidy, ready for Annie to surprise me and come home anytime, but the place was filled with the spirit of a defunct motel room. The house rang with emptiness. The chill on Annie's side of the bed woke me when I rolled over with the abruptness of a bloody nightmare. But I decided, sipping my chai, when she did come back to me, I was going to kill her for leaving.

I couldn't sort us out. Where did AnnieLaurie end and I begin? I didn't even want to know. I liked us all mixed up together. I thought that was love. As far as I was concerned, twenty-some years ago we made a deal: she'd take care of the mushy stuff, except when I wanted to do some, and I'd take care of the practical stuff, except when she wanted to do some. Of course, by the time the boys were born, the store needed Annie's attention, and that plan turned into each of us rushing from one thing to another to keep disaster at bay. And though it had come down to Annie not caring much for the business lately, she had gotten hooked as I did in the beginning years of its growth. She didn't just dabble; she brought the babies and all their gear into the store and took over big chunks—to my relief. Annie had a head for business; I didn't.

But that was when things started to mix up between us. Pretty soon I was full-time baby soother, some days walking the aisles of demo skis singing "Humpty-dumpty doo, humpty-dumpty dee" over and over in my flat, toneless voice, trying to vibrate away colicky pains in a tiny tummy, while AnnieLaurie fought for our financial life in the office with a banker or just alone with the ledger. I guessed I'd gotten us in quite a mess before she came on board.

I finally warmed up and shrugged out of my jacket. The rule for getting warm the fastest was to remove your coat immediately inside a heated place, since the coat trapped icy air. But who could get themselves to take *off* clothes when they were frozen to the bone?

Bethany brought over a scone and napkin for me. "On the house."

"Thanks, Bethany. Looks great." I must strike her as needing some special attention. Maybe word had gotten out about Annie. This was a small village, despite tourists arriving in the tens of thousands. Didn't like to think that other people were in on my private heartache. Hadley was okay. She'd been in on everything from arguments between Annie and me to teenage trouble with our sons over the years, and she knew how to keep secrets. Maybe Bethany just had an extra scone lying around. I broke off a bit of it and popped it into my mouth, while resuming my stare out the window.

I loved caring for our boys, and customers thought it was charming to see me sell skis and hiking boots with a barefoot baby in one arm. People were always telling Annie what a gem she had for a husband. I remembered she asked me once if people said things like that about her to me. But they didn't. They didn't see her that much. She was holed up in the office. Anyway, things got all mixed up then. Suddenly one day five years ago she wanted to separate it out again. Decide who did what, regulate our hours. Well, you couldn't just do that in a day.

Was that really five years ago? Guess we could have made some progress on that if we'd tried. I supposed now that it was more important to her to have some independence than I thought. Maybe she had been unhappy about that. But what the hell? That was only five years at the end of a long marriage.

My breath caught in my throat, cutting off my ability to swallow my sip of chai.

I corrected myself: only five years *out* of a long marriage.

Eleven

Annie

This morning when I woke up, I realized four days had passed since Dad left, and I was boldly going nowhere. Creating my instant home took only an instant, and now I needed a life to live in it. I could no longer lie here in bed, patting my head over how brave and wonderful I'd been to set up a home for myself in a new place. But in a fresh swell of pride, I patted my head again anyway.

Surrounded by strangeness, I had replayed the lesson I'd learned two decades ago as a new mother: whatever you fed and tended repeatedly became your own—no matter how red and alien it was or how shrill it screamed. So I had filled my new shelves and cupboards and corners, then tended my odd assortment of trinkets and—snap your fingers—I'd created a place I cared about.

By now moldy leftovers even resided in my refrigerator, I discovered when I padded out to the kitchen in my nightgown. I peeked inside a plastic dish. In Florida you didn't just toss food into the trash can; the process of decay began the moment anything left refrigeration, and the process moved fast. Which was the reason, my father claimed, that the residents rarely left air-conditioned homes, cars and shopping malls. "You begin to rot the minute you step out the door," he'd said.

I returned the food to the refrigerator, made coffee and gathered my breakfast to carry to the porch. My first delivered newspaper lay on the landing, wisely sheathed in plastic. Wisely, since a hit-and-run cloud could spill tubs of water without notice of wind or thunder. This very crime of nature probably accounted for the beads of water filling the porch screen and jeweling on top of the newspaper's orange plastic wrap like garish sequins. I dabbed a toe in a pool of rain water on the landing and found it warm. I stepped in with both feet and watched the blue-green triangle of ocean over the rooftops.

I felt listless—literally without a list, a to-do list—for perhaps the first time in my adult life. Back home I had yearned for days with nothing scheduled and had savored the idea of their emptiness with a kind of mental sensualism. I wiggled my toes in the puddle, then stomped, splashing water up my ankle bones. With the morning's heat this puddle could dissolve sugar. So warm, organisms were probably hatching between my toes. For a painful moment I longed to stand on my log porch in Wyoming, cross-country skis in hand, breathing cold, slicing air, ready to head out with my three dogs before going to work. I pictured on the door the wreath that I'd made from scavenging the slopes and folds of Snow King Mountain behind our house. Leathery Oregon grape leaves in purple and scarlet, sagebrush, wild rose hips, juniper and snowberries. And on top, a robin's nest from last spring. She had built her nest on the wreath, then laid four blue eggs in it. Jess and I had to stop using the front door for a few weeks, but we got to watch the whole drama of baby birds hatching, being fed by a pair of solicitous parents and then applaud when the young birds learned to fly to the porch railing and back.

This morning I felt like both the baby bird testing its wings and the anxious parent looking on.

I returned inside the screened porch for breakfast and found my coffee was the same temperature as the puddle. I opened the newspaper. Along the edge of the third page a large ad announced *Last day to sign up.* This was either synchronicity or any old idea would have sounded good to me, due to my need to accomplish something tangible with my time down here.

*   *   *

Only a dozen of us stood in line to sign up for late registration, probably because it was so late. Classes would begin at the Gold Coast College Monday, after the weekend, but I had just realized this morning that a college campus accounted for the spread of trees and grass where I had been taking walks when I didn't go to the beach. I sincerely hoped my mental fog would lift soon, as I was apparently missing quite a lot with my head down, lost in thoughts about Jess and home.

The campus had once been a pineapple plantation, and I read yellowed newspaper clippings about life on the plantation, framed beneath glass, as the line moved along the hallway, until I ran out of them and was left to stare at a huge map of the United States hanging over the registrar's desk.

From behind me a woman said, "Ever notice how Florida hangs off the continent like a flaccid penis?"

I turned, knowing I'd see someone interesting.

"The entire state," she continued, staring up at the map, "says to the world, 'I'm just not that into you.'" She grinned when I laughed and said, "Hi, I'm Marcy 'Empty-nest Syndrome' Marden. What have you decided to be now that your divorce is final?"

"Gosh, is it that plain?"

"I hit it right on?"

"No, you're actually off quite a bit. But similar setup."

"After we're finished here, let's meet at the Green Bottle Café, and you can tell me how psychic I am."

I signed up for five classes, a full load. When seeking diversion, accrue college credits at the same time was my motto. Besides, I'd always felt slightly embarrassed about not having a full four-year degree, since I had dropped out after two years when Jess and I married and moved to Jackson Hole. After that, life never sent a strong enough invitation to finish off the final two years. The nearest college to Jackson Hole was a hundred miles away in another state and over two scary mountain passes, often closed due to avalanches in the winter. Cam and Saddler attended the only university in Wyoming, located on the other end of the state in Laramie, four hundred fifty miles away.

But I was receiving a strong enough invitation now. A sense of accomplishment could only help my case down here, feeling as I did that I was playing hooky from my real life. Now I had a reason to be here. "Oh yeah, I left my home and husband abruptly because I needed to get down to this little town in Florida real quick and sign up for college classes."

That may take some editing, but it could possibly work as a general excuse back home.

My best friend and old college roommate, Gina, probably wouldn't fall for it, and neither would my sons. I had plenty of time before meeting Marcy for lunch, so I strolled around campus and chose to sit on the low, sloping trunk of a palm that grew almost horizontal before lifting its bristly brush of fronds into the sky. I hadn't called my sons yet and hoped to practice with Gina and maybe learn a few tips from her about telling the boys my story. Since Cam and Saddler had just been home for Christmas and New Year's, they would have been alarmed if I'd phoned too soon after their return to school. By waiting to call, I hoped to set a more relaxed tone for my news.

Gina covered her shock at hearing about my marriage sabbatical as smoothly as I knew she would. I told her I was worried about telling the guys about it.

Gina said, "Just tell Cam and Saddler the truth, like you did when they were toddlers: 'Mommy loves you very much and everything is going to be fine.'"

I said, "That worked remarkably well once. Maybe it will again."

"But tell me the grown-up version. What's up, sweet girl?"

"This is as much as I know for sure: Jess has been AWOL from the marriage; I've been AWOL from myself and somehow I got the bright idea that a winter in Florida would solve everything."

"Your bright ideas are always on the mark, Annie. Just follow the lights along the path one step at a time, and you'll come out right where you want to be. I believe in you."

"Don't make me cry. I'm in a public place."

"Just to let you know you're heading in the right direction, concerning Jess, both Jim and I have felt his distraction the last couple years, too. He's such a bighearted guy and so much fun to be around, but his avoidance patterns have seemed to pop into stronger relief lately. It always makes me think about his mother's accident. Not to be too simplistic, but with both the guys off to school, life is opening up all over again for the two of you. . . . It's just a time, Annie, for stuff to come up. Maybe Jess is thinking about things."

"You and Jim are going through the same thing now with your kids gone."

"And we're bumping up against each other in whole new ways. We don't have any serious trouble, but neither of us has any traumas in our backgrounds either, especially ones we don't talk about to anybody. Jess does." Gina added, "Sorry. I may be way off here. I'm just scrambling to give you a handle on this."

"No, you're right. That is a big piece of it."

Gina assured me that I'd figure it out and reminded me to try to enjoy myself while I was working on it. I told her I met a woman whom I was having lunch with today.

Gina said, "That's good. But don't like her better than me, okay?"

"Fat chance."

I snapped my phone closed and held it in both hands on my lap. Thank goodness for Gina. I could use half a dozen friends like her, but never had time to make them. Then I straightened my back and called my older son, Saddler.

"Hello, baby boy." I loved calling him that. It always reminded me of the moment the obstetrician held the newborn Saddler up to me in the delivery room—twenty-two years ago now—and said, "You are the mother of a baby boy." All that first night I didn't sleep, but just repeated those words to myself, "You are the mother of a baby boy." I followed Gina's advice in that I confirmed that I loved him and paraphrased Julian of Norwich, "All shall be well. All manner of things shall be well." I had been reading about this thirteenth-century nun in one of those secondhand books I had piled beside the sofa.

Saddler surprised me by saying, "Mom, you guys will be okay. You love each other too much. Come home soon, but have some fun while you're in Florida, okay?"

I promised I would, noting that was the second time I had gotten the advice to add some pleasure to my life. Then I phoned Cam. A similar assurance from me and another surprising response from my second son. "Dad won't know what to do with himself."

"He won't?" That didn't sound like the man I knew, busy with his sports and search-and-rescue work, always outside, checking on the wildlife. "He's pretty busy, Cam."

"But he schedules everything for when you aren't available. I'll call and see if he wants to come down for a game or something."

When I hung up from that call, I sat a moment, smoothing my hand over the tree trunk beside where I sat. In the mirror each of my sons held up to my marriage, I saw that Saddler reflected the strength of love Jess and I held for each other, and he was right about that. From Cam I saw that he viewed his father as designing his life around mine, almost propped against mine. I'd have to think how right that was, because all along it had seemed the opposite was true: I designed my life around Jess.

When I arrived at the Green Bottle Café, I found I wasn't the only person Marcy had recruited. Two other women sat in the booth with her. Also strangers to each other, they were just introducing themselves as I approached.

"Sit," Marcy commanded, and moved over to make space next to herself, facing the windows. Plate glass stretched the entire width of the café's front, broken only by a door in the center. Glass shelves across the windows held—who would guess?—green bottles. Hundreds of empty green bottles. Tall, squat, plain, fancy. I felt as if we were sitting inside an algae-covered aquarium. When I was introduced to Perry and Sara, I expected our words to bubble up toward the ceiling. I was feeling nervous as I repeated their names in my head: Perry and Sara.

I said, "Hi, Para and Sarie. I mean Perry and Sara." If I'd been a blusher I wondered what color that would have made my face in this greenish light.

"Sara," Marcy said, tipping her open palm toward a woman with a short single braid over her shoulder, "is returning to school for a paralegal degree because her husband says that brings in the most money.

"Perry, here . . . " Marcy moved her palm to indicate a soft-featured woman with a clipped boy cut, long blond bangs to one side, somewhere in her early to mid-forties like Marcy and Sara. "You tell, Perry."

"I am resorting to pleading with total strangers to listen to complaints about my husband, because I'm afraid I'll leave him if I don't vent, and to please don't tell anybody what I say, because people know my family around town." She took a big breath and looked around the café. "I might take up drinking. Do they serve liquor here?"

Marcy said, "You don't need to take up drinking; you just need friends. AnnieLaurie is leaving her husband, too. We're all a mess. That's why I picked you to have lunch. That and your age—you're all grown-ups."

"What age?" Sara asked. Perry mumbled a humorous thanks,

and I felt glad to be sitting on an outside seat of the booth and began making up excuses in my head to leave.

"I thought we grown-ups could bond," Marcy said. "Have you noticed we're in the minority on campus? And in town, for that matter. At school we are surrounded by children, in town by old people. Excuse me: 'senior citizens.'"

"I'm beginning to hate that phrase," I said. The term was used excessively by advertisers in this state.

Sara said, "I'm not a mess."

"You are if you're studying for a career your husband chose for money reasons. I know, because I often threaten to leave mine for saying annoying things like that."

The waitress approached to take our orders, but I believed, like me, probably everyone except Marcy was thinking how they could get out of staying for lunch. Nobody ordered, but kept eyes glued to the menu, like me, probably without reading it.

Marcy said, "Oh, come on. I get better. It's just because we're all total strangers that I'm acting so bold." None of us looked convinced. "You'll see, once I get to know you, I'll become meek and reticent."

We just stared at her.

She added, "I promise."

The waitress shifted her weight to the other hip, and Marcy said she'd have the special, a crab salad. Long pause, then one by one we mumbled agreement, we'd have the special, too. Marcy said she'd have a glass of white wine. We all agreed again—even me, who much prefers red—and it was as if we had just voted Marcy leader of the group by way of our lunch orders. After the waitress left we all turned to Marcy to tell us what was next.

Marcy said, "I need somebody besides my husband and kids to ignore everything I say. I'm seeking diversity."

Perry said, "I'm not really leaving my husband."

I said, "Me, either."

"See?" Marcy said. "Already we've saved two marriages. We're going to be great together."

We laughed. Then I explained my situation. They liked the idea of a marriage sabbatical.

"But why return? Leaving is the hard part." Marcy took water glasses from the waitress and passed them around.

She got that right. Leaving was the hard part. But my heart squeezed a bit remembering Jess and how angry I'd felt around him lately and also how hard I laughed with him and enjoyed his company.

I said, "I'm returning because he's my favorite person in the world." I thought a second and added, "Along with my sister. But I just can't live with Jess right now." I sounded like our son Cam when he was five. He told my mother he had two friends in kindergarten, but one of them he didn't like. That had become a family joke over the years. I considered telling that story to my new friends, but Perry leaned over the table to speak.

"Leaving Alex is just a fantasy I indulge in once in a while, but I will never do it." She lowered her eyes a moment, then looked up. "It would break his heart."

"Listen to us," Marcy said. "We let them rule our lives."

Perry dipped two fingers into her water glass for ice chips and cracked them with her teeth. "You would have to meet Alex to understand." On her left arm Perry wore gold bangles that moved from wrist to elbow as she gestured. Some had diamonds embedded in them. "I know." Her arm shot up. "Come to our lawn party this Sunday. You'll meet Alex and his parents. His mother is the one who gives me these." She shook her arm. "She's a dear. She also wears an armload of bangles, and when she becomes especially pleased with me, she wriggles out of one of them right on the spot, squishes my fingers together." Perry demonstrated. "And twists the bangle onto my arm." She looked at all of us with regret. "I'm talking too much. Somebody else take a turn."

Wine arrived. Food arrived. We ate and talked and laughed and got directions to Perry's house.

Marcy said, "My God. You live in that beautiful pink-and-yellow gingerbread on the beach?"

"I live with my in-laws. It's their house."

"Poor baby." Marcy looked genuinely dismayed.

"No, it's okay. It's the only way . . . really. Just come. Meet everybody. I never have my own friends to invite to these affairs. Promise you'll all come."

We promised. And I decided right there: if none of these women turned out to be kleptomaniacs or child abusers, I could handle the relationships and I could sure use the friendship.

It looked as if I were acquiring my friends in the same way I acquired my household furnishings: accepting whatever came my way and trusting it would fit together—Mexican vases, amateur seascapes, a truckload of vinyl and particle board from K-Mart. Marcy, Sara and Perry. The same way I set up my class load at the college; I took whatever was still open: textile design, introduction to basic art, contemporary crafts, psychology, English literary masterpieces.

When I left the Green Bottle Café and stepped into the bright Florida sunlight, I felt a strong desire to set up an aquarium. Though I knew what I really longed for as a pet was a puppy, like Mitzi. I decided to talk it over with Shank and Lucille. I also decided to talk to Jess and end the moratorium on phone calls. I felt established enough in my new life to open up to him, and I also wanted to tell him I would be down the coast at Daisy's until Sunday.

Twelve

Today the sky was solid blue. A Western blue, not like in the East, where the thin haze of humidity watered down the color; this was a blue with no white in it, a blue almost purple. And the iced Tetons shimmered with silver against it. Possibly this ski trail was one of the best places on earth. A flat track began below the Taggart Lake piedmont and wove in and out of trees and meadows to the shores of Jenny Lake, and along the whole way the frilly, yet craggy, spires of the Tetons rose straight up beside me. On the return ski I veered off trail to evade a bull moose browsing along Cottonwood Creek. I drove home, watching the sunset drape gold along the silvery peaks.

I pulled into the driveway at last light, with the sun fallen behind the mountains, temperatures sinking toward twenty below for the night. I walked into the dark house and I was slammed by the sight of a note I'd left on the table by the door for Annie.

Gone to the park.
Home for dinner.

My God, I had done that out of habit. Just scribbled the note with one hand, grabbed my car keys with the other. I stood there, hand on the doorknob, starring at the note. The dogs sat watching me, a little miffed that they were left behind for the day, a little puzzled that I wasn't greeting them. I couldn't believe I had done that, written a note to her before I'd closed the door. And yet I could believe it, because I halfway expected to smell dinner cooking when I'd opened the door.

Right then the phone rang. I picked it up.

Annie said, "Hi."

No greeting from me. I just said straight out, "I'm going to win you back."

She didn't take a breath. "Then that would make you the winner, wouldn't it, Jess? And make me the loser."

I said, "Damn it, Annie. I keep trying, but there's just no . . . winning with you."

"Right," she said. "No winning, no losing. This is a love affair not a political race."

"Semantics. You know what I mean."

"You always see us in competition, Jess. It's not a relationship of equals with you—it's one person winning over the other. A power game. You don't even mind losing once in a while, because to you losing once in a while is fair. And you try to be fair because *you're such a nice guy.*"

There was a sarcasm in her voice on those last words, but I said, "Thanks."

She didn't acknowledge that and went right on ranting. "But you have to win most of the time, and in certain areas you have to win all the time. You know that isn't right in a marriage, but you just can't let go of the idea of a hierarchy, and you want me to hold that idea, too. But I don't hold it. You get that, Jess? I am not to be 'won over.'"

I said, "Hell, you don't have to get angry about it."

She said, "But I do. Anger gets your attention. You don't budge unless the flames of my anger singe your pant legs. At first you think, 'I'll just spit at this and she'll subside.' You dismiss me, saying that I'm exaggerating or that I'm too touchy. And then when the fire doesn't go out, you unzip your pants and pull out the big fire hose. . . ."

I said again, "Thanks."

I figured she wouldn't acknowledge me this time either. But there was a silence. Then I heard the sound that—I swear—was the adhesive that held us together. Laughter.

We laughed harder than my stupid joke deserved. Ripples of pleasure came together in the phone lines.

I said, "Isn't phone sex great?" It felt like sex. When I reached into the center of Annie's feelings and tapped her funny bone and sent her into orgasms of laughter, then joined her with my own, it always felt like sex. No matter where she was, in my arms or, like now, three thousand miles away, no matter what she was thinking or feeling, even when she was angry with me, I could get into the center of her—the absolute core of AnnieLaurie—and trigger her pleasure. And every time she accepted me—even the weakest attempt on my part, the lamest joke.

She said, "Yeah, phone sex is great." And she laughed again.

I filled with love for her and met her laughter with my own. Who said coming at the same time was rare?

I said, "Annie, I love you with my whole heart." Tears came to my eyes and my voice cracked at the end. I had to love her to be whole. I didn't care suddenly whether or not she loved me. I just needed to love her.

"Oh," I said out loud, getting what she meant about winning and losing and how that didn't belong in a marriage like ours.

"Oh, what?" she asked, her voice low and soft, almost a whisper.

"Oh . . . nothing."

Thirteen

Annie

When I reached Daisy's house, no one was home. She and Marcus never locked the doors, so with my new puppy, Bijou, in my arms, I walked in and looked for a note. The red light on the message machine winked from the desk. Thinking Daisy might have put a message on it for me—she had done that before—I headed there. Knowing Daisy, I assumed she probably couldn't find a pen or paper—I looked around—or a cleared surface to write a note on. No wonder Daisy trusted leaving her doors unlocked. A burglar would take one look at this mess and back right on out, figuring someone had already ransacked the place. Even I thrashed frantically around in my mind for an excuse to get a motel room, but I knew I was not allowed to do this and remain her sister.

I set Bijou on the floor and pushed the PLAY button. My own voice startled me—Daisy had insisted I call the very second I was leaving so she'd know when to worry. I sounded like Mia Farrow on antidepressants. The voice informed whoever listened that I would arrive about five o'clock. I remembered hoping this might suggest pushing toys off the guest bed or—ever optimistic—putting dinner on the stove. I looked at my watch; I was an hour early.

Really, Mia Farrow? I played the message again. Yep, same pauses and emphasis and same intensity of speech. As I listened, even I wondered if the person speaking had a very slight British accent.

"I say," I said, punching the DELETE button on my message. "Bloody awful here." Bijou stalked piles of clothing on the floor and pounced on them in viciously friendly attacks, tail wagging.

I walked into the kitchen. A child's dirty sock rested beside the sink, which was full of melon rinds and cereal bowls with Sugar Pops dried to the sides. I said, "Bloody awful here, too."

I felt hungry and picked up a banana from the fruit bowl. A flock of tiny insects lifted into the air. I dropped the banana and opened the refrigerator. The butter dish was smeared with grape jelly and the stick of butter itself encrusted with toast crumbs. I always forgot this part. I felt so eager to see Daisy and Marcus and the girls that I could hardly get here fast enough and I always teared up when I left. Yet in between I could never find a place to sit in this ten-thousand-square-foot, six-bedroom house. Marcus' T-shirt was tossed on the nearest end of the leather sofa, probably sweaty from one of his ten-mile jogs, one of the twins' half-eaten sandwich lay on an upholstered chair, an uncapped tube of toothpaste on another; books and magazines were mounded into precarious heaps on seats around the kitchen table.

I gave up the idea of finding a snack and closed the refrigerator door. Like a narcoleptic, Bijou had fallen into one of her spontaneous naps: all but her tail and hind paws was burrowed beneath an abandoned towel on the floor of the family room. I lifted the towel to peek at her. She was so small and beautiful in her variegated black-and-white shagginess. She would grow about three times her size now, but would still be no bigger than any of my Wyoming dogs had been as puppies. Even so, her mother looked sporty rather than frilly, and I counted on Bijou holding her own in the Wild West later on. I loved her immeasurably. She was sister to Shank and Lucille's puppy, Mitzi, and they were happy that I was providing a playmate for their energetic pup.

I found a clean towel in the clothes dryer, left the bathroom door open so the puppy could find me when she woke and began to strip for a shower. Though this was one of the guest baths, the twins had five flavors of toothpaste in pump bottles lined around the faucet. I chose bubble gum. I held my towel under one arm and my clean clothes between my legs while I brushed my teeth, since I couldn't find a cleared space to set anything down. Soap and shampoo smears covered the counter. I returned to the dryer for another clean towel to spread out and lay my stuff on. Marcus teased Daisy that she treated the dryer as a combined linen and clothes cupboard; everybody knew to go there for their needs, apparently even me.

While irritated at the mess, I was also admiring of Daisy, because she hadn't caught our mother's tidy disease. Our mother didn't make a home for us—she kept a house. She wasn't so much a neat freak as devoid of a personal taste she felt comfortable displaying. A house of cleared surfaces. No knickknacks on shelves, no pillows on sofas, no canisters on kitchen counters. Everything was tucked away in closets or drawers or else given to the Salvation Army. She and my father had kept life stripped to the minimum when it came to belongings, and that included family photographs—there were none. If a friend or relative sent pictures of us or themselves, our parents admired the photos, then tossed them in the wastebasket as easily as yesterday's newspaper. When company came it was the height of embarrassment for our mother if any room displayed a trace of human presence. I took the middle way in my Wyoming home; I liked to think of my decorating as Zen spareness mixed with evidence of a full family life. Daisy just went with the full family life.

I let cool water drum onto my head, shampooed and rinsed. Once my ears were freed of the spray of water, I heard rustling sounds and, thinking it was Bijou, I peeked out the shower door. Nell and Libby, dressed in ruffled sun dresses and jelly sandals, were preparing to surprise me outside the open bathroom door. Their whispered plan was to jump out at me as soon as I appeared.

So busy plotting, they didn't see my face above them. I ducked back into the shower and began humming "Oh, Susannah." I heard them giggle. I reached for my towel, slung over the shower door, wrapped it around me and stepped into their trap. The girls leaped into the doorway with gleeful shouts, arms raised and waving; I pretended to nearly faint and they broke into hysterics. I burst into teary laughter and knelt down and swooped them into my arms.

This morning on the phone, Daisy had said Marcus planned to stay overnight on the boat he docked in Palm Beach an hour down the coast, where his office was located, in order to give Daisy and me some private time. When Marcus was gone, his presence resided in the status symbols he surrounded himself with, and sometimes that was true even when he was home. Whenever I asked him, "What's new?" he answered by telling me what he had purchased lately. Though in Marcus' favor, he was generous and enjoyed setting up good times for his friends and family. His latest plan was a Conestoga trip for him, Daisy and the girls through Yellowstone this coming summer.

Daisy first dated Marcus when he worked with her in Dad's Palm Beach store; then suddenly he received a huge commission as a part-time real estate agent selling a cattle ranch outside Ocala and turned to real estate full-time. A year and a half later, he and Daisy married. I knew Daisy truly loved her husband, yet it was also true that a person needed leverage around Dad, and Marcus had so much money and so many powerful friends that his leverage was without question in the vicinity of our father. Jess even joked that Marcus was impressive enough that he could have been a black Jewish transvestite and our bigoted father still would have approved of him as a son-in-law.

My leverage with Dad, Daisy claimed, was that Jess had been artistic and poor and comfortable with that, plus Jess and I ensured ourselves of a certain autonomy with distance. Three thousand miles was good leverage. Mostly though, Daisy's theory was that I chose the opposite values of our father, whereas she chose similar values intensified.

I stopped to think, while I toweled dry and the girls waited outside the door, what Daisy's leverage might be with Marcus. I buttoned up my skirt, pulled on a tank top and slid into sandals. Her indifference to the status symbols he surrounded them with, I decided, as I sauntered through the family room again with its giant stereo system, large-screen TV, pool table with a load of laundered sheets lumped atop it. Nell and Libby skipped ahead, leading the way to their mother.

We found Daisy waiting for us outside, near the pool.

She jumped up from her lounge chair, held her arms out wide, and I stepped into them. Daisy hugged me tightly, then held me for a long moment against her and smoothed the back of my hair. When she stretched her arms to look at me, she said, "I was banished out here so the girls could surprise you."

I got teary again at the soft, caring look in her eyes and the relief I felt to be with someone I knew would understand all of me. This time the teariness swelled into chest-heaving sobs and I was back in my sister's arms. Daisy told Nell and Libby to find some treats in the kitchen for us and held me and patted me until I subsided into wet whimpers.

The trouble with my marriage and the hopelessness that had brought me here to Florida rose to the surface and swamped me all at once. Filled with confusion and misery, I dumped our age-old manner of speaking about our husbands anonymously and blurted, "I love Jess, but I am drained. Just depleted by his stuff, his unfinished, unacknowledged, repetitious stuff." I sniffled, accepted a tissue and blew my nose; sobs threatened to take hold again.

"I know."

"We can be getting along fine, feeling especially close. Then *bam,* Jess hits some invisible wall."

"I know."

"Like last night on the phone. I talked to him about his urge to win all our encounters, when it isn't a contest, and I know he finally got what I meant. But could he say so? No. He maintains the upper hand, a certain distance and control when it comes to intimacy with me. He drops out, acts indifferent. And I am left hanging there, wondering what happened, where he disappeared to." What was I ranting about? Why couldn't I stop? Since Daisy kept saying she knew, why couldn't she tell me?

"And you take this personally," Daisy said. "But it has to do with his limits, even if it feels like he's deliberately withholding from you."

"How can I separate from him enough to live my own life while staying connected with what I value about us together?" My voice sounded desperate. "I have to figure this out."

"You will."

Daisy had set a small table in between two lounge chairs here on the shaded patio. Two glasses and an opened bottle of cabernet sat on the table beside a box of Kleenex. I mopped my face, and she poured a glass of wine for me and another for herself, and we sat knees to knees on the ends of our lounges. "I have to find rules," I said.

"Good luck. If you succeed in finding rules, you'll make a lot of women happy."

"This is my job down here. I need to rest and recuperate and find rules. Something I can remember when I go home again. In the past, every time I felt I'd figured something out, I lost it in the chaos of gunfire during the problem at home. This move down here is an effort to get clarity and some concrete perspective."

"What is it exactly that's so hard with Jess?"

I blew my nose a final time, trying to clean up before the twins returned. "I knew somebody was going to want that laid out sooner or later. I don't know. . . . I can never organize it in my head. It's like the bruises fade the moment I try to describe them. Emotional bruises, I mean. I just know I feel knocked around."

Nell and Libby walked toward us, slowly and on wobbly legs, each balancing a plate. Nell's plate had Oreo cookies smeared with peanut butter.

"Oh, Nell," I said, "this looks fabulous."

"Libby's is fablis, too," Nell said.

"Indeed it is," I agreed, taking the plate from Libby to set on the table.

"Indeed it is," Libby repeated and giggled, bent at the waist with her hands wrapped tightly into her skirt and stuck between her knees. Daisy and I exchanged looks.

"What do you have here?" Daisy asked Libby, her voice admirably serene.

Nell explained. "This way you don't have to put the cheese on top of the crackers and get the knives dirty."

It became clear then that the mess we were viewing was Boursin cheese with crackers broken up and smashed into it. The hands that created this ingenious dish were not entirely cleaned of the peanut butter that had been used on the first delicious canapé.

We had to eat one of each while the twins stared at us. They offered to find some more treats, but Daisy dissuaded them. To play my usual role of loving aunt and troublemaker, I said, "Oh, please? Some more?" Then I remembered my new pet and sent the girls on a mission to find Bijou and potty her in the yard. I felt guilty that she'd probably done that in the house already, but knew I wouldn't have to confess anything since it wouldn't be discovered for years.

Later, after the sun set, laying wavy stripes of reflective pastels across Daisy's pool, she and I went inside. I called Dad to tell him I'd arrived. He filled me in on his latest intestinal developments.

"So, Dad, what do you think caused this?"

"I don't know. I been eating good things."

"Like what?"

"Muskmelon."

"That's good for you," I said, relieved it wasn't a sack of peanuts for dinner three nights in a row like once before.

"That's what the dietitian said. She said, 'A little melon is good.' So I figured a lot would be great. And then I get diarrhea. That gal doesn't know her stuff."

I took a big breath. "Like how much is a lot?"

"Just one."

"One piece?" This sounded too normal. I suddenly caught on. "One whole melon? You ate the whole melon? At one time?"

"In a meal or two yesterday."

"Well, no wonder."

"Oh, *you're* a doctor now."

"Well, I know not to eat a whole melon."

"That's what you have to do when you live alone. You want a little melon, you have to buy a whole melon. Then you have to eat it before it goes bad and then you get sick."

"I'll get a melon before I leave, and we'll share it," I said.

"No. I don't eat melon anymore. It's not good for me."

I just wanted out of this conversation. I said, "Isn't the news on soon?"

"Oh, you're right, honey. I'll talk to you later."

We made plans to see each other and hung up. I pictured Dad sitting before the television gathering more material to depress me with when we met for breakfast.

When I got off the phone, I told Daisy, "He needs a woman in his life."

Daisy said, "He's got one. Me." And she filled me in on how Dad was transferring more and more of his business at the store to her and called her on the weekends to accompany him socially. We decided he was way too young to be giving up like this and that she had to harden and refuse to accept his assignments. But I knew in the short time I'd been in Florida that I wanted to fill all

Dad's needs myself and found I was thinking often of how I could entertain him or solve his complaints.

Daisy and I talked while we started dinner. She'd been at the grocery store when I'd arrived, and only put away the foods that needed refrigeration, so first we unloaded grocery bags into the cupboards. I was little help. I just stood in front of the crammed cupboards with packages of pasta in my hands and shook my head.

"Here," Daisy said, and handed me a pineapple. "Prepare this."

The counter seemed to be moving. I looked closer. Tiny infinitesimal ants, nearly invisible, skittered around the countertop. I stood staring at them, feeling hopeless that we could ever prepare food here, that the huge number of ants indicated the only solution was to burn down the house.

This happened to me lately. Defeat loomed early in a situation and suddenly overwhelmed all hope that life could move forward.

Daisy said, "Use this." She handed me a clear acrylic cutting board. "For some reason these little sugar ants can't climb on that."

I looked at her blissful countenance with some envy, some disbelief. She continued to put away groceries. I set the cutting board down on its rubbery four corners in the midst of ant Olympics, and as eventually happened in Daisy's house, I dissolved my fastidiousness and lowered my standards. My shoulders relaxed; my stomach muscles eased. The acrylic cutting board became an island of hygiene. The ants slipped off the beaches and soon gave up storming the edges of my sanctuary. I cut off the spiny leaves at the top of the pineapple, then quartered it.

I said, "I have this trouble when it comes to naming what's wrong with my marriage or describing what's hard about living with Jess. I tried telling Lola, a therapist Jess and I were seeing once. It took all her patience, but she listened to my fumbling complaints about how careless Jess is, how he leaves jobs unfinished, drawers unclosed, loses mail, phone messages; how he offers to go to the grocery store, then returns without getting half the list. I told her about the vast amount of small but constant mistakes and messes Jess trails behind him throughout his day. And I felt petty doing it."

"What did the therapist say?"

I singsonged Lola's words. "'So what are you so angry about, Jess? Those are the acts of a man who's angry and not comfortable about it. It'd be easier, Jess, if you'd just acknowledge your trouble with your wife straight out.'"

"She didn't dismiss it."

"Not at all. But Jess denied he was angry, and Lola turned to me, raised her eyebrows and said, 'The end.'"

"Whew," Daisy said.

"Lola ended up saying to Jess, 'Well, Jess, you sound like a cuddly predator to me.'"

"She did?" Daisy turned to face me with a tower of instant oatmeal boxes in her arms.

"That's when I knew Lola understood completely, that he was both lovable and menacing." I sawed at the tough outer edge of peeling on one quarter of the pineapple. Daisy's knives were dull; she didn't own a sharpener and in the past just bought new knives if I complained. I said, "Lola quoted Marion Woodman—I looked this up and memorized it, I loved it so—'His sin is not so much in doing wrong as in not being conscious of the effect of his actions on other people.'" I said to Daisy, "Isn't that Jess exactly?" I set down one quarter and started on another. "Here's the rest of that quote: 'His lack of emotional empathy shelters him from the conflicts that lead to manhood.'"

Daisy said, "How did Jess take that?"

"He said Lola was welcome to her opinion. He wasn't even insulted."

"Which proved your therapist's point, not to mention old Marion's. So then what?"

"So then nothing," I said. I cored one of the quarters. "Lola said right in front of Jess that he was passive-aggressive, and unless he recognized that, there was nothing I could do but leave him." I stopped my work and looked at Daisy.

"I said to her, as if Jess wasn't even in the room, 'But I love him.'" As I looked at Daisy, I felt my face assume the hopeless perplexity I had experienced that day in Lola's office, eyes widening and beginning to water. And now, so did Daisy's.

Daisy and I stood quietly in her kitchen a moment; then she asked, "What did Jess do?"

I recalled how my words had brought Jess to the edge of the sofa we shared, his elbows on his knees, hands hanging loose between them. He looked at Lola as if she were the judge in a custody trial about to separate us and was powerless to stop her. He said, "I love AnnieLaurie." His voice was husky and pleading. I remembered how we reached for each other's hands, the two of us against Lola and her bad news.

I told Daisy, "Jess told Lola he loved me and that he would do whatever he had to do to make our marriage succeed. Lola said that would take considerable work on his part, but she was willing to help him, if he chose to do it."

Jess indicated his willingness, I remembered now, but never proclaimed it. And never acted on it. Never followed through on further appointments with her or any therapist.

"Lola confessed that she watched us every week as we held each other in the parking lot after leaving her office—she apologized for this, but it all happened right outside her window. She said our deep love for each other was very clear to her and moved her beyond words. She even thanked us for letting her witness this, saying that it allowed her to go on with her work, strengthened and renewed."

I put my juicy hands down in the midst of the ants, and said, "Isn't that something?"

Daisy said, "She sounds pretty special."

"Before we left that day, she looked straight at me and said, 'Take care of yourself, Annie. That's the best thing you can do.'"

"Wow," Daisy said, "she was sure sending you a message."

I realized I'd unwittingly committed mass murder of the ants and moved to the faucet to rinse my hands of tiny ant corpses.

"I ignored that message though. Until now, anyway. That's what I'm trying to do down here."

I rooted around a drawer for a better knife for slicing the pineapple into pieces.

I stopped shuffling through the drawer and looked up. "I love him."

"The stinker."

"Yeah," I agreed. I gave up my search for a better knife and resumed slicing the slippery pineapple quarters.

I hadn't seen Bijou for a while now, and her nap should be over. I called Nell and Libby. "Did you take the puppy outside?"

Nell said, "We couldn't find a puppy."

Libby said, "We thought you just wanted to tell secrets to Mommy."

"No, really, I have a puppy." I nodded to Daisy. "Really."

"I haven't seen any puppies," Daisy said. Did I detect a hint of disbelief?

"Oh, my gosh." I rinsed and dried my hands. "She's got to be around here somewhere." I began to lift clothing strewn around the family room. "Careful where you walk, Daisy; don't step on any piles."

"What color is this puppy?"

I abruptly stopped my search. "Daisy, I know I'm a mess, but, honest, I have a puppy." I scooped a load of damp beach towels off one end of the leather sofa and looked beneath it. I said, "She's got to be hungry. She hasn't eaten since early this afternoon."

The twins wiggled their tiny bodies behind the sofa. Nell found a baloney sandwich.

Leaning against the kitchen counter with her arms folded, Daisy said, "Well, don't worry. If there's a puppy in here, it won't starve to death."

"*If*?" I said. "*If*? I own a puppy; her name is Bijou. Now help me look for her."

"If Marcus calls and finds out we have an animal loose in the house and that nobody's seen it for an hour, he's going to start in about my housekeeping again. It'd be a lot easier on me if this puppy was a figment of your imagination."

"Bijou!" I called.

A moment later she trotted down the stairs with one of the twins' dollies in her mouth, wagged her tail at all the smiling faces staring at her. She accepted Nell's and Libby's squeals of pleasure and their four chubby hands reaching for her.

"Aw," Daisy and I said in unison.

Fourteen

Jess

She answered on the second ring. I didn't even say hello.

"No dating," I said.

"No dating?" she repeated, sounding puzzled.

"No dating."

I hung up.

I drummed my fingers on my desktop in the back office of TFS. I did not feel reassured. Furthermore, I doubted Annie had considered dating. Maybe I'd given her ideas. And beyond that, I suspected I had, as usual with Annie, said more about my own thoughts than anything else. And worse, that was just what Annie would pick up. My neck heated.

Shit. I had just announced to my beloved that *I* was considering dating.

Now she would think less of me than ever, and she wasn't in Florida to think good things about me as it was.

The adolescent boy left without supervision for a couple weeks was eyeing other women—that was what she would think.

I heard Hadley scrape snow off her boots on the grate outside the store's front door, then insert her key into the lock and turn the bolt. Soon the rest of the staff would follow and the workday would begin, ready or not.

I wondered if Lizette was scheduled to come in today.

I wondered what she'd be wearing, how she'd fix her hair. Sometimes she left it down and all those curls would swing in sync with her short skirt. I wasn't the only one watching her, I had noticed. But I didn't think she was encouraging the young guys.

Then the flip side of my phone call occurred to me. Maybe Annie would get jealous. Maybe she would worry. Hurry home and claim me.

Then my mind flipped again, and I realized that if I was experiencing sexual thoughts about another, she might be, too. Now I was back where I started, back when my hand had reached for the phone.

I sat at the Snake River Brew Pub that night thinking I'd have paid any price to undo that "no dating" phone call to Annie. She heard those words and knew right off what was going on with me. I doubted it scared her, either. It won't make her rush home to keep me from straying. I knew Annie. She'd figure if I was so damn shallow to start an affair as soon as she left, she wouldn't want me. I don't know—am I that shallow?

I had known the guys sitting at my table here at the pub for years and had begun coming after work to have a beer with them since Annie left. Usually I stayed to order some dinner. Gerry Spence's private detective was here tonight, along with Harrison Ford's ranch manager, the helicopter pilot responsible for most of the mountain rescues and a friend who had the smartest search-and-rescue dog I'd ever seen in action. Buster, a border collie–blue heeler mix with gold eyes lively as small suns, found a man buried in fourteen feet of snow in three minutes flat. Great storytellers, all these guys. And though the talk was good as always tonight, I kept tuning out of the conversation to watch my hands wipe sweat off my beer mug and feel sorry for myself about spending dinnertime here once again, drinking Snake River Pale Ale and having the pasta special.

Maybe Annie didn't give a damn, but Lizette was beginning to notice me watching her. I swore there was an extra swish to her butt moving around the store when she knew I was in sight.

Aside from that, the store was doing okay without Annie. In some ways she was too intense for a resort business. Once a guy came in, just browsing, saying he was killing time. And Annie said, "That's a terrible thing to do to time." She was always bringing people up short like that. I remember one fellow shot back, "What the hell? Time's going to kill me."

The racket in this place was getting to me. They designed restaurants these days to increase the noise level, instead of reducing it as they once did. The pub was two stories of metal stairs, supports, rafters and brewing equipment, all of it ringing with voices and the clink of glass and pottery. The din was supposed to jack up the belief you were having fun. Tonight, it wasn't working.

Ford's ranch manager was telling how they sneaked the Dalai Lama and his entourage on the ranch last summer, because he needed a rest. Painted a pretty humorous picture of orange-robed monks and cowboys milling around the corrals together. When the story was over, I said good night to the guys, using the dogs in the car as an excuse—didn't want them to get too cold. In the parking lot I scraped off a couple inches of fresh snow from the windshield to expose their three noses smearing up the other side.

I wished I'd thought before making that stupid phone call—"No dating." It was the image of all those exposed bodies in Florida. Naked tanned chests, bare muscled legs. Annie, half clothed herself, walking the beach, strolling along the boat pier. Men would look at her. And, unlike me, they would really see her—topaz ear studs and all.

Fifteen

Annie

*J*ess hung up on me, and I looked at my cell phone and said right out loud, "Jess, you dumb nut."

Across the table from me at the Osceola Café in Old Town Stuart, where my sister, nieces and I were eating a late breakfast, Daisy halted her motions a moment, then busied herself cutting up an egg-and-bacon croissant into small pieces for her daughters. A bit dazed, I tucked my phone back into my tote. I kept my head down, my hand holding the phone inside the tote on my lap. I shouldn't have allowed phone calls. I had enough garbage to wade through without him adding more crap.

Two words, "No dating," and he'd hung up.

As was typical of Jess, he attributed his own feelings to me, which left him off the hook for needing to acknowledge or be responsible for them himself. Instead, he picked up the phone and issued his demand, *no dating,* as if I were the one plotting such a thing. But I knew what he was thinking even if he didn't. He was thinking that it'd be a lot easier to fall into a sexual attraction with another woman than to trouble himself solving this thing with me. All I could think was, Oh, Jess, you wouldn't, would you?

My nieces picked up on the charged atmosphere around the table. I felt them staring at me. I looked up.

Libby said, "Mommy has hair on her vagina."

Nell asked, "Do you, Aunt Annie?"

Yanked from my dark thoughts, I barked out a surprised laugh, set my tote on the floor and said, "Yep."

Satisfied, the two girls resumed eating. And Daisy said, "Everything okay?"

I told her what Jess had just said on the phone. "The next time I talk to him, he'll minimize his words, experience a loss of memory about the call or say that I had misunderstood. I'll bet money on it."

The door of the café was open, propped by a potted palm, and sweet breezes from the Indian River one block over skated through, rolling smoothly over our table, lifting napkin corners and tickling my face with my loose hair. I took a big breath and then a bite of my omelet.

Two more bites and a sip of coffee, and my phone's muffled ring came from my tote on the floor. I resisted smirking at Daisy, reached for my tote, checked the ID and said, "Hi, Jess."

"I don't remember exactly what I said, but I thought you might misunderstand. I was just thinking we hadn't talked about certain things."

He used all three excuses. Should have made that bet.

"Okay, thanks. Bye-bye." I sounded friendly and even felt that way, always grateful for any sort of acknowledgment that could be construed as an apology from Jess. Then—as I typically did—I began my descent into forgetting my negative feelings toward him once we patched things up. If it wasn't for talking to Daisy, I knew I would not be capable of recalling what had upset me.

After first checking that the girls were preoccupied with their own conversation, I said to Daisy, "It's as if I lived with a wife beater who, after bloodying my nose, fell to his knees to swear his deep love, and I only remembered the words of love. I am so eager to forgive, to slip back into the good parts of our marriage, that I sometimes cannot actually recall the trouble that led to our makeup kiss."

Feeling hopeless, I shook my head. "Marital amnesia."

Daisy said, "Sounds to me as if you both use 'marital amnesia.'"

"But he uses it *against* me; I use it *for* him."

Daisy and I could talk freely to each other without suffering guilt over betraying our husbands, because we loved each other's mates enough to bear the knowledge of their imperfections. Marcus' wonderful curiosity and wide intelligence made him a benevolent listener; he wanted to understand everything and everybody and rarely made judgments, feeling as he did that he always had more to learn. I adored him, and Daisy could count on it, even while she complained, as she did after breakfast while we browsed together in Barnes & Noble.

"Marcus will have a fit if I come home with more books."

I said, "More books bought with your *own* hard-earned money from working at Teague Family Sports three days a week?"

We had positioned Nell and Libby in the children's book corner, then strolled the nearby shelves while we talked.

"Daisy," I said, "why can't you buy all the books you want?" The two of them spent money like kids betting toothpicks. "It's *your* money."

"We pool our money. We've done that since we began living together. You and Jess do, too."

Abruptly I was struck by the immaturity that sharing money required of marriage partners. Why in the twenty-first century were adult men and women bound to each other by money in ways that curtailed their personal freedom? I thought how Jess tossed his opinions around every time I bought beautiful gift wrapping, saying it was just wadded up and tossed out after one use. And how I rolled my eyes at his ever-expanding collection of Hawaiian shirts.

I said, "You know, Daisy, we had more independence as twelve-year-olds with our allowance from Mom and Dad than we do as adult married people."

Daisy hugged a book she wanted to her chest and looked at me with some surprise. "That's so true."

"We are making mommies and daddies out of our marriage partners. Didn't we work hard at growing up and getting out of those confines? Adults should have their own money."

"But it would be too hard to separate money out," Daisy said. "Besides, most men make more money than women do and . . ." She glanced off toward the girls. "There're just too many problems with that idea."

"I think there are too many problems without some separation." I thought for a moment. "It can be worked out. Different-sized paychecks like you and Marcus have can be dealt with through percentages. You know, twenty-five percent of each of your paychecks goes for housing . . . like that. Adults should have their own money. Period."

Like most couples, Jess and I endured hours of argument and resentment over money. I accused him of rash spending and he accused me of penny-pinching. The truth was: we each deserved to have our own styles of spending. If I could clear away this issue for the bulk of our expenses, it would reenergize us both.

I had reminded Daisy about the husbands and wives who came into our stores—mine back home, hers there in Stuart—expressing guilt over what they were purchasing, because their partners would complain.

"Sometimes it's as small as"—I searched my mind—"as this book you want." I took her book, said I'd buy it for her and stated again that this idea of mine was a good one.

I ended up buying three books for Daisy so she didn't have to deal with Marcus about them. His view on book buying was founded on his position as board member and financial supporter of the Martin County Library: Daisy could buy a book if the library didn't carry it. Sounded like a transaction a parent might make. You can have a cupcake if you finish your green beans.

I told Daisy, "Marcus gets to have his view; he just doesn't get to inflict it on you." I assured Daisy she wasn't undermining her husband by buying a book she wanted to read. Having stirred up enough trouble, I bought Nell's and Libby's books, too.

During the two-hour drive home from Stuart Sunday morning, I thought about this idea of separating money. It could be harder for Jess and me to separate financially because we ran a business together, pulled a joint paycheck. But if I could figure it out for us, then any couple could do it. For a partner who stayed home to keep house and care for children, an hourly wage for their many duties would take the place of a paycheck. For starters, Jess and I should be given the same benefit we had given our sons as they grew up: personal money to spend. When we cashed our paycheck each month, we could budget for separate discretionary money for each of us.

I considered the money issues Jess and I argued about most. We had an envelope of grocery money set on the kitchen shelf each month, and each month I became annoyed that Jess used it to buy food he let spoil or grabbed all the cash, stuffed it in his pocket on his way to the store and never returned the remainder. I accused him of carelessness; he accused me of being a Nazi banker. What if we separated that out, too? He got half the monthly grocery money; I got the other half. If we spent it unwisely, we had to dig into our discretionary money.

He used debit cards without recording the transactions and credit cards to order things I never saw, so couldn't budget for. Okay then, separate debit cards and credit cards to be paid from separate checking accounts, in which we deposited our personal money. His and hers. But what about house payments, the boys' college fund, vet bills for the dogs?

Sixty-five miles of driving had passed in a mindless blur when I said right out loud, "Everything can be separate." In a flash I saw it, clear and clean. Jess and I would receive separate paychecks and each make payments into a family checking account for the mortgage, insurance, household bills and repairs. From our separate accounts, we'd each be responsible for all personal spending—our own clothes and our own share of the groceries. Even our own car and its gasoline and repairs could be included. If any of that didn't work for some reason, we could put the expense back into the family account. I yelped right out loud with glee over my liberation.

Marriage Rule #1: Establish Independent Money.

The marriage sabbatical was working.

Sixteen

Jess

Sometimes I was so convinced Annie was on her way back to me, so sure she'd realized how dumb this marriage sabbatical was, that I'd reach for the phone and dial her number. If voice mail picked up, she'd packed and was on the airplane. It was all I could do to keep from driving to the airport to surprise her when she landed. Fortunately, I just kept dialing, and unfortunately, she eventually answered. Except for today. Five in the evening, almost dark, and she hadn't answered yet. I knew for a fact that Delta's scheduled flights between here and Orlando allowed her to arrive home by now. I didn't go so far as to show up at the airport, but I bought five red tulips on the way home after work.

I pulled into the driveway with all the anticipation of a birthday kid suspecting his surprise party. I got out of the car, tulips sheltered under my jacket so the freeze wouldn't kill them and Annie didn't see them, held the car door open while the dogs tumbled into the yard, and walked toward the house. Then I noticed. No footprints in the snow. And another thing—why did it take me so long to see something so obvious? There wasn't a single light on in the house. I opened the front door anyway with a limp scrap of hope.

Nobody jumped out, shouting, "Surprise."

It was possible that I was going crazy, and the idea sounded good to me.

First I had left a note for Annie a few days ago without thinking; now this ridiculous and overwhelming certainty that she was waiting for me in our home. I found a vase for the tulips, filled it with water, and carried out my plan to set it before the dining room window: red tulips with the backdrop of white snow and dark gray sky. This was the kind of thing Annie never thought to do, but she loved it when I did.

If I did go crazy, I wouldn't have to spend evenings alone in this chilled and empty living room. Eventually someone would come and put me in an institution; there would be company there, someone to eat dinner with. Acceptance meant I'd have to go on like this for months, because AnnieLaurie wasn't coming home soon.

She had started college classes. Most of them involved Creativity—capital C, of course. She couldn't just lie on the beach and do nothing. She actually sounded interested in getting a degree down there in Florida so she could be a *legitimate* champion of bad art.

I called the dogs, got in the car once more and drove downtown to eat at the pub. It started snowing again. Dark had descended for good . . . or bad. What the hell did it matter?

On the drive home from the restaurant, the streets were completely white from the fresh snow, no dirt in the tire tracks. Where else in the world do you drive down a busy highway, the busiest in the state of Wyoming in fact, and see total whiteness on the road? And Annie was missing this. Even if she was here, she'd need me to point out these things.

I thought about how much Annie lived in her head and how since she was gone I'd started doing the same thing. Because I missed her I seemed to take on some of her characteristics. I'd noticed the same thing when my dad died. He had this habit of lightly knocking his chin with the first knuckle of his fist, a kind of John Wayne tough-guy mannerism. Since I'd grown up watching him do that, I never consciously took notice of it. Then he died and I found I was doing it myself. Still do. So here I am thinking about stuff every time it gets quiet, just like Annie does.

Annie reminded me once that the largest erogenous zone in the body is the brain. I said, "Only if your dick is stubby." She laughed. She laughed at all my jokes. She was generous that way. Still, who could imagine living with someone who was always thinking? Even in bed? Even making love? That was when she said that about the brain. Hell, I tried to make her laugh in self-defense; if I didn't, I'd be on my elbows, above her, midpump, listening to her philosophize.

I pulled into the driveway.

Before going into the house, the dogs and I walked around the neighborhood to give us all a little exercise and them some sniffing time. I got a kick out of the way they buried their noses deep into a snowbank and just stayed there a while savoring the cold. No traffic at this hour, everybody home on the sofa after dinner, so I walked down the center of the street on the snowpack and the dogs wandered along the high banks of plowed snow on both sides of me. The snowfall had stopped. Above us the clouds were thinning in the black sky and stars popped through, looking like snowflakes caught in gauze netting, as if not all the snowflakes had fallen, but some stayed put to sparkle.

I didn't analyze myself or my life, the way Annie did. Or I didn't put it to words. I just found myself going in some direction. Like my dogs, I wandered over to the food dish before I acknowledged my hunger in any words in my head. Annie always knew by looking at me what was going on. She'd say, "Why don't you take an aspirin?" And I'd wonder why the hell I should, and she'd say, "Your face is all screwed up. You hurt somewhere, right?"

Well, I hurt somewhere now. I thought how I'd sat there staring at the staircase that night Annie left—the same way our dogs stared up the street whenever I took my fishing rod to the creek without them. They never moved, just faced the direction in which I'd left and waited, primed to greet my return. In my mind, I sat primed to greet Annie's return.

Yellow lamplight warmed the fronts of houses I passed. About a quarter of them still had their Christmas lights up. Even the town square sparkled with holiday decorations a month after the holiday was over and, like other years, it would probably stay that way until spring. Never saw a community so reluctant to give up its colored lights. Maybe the six-month-long winter had something to do with that.

Once I said to her, "Take it easy, Annie. Go with the flow. You don't have to do everything the hard way."

"The hard way," she repeated, stretching her eyebrows into high arches. I should have recognized the trap. "Versus the easy way of leaving it for someone else to do . . . like, say, your way."

She did a lot—I'd grant that. But she didn't think about stuff like red tulips against a snowy background. Why didn't that count in my favor?

Our walk circled back home, and I rounded up the pups on the porch and brushed snow off their underbellies the best I could before we all went inside. Last week the dogs and I moved out of the bedroom and into the guest space; I slept better in the loft, a large open room with curved windows on each end. The view to the south overlooked Snow King Mountain; the view to the north held a wedge of Tetons looming over the saddle of a butte. I sat up here in Annie's rocker before these floor-to-ceiling windows and rocked and thought until I eventually stretched out onto one of the guest beds for the night. Annie always did accuse me of getting sleepy when I tried to think.

Tonight the rockers on the chair bumped on the ridges of the old wool braided rug lying before the windows. The jagged peaks of the Tetons had snagged all the clouds in the sky now and lay bundled in them for the night. Bannon, Leidy and Ranger lay beside me and plucked ice balls off their paws and lower legs and crunched them in their teeth. It was almost as noisy up here as at the pub during dinner.

The first years we were together, my love for Annie used to consume me in its totality. I couldn't take my eyes off her. She was my friend, my sister; the next thing I knew I was undressing her, wild with lust and confusion. That girl burrowed deeply into my insides. She weaseled out my secrets, secrets I never knew I owned and dreams I didn't know I carried until they were unearthed by her, formed into words and set out before me.

Then, of course, once she knew my secrets, my story, she was armed with weapons to use against me. More than once she'd said, "If you'd face up to your background, Jess, instead of trying to forget, it would help our relationship." Like stuff from twenty years before we even met had anything to do with our marriage.

I had two choices with Annie. I could freeze her out, just turn on the TV and not take much notice of the household events. Or I could melt into her, turn into a shapeless blob like a gingerbread man baked with too much butter—or whatever it was Annie did wrong one Christmas. Spread all the hell over the cookie sheet, no definition to him.

Now I rocked with one hand rubbing Leidy's head where she'd set it on my thigh. Plainly, I was in foreign country when I fell for Annie. I felt envy now for the guys who talked about *the wife,* because those guys never felt like they were blobs without any edges to their skin when they made love to their life mates. No mix-up there, by God. She was *the* wife. He was Head of the House. Leave Daddy alone—he's tired. Could I have some money, honey?

These were not words heard in our house. And it wasn't that I wanted them said. It was just that I'd like that to be the understood standard, and that it was recognized that I gave AnnieLaurie the gift of our relationship being more. I wouldn't mind a thank-you once in a while. I wouldn't mind a little credit for being a decent guy who didn't lord it over the family, like our store manager's husband. Hadley married this guy who'd told me once that he jacked the heat up to eighty-three degrees but had the thermostat read sixty-eight degrees. Just liked to keep Hadley off center. I wouldn't go that far, but sometimes I knew how the guy felt.

I tugged my boots off and stretched out on the bed.

She'd been gone half a month now, yet I still heard Annie's voice in my head as if she were in the twin bed next to mine up here, whispering in the dark, "Yes, but, Jess, that is just your desire to be in control. Two equal partners cannot play power games."

It was no goddamn game. I wanted the power, no playing around about it. It'd been that way for centuries—men held the power. Yet I was willing to go with the change (Annie would say, when I felt like it). I cared for the babies, cooked, cleaned house. Maybe inconsistently, as she claimed, but those were her jobs; I was just helping out. Didn't I get any credit for that?

Maybe she had just meant to rock the boat when she left, but she'd tipped the whole goddamn thing over.

Seventeen

Annie

I climbed the stairs to my apartment, leaving my suitcase in the car, because I had Bijou's dishes and food in one arm, a birdcage in the other. I couldn't resist the bird when I spotted her at the pet store while getting chew toys for Bijou. After staying at Daisy's I feared there wasn't enough company at my place with only a puppy and refrigerator mold.

Kia was a beautiful, tiny Fischer lovebird. Only four and half inches high with feathers of exotic greens, reds and yellows. White eye rings pounced out of her face above a brilliant beak that looked as if she were wearing shiny red lipstick—my mom's old favorite Cherries in the Snow by Revlon. The tiniest parrot in the world and I took to her immediately. Already she ate out of my hand.

"Don't you, pretty bird?" Kia scrambled over to the side of the cage nearest my voice. I set her cage on the kitchen counter, reached into my pocket for a sunflower seed and held it out to her with my fingers between the bars of the cage. She tipped her head sideways and took it, showing her tiny tongue. I had confessed to Jess about acquiring my second new pet while he was still feeling regretful over his "no dating" phone call to me. Then I turned my phone off; I needed a break.

Talking to Daisy over the weekend gave me confidence in my decision to take a marriage sabbatical. I'd seen too many divorces among friends in which the good parts of the marriage were discarded with the bad. I intended to save the good parts. Yet marriage as a completely shared life—from bed to business—needed loosening. MARRIAGE RULE #1, Establish Independent Money, pried open new avenues of thought. I couldn't tell yet where that would lead.

From the car I gathered an armload of shopping bags, my tote and suitcase. Lucille opened the back door as I closed the gate.

"Welcome home."

"Good to be back."

Mitzi barreled out to give Bijou a frenzied greeting. The puppies collided and locked into a black-and-white furry knot that tumbled in the grass.

Upstairs I opened Kia's cage door and she immediately flew to my shoulder. She accompanied me as I moved from room to room, opening all the windows in my stifling apartment. I checked on the puppies, then gathered ingredients to put together a salad for lunch. Kia nibbled on a lettuce leaf I held up to her, perched on my shoulder. Then she flew down into the sink to play in the drizzle of faucet water. I laughed as I watched her flutter her feathers and begin a little dance accompanied by quiet murmurs and clucks. She lifted one wing, tucked her head, lifted the other wing, tucked her head, turned in a circle.

Two hours until Perry's party. Plenty of time to unpack, settle back into my new home and get showered and dressed. I should have asked Perry how formally to dress for a dinner party on the beach. When a dressy event was held outdoors in Jackson Hole, invitations read "Mountain Cocktail Attire." As far I could tell no one had figured out what that meant—clothing ranged from Levi's to lace. I hoped the same loose criteria reigned for a lawn party in Florida. My new orange cotton dress with the flared skirt and crazy assortment of white buttons down the front, dressy sandals and sunglasses might do.

My friends greeted me in the wide circular drive as soon as I handed my car keys to an attendant. Then Perry took us all to meet our hosts, her parents-in-law, Ralph and Anna. Next, with chilled glasses of white wine in hand, we sauntered across the bouncy Florida grass to the tennis courts where Perry's husband, Alex, was playing. Lobbed balls stunned the silence. I took in Alex's startling good looks, blond, slightly curling hair and tanned, muscled body. He grinned at his two opponents with bright, playful eyes as he crouched in anticipation of a ball served from the far corner of the court. We watched Alex beat the heck out of his two guests, teenagers who worked hard to keep up with this forty-year-old. Alex leaped over the net and shook hands with the losers.

Marcy said it for all of us: "So . . . rich *and* married to a movie god."

"And on top of that, she's blond and beautiful," Sara added.

Perry said, "The blond may be symbolic of it all—my real hair tends toward a dull rusty brown and the rest . . . You'll see. And I'll explain everything at lunch on Tuesday."

What could possibly need explaining? She looked content and happy.

"Alex." Perry waved. "Come meet my friends when you can."

It was a beautiful day and a beautiful place. The house was huge, painted pink and yellow, its gabled roof tiled. It stood against a blue sky and was surrounded by lush, deeply green grass on three sides. The mirror of ocean stretched behind it, where sunlight sparked on the waves over the dune, like mysterious signals from beyond the sea oats. I checked my friends' faces, and they were all enthralled by the physical beauty of Perry's home . . . and her husband.

Alex jogged over, looking invigorated, while his partners slumped on a bench, looking exhausted. Up close a long, raised scar beside Alex's hair line was visible, but didn't deter one bit from his handsome, perfect features. His teeth flashed bright as the sunlit waves when he smiled at Perry, then at us. Perry made the introductions.

When Alex learned I had just come for the winter, he asked, "Have you gone to Disney World yet?

"No, I haven't. Probably won't," I added.

"Oh, you have to go; doesn't she, Perry?"

"Alex loves Disney World."

"I love it," he said simply.

"I have a business at home where I deal with lots of tourists, so I don't usually go places with crowds." I expected him to ask about my business now; I was looking forward to telling him. Something dramatic-sounding to Florida people, I had learned, about a ski shop in Jackson Hole, Wyoming. All those snowstorms, cold temperatures and steep mountains. I was happy being in Florida, but I missed Jackson Hole enough to want to talk about it every chance I got. Giving the weather report back home was a sure way to stir reaction. I had come prepared: snow three feet deep on the valley floor, thirty feet in the mountains. Temperature: eleven below zero.

"Disney World, though . . ." Alex looked to Perry for the words. Perry glanced to each of us, as if gauging something, and I wondered if perhaps not everyone liked to talk about Disney World in Florida. I checked Sara and Marcy for their reactions. There were none. They were just smiling at Alex and Perry, eyes expressionless. Much as I was doing. Maybe the family's obvious wealth—I glanced toward the enormous Key West–style house rising above the beach, with pool and gardens—was making us all stupid.

When Perry didn't step in to supply the words, Alex said, "Disney World has Space Mountain."

"Space Mountain?" Marcy spoke as if taking her first verbal step out of a trance. You could feel her gathering herself together and trying to pretend that she had been part of the conversation all along, not off somewhere trying to put two and two together and coming out with five.

"And you can get married at Cinderella's Castle," Alex said.

"My girls used to dream of doing that when they were little," Sara said. "Hope they've gotten over *that* by now." Sara tucked both lips between her teeth, realizing that she should have omitted that last sentence. She added, "Because it's so expensive." And she dashed a look around the circle to see if she had reclaimed her good manners.

"That's what we did; we got married at Cinderella's Castle. Perry was Cinderella, with just the right color hair. And I was Prince Charming. I carried the ring in a glass slipper."

"You mean . . . ?" I didn't even know where to go with this.

"They really do that down here," Perry said. "I was surprised, too, when I first heard about it."

"It's the dream of a lot of Florida girls," Sara said. Her lips disappeared between her teeth again. Then she added, "And boys."

Marcy, still looking a bit dazed, right when we needed her brashness for asking all the questions we were afraid to ask, said, "Well, it's all just perfect, then."

Alex said, "It was perfect. The fireworks went off at just the right time in the background."

Perry said, teasing him, "And you were so busy watching them, you almost missed saying your vows."

"Perry poked me." Alex grinned at us. "Then we went on a Mickey Mouse honeymoon."

"Better go shower and change your clothes now." Perry raised up on her toes and kissed Alex on the cheek. "They're all laid out on the bed."

"I'm okay."

"We're going to eat soon. See? Mr. Raul is grilling."

"I don't need to change."

"I'll come with you." Perry turned to us and said, "Please help yourself to canapés and more wine. I'll be right back."

Not one of us said a word or even exchanged a single glance. We were Perry's friends; she'd tell us what she wanted us to know during lunch this week at the Green Bottle Café. We moved together toward the tables set with food beneath colorful umbrellas and then, as if it were too great a burden not to look at one another without question marks in our eyes, we each reached for a canapé, turned and sauntered off in three different directions.

I struck up a conversation with a woman in her twenties I had seen knitting beneath a bottlebrush tree on campus one morning last week.

"You made me remember I really liked knitting," I told her. "But I've only done square things. Well, dishcloths. It looked as if you were knitting a sweater."

"A summer shell. It soothes me to knit and helps order my thoughts," the woman said. "Mostly, though, I'm just hooked on it."

We talked for a while, exchanged names; hers was Caridad. She said she was also a student at the college, her family was from Cuba and she had recently moved up the coast from Miami. She gave me the location of her favorite yarn store and the phone number from her cell, which I copied into mine. The desire to hold knitting needles in my hand rose suddenly and urgently, a physical thing. I wanted to knit right now. Caridad invited me to sit under the bottlebrush tree and knit with her between classes; then we parted when people were called to dine. I headed toward the patio, with fingers that itched to hold beautiful yarn and a pair of those bamboo needles that I'd seen Caridad use. Like her, I needed soothing. I needed to order my thoughts.

Urges seemed to come on hard and fast for me lately, as though my inner landscape were cleared of brush and tilled for seeds. I thought of my new bird, and before that Bijou, my college classes, those sudden longings for the beach, in which I dropped whatever I was doing and left. When was the last time I felt this much in touch with myself? For the past two decades I had held down a full-time job, along with mothering two sons and trying to keep a marriage together. Breakfasts and lunches were eaten at my desk. I smiled to myself; it was a nice surprise to discover I still had urges.

Marcy, Sara and I carried our plates, heaped with lobster ther-
midor, shrimp, crab cakes and colorful fruit, to the upper deck of
the pool house, overlooking the ocean. Perry popped by our table
in between hostess duties and perched on a chair to join our talk.
The water stretched before us, calm and silky, a navy blue against
the softer blue of the sky. Once our empty plates were collected by
a waiter, Perry led us to the dessert table, and I hung back a bit,
stepped behind an oleander and called the yarn shop to see how
late they were open on Sundays.

The four of us sipped coffee, talked lazily and tested bites of
one another's dessert choices until the colors of the sunset faded
from the garish shades resembling the sherbets dolloped beside our
small cakes to the soft pastels of our dinner mints. Discreetly I
checked my watch, discovered it was a quarter after five; the yarn
shop closed at six. I hugged my friends goodbye. I found Perry's
in-laws and offered my appreciation for the wonderful afternoon,
then hurriedly jumped in my car and headed for town. Who but
me would be so eager to knit another dishcloth?

Monday morning I phoned the store. A young woman answered in
a little-girl voice with a deep come-on to it.

"Could I speak to Jess?"

"Like . . . who's calling?"

"His wife."

"His *wife*?"

"Yes," I said, and mimicked the young woman, "his *wi-ife*."
Then I changed my mind. "Let me speak to Hadley."

I heard the young woman call Hadley and say before handing
the phone over, "Jess is mar-ried?"

"Annie?"

"Does she look like she sounds?"

There was a pause, the clunk of a door shutting; then Hadley
answered, "Bustier."

"Oh, dear."

Hadley said, "Come home."

"Oh, dear."

Jess had said our phone talks were our mating calls. Like birds, he'd said, calling from tree to tree:

"Are you there?"

And answering, "I'm here."

"Are you there?"

"I'm here."

This time, no answer from Jess.

He wasn't there.

Eighteen

Jess

I stared out windows so often at work lately that several times a day Hadley tapped me on the shoulder to get my attention. I was going to have to give her a raise for adding one more job to her list of duties as store manager. If I was correctly reading the footsteps approaching my office door, she was about to catch me daydreaming again.

She said, "Jess, I'm sorry to bother you."

"When I'm this busy," I added, and conjured up a smile for her, as I sat stretched out in my desk chair, feet on the overturned wastebasket. She and I were the only grown-ups, as I jokingly called us, who worked in the store this ski season. The rest of the staff was college kids taking the semester off to winter in Jackson Hole or kids who did that last winter and still hadn't left.

Hadley shifted a pair of new skis that were about to fall across the doorway. Then she faced me.

"Lizette is crying in the washroom. She's dropping heavy hints to the others that it has to do with a love affair she must keep secret."

"Really? What's that about, do you suppose?"

Hadley gave me a stern look and stepped closer to my desk, where I sat with my chair cocked back in order to see the ski slopes out the window. She said, "Jess, it's none of my business." She stopped and propped her hands on her hips. "But I do believe Lizette intends on *making* it my business and everyone else's business who works here. I thought you could use the warning."

"I don't get it." Maybe the window staring was dulling my wits, but the past few weeks since Annie left, I hadn't been too sharp; no one's words seemed to come through clearly the first time around. Annie used to accuse me of using stupidity to relieve myself from responsibility. What-I-didn't-know-couldn't-hurt-me kind of idea. Once she got angry and she said, "You know, Jess, your IQ could rise to intimidating heights if you didn't try so damn hard to keep yourself uninvolved."

I asked Hadley, "Warning about what?"

Hadley stared straight into my eyes for a breath—in, out. Then she stepped forward to the edge of my desk. Hands braced on my desktop, she leaned toward me. "Jess, if you're not having an affair with Lizette, you're in big trouble."

"I thought the opposite would've been true." My voice sounded sulky, like the voice of a little boy who had missed out on extra candy due to a misunderstanding of the rules.

"Well, I mean . . . either way." Hadley stood straight. "She's intent on making trouble. Either way."

I had imagined having an affair with Lizette so many different times, in so many different ways and places, I felt guilty enough to question myself: did I lick that shiny round shoulder, or hadn't I actually seen Lizette's bare shoulder? Her pubic hair was light brown, wasn't it? Or was I just assuming that her natural coloring was three shades darker than her light-catching curls piled so carelessly on top her head?

"Trouble, Jess." Hadley pulled me out of my immobile, blank-eyed stare. "Either way." She raised herself to her usual abbreviated but dignified stance, tugged the bottom of her wool vest over her hips and added again, "None of my business."

"But you'll kill me in my sleep if I've cheated on your angel friend AnnieLaurie." I sounded a bit sour to myself. I wondered if I was mad about being accused of something I hadn't enjoyed.

"Kill you with your eyes wide-open . . . if you've gone against your own best self." Hadley took a breath and softened. "We can't really understand somebody else's bad spells. None of us acts our best during them."

"This is a bad spell, all right. But I'm clear on this one, Hadley." I sat upright, kicked the wastebasket aside. "I know where I want to end up. Annie and I . . . we'll be okay in time." I brought myself fully into the moment and stood. "What's up with this Lizette deal?" I took a swig from my water bottle.

"You have to admit purple emanations have throbbed from this office since Lizette walked into the store last month. No one has been unaware of that, so this looks bad for you. She could turn into very big trouble, Jess."

"Big trouble? I haven't done a thing. The office door has always been open. Everyone should have been aware of that, too."

"If you have no need to shut her up, Jess, then fire her."

"Fire her? For crying?" I sat back down in my desk chair. That didn't sound fair; besides, I needed Lizette to fantasize about. I'd go nuts if I couldn't exchange purple throbbing emanations with Lizette. I swiveled my chair away slightly, folded my hands and pressed my lips with my index fingers. God, did this mean I was sexually using Lizette? She was a kid in her early twenties; I was a grown man in my late forties.

To give me time Hadley evened up the edges on a pile of invoices on the desk. I swiveled back toward her.

"Take a look at that one," I said. "We never received those ski helmets."

While she read the invoice, another thought hit. I stood back up and walked to the window. I was Lizette's boss; this was the workplace. Men have been alerted to cringe in terror at that certain phrase: "Sexual misconduct in the workplace." Shit, was I a depraved older man using young Lizette's presence in the store like some guy might use a model in a porno magazine?

I wanted to hole up with a strong drink and think about this. I looked back over to Hadley. She laid down the invoice and raised her eyebrows at me. I wasn't going to get that chance. I nodded. Hadley led the way out the door, and I followed her to the employees' washroom.

Lizette sat on the edge of a bench with her face buried in a cloud of toilet paper held scrunched in her hands. Four other employees stood inside the washroom, watching her, and two others sat beside her on the bench, patting her.

"What's wrong here?" I said, bracing myself in the doorframe. Nobody volunteered an answer, but six employees offered less than respectful looks toward their boss. Lizette had won their hearts with her muffled mewing. Hell, mine, too. I felt like beating up the guy who had done this to Lizette.

"Lizette?" I spoke gently.

"You know what's wrong." Lizette lifted her face long enough to shoot me an accusing glare from her pink-rimmed eyes, her upper lip swollen into a sweet pout. The six others glared with her. Saundra, darn close to being obese, was in her usual process of twisting one strand of her brown hair into a thin rope, which she kept tightening until it stiffened like a spike and stood straight out from the side of her head, before unraveling into limpness. She sat on the bench rubbing Lizette's back with the hand that wasn't busy twisting hair. On the other side, Molly sat patting Lizette's knee and Tawnya leaned against a wall with the three guys. Hadley stood beside me in the doorway, her short, slender body just fitting under my left arm, which was raised level with my own head and gripping the doorframe so hard I could hear it creak, unless that was Lizette squeaking when she breathed.

I took a big intake of air myself and I cursed the day Lizette walked into my store and I cursed the day Annie walked out of it. Then I heard Annie accuse me of avoiding everything unpleasant in my life by blaming it on something else, or refusing to notice it, or diminishing its importance, or forgetting about it altogether.

I ran through that list one more time to see if any of those responses might work here.

I had to hurry; the silence felt lethal. If this had been a movie,
huge Japanese drums, big as a house, would have been resounding
throughout the theater.

Finally, I decided I'd better just grab ahold of this one and see
if I could bring us all out the other side. What other choice did I
have?

"Lizette, we don't know what's wrong. You're troubled. How
can we help?"

"We," she said, the sneer loud enough for all of us to hear, and
I thought, Heck, there goes my first bright idea: to make this a
community problem. But maybe I wasn't forced to drop that position yet.

"Can you tell us, Lizette?" I used my best grown-up, man-in-
charge manner, measuring carefully my warmth and distance.

"I can tell you privately."

Trap, trap, my brain hollered. I shot a look at Hadley and her
eyes yelled back at me, *Trap, trap.* But I read another thing in Hadley's eyes as well. Hadley wondered if I was willing to step into this
trap. I wondered a moment myself. Holding moist, limp Lizette in
my arms behind the closed washroom door. Practically legitimate,
because, heck, there was no sneaking here, everybody knew for
God's sake. I was Lizette's boss; she needed my private authority.
You heard her ask.

A noise came from the front of the store.

"Is there a customer out there?" I said. I thought about who
to send. Saundra, twisting her hair? Nah, she didn't have much
fun in her life. She was practically in the spotlight right now; it
would be cruel to remove her. One of the guys. Todd. He had a big
crush on Lizette. No, that was mean, too. Rafe, he had a crush on
Todd. Who didn't have a stake in this? Casey. He didn't have a stake
in anything, even his own life, just rolled with whatever. "Casey,

tell whoever's out there that we're closed. Then lock the door and come back."

Whether I wanted to or not, I had to get on with this problem, and I had to move from my safe place in the doorway, where I was neither in nor out of the room, if only to let Casey through. I dropped my casual stance of arms supporting my weight against the doorframe, like a coach leaning into the locker room to wish his players well, and I drew myself together and stepped farther into the washroom.

I said, "Lizette, this is about as private as we get around here. Periodically, we all scrunch into the bathroom together and talk things out." I looked around with smiling eyes, stupidly expecting support in the form of laughter to my witticism. My humor was not appreciated. Neither was my position of spokesperson for "us workers." This was *my* problem, those faces said. I felt like firing the bunch of them. Start over.

Maybe keep Lizette.

Hold it, buster, I counseled myself. This is serious stuff. Besides, at the actual thought of touching Lizette, not in the fantastical future but now and here, I felt a great resistance rise in me. I bought time to sort out this surprise piece of news by pretending we were all waiting for Casey.

Annie can rub her snot all the hell over me, but please don't make me have to deal with some other woman's snot. In fact, I didn't want to deal with another woman, period. Not her snot, not her emotions, not her sexuality. And now I understood how I had messed up. I had not treated Lizette with the dignity deserving of a real person, but rather had used her as a receptacle for my imagined longings, and it was no more right than if I had dishonored a woman by paying for sex with her. Maybe that was putting it harshly, but Lizette clearly felt abused and I needed to try to fix that, if I could.

Casey returned, took his place, leaning against the wall. "Locked up, but we're losing money, boss."

"We've got a different kind of business to attend to here." I moved to the bench. "Molly, could I trade places with you?" I took her seat beside Lizette. "We could use some more toilet paper here." Todd handed me a wad and I gently removed the damp scrunched-up mess from Lizette's hands. Now that I saw her as a real woman, I didn't mind Lizette's snot as much as I had thought I would. I'd still rather have been dealing with Annie's snot though. God, how I ached for Annie. Suddenly it seemed as if my own emotions surfaced along with Lizette's. I felt my upper lip begin to swell, and I wondered if everyone in the room was feeling especially close to sad parts of their lives.

I never handled personal problems with employees or even our sons, if I could avoid it. Annie did that. The only way I was going to get through this deal was to imagine what she might do. I'd watched her enough over the years. Often she began by stating the situation; so I did, too.

I tipped Lizette's face up with my forefinger to meet her eyes. "Lizette, you are a very pretty woman. I like to look at you. I have been looking at you a lot lately." I took the new bunch of toilet paper and dabbed at Lizette's tears and held it to her nose. "Blow."

Someone handed me more toilet paper. I got Lizette to blow again.

"I've been rude about it, this looking at you." I fought back the excuses that flooded to my defense, the remarks that suggested this was not typical behavior of mine, that it was prompted by my loneliness for the woman I really wanted to stare at. I came close, but I heard Annie's voice tell me to grow up and own up. I heard her accuse me of slippery behavior, of hiding behind a "nice guy" persona. I felt such a powerful pull to slide into those old slots that I dug in my mental heels and forced myself to resist.

In the disturbed ground that resulted from the struggle, new thoughts surfaced that promised to serve us all better.

"I regret how I have treated you, Lizette. I haven't learned who you are."

More than that. I *avoided* knowing information about Lizette. I was afraid it would blow my fantasy. She would hate fly-fishing or rodeos or beer or mystery novels. I just looked at her and let her see me looking at her and that was all I wanted from her. I felt full of regret for my refusal to know who this young woman was. And disgust. I had told myself it was okay to think anything I wanted, just not to act on it. Well, it was not okay, because all thought begat some kind of action. And because I was responsible for what I put out in the world . . . even thoughts. I did a disservice to this young woman and to Annie and to myself.

"My wife, Annie, and I are trying to spend the winter apart. Instead of thinking about some of the questions she and I want to settle between us, I just daydreamed looking out the window and when I wasn't doing that I daydreamed looking at you. I wish now I hadn't put you in that bad spot."

Lizette looked puzzled. This wasn't what she had expected. She was young enough to enjoy creating dramas and she was pretty enough to have experienced control over them. In this drama, *my life* depended on the outcome, and Lizette hadn't counted on that.

The others were still and attentive. Saundra was twisting a new piece of hair and crying quietly.

I was unsure of what to do next. One thing I recalled was how Annie made sure all of us in the store knew one another personally. So I said, "I enjoyed your prettiness without taking into consideration your whole self. For instance, I know Saundra has two hamsters, Twiggy and Penelope, and that she reads a romance novel every three days. And Todd here comes from Bill, Wyoming, where they only have a single parking meter—imagine that. He likes to fly-fish from opening day throughout the season. We practically want to wear black in honor of his misery closing day. But I don't know anything about you. That might be one of the hard parts about standing out physically—that's all anyone acknowledges about the person, the physical sight."

"Everybody just thinks of me as fat," Saundra said to prove my point. She nodded to everyone to acknowledge that she meant to be helpful. A new tear started at the corner of her eye.

I tore off some of the tissue and passed it to Saundra. By now the fresh end of the toilet paper was in my hands, while Todd held the center of the roll itself, which was huge and refilled one of the industrial holders we had in the toilet stalls around the corner. He rolled it loosely in his hands, letting it unwind as I needed it.

I wasn't sure Lizette liked the way things were going. She had created this scene, I suspected, to move me out of the hands-off staring track I kept myself in, and because she was used to playing center stage and maybe because it was Groundhog Day, which came along with the bleak reminder that we were only halfway between the first day of winter and the first day of spring. But I felt a sense of peace and cleanness of spirit pervade our group's intimate space, so I kept going.

"Tell me, Lizette, do you have any pets?"

"No."

"Where does your family live?"

"Here."

"Here?"

"I was born here."

"You're kidding. I didn't think anyone was born here. That's what I tell tourists who come in the store and ask me if I was born in Jackson Hole. I say, 'Nope, nobody was.' Now I'll have to send them to you with their questions."

"We moved when I was a month old. Then we moved back this winter."

"So you feel new here. Do you like it?"

"Not much."

"It'll get better. Do you like to read?"

"It's okay. I read sometimes."

"We should start a book trade. Bring in our old books and borrow from one another. I've got a bunch I can bring."

"Boy, do I have a lot," Saundra said. "Hope someone else reads romances. I could save a ton of money if I didn't have to buy so many."

I checked my watch. We usually closed at eight; it was now a quarter to six. "How about we all head over to the Mangy Moose and order some dinner? My treat." I looked around and was met with agreeable faces. I smiled in gratitude for their forgiveness.

I said, "Celebrate this book-trade deal." They laughed to let me know we were all square. Hadley was beaming. But I felt one more piece of closure was needed to cement the situation.

"Lizette, I ask your forgiveness for the trouble I gave you."

"It's okay, I guess."

"Todd, wait for Lizette while she gets ready for dinner, and we'll meet the two of you at the Moose."

I realized I was playing favorites here, but I didn't think Rafe had a chance with Todd.

Nineteen

I sat on the top step outside my porch, feeling the luck of the draw with my college classes, Bijou on my lap. That morning I had attended introduction to basic art with happy anticipation—and some terror that I'd be asked to draw. But the instructor planned to concentrate class assignments on understanding composition, perspective and the color wheel, with preliminary steps into various media. Next class, he said, we'd mix paint colors and learn about their warmth and coolness. I could do that.

I was also enrolled in an art class that involved creating with textiles. And a contemporary craft class, which was a study of craft as business and innovation. There, I was expected to design a pretend business and be innovative about it, to boot. The two remaining classes—psychology and English literary masterpieces—involved mainly reading. I loved to read, so felt I could handle my full schedule. I sat in the warm sunshine and fairly buzzed with excitement over my new textbooks and especially my art supplies, all set out on my worktable ready to use.

I smoothed Bijou's ears. My new life was taking shape. I found it pleasant to concentrate on myself and my own interests. And though the busty young woman who was surprised that Jess was *"mar-ried"* intruded on my thoughts now and then, my response was impatience, annoyance. Anything more would have reflected the old pattern of my married life, in which I offered my primary attention and energy toward Jess and directed the leftovers to my-self. Briefly, I even wondered if Jess had set up a situation designed to draw my attention back to him.

These weeks away from the store reminded me that I never meant to make a career out of the retail business. I began studying the ledgers of TFS to see if I could save the business from the threat of bankruptcy, resulting from Jess' disregard of the financial aspects of the store. Once I packed up Saddler's portable crib and carted it into the office, I never got away again.

I succeeded in resolving the financial problems, then became engaged in the challenge of maintaining a thriving sports store in a world-class resort. Our second son was born, and both Jess and I assumed I'd bring him into the store, as well. I worked in the office and Jess minded the children while he waited on customers. We were pleased with ourselves for stepping outside the traditional gender roles of husband and wife. Yet somehow the confusion of dropping those barriers instilled an imbalance in our workloads, and the bulk of responsibility landed on me. How could I have created a life so full and hectic and challenging that I never once paused to notice that it wasn't fulfilling to me?

I saw now that intimacy in my marriage was how I had defined the path to my sense of self. And I saw, too, that often I was so engaged in the pursuit of it that I didn't notice it wasn't reciprocated. These two ideas—intimacy within my relationship and an independent sense of self—described my struggle. They had been the two conflicting pulls on my marriage. Intimacy with Jess had often opposed my need to become an individual and any individual choices seemed to encroach on my intimacy with Jess. I thought especially of the time I cleaned the dining room table of my craft projects.

How did I come to feel that abandoning myself for Jess was proof of my love for him?

Breezes ruffled Bijou's fur and brushed the fronds of a coconut palm against the screen on the porch. I recalled leaving Perry's house at sunset Sunday, the dark descending quickly, and as I waited for the attendant to bring my car, early stars sprang out and dangled on the frond tips of a palm as tall as this one beside me. Despite the reason for being here, I enjoyed the enchantments of living in the tropics.

I ducked inside, grabbed a ball and my new knitting project and raced the puppy down to the yard to play awhile before meeting my friends at the Green Bottle Café. "Tuesday. I'll explain everything," Perry had said again before we parted. I recalled glancing across the lawn then to Alex, her husband, dressed in pale linen pants, a short-sleeved knit shirt and leather sandals, talking to friends of his parents. He looked happy and at ease. A handsome Prince Charming.

I tossed the ball across the yard, and Bijou peeled after it, caught the ball as it rolled and somersaulted over the top of it. I laughed. She took the ball in her mouth and lay in the grass and chewed on it. Not a retriever, I reminded myself. I moved over to the shade of an acacia tree, sat and pulled out my blue ribbon yarn and needles. Time enough to work a few rows on the scarf the yarn shop owner had talked me into tackling, graduating me from both dishcloths and the simple knitting stitch. She had taught me the "drop stitch," which created a lacy pattern, with holes I *deliberately* knitted in. Daisy would look great in it. And when I met Caridad under the bottlebrush tree to knit between classes, she might find this project more interesting than a dishcloth.

I had almost forgotten that elated feeling I used to get in a yarn store, with all that color and texture sparking the air. Along with my other craft projects, knitting also had gotten put away a few years back. Now I felt a rush of energy, thinking about all the free time I had in which to do the things I liked.

I rested my needles in my lap for a moment. Some unspoken tug-of-war had been going on between me and my marriage. And though I didn't for a minute believe that Jess had understood this, I did believe that he picked up on it unconsciously and tugged with all his might on the rope that kept me from moving in one direction or the other.

I watched Bijou roll onto her back and hold the ball between her paws to mouth it like an ice-cream cone. I held up one of the ear-shaped leaves that had fallen from the acacia tree above me and traced the inner curve of it.

I was struck by the realization that it didn't work for Jess to have me fully invested in intimacy with him or to create any sort of life without him. It worked best for Jess to keep me striving for footing and never quite succeeding balance. For Jess, it worked to have me off center and scrambling.

Intimacy and selfhood, those were the two ends of that rope.

My landlord, Shank, drove into the driveway alongside the picket fence, interrupting my thoughts. Probably home for lunch after doing errands, which reminded me that I needed to leave for the café soon. Shank had retired from the maintenance department at the college and his wife, Lucille, also retired, had taught history there. I said hello to Shank and he wandered over to pet Bijou and praise the weather, which was soft and warm and the exact reason people loved Florida in early February.

"Cille says you're attending classes."

"I am and I'm enjoying it, too. Attended my first classes this morning."

"Good thing somebody here is going to the college, now that Lucille and I are retired. How's the place doing without us?"

"Falling apart and grieving," I said.

He laughed his deep, rich chuckle.

And I joined him and got up to walk across the yard with him, then on up my stairs.

We met inside the mossy air of the Green Bottle Café. The day was so beautiful, we decided that even eating outside on the deck wasn't good enough. We ordered carryout, piled into Perry's car and drove to the savannah for a picnic. Twenty minutes inland got us to a vast, waving land of tall grasses, hidden ponds and paths wending through it all. We laid a blanket from Perry's trunk in the shade of a scrub pine near a pond and opened our lunch bags, screwed tops off our drinks. The loveliness and silence of the afternoon sun were stapled in place by the soft, lazy buzz of insects and an occasional breeze that lifted our hair.

Sara said the best time to come was early morning or sunset. "We aren't likely to see the animals in the heat of the day."

I said, "I hope that includes alligators."

Marcy said, "There're always alligators. Good thing you didn't bring your little dog. That's their favorite afternoon snack."

Sara said, "If it were later, we'd see white-tailed deer, turtles, rabbits, maybe raccoons."

We laid our food out on opened napkins.

"The party was wonderful," Marcy said to Perry. And Sara and I agreed, and we all lavishly praised the wonderful food, beautiful surroundings, the lovely people we met.

"And it was nice to meet your husband," Marcy concluded for us, bringing up the subject we had been avoiding so far.

Perry probed her salad with a fork. "I'll just start from the be-ginning, I guess, before Alex." She took a sip of her lime soda. "I left Kentucky and came down to Florida to hide out. I had got-ten beaten up by my husband quite a lot, which had caused three miscarriages. The last messed me up for ever having children." She looked at each of us and addressed our sorrow over this news. "It's okay. That was fourteen years ago. Things have been looking up since."

She took another drink. "I worked as a checkout clerk at the K-Mart here in town and Alex was a shelf stocker there."

"Really, a stocker?" Marcy said.

"I'll get to that."

I had assumed that Alex either didn't work or worked with his
father in some capacity. I couldn't picture anyone who lived in that
beautiful home working as a stocker at K-Mart. But Perry continued.

"Alex was hit by a car when he was eleven and suffered brain
damage. His intellectual development was halted at a fourth-grade
level, and that is as far as he will go." I recalled the deep scar that
marred Alex's beauty and expressed sadness at that news.

Perry said, "At work Alex always told new people about his
problem and explained that many things were hard for him. That
was the opposite of how I had been brought up, in which you felt
shame and tried to hide personal things. He made people comfortable around him. I was drawn to Alex right away because of his
kindness."

"That's remarkable," Sara said. Marcy and I agreed.

"Alex has a big heart. He knows how different he is, and even
though he is frustrated and sometimes even angered by his situation, he makes sure other people are at ease." Perry's nose reddened
and her eyes watered. "So, anyway, after a year of working with
Alex and sharing lunchbreaks, his mother invited me over. She said
I was all Alex talked about and she wanted to meet me. Next, they
took me to Disney World with them for Alex's thirtieth birthday.
As you can tell, Alex *loves* Disney World."

Perry laughed. "Our joke is that I was his second choice for a
wife; his first choice was Minnie Mouse."

We all laughed with her.

"Anyway it went on like that for another year or so. Then I realized that I had never felt so loved in my life as I did by Alex and that
I loved him. I let the relationship become sexual." She paused. "We
told his family about that and they supported this turn of events.
And, though they are dear and honest people, I suppose they saw
benefits in my becoming attached to Alex. He is their only child,
and they worry about what will happen when they are gone."

I felt each of us registering her story in the silence that followed and could practically hear the unmatched pieces of Perry's life we had witnessed at the party snap into place.

"I should tell you," Perry said, "I wasn't any prize. Sixty pounds overweight, had no education, didn't even shampoo my hair all that regularly. Back home we did that—like the old joke goes—on Saturday nights. I had very little self-esteem. Barely enough to escape my husband. I still feel amazed that I stepped on that bus one afternoon. Got off here because I needed to go to the bathroom and the bus left without me." She laughed. "Meant to go to Miami; it was the only city in Florida I'd ever heard of back then."

I could hardly swallow my food, imagining young Perry lost and alone in a strange place. I tried to transform the stylish, confident woman before me into that ungroomed, frightened girl she described. Perry seemed born to her gold bangles and blond bob.

"Anyway, I divorced my first husband, and Alex and I married." She laughed again. "If we get right down to it, it's both he and his parents that I married; it was certainly his parents who proposed."

We all laughed along with Perry, without actually realizing what was funny about that. Her story was too different from our own lives for us to see the humor.

"So although Alex didn't fully grasp the concept of marriage, he did fully grasp the concept of us sleeping together every night and playing together every day. And he was pretty excited about having a wedding at Disney World."

Perry bent over for a bite of her salad, and while she chewed, the rest of us remembered our own food. For a few moments there was the rustle of potato chip bags, the scrape of plastic forks against Styrofoam. Then Perry went on.

"A wedding at Disney World worked perfectly for our two families. If there is any place on the planet that Alex's family and mine could spend time together, it was there. My family went nuts with all that glitter, and there was Alex, leading the way through it, their own personal Disney guide."

A pair of sandhill cranes flew overhead, calling, and we all looked up and watched them land in tall weeds on the other side of the pond.

"Ralph and Anna treat me like a beloved and treasured daughter. At home, I was barely tolerated as were the rest of the seven kids. Daddy drank a lot, still does; Mama was angry and tired all the time, still is. I'm the only kid that left.

"Down here I became Perry instead of the misspelled Perris—P-E-R-R-I-S—named after . . . you guessed it: Paris, France. Nobody where I lived ever caught the misspelling. But I changed over legally when we got the marriage license."

We had all forgotten our food now, swept up in Perry's story.

"When I first met Alex I couldn't afford a car, so I bought a used bike to get to work. Alex has always had so much energy, he'd take me on twenty-mile rides on the weekends, stopping often for me to gasp and wipe sweat. In little more than a year I had lost weight, cut my waist-length hair, become blond and . . . after meeting Alex's parents, I began to jangle." She shook her arm and laughed. "Like my mother-in-law."

Marcy said, "She's quite lovely."

Sara said, "And very nice to your friends."

Perry said, "Anna and Ralph are truly wonderful people, and I'm lucky they're my family now."

"My God," Marcy said, sounding breathless, "what a life."

Perry's eyes softened as she said, "There may not be a human on earth who is as loving and sweet as Alex. So patient and caring. Which makes him a wonderful lover, believe it or not." She smiled shyly. "We share some other things: tennis, golf, swimming, and, of course, bicycling. And he picks out all my clothes. Don't know where he gets his eye for things, but when we were dating, it was Alex who took me to get my hair cut and out to buy clothes . . . size eighteen at the time. Down to eights now. All that playing he's gotten me to do."

It was hard not to stare at Perry. I wanted to study the eyes that had seen so much. I suspected Sara and Marcy felt the same way, because when Perry began to eat again, we all turned our heads away from her, toward the water, where not even a dragonfly stirred in the still afternoon air. Then we all darted glances back to her at the same time.

Perry caught that and laughed. And we all followed. It provided the release we needed.

"I'm never going to leave Alex. I just get bound up in how static things are and always will be, rant a while, then realize that it's up to me to change things and eventually I do." Perry looked sad, and I remembered how tightly wound and frustrated she had seemed at our first meeting at the Green Bottle Café.

"I'm going to school now," she said. "And later I'll begin a career that I like. I realize since we all met"—she circled her palm around to each of us—"that I have needed my own friends. Living with Alex means I have many family friends, but no personal friends. This is what is going to save my marriage."

I nodded, recognizing my own lack of personal friends and seeing how they helped one's perspective and sense of independence. On the drive to the savannah from the café, I had talked about my realization that what I wanted most from my husband was intimacy, and in striving for that, I had lost sight of myself. Sara added her thoughts on how strained intimacy became as the marriage matured with children, mortgages and careers. Marcy also joined the conversation, but Perry had been quiet on the subject.

She said now, "I don't share this intimacy you all talk about in my marriage, but where I come from, we don't know much about that, anyway. Who has time for intimacy in the hills of Kentucky? Starting in the early teens, women have baby after baby and men work job after job. Kids, work, church. Weddings, births, deaths. No intimacy."

"Then you've never expected it," Sara said.

"That's the key to my whole marriage: I don't expect anything." Perry shook her head. "Because if I've painted a picture of rosy riches and handsome husband, I need to tell you the hard parts. Living with Alex is like living with an eleven-year-old boy. He is self-involved, doesn't notice whatever mess he is making, repeats the same mistakes over and over and will never learn from them. There is no progress and there never will be. He is stuck right where he is and I am stuck right there loving him."

"Sounds hard," Marcy said.

Perry said, "Tedious."

Sara said, "I don't mean to diminish the difficulty of what you've told us, but I'm struck by how much of your description of Alex's behavior resembles my own husband." She spoke seriously.

Sara said, "Steve runs a corporation but he can't seem to remember to turn a stove burner off."

Marcy said, "You're lucky. Mine can't remember how to turn one on."

I found that Perry's wisdom in not expecting anything was something I should take on myself. I said, "My expectations keep me in a righteous position with Jess."

Perry said, "Well, perhaps you have good reasons for your expectations, but maybe, like me, they end up making you dissatisfied."

We gathered up our picnic remains and headed back to town and our separate cars. While we drove, Perry told us Alex's situation wasn't hard for only her, that Alex himself often felt worthless and depressed over his limitations. "He is fully aware of who he is and how he measures up with others. I love him too much to ever add to his low self-esteem. I understand it so well myself."

I kept thinking about Perry's words while we drove back to town. I held high expectations for Jess, which just set him up for failure and me for disappointment. If I stopped holding out hope for certain changes and worked instead on acceptance, how much of a difference would that make? It was an experiment I wanted to try. The truth was coming clear: there were many ways to conduct a marriage. Thanks to Perry telling her story and creating a fast bond among the four of us, I was discovering the value of women friends for sharing thoughts and opening new perspectives on how others conducted their lives and relationships.

Once home, I realized I had acquired MARRIAGE RULE #2: Enjoy Personal Friends.

Twenty

Jess

"Hi, Annie," I said, then checked my watch quickly. Kept forgetting it was two hours later in Florida. "In bed yet?"

"It's nine thirty. Night's young. I'm getting ready for a date . . . with my psychology textbook, that is."

"Is there a chapter written about me in there?"

Annie said, "That's advanced psychology."

"Good. Don't want you down there trying to figure me out."

"I'll figure you out, then write the advanced book myself."

I wasn't sure if she was teasing me or insulting me. I decided to skip it. "Got bad news."

"Oh, gosh, what's wrong?"

"Wolf No. 9 was kicked out of the pack."

"No! How can that be? She's the leader of the Rose Creek pack."

"I know. Her daughter's alpha now. Nobody has spotted No. 9 anywhere."

"That just kills me. She is so special. She's the movie star of the whole wolf-restoration program in Yellowstone."

"The worst part is the weather." Early February in Yellowstone. Subzero temperatures day and night. Shelters snowed over, food scarce.

"How is she going to make it? She's seven years old now. That's old for a wolf."

"The naturalists are saying she can't last long. Can't take down an elk on her own. And, of course, the pack is chasing her off of their kills, won't share with her anymore." I paused and let Annie groan. "They figure she'll only last a couple weeks at the most."

"I could cry for her."

Annie sounded as though she identified with No. 9, as if she, Annie, had been kicked out of her pack and left to fend for herself. I considered reminding her that she'd left on her own. Anger with her stirred beneath the surface of my words, but I missed her and resisted indulging in it. I needed a friendly phone call tonight.

I said, "You're not the only one upset over this. She made the headlines once again. *The Jackson Hole News & Guide* said she is everybody's favorite wolf." They had a stock photo of No. 9. Her large, black-furred body was posed against the frozen surface of the Yellowstone snowfields, alert to the photographer hidden somewhere above her on a hill. If she was still alive, she'd be keeping in constant motion, checking all sides and behind her, as she made her way miles and miles over the rugged winter landscape.

Annie said, "She has such an amazing spirit—no wonder she's everybody's favorite."

"Think back," I said, "to when we heard about her coming to Wyoming and how exciting it was to have wolves back in Yellowstone." I remembered that right off her mate was shot by a poacher. No. 9 and her eight pups had to go into an enclosure pen and be fed so they'd all survive.

Annie said, "My favorite part of her story is how the male from the Crystal Creek pack sat outside the pen waiting for her release."

I said, "I'd do that for you."

"I know you would." Annie's voice sounded soft and warm.

I said, "You're welcome back to my pack anytime."

Annie said, "I'll be back."

"Kawabunga, babe."

*   *   *

This morning I scraped ice off the driver's side of the windshield. Muffled explosions from across the valley pounced on the quiet like Annie's fists punching a pillow into shape. In the village, the ski patrol was shooting into the snowpack on the slopes, trying to provoke avalanches—a morning ritual performed before the slopes were opened to skiers.

Sometimes it had seemed *Annie's* morning ritual to shoot insults at me, trying to provoke a response. She might have hoped for an avalanche of some kind from me, but instead, I'd freeze her out. When we were seeing a therapist together, the woman had said Annie was just trying to get me to participate in the marriage. I said she should find a better way, but when Lola asked for my suggestions, I didn't have any.

"So, Jess, perhaps you just want to be left alone," Lola said.

I said I didn't know. So then *Lola* accused me of not participating in the *counseling.*

I walked to the passenger side, leaned over and scraped the windshield. The dogs romped in the yard. The idea was for them to do their business before getting in the car and riding to the store, but if they kept up this playing, their feet were going to start to hurt in the snow, and they'd be lifting a paw and pleading with mournful eyes to be carried out of it. Each of them was as big as a small pony, so that wasn't going to happen. Took only a minute or two for them to feel pain when it was this cold—twenty-three below this morning. The weatherman on the radio announced that we were heading into a temporary thaw; often happened about the third week of deep cold, when all the valley residents, worn down by weeks of severe temperatures, were beginning to eye their luggage.

The weatherman reported that today we'd be "warming up to freezing." Where else but in Jackson Hole would somebody have the nerve to say such a thing?

Gladdened my heart, though. By that afternoon we should get a fifty-degree climb into the low thirties. It would feel like a heat wave, and I'd be driving home from work with my car window down and elbow sticking out. By tomorrow or the next day, it would pass and winter as usual would return, yet without the deep subzero drops.

"Leidy, Bannon, Ranger. Load up." I stood with the car door open and twelve legs scrambled into the backseat and stomped around for the best spot. I had forgotten to notice whether they— as Annie insisted on saying—"pottied." She had the dogs trained to that word—they'd practically go on command for her—but I refused to use it. "Potty," I said scornfully, slipping behind the wheel in the front seat. Then, looking in the rearview mirror at three perplexed faces, I said, "No, no. Not now, girls."

I felt irritable, wasn't being kind with the dogs, the customers or anybody, really. Last night before I'd called Annie, someone had knocked on the front door of the house and I'd answered to two Seventh-Day Adventists wanting to pass out literature and talk to me about God. I said, "You know, I can't imagine why someone goes door to door trying to discuss religion, or sex, or any other intimate topic with complete strangers." I paused. "This seems like a matter for the police." I was probably a little harsh.

The road to Teton Village this morning was freshly plowed, no ice. I was coming to my favorite part of the drive, where the road cleared Gros Ventre Butte and I got a sudden grand sweep of the Tetons. *Ba-he-du-wuh-nu-d.* Shoshone. Meant "Hoary-headed fathers." They were hoary-headed today, all right. We were lucky to end up with as simple a name as Tetons. The French won out there, though as far as the Shoshones were concerned, the French won out everywhere. "Teton" meant breast. According to the legend around here, the French fur trappers named the mountains for a female body part they hadn't seen for some time. This was a man's valley in many ways. Annie would say: you mean *boy's,* don't you?

She would be referring to the large number of guys who lived here only to play in the mountains—skiing, climbing, bouldering.

I looked in the rearview mirror again at the three beautiful, attentive faces of my dogs, looking out the window, watching the Herefords in the pasture beside us follow the hay wagon that spread their breakfast in the snow. The dogs didn't miss a thing. If I were to drive off onto the rough shoulder, one of them would nudge my neck with her nose to alert me. It'd happened before. When it came to God, emotions and all those other topics Annie accused me of avoiding, I was kind of like my dogs: I knew plenty, just didn't say anything.

Since Annie had left, I felt like I was in "time-out," our usual punishment for the boys when they were little. We sent them off to think about their behavior. Except in this case, I was left alone while Annie went off. I guess, to think about my behavior.

Kind of like the God topic, I didn't know how to think about my behavior, either. I just did what came along, didn't do what didn't come along. I told that to our therapist, Lola, back when Annie and I were seeing her, and she said, "You know, Jess, you are something of a cuddly"—she searched for the proper word—"predator."

I said, "Hey, I just leave everybody alone."

She said, "That's the cuddly part."

From there I tuned out. Or tried to. Annie grabbed my arm, said, "That's how it feels, Jess. As if you're a . . . a passive sort of terrorist. You go around not allowing yourself to know the swath of damage you leave in passing through life. All the while not meaning to cause harm, but not meaning to cause . . . anything. Anything. You refuse to be present . . . or aware." She ended by saying, "It's terrorism by omission, if that makes sense."

It didn't to me.

Then she started to use the term "nice guy," as if she were talking about a pathological killer. What was so wrong about being a nice guy?

If Annie was having trouble with that, she would have loved me yesterday at the store. I was no nice guy then. I told a customer, an older guy who reminded me of the Skipper, that our beanie hat with the propeller on top—a hit with the young locals—was what the Olympic ski jumpers were using to successfully gain air. The newspaper that morning had headlined a story about some European teams training on the mountain. The customer said conspiratorially, "Is that right?" as if I had let him in on a ski-industry secret. Hadley shooed me back to the office then and took over up front. Good thing, too, because he was one of those men who were creepy about their money. Instead of handing over his twenty-dollar bill, he balanced it on edge lengthwise on the counter, the theory being that if more than one was accidently stuck together they would fall apart and you'd catch the error. I'd had men stand rubbing their fingers over a twenty-dollar bill for a full thirty seconds before handing it to me, just to be certain they were giving me only one. I had no patience with such crap.

I wasn't getting out on the mountain as much as I was used to. With Annie gone, I was stuck in the store more. Besides that, this long subzero stretch took the fun out. So damn cold I had to leave the shower door open in the bathroom at home or the drain froze. At our house even the *inside* knob on the front door was white with frost. At the top of the tram yesterday, the temperature with wind chill was minus eighty degrees—instant frostbite on any exposed skin.

That didn't keep the Jackson Hole Air Force home. Those guys skied anything, anytime. They got their name from jumping couloirs that made my heart shrivel to look at—steep, skinny, nearly vertical gullies, strewn with boulders, heaped with snow.

I pulled into the village parking lot, and the dogs tumbled out to begin their day, greeting customers at TFS. The sun was shining over Sleeping Indian Mountain and flashed on the windowed storefront with displays of our ski clothing lines—lime ski jackets, strawberry knit hats, skis, boots, poles.

Before unlocking the store, I stood a moment looking at the place, thinking about yet another day of working there without AnnieLaurie.

Suddenly I got so damn mad I could have exhaled soot. Who the hell did she think she was, walking off and leaving me with this place?

Then I decided on the spot to call that therapist Lola and see who she thought was the bad guy now.

Twenty-one

Annie

During lunch Tuesday at the Green Bottle Café, I poked around my food, my mind on last night's phone call with Jess. He had ended it with an old joke from a Florida vacation a few years back. We had watched a sixty-year-old surfer, long gray braid stuck with a gull feather, grab his board off the top of his rusted Volkswagen camper and trot off toward the surf. He'd hollered over his shoulder to his lady, waiting on the beach for him, "Kawabunga, babe." It had been our sign-off ever since.

Marcy looked over at me. "You eat like a bug."

I told her and Sara and Perry about Wolf No. 9, first filling in her unique story as a contributor to Yellowstone's wolf restoration. "And now she's been kicked out of the pack."

"I know why," Marcy said. "She gained weight."

The women joked, and I stared out the window through the green-tinted bottles to Bougainvillea Street, where the town went about its business of banking and browsing and shuffling through the table of dollar hardbacks outside My Ex-Husbands' Bookstore across the street. Like Wolf No. 9, I missed my pack.

Jess missed me, too, I knew. Yet he often set up barriers between us. I remembered a morning several years back when I woke to find Jess staring at me. He'd said, "I don't know who you are anymore." And I'd felt heartened over his realizing that. I agreed that he didn't, and he cut off the moment, swinging himself out of bed and saying, "I'm taking a shower."

I was staring out through the green bottles again and finally got the joke on the bookstore's sign.

"Oh," I said to my friends. "I just noticed where the owner, Talia, put the apostrophe in her store's name. Buying that place apparently took alimony from more than one ex-husband."

Marcy said, "That's called ali-*money*."

After lunch I went home and picked up Bijou for a walk on the beach. The day had turned gray and sultry, the sky a flat tin lid, capping the town in stillness. No breezes, until Bijou and I dropped down off the dune steps; then warm, heavy air blew along the shore. I clipped off the leash from Bijou's collar and shucked out of my sandals. I felt such longing in my throat today—a lump like bread dough, warm, malleable, about to swell. Was it the image of Wolf No. 9 walking alone in the snow? Or of myself walking alone on the sand?

I'd been carrying a vision of fulfilling my sense of selfhood while also creating a magic kingdom within my marriage, yet somehow, while heading for those two goals, neither seemed in sight. At times here in Hibiscus, I felt that I was after something tangible: independence, selfhood, marriage rules, college classes. Then other times, like now, none of that mattered, and all I felt was a sense of estrangement from myself and those I loved most.

Considering my choices during the past twentysome years, I wondered: did I hold enough personal power to meet my goals? When I first left on my marriage sabbatical, I was empowered by anger, but that was a short-lived source of strength, and now I needed an authentic sense of authority to accomplish the goals I had set for myself.

In the beginning of our marriage, I had contributed my time and effort to helping Jess. I had thought that giving to him was the same as giving to myself, having willingly relinquished my individuality for the sake of our togetherness. Or at most I had considered my offering as an investment, something that would be reciprocated when it came to be my turn. Yet, if that time came, I never recognized it or knew any longer how to fulfill my sense of selfhood, after having once merged it so completely with my husband's.

I walked along the hard sand near the water's edge, with an eye out for blue jelly fish. If the poisonous Portuguese man-of-war was in the area, a notice was usually posted at the steps that led down to the beach. Still, I was watchful on Bijou's behalf. The wind had come up stronger now, and the waves were frothing, slapping the shore and leaving behind pearly bubbles. I stopped and faced the sky and water, my feet catching the ebbing waves The bubbles broke against my skin and tickled my toes. I gathered my hair into a ponytail to keep it from whipping my face. A black cloud sat on the horizon like a massive tea bag about to dip into the ocean, suggesting a storm was steeping in this muggy air. I had walked about a mile down the shore, but now turned toward home.

I recalled a story I used to read to the boys when they were little about a tree that gave and gave of itself, without regard to its own well-being, until it was a stump and could give no more. Seemed for me, if I hadn't taken this time out in Hibiscus, I was in danger of becoming a stump myself.

By the time I climbed the dune steps, rain was slashing against my bare arms, and all about me, the dark air was dense with wind and water. Yet inside, I felt something had lightened, been washed clean. Missing my family had clouded the value of my marriage sabbatical. Understanding that, I felt renewed in my determination to find the path that included a sense of personal selfhood along with a loving intimacy with my husband.

I realized two things. I needed to send for my sons and I had discovered another rule.

Marriage Rule #3: Claim Personal Power.

Perhaps the centerpiece of my rules was this third one. Marriage Rule #1, Establish Independent Money, referred to separate money, which represented in the outer world what personal power did in the inner. Money was a physical form of power. Marriage Rule #2, Enjoy Personal Friends, was also the outworking of a claim for retaining a sense of self and individual perspective. I'd have to see what more I learned during my marriage sabbatical, but to claim personal power seemed the keystone holding up the whole structure.

Certainly Wolf No. 9 had no hope of surviving this winter unless she had gathered enough personal power to pull her through.

Once Bijou and I got home and dried off, I called Jess. I held the phone in one hand. With the other I mopped up from the sills and floor rainwater that had blown in the opened windows.

"I need to see Cam and Saddler."

Jess was quiet a moment. "It'll cost like hell at this late date," Jess said, "but next Monday is Martin Luther King Day, no classes. It would give you a three-day weekend."

"Perfect." I paused with the wet towel in my hand and felt awash with relief and filled with gratitude to Jess. "You're wonderful for understanding this."

"Of course, I understand. You call the guys and I'll get on the tickets."

This was Jess at his best. I felt very loved.

I was excited about seeing my sons. A bit uneasy, as well. Recently Jess had driven to Laramie to attend a weekend basketball game with the boys. After he'd returned, I'd asked him during a phone call, "Are the guys worried about us?"

He said, "I don't know. They never talked about it."

I said, "Well, what did you tell them?"

"Nothing. Just that you needed to get away, get some sun."

Sure, an old family pattern: parent flees cross-country without notice, suitcase, or destination in mind.

The annoying thing was that the boys typically let Jess get away with ducking uncomfortable talk, but I couldn't expect that from them. I would have to explain my actions to my sons and didn't have a clue how to do that.

The guys were due in at ten Friday night. I drove to Orlando in the afternoon to check out the yarn shops. I walked with Bijou around a small lake in a pretty city park, and sat beneath a huge shade tree and read and knitted while she played near me in the grass. For dinner, I found a nice outdoor bistro, then caught a movie before heading to the airport in time to meet their flight.

Now, past eleven o'clock at night, Cam and Saddler and I drove through sparse traffic until we reached the stretch of dark inland swampland on the way to Hibiscus. Along this part of the route traffic was practically nonexistent.

Saddler, sitting in the front seat next to me, said, "I can't believe how black the night is around here." My older son took after Jess with his tall, dark-haired good looks. Yet he had a head for business that I liked to claim.

It was so dark that I had dimmed the dashboard lights, because they glared and bothered our eyes.

Cam agreed from the backseat, sitting behind his brother with Bijou on his lap. "I thought Wyoming was the darkest place in the country at night with cities almost a hundred miles apart, but here it's like these swamps suck up starlight." My younger son carried golden tones in his hair and skin and this extended to his personality. He glowed with goodwill.

"Weren't you scared driving all alone on this road late at night when you first got here?" Saddler asked.

So I didn't have to wait as long as I had feared for this tender topic to open. With relief, in the comfort of the dark car, on this narrow road, crowded on both sides with walls of solid growth, I said, "I was too surprised by my actions to be scared."

Yet the whole truth was that I was too miserable. I remembered how the outside bleakness of dark and lonely road mirrored my inner hopelessness. I didn't say so out loud, but that night some part of me had invited disaster. That feeling had scared me. Inwardly, I had beckoned a horrible accident to occur, as if that would explain or match the mangled way I felt inside.

"I love your father. I loved him the night I left. But I had become unhappy with my life and my relationship with him. In order to save my marriage, I temporarily left it. When two people fill their lives with the love and care of their children and those children move on, *as they should,* into their own lives, it takes an adjustment. The old rules no longer apply. Instead of thinking what was best for the family as a whole, I had to consider what was best for me. I had lost the knack. Your father adjusted better than I did."

From the backseat Cam said, "That's because he'd been practicing all along."

"What?" My whole body became an ear in the darkness. I felt myself tense with the need for absorbing those words.

Cam repeated them and added, "Dad knew you were taking care of everything, so he could pretty much do what he wanted."

Saddler said, "It's a male thing from your generation."

"It is?" I felt like a child, as if my sons and I had exchanged places in this disembodied blackness.

"Yeah," Saddler said. "Men from your generation learned how to take over from watching their own fathers, but they don't get how to share being in charge."

Cam said, "It's like you two tried to be less traditional in your marriage than Grandma and Grandpa were, where he went to work and she stayed home. With you and Dad, nobody was in charge either place. So you took over both places and Dad just helped . . . when he wanted to."

Saddler said, "We're not on anybody's side or anything; we just noticed this stuff."

"I want a marriage just like you guys have," Cam said. "But I want both of us to have fun."

Saddler said, "You should have more fun, Mom."

My throat swelled and ached; I kept swallowing. The top of my nose stung, and my eyesight blurred with the tears that lined my lower lids. I blinked, hoping to absorb them, but more tears gathered and they slid down my cheeks anyway. I felt safe in hiding my wet face in the density of the swampy night. No faraway town lights, no moonlight visible through the narrow slit of sky directly above the road. Then the headlights of a rare oncoming car gave me away.

"Aw, Mom, don't cry. You made her cry, Cam." Saddler rooted around in the glove department for tissues, and I sniffed and wiped the back of my hand across my face. Saddler was as uncomfortable as Jess with negative emotions, and often assigned blame.

Cam found my purse in the backseat, handed me a tissue from inside it and said, "Pull over. I'll drive." The sensitive son.

My chest felt crowded and my breath was ragged in my attempt not to sob out loud and alarm my boys. I pulled over, and we all got out for the shift in seating—Saddler was going to sit in Cam's seat in the back so I could sit up front. Outside, on the edge of the road with the car motor off, the air sang with the watery sounds of frogs and the rasp of insects. Cam handed me another tissue and I blew my nose loudly. The noise of that created an abrupt alert to the swamp creatures. Utter silence descended.

In the dark, it felt as if all my senses were cut off. Then my sense of smell was alerted by a powerful sweetness that perfumed the silky night. I inhaled deeply.

With wonder lacing my voice, I said, "Blossoms." And I stuffed the tissues in my pocket, tipped my head back to take in the heavenly fragrance. Cam and Saddler did the same and we stood together silently. Bit by bit the sounds of swamp life returned. First a single night bird chirped; then frogs croaked in unison, and a soft insect buzz stitched in the background. My eyes were adjusting to the night and I caught both guys watching me. I grinned at them, pleased to have them with me, proud that they had become such good, caring company.

Cam reached over and hugged me. After a moment, I pulled Saddler in with us. We stood together for another moment, arms around one another with our heads tossed back, inhaling the perfume and listening to the noisy night. It seemed as if the wildlife was celebrating something wonderful with us.

When we got back in the car, I considered Saddler's hesitancy in hugging me just now and earlier at the airport. Over the years I'd found this to be a sure signal. When the guys had girlfriends, it was harder for them to sort out their demonstrations of affection, and I was rightfully the woman set aside. Greetings and goodbyes turned briefly into stilted affairs, until the girlfriend became more familiar or the relationship moved on. I always honored that insight into their private lives.

I turned sideways toward the backseat. I said, "Saddler, do you have someone special in your life now?"

"I don't know."

Cam glanced in the rearview mirror and said, "Tell her, Sadd."

"We weren't finished talking about Mom's stuff. We should finish that."

I said, "Well, to sum it up: it's entirely possible that you're both right, and much of my misery over my life and marriage could be healed by having more fun." Such a simple idea. Yet it struck a note of pure truth with me. "I'll begin having more fun this very weekend with you two. Now tell me about your girlfriend."

"Her name is Ella." And from the darkness of the backseat while Saddler held the sleeping Bijou on his lap, I learned—more from what Saddler didn't say than from what he said—that my elder son was in love. I had thought at the airport as he approached me that he looked so much like Jess when I'd first fallen in love with him. Dark, wavy hair; tall, athletic body that could as easily climb rock walls as contort itself into a kayak and somersault down fast water. Ella, I learned, was a junior along with Saddler. They planned to live together this summer, probably in Telluride, Colorado, where Ella's family had a vacation cabin, but that was still pending on what jobs became available. They were both acquiring degrees in hotel management and would look for experience in their field. Saddler had loved Ella from afar last year while she was still involved with a boyfriend from home.

"Finally she wised up," Saddler said, and laughed.

"She's a looker," Cam said. "And really nice." He added, "I'm glad I haven't found anybody special yet."

"Me, too. You're too young." Though at the moment, I was feeling Saddler was too young, as well—a mother's perennial perspective, I guessed. He was two years older than me when I decided to marry Jess. But they weren't talking about marriage, I reminded myself.

We drove several miles in silence.

Then Saddler said, "I just don't know why it doesn't work sometimes. I mean, when you love somebody, why doesn't it last, like you think it will?"

The question at the crux of separation. The ripples that disrupt more than just your own life when a marriage doesn't work. Cam and Saddler were in the process of building their understanding about long-term love, and I had slipped out some key supports when I left their father, even though temporarily. I owed Saddler and his brother an answer that lent strength to their understanding. I considered what I wanted to say. That old fairy-tale ending of happily ever after would never pass muster with this generation of kids, whose parents had a divorce rate that exceeded by far any before them.

"People fall in love for all kinds of reasons—some healthy, mature, and realistic; some not. When choosing a life partner, you question yourself about this quality of love and whether it has components of need to it that will burden the relationship."

I thought for another moment and continued. "What can't be factored in is the uneven growth patterns of individuals. So this love has to hold patience within it and acceptance."

And then to lighten up the conversation, I added, "But you guys are lucky. Your mother will choose both your wives for you."

They'd heard that empty threat before, but laughed anyway.

Like his father, Saddler was a collector of brochures. By the time we'd ordered breakfast at the Green Bottle Café the next morning, he'd wandered off to the rack by the front door and picked up brochures about every adventure opportunity within a couple hours' drive. We passed them around to one another, discussing their merits while eating, and decided by the end of breakfast to kayak the Loxahatchee River that afternoon.

We loaded one of my canvas grocery bags with drinks, chips, cheese, salami and three apples, drove an hour to the river and rented kayaks from a man inside a shabby trailer. The adventure was advertised in the brochure as Florida just as it appeared in the 1930s. The boys and I joked that meant the owner's residence and his lack of plumbing.

Outside, behind the trailer, a big hand-painted sign warned about the danger of alligators. NO SWIMMING, it said. The owner's son outfitted us with three muddy and faded kayaks and eased us off the banks of the Loxahatchee into shallow red-brown water, where a gentle current floated us around a bend and into the silence of a bald cypress swamp.

Immediately our faces opened in delight at the strange environment. Hundred-foot bald cypress trees arched over the river, the limbs leafless at this time of year, though draped elegantly in Spanish moss. I had always read about cypress knees and had wondered what they looked like. They looked rather like the knees of scrawny skeletons, and they poked out of the water a couple of inches or a couple of feet, as part of the trees' vast root systems.

Cam spotted the first alligator.

"Hey, look," he whispered, lifting his oar and pointing left toward shore.

Saddler paddled up near his brother. "Mom, check it out."

"Oh, my God. Keep your hands in," I hissed in a loud whisper. "Boys, do you hear me? Keep your hands in the boat and get out of here. Quick." I paddled up behind them. "Go, go." Sweat plastered my hair to the back of my neck. Forgetting I was the mother of two men now, I felt suddenly responsible for putting children in danger.

Both of them laughed at me.

"Let's go pet it," Cam teased.

By now we were back-paddling in order to maintain a steady view of the alligator. The river water was a rusty brown around us, except in the sunny spots where it looked orange-red. The alligator's five-foot-long body was lying in a slice of orange, sunlit water near shore. Its bumpy-skinned shape was wedged among cypress knees, its head lay floating on the surface of the water and it looked far more at ease than I felt, even shielded in a kayak and sandwiched between two men. I wished we were wearing armor and helmets. When the alligator failed to leap out of the swamp and swallow one of us, I eventually relaxed.

Saddler started to laugh quietly. "I was just remembering when I turned sixteen and we were walking to our car after getting my new driver's license," he whispered.

I whispered back, "I remember that day."

"We came to a busy street and you reached out to hold my hand before crossing it, like I was still a toddler." Saddler laughed again and Cam joined him.

I said, "I remember that, too. The best part was that you didn't say a word and just let me hold your hand all the way to the car." I smiled at the memory. "That's when I knew you had grown up."

We paddled on. Half an hour later, we came to a dam built of logs, where the water spilled several feet lower into a rowdy swirl of dips and waves, nothing like Wyoming whitewater, but fun for the guys and intimidating to me. Cam and Saddler swooped over the dam with ease.

I gave wide berth to the fast-running water, in order not to get pulled in, and worked my way toward the portage.

"You can do it, Mom. Cowboy up," Cam called.

"I don't think so."

Saddler said, "It's easy for a Wyoming Woman."

I wanted to be a good sport, and my sons were longtime judges of what I was capable of. So I paddled over to get in position to take the rapids.

My sons were cheering, "Red rover, red rover, send our mother right over."

I entered the spill and paddled like a fool, trying to keep nose forward, but the water pressure on the tail of my kayak pivoted my boat around and lodged it sideways on a log. Abruptly my kayak tipped and took in water. It all happened so fast. One minute high and dry; the next minute, river water swirling around my waist.

I remembered the alligators and thrashed around trying to get to my feet. Was it thrashing that drew their attention or was that sharks? I rose halfway up and fell with a splash. The logs were slimy with algae. I used my paddle for leverage, stood up halfway, lost my footing and fell back down again with a big splash. Exhausted, I looked up. Cam and Saddler were laughing so hard no sounds were coming out of them yet. Then sudden explosions bent them over at the waist and they howled.

What the heck? I thought. I joined them.

They were both strong guys, strong enough to paddle *up* the

log dam. They secured their kayaks, waded into the river and together tipped the boat and poured out the water. We continued
downriver, even more charmed with our environment now that we
had completely *submerged* ourselves in it.

Lucille caught us piling out of the car and into the backyard, our
clothes sticky with river water. She stepped from her back door,
smoothing hands across her apron, and I introduced her to my
sons. She'd been keeping an eye out to invite the three of us to join
her and Shank tomorrow morning for tea.

"Eleven o'clock every Sunday morning. We never know who
to expect: some old students from the college, some new students
that hear about it, teachers, maintenance workers, administrators."
Behind her, Mitzi was up on her paws, peering at us through the
screen and emitting an occasional whimper to remind Lucille that
she'd been left behind. Lucille ignored her.

"Shank and I started the tradition when we first got married
to help pull our separate friends and colleagues together. You folks
come and join us tomorrow."

Sounded more like an order than an invitation, but we were
happy to accept. "We'll be there," Cam assured her.

"I'm baking my muffins right now. Blueberry oatmeal and
orange almond."

"We'll be there *early*," Saddler said, which made Lucille laugh.
Then she frowned and cocked her head to the side as if listening to
something deep in her house. "Shank!" she hollered. "You get your
boots out of that kitchen right now."

Her voice sounded severe and mild all at once, as if she darn
well meant what she said, but already had moved on to forgiveness.

"Every week the same thing," she said to us. "I make the batter;
Shank sneaks in and eats it. He's going to get salmonella poisoning
from raw eggs. But telling him does no good." She reached for the

screen door handle. "I better get in there or we won't *have* muffins in the morning."

The boys and I grinned at one another, then trudged up the stairs to the whimpers of my own puppy behind the screen door on the porch. How nice it was to have such a sturdy, conventional couple as Shank and Lucille in my acquaintance, while I was wrestling with my own marriage. Not that my aspirations included making muffins every week and snapping at my husband to leave the batter alone, but I liked thinking that such close and cozy partnerships as Shank and Lucille's were alive and well.

The feeling reminded me of when I was young and enjoyed the same sense of stability with my parents' relationship, while I dreamed about the different kind of marriage I wanted for myself. My parents' marriage served as a springboard for my ideas. My sons were right when they said that Jess and I wanted less rigidity to gender roles, but were unsure how to express that. We didn't intend to plow down the barriers that held our parents' gender roles, just bend them to our liking. While thinking we were just experimenting, just opening ourselves to new ideas, we had instead taken interim steps to change the concept of male and female roles in family life. My sons would take another step and their children yet another.

My cell phone rang. I looked at the screen and told the boys to go ahead with their showers. I'd take mine last.

"Perfect timing," I greeted Gina. I opened the door for Bijou and walked with her down to the yard. Shade from the acacia tree graced the grassy area in the late afternoon.

"How's it going down there?" Gina asked.

I filled her in on the boys coming for a visit and how helpful Jess was in setting it up.

"He's such a good guy," Gina said. "We have to remember the positive when we're struggling with people."

"That will be your job," I said, "because sometimes I have trouble remembering." I asked how she was doing and we got all caught up with each other while I waited for my turn in the shower.

Later, on our way to an early dinner, I gave the guys a tour of campus, telling them all I'd learned about its history as a pineapple plantation. I spotted a familiar figure sitting in the distance beneath the bottlebrush tree, knitting needles wrapped in fluffy yarn and flickering like bird feathers in the speckled shade. I guided the guys over.

"Caridad, meet my sons." As a sophomore in college she was right in between the boys. We sat on the grass with her. She told us her first knitting project was an afghan for her parents.

"By the time I had finished it, I'd dropped so many stitches that instead of square it came out almost triangular. My dad took one look at it and said, 'How clever. It's for the bunk in the prow of the boat.'"

We laughed. Soon after, we parted and the boys and I headed for a restaurant on the beach. Saddler collected more brochures while we waited to be taken to our table, and I knew that after tea with Shank and Lucille in the morning, I was in for "more fun in my life" tomorrow.

Twenty-two

Walking Therapy, Lola called it when I made my appointment. Probably it's a Jackson Hole thing. Nobody in this valley could stand staying indoors. Mornings you saw people climbing Snow King Mountain with their dogs in the dark, then skiing down in the gray light before starting their day in the office. Special lunchtime ski passes were sold for the bankers, doctors and office workers who'd rather ski than eat. So now there was Walking Therapy. What next? Outdoor surgery?

Lola said: meet her at the Cache Creek trailhead at eleven o'clock and bring my dogs. So here we were, watching her pull into the snowy parking lot with the Bernese Mountain dog I remembered greeting clients in her office a couple years back. I watched the two of them walk toward us, Lola depositing her car keys in a pocket.

"So, Lola, lose your office? We all know real estate is expensive in Jackson Hole." In fact, Teton County was just named "Most expensive county in the U.S." for yet another year. That's what happened when you had the Grand Tetons in your backyard and only four percent of the land available for private purchase. Still, my greeting sounded sharp and implied Lola wasn't successful enough to pay high rent. Her expression didn't change, but there was an almost imperceptible halt in her step as she came toward me. I wasn't looking forward to this session, and I guessed she knew that now. Just covering my butt by petitioning support against Annie's "marriage sabbatical." This was the price I had to pay.

"Jess, good to see you."

I petted her dog; she petted all three of mine.

"I save this for special clients," Lola said, pulling on her knit hat. "Thought you'd especially find this comfortable. I remember our last visits. You didn't say much. Being outside is more your style."

That was different. Whatever resentment I was holding against her—for whatever reasons—melted. The fact was that I did appreciate being out here this morning. The day was a beauty and not too cold. We headed up the canyon on a snow-covered dirt road I knew well. The road wended up and down hills, between wooded mountain slopes, for the next few miles, and the dogs could run unleashed.

I blurted, "Annie left "

"Uo-oh." Lola stopped dead in her tracks. "Oh, Jess."

Nobody had sounded so compassionate about this news before, and I was afraid I'd start to cry. Of course, nobody got the news straight out like that, either. When I told the boys, I'd softened it to the point of sounding like Annie just needed some sun. And I tended to do the same with anybody else who asked.

We walked on. Our dogs ran in a happy pack among the trees, over the frozen creek, up and down the slopes beside us. All my intentions for tattling on Annie being a bad wife and leaving me with all the work just dropped away. Suddenly I started talking; I had not a single idea that I would tell this.

"A lot of people, Annie included, would like to use my story to figure me out. It happened all the time as a kid in school. I'd get a new girlfriend, and pretty soon somebody would whisper in her ear, 'You know what happened to him when he was a kid, don't you?' Like this accounted for who I was, for everything I did or didn't do."

I heard the call of a raven and looked up. Snowy cottonwood limbs laced across the path above us, black and white against a deep blue sky.

Lola said, "Tell me your story, Jess."

"Hell, I don't even remember it. I was only four years old. Sure, it's a big deal when your mother dies, no matter how old you are. And before I fell in love with Annie, I used to carry this mild ache in my chest, a kind of yearning I didn't notice until it went away. But, really, I was four years old, for God's sake. I can't carry any blame. And after she died, I still had a pretty decent life. People took care of me. My dad, an aunt. My mom's mother, Gran Genie, lived with us till I started second or third grade. The point is, the accident happened. It wasn't my fault—everybody said so—and I grew up."

Words rolled out of me, like a boulder falling downhill. I couldn't stop, didn't want to. The push inside me almost hurt. I leaned over and grabbed a handful of snow and patted it between my palms as we walked.

"I never got the whole story in one sit-down explanation. Families work like that. I remembered when our son Cameron was ten and learned for the first time about his grandmother's death. He was put out that nobody had told him, even though it was one of those family facts we all freely alluded to. It was kind of like that with me, too. I said to him, 'Cam, heck, I never did hear the whole story myself. I'm darn near forty, and I just learned a few months ago from your great-aunt Tula that your grandmother was driving to an art class when our car was hit.'

"He asked me, 'What kind of art?' Painting, I told him. I told him, 'Tula said, in fact, it was the art instructor who stopped to help us.'"

I felt driven to tell this as if I were in a spell and not really here in the canyon, not really in my body. Yet my bare hands ached with the cold from pressing the snow into a hard, icy ball. I tossed the snowball ahead, and all four dogs leaped at once to try to catch it before it fell through three feet of soft snow and disappeared.

"Cam looked kind of like those old pictures of my mom, I was thinking that day. Sandy hair, perky nose, expressive eyebrows.

Those eyebrows said he was going to make me tell the whole god-damn thing."

I glanced at Lola. She walked with her eyes on me.

"Fact was, I'd never told the story to anyone. Instead, the story got told to me. In bits and pieces, it dribbled my way, and all I had to do was fill in a detail here and there from what someone else passed on. Even with Annie, others got to her first. 'He watched his mother die right before his eyes.' 'They found him lying in so much of his mother's blood the EMTs didn't know who to work on first, but turned out it was too late for her and he barely got scratched.' I tried to send Cam to Annie for the story.

"He said, 'Come on, Dad.'

"I said to him, 'Cam . . . my mother and I were driving to her class, like I said. We got hit on the driver's side. Icy road, drunk driver. He was injured, too. Unconscious, I guess. This art teacher came upon the accident, got us covered up with some old blanket from his car, then took off for help. He told me before he left to press this shirt of his against my mother's thigh.'"

Now I took a shaky breath, and despite the cold, sweat seeded my forehead. My throat felt tight and achy. I took another breath.

"I said to Cam, 'I was supposed to keep this cloth tight around her artery—I didn't get that then, but I did get that I had a job to do and that it was important. I had to push on this shirt knotted up under her skirt until this man came back.'"

I had to stop walking. I bent over at the waist. I remembered Cam saying, "I guess it didn't help, huh, Dad?"

Lola patted my back. I hung there a moment. She pulled fresh tissues out of her coat pocket. I stood and blew my nose.

"I loved that kid, and I knew he was listening to this story of mine the same way he'd listen to any story I read to him before bed: putting himself into the role of that little boy on the roadside, soaked in his mother's blood, and next he would be feeling that little boy's . . . that little boy's . . ."

"What, Jess?"

"Shame," I whispered.

More tissues emerged from Lola's pockets. My chest heaved as I tried to keep my sobs inside my body.

"Then I told him. I said, 'Cam . . . he, uh, I . . . fell asleep.' I buried my face in a big hug to my kid. I didn't cry. I didn't even want to. It was Cam I was worried about."

I blew my nose on tissue after tissue. I checked on the dogs. They were sniffing scent marks with wagging tails and leaving their own scent marks on snow-covered logs and boulders beside the old road.

I looked down to the creek bed far below the edge of the path, a sheer drop, and I wished for a single bleak second to toss myself over. As if alerted to the drastic thought, my dogs came bounding back down the trail and gathered around my knees, whimpering softly. I smoothed the ears of each of them and seemed to come back into myself.

I said to Lola, "Cam's eyebrows slanted down along the sides of his eyes in sympathy." I nodded to Leidy, Bannon and Ranger. "I've fallen in love with all my dogs because they have this same slant to their eyebrows. It gives them the look of a wide and loving understanding." I turned toward Lola. "Don't you think?"

She said softly, "Yes, yes, I do." She pulled more fresh tissues out of her pockets.

I used those and she pulled out more. I joked to her, "I thought you had gained weight, but it's just all these tissues puffing out your coat." She had them stuffed all over her, inside and out.

She laughed. The dogs led the way and we started walking again.

"I don't know to this day what that little boy felt when he woke up and they told him his mother died, bled to death."

Lola said, "Jess, that little boy is you."

I said, "You know what Cam said?"

"What?"

"Cam said, 'It wasn't your fault, Dad.'"

Lola said, "And what do you think, Jess?"

"I don't remember much about it." I looked up to the peaks rising across the creek bed. Annie liked to say I didn't remember much about anything in order to remain guiltless about everything. She had to be very angry at me before she'd bring up "The Story." But I was expecting to hear about it any day. Now that I thought of it, I was expecting to hear that I'd have to see a therapist and address my mother's death before she'd return. Well, now that was done.

Lola and I turned around when the road narrowed with only ski and snowmobile tracks and no footpath tamped down through the deep snow.

Lola said, "Jess." She took a big breath. "Jess."

I looked at her and she was fighting tears. I wrapped my arms around her to soothe her. Hugged her hard and hated to let her go.

When we walked on she said, "Jess, you are a good hugger."

"Well, you needed it."

She stopped right on the path. "But you didn't?"

"Don't get sappy on me, Lola."

"Jess, you told me that long, hard story about your life, yet told it from your son's point of view. Next time I'd like to hear it from your point of view. Next time, the pronoun must be 'I,' not 'he.' It will be difficult at first, but then I promise you, it will be easier and then easier yet."

Twenty-three

Annie

*D*ad had seemed at loose ends. So I invited him to come for the weekend, even though I'd just taken my sons to the airport on Monday. Too, Daisy could use a couple days free of phone calls and drop-in visits. Despite having lived in the same place with many friends for decades now, Dad refused all social invitations unless Daisy accompanied him, because he said the world was made up of couples. And in his world, that was true. Mom used to say that the old conventions were ridiculous, considering how many single people there were in their age bracket. Still, parties at their golf club were like Noah's ark, everyone arriving in twos.

Dad flung open the bathroom door. "Biko, Biko-o-oo, Biko." His beautiful singing voice reverberated off the tile walls. At church, when I was a child, the first note to ring out in any hymn was Dad's, as if he felt it was his duty to lend the timid and straggling voices of the congregation his own confident resonance.

I said, "Gee, Dad, you don't usually remember songs. 'Silent Night' is a brand-new tune every Christmas." Once again I decided to hold off on telling him who Biko was and his story of being a freedom fighter in Africa. The anticipation of revealing that news gave me too much pleasure to squander too soon.

He said, "This song sticks to me like hot cheese. It gives me the wimples."

"Wimples?"

"You know." He wriggled his upper body.

"Shivers."

"Wimples," he repeated and bent down toward the sink to splash water on his face in preparation for shaving.

I spoke to the back of his neck. "You're letting your hair grow longer. Is this your idea or your hairdresser's?"

"It's hers." He glanced up to the mirror. "She said I need a scalping lotion." He pointed the shave cream spout onto his left palm and spread squiggles of deep aqua gel over it.

"You tee her off?"

"No, she likes me." He rubbed his palms together and magically the blue gel turned into white foam, which he spread across his cheeks and chin.

Puzzled, I said again, "Scalping lotion."

"You know . . ." Dad carved shapes in the air around his head with his foamy fingers.

"Oh, *sculpting* lotion."

"So I got some. I'll use it for my next appointment with her."

"I don't think that's what she had in mind, Dad. She meant for you to use it every day after your shampoo, like now. She didn't mean for you to look good just for her."

"I don't know about that. She likes me."

I began to drift into a different direction of thought at this. In Dad language this meant *he* liked *her*. And it meant not just as a hairdresser. I watched his razor carve pathways down his cheek, and for a moment I felt homesick, as it reminded me of skiing down the snowy slopes of Casper Bowl.

"What's her name?" If he knew her name, this was serious.

"Her name is . . . something sweet." He rinsed his razor, then banged it on the edge of the sink a couple times.

"Candy?" I could just picture her. I hated to ask this next question, but something about Dad's manner alerted me. So I asked, "About how old is she?"

"If you have to know, she's a lot younger than me. Maybe your age. But I don't give much of a darn about that."

You hear these stories. You never think it's going to be your dad. Would it have to be the whole deal? Younger woman seeks out older, richer man, woos him, takes his money, disrupts the family, breaks his heart, leaves much older, much less richer man for children to put back together again? Made me tired just to think of it.

"I don't think it's Candy—something like that though."

And yet . . . Daisy had been worrying about Dad's memory. She had given him extra vitamins, since she'd read that a lack of one of the B vitamins could account for memory loss. Mostly we concluded that he was bored, lonely, a bit depressed. A new love interest could perk things up and offer Daisy some needed time off.

"Might be something to drink," he said.

Of course. "Brandy."

"Close. She's nice. I'm going by after her work Monday so we can get to know each other. Go out for a drink and, if that goes all right, dinner."

So this was moving along. Might as well jump on board. I said, "You could take her out to that nice place in Old Town we all like, Flagler Grill."

"You're making my wallet quiver now."

I laughed. He looked ten years younger just talking about Candy/Brandy. For a guy who had been married for nearly fifty years, living without a partner for the past four was lonesome.

This could be good. The last emergency he called Daisy to check out was an animal Dad said was chirping in his house. Claimed he'd looked all over the place, moved furniture, rooted through closets. The thing seemed to move. He'd be in the bedroom and hear it, then in the living room and hear it, before he could get back to the bedroom himself, the creature had somehow scampered ahead of him and was chirping in there. Daisy climbed into her car, drove the three miles to Dad's place, opened his front door and immediately heard the alert that smoke detectors sounded to warn batteries were low. *Chirp, chirp.*

Daisy fixed the problem, then told Dad he had to start getting out of the house and doing more. He'd told her, "These are my reclining years." Daisy said to me on the phone afterward, "I guess he meant his *declining* years, but he's *declining* too fast and *reclining* way more than he should."

We had both feared that after taking care of Mom for so long during her illness, shutting himself off from his friends and his usual social routines, he would find it hard to get his life going again.

Now this new development. I could hardly wait to phone Daisy.

But I sympathized with Dad. I knew now how difficult it was to rouse energy when you were grieving. In many ways I was grieving for Jess, though I realized more and more that I was grieving for my image of Jess—my imagined husband, my imagined marriage—something not wholly based on reality, but on expectations and dreams. Hearing Perry talk about marriage to Alex clued me in to how much of my trouble depended on expectations I carried and how important it was to let them go. Jess may never address the childhood guilt he carried, may never accept responsibility, may never choose to fully come awake to me or his own life. And now, instead of feeling angry because I was not receiving what I had felt to be my rightful due, I was feeling a kind of grief, an emptiness in that place of expectations and dreams. And the grief made me lethargic, as if all my energy was being sucked into that emptiness or taken up by its management.

As I hung in the doorway talking to Dad while he finished his turn in my single bathroom, I thought how comforting it felt to be around maleness, watching male activity. He poured cologne into his cupped hand, and in the way many men started their day, Dad began slapping himself in the face.

I had become used to having male energy in my vicinity with Jess and our sons. And I missed it. I'd begun taking walks on the docks in the late afternoon when the fishermen came in. Men boning their catch, hosing the decks. Guides standing next to their clients who were holding huge fish and grinning for photos. Sometimes the men flirted with me, and it felt good. I put lip gloss on now when Bijou and I walked there. One guide in particular I found especially handsome. He didn't flirt or even smile, but he looked. Maybe Dad and I would amble down that way before dinner tonight. Right now we were going to the Green Bottle Café for breakfast.

"You about ready?" I asked Dad. He seemed to have arrived at the final step, tidying up the part in his hair with his comb.

"I'm losing my hair."

"You are not." Dad had a dense head of hair, another one of his vanities along with his singing voice. His silver hair was so thick that up until this visit he had been wearing it in almost a military-style crew cut. With his tanned face and blue eyes, he was the picture of radiant health. I said, "You have piles of hair, more than me."

"You should see the pillow. When I lift my head in the morning and look down, I think I'm still there—so many hairs cover the pillowcase."

"It's just because your hair is longer now; you haven't worn it that way for years."

As we walked out the gate and headed for breakfast in town, I told Dad, "I'm glad you have a new friend and something to look forward to when you get home Monday."

He said, "Make a new friend around here and before long they up and die on you. That's why I'm dating younger women now."

That would be Candy/Brandy. Daisy was going to scream.

We sat at the counter so Dad could gain the favor of the waitresses (he felt that gave him an edge with any food dropped in the kitchen they might consider sticking back on the plate) and also so he could strike up conversations with strangers. He was always at his best with strangers. Came from working in a store most of his life. I wondered if I'd become like that after working in my store for many years, mostly interested in shallow conversations with people I'd never meet again.

He started right off before our coffee arrived with a fellow probably in his seventies, tan and strong-looking, wearing a khaki fishing cap, shorts and plaid cotton shirt. The man sat one stool down from Dad and was writing a postcard.

He looked up at Dad's greeting, raised his pen, said, "My ninety-five-year-old mother has to know where I am every day."

Dad opened the menu, said to me, "They have that drink stuff you like." Meaning mocha lattes. "Guess I'll have fried eggs, potatoes and sausage."

"That's not on the menu."

"I didn't see it either," he said, "but tell them that's what I eat."

"Dad, they don't serve that here, but I'll order something good for you."

"No, you won't; you'll order something *inter-esting*."

He never cooked at home, except popcorn in the microwave. His stove top was used as a fireplace mantel. Photos of his grandchildren that Daisy and I gave him lined the backside of the stove, leaning against the burner knobs.

When our food arrived, I found myself watching Dad's eating manners; since living alone he'd relaxed them. On my last visit, he had pried out watermelon seeds with the pen he was using for his crossword puzzle.

When the afternoon cooled, we set off with Bijou to walk along the pier.

"Beautiful day," Dad called to the fishing guide who always looked, but never smiled at me.

The guide tipped his head up, checked the sky, said, "You're right. Severe clear."

"Sounds like pilot talk to me." We paused and Dad asked, "You a pilot?"

"Yes, I am . . . or was. On the water more these days." The man was cleaning a small part with an oily cloth; he flung that aside, set the part down and, while wiping his hands on a cleaner cloth, came over to the side of the boat and introduced himself.

"Daniel." He stuck his right hand out toward Dad.

Dad shook it and said, "Skip. And this is my daughter Annie Teague." Dad didn't use my married name, never had.

I shook Daniel's hand, looked up at him, and I felt a brief sexual jolt at meeting his clean penetrating gaze. For a second it threw me completely off balance. Daniel nodded imperceptibly as if confirming the jolt. Then he directed his attention to my dad, who was bent over, checking out the engine on view inside the open hatch cover.

During their small talk I rearranged any trace of response lurking in my facial expression. It was as if this man had passed me a secret note, a small key, acknowledging with his nod that it was intended expressly for me. I'd felt a vibration in the center of my palm, sharp and brief. To ease the weight of my sudden self-consciousness, I worked to convince myself that it didn't happen.

Maybe he had one of those practical joke hand buzzers.

I greeted Daniel's dog, who had gotten up, stretched, then sauntered over to check us out. I petted the sleek black-and-white dog that Daniel said was named Jeter. Then he and Bijou sniffed each other.

In between his casual questions to my dad—Live around here? Do you fish?—Daniel answered enough questions of Dad's to make him feel comfortable—Don't guide much, used to fly cargo, been around Florida a few months. But through my father, Daniel gleaned more information than he offered, slowly and methodically, and with no help from me.

Then Dad said, "That fellow over there down the beach—he's watching you with his binoculars. Did you notice?" Dad directed our attention back toward the grassy park, where the picnic tables sat beneath the shade of Australian pines.

Daniel didn't glance over in the direction my dad indicated, but said, "Lots of tourists around, interested in boats."

I turned to see, though.

I said, "He looks as much like a tourist as the Secret Service who accompany Vice President Cheney on his trips home to Jackson Hole." Even from this distance you could see the sun reflecting off the smooth fabric of this man's dress pants, and though he didn't wear a tie, his shirt was collared with long sleeves. Back home the Secret Service started off wearing dark suits and ties, and when all the locals greeted them with questions about the weather in D.C., they switched to khakis and fishing vests, which handily concealed their guns and communication equipment. Whether they actually had the dry cleaners starch and press their fishing vests was uncertain, but somehow the way they wore them gave off that impression. We still asked about the weather in D.C.

I'm not sure why, but when Dad tried to pursue a discussion about the man with the binoculars, I conspired with Daniel to change the subject, as if I were in on the mystery and trying to protect it along with him. And there was a mystery. I didn't know who Daniel really was or why he was posing as a fishing guide or why the man in the pressed pants was watching him, but I wanted the mystery for myself; I didn't want to share it with my dad.

Luring Dad away from the topic, and then soon after away from Daniel's boat, set me firmly into an alliance with this stranger. Unless I chose not to come walking on the docks again, not to talk to Daniel again. Then, of course, no alliance could possibly exist. I suspected I would be back. I didn't know whether Daniel would stick around or not.

Twenty-four

Jess

I remembered how endearing AnnieLaurie looked on extremely cold skiing days when the baby fuzz along the hairline in front of her ears froze and the ice crystals sparkled like party glitter. Temperatures finally crawled stiffly into the lower single digits, so to hell with the business, I was downhill skiing all day long. As I poled into the lift line at Teewinot for my first run, I searched for that glitter on other women's faces. The darnedest thing was, it tended to look stupid on other women, even masculine. I never noticed before how many women had hairy faces. I swear, one woman had a heavy ice mustache and goatee. Looked like Sigmund Freud on skis.

The slopes were filled with a lot of unattractive women. Or so it seemed today. Other days all the women looked beautiful to me and reminded me of Annie in one way or another, as if the ski slopes were filled with her sisters taunting me out here.

The line was long, so I tucked my poles under one arm, pulled out my cell and called Annie. I hadn't decided yet whether to tell her about my session with Lola. The fact was, I didn't like thinking about it.

"Hi. It's me. I miss you."

"Hi, Jess. I miss you, too."

"Yeah, but I *really* miss you. I'm skiing this morning, and all I can think about is how much I wish you were skiing with me." I glided my skis up the line as it moved, trying to keep my poles from poking someone's eyes out behind me.

"But I hardly ever skied with you. I was usually in the office working."

"I just miss you a lot, Annie, and I'm anxious for us to be together again." I didn't call to bring up how much she worked and I played.

"Well, I'm getting a little annoyed with that line, Jess." She took a big breath and let it out. "Mushy talk about missing me and how much you want me home is your avoidance scheme. You're beginning to sound like a broken record."

"That's the love of my heart, insulting me when I say nice things." I looked around to see who might be listening and smiled at the strangers surrounding me. The tricky part of getting into the chairlift with poles in one hand, phone in the other was approaching. Should have thought this out. "Just a second, Annie." I decided I better give this up, especially if the conversation was going to get difficult. I maneuvered under the rope that kept the lift line in place, held the phone up to my ear again. "I'm back." Without using my poles, I slid down the gentle slope toward a bench in the sunlight. "Where were we? Oh, yeah. 'Broken record.'"

She said, "More like a broken record that thinks it's endearing in that condition."

I rested my poles against the bench. "Shit, Annie." I guessed this was going to take a while, so I worked out of my skis in order to sit comfortably.

"You're in denial, Jess. And grasping for the innocent position— missing me, telling me you love me. Staying firmly in the same spot that you've always clung to—blind, blameless, refusing to see reality."

I sighed audibly into the phone. Leave it to Annie to turn a genuine sentiment of mine into a fault I should feel guilty about.

"Move it along, Jess. We're having problems. Let's work on them."

Maybe this was the time to tell her about seeing Lola. But

then this conversation would really get uncomfortable. I changed the subject with her instead, said, "Okay . . . so what's up with school?"

She allowed a long pause, then gave in and answered me. "I love school, Jess. I want to go for a degree, do something with this education I'm getting."

Her voice sounded as if her face were all aglow, eyes lit, cheeks lifted in a soft smile—the way she used to sound and look while talking about us. "A degree in what?" Here it comes.

"Creativity."

Again I sighed into the phone. But I kept quiet, let her talk. I leaned against the back of the bench and stretched out my legs. From here the entire mountain range spread out before me, and it made my heart buzz to see the peaks all lined up, glimmering in the bright morning light against the sky. The drainages were folded in between the slopes and crowded with the spires of dark pines. The sun felt great. I'd missed some of what Annie was saying. I tuned back in.

"I just think people must honor one another's creativity," Annie said.

"Not if it's crap, we don't."

"Jess, you're such a severe critic."

A woman coming off Apres Vous skied into my line of vision, and stopped to wipe the fog off her goggles before getting in the lift line again. I checked how the frost had decorated this woman's face and she had a long, icy chin hair. I bet she would have died if she knew that hair was even growing on her face. And here it was frosted, catching sunbeams and flashing them over the mountain like SOS signals. I didn't respond to Annie, so she went on.

"You're harshly judgmental toward other people's creative pursuits and the reason may be because you're not creating much yourself."

I still didn't respond.

"Maybe if you'd completed any of your projects or stood ready to back them up as the best that you could do—"

I interrupted, "Then I'd miraculously have low enough standards and crummy enough taste to applaud everybody else's efforts. Great theory."

"I'm just saying, Jess, that you're as severe with yourself as you are with others. It's as if you're privately sneering yourself into immobility in the creativity department."

"I hate that damn word 'creativity.'" I stood up and took a few steps in a small circle before the bench. "I have a degree in design. I know good work when I see it. And I don't see it often." I sat back down. People settled for junk these days. They were too lazy to hold out for good work, either making it or buying it.

She said, "We don't go around judging the quality of people's prayers, and so we shouldn't be doing that to creative efforts. Just as with prayer, we should stand reverent in the face of it, whatever it is."

She was on a soapbox now. I leaned up, propped my arms on my knees and held my head in my hand.

"Art, no matter how it's judged by the contemporary world," she continued, "is the reach toward the sacred, that which is larger than ourselves." She paused. "Being creative is a way to experience the divine."

Oh, geez. Good art is good art. Not much of it in the world and no use trying to squirm around the fact. I won't hurrah someone just because they got their crayons out and tried to draw a barn.

I said, "Write it for your term paper." I meant, *And spare me.* But that just encouraged her.

"I'm finding out for myself that it's a path to self-knowledge, a kind of education that enlarges my awareness. This is important to me, Jess. Creative energy feels like medicine to me, a way to heal myself, and I want to learn to offer that to others."

That was it. I got mad. I stood up, turned my back to the skiers going past and tried to keep my voice low.

"Annie, you are no goddamn good at drawing a fig tree, you can't sing 'Happy Birthday' with a bunch of off-key five-year-olds and you dance with the rhythm of a wombat. You're just looking for an excuse to elevate these facts into something else. Stick with the ledgers."

Long silence.

"Thanks for the support, Jess." Her voice cracked. "Maybe I'll follow your suggestion. Come back home to the ledgers . . . and release you to the ski slopes. That what you had in mind?"

"Oh, shit, Annie. I'm sorry." I don't know what sets me off when art gets into the picture. I hear this passion in her voice . . . I see my mother on the road, her painting tools lying in blood. I said, "I got to go."

I pocketed my cell, snapped back into my bindings and poled off to stand in the lift line. I'd have to apologize again for all those insults—not that they weren't the naked-ass truth, except for the wombat part. Even Annie once admitted she couldn't draw a happy face. "But," Annie had followed, "that isn't what matters." And, of course, we knew what mattered. All together now: "It's the big C."

I slid onto the chair, a double that I was sharing with a woman I didn't know. Not interested in chitchat, so I just said, "Nice day," and turned my head away to admire the slopes laid out in the sunlight below to my left.

The chair reached the top of Teewinot, and the woman and I slid off, skied across each other's path. She skied toward the left to go down the short slope and I skied toward the right to stand in line for the Apres Vous lift that went to the top.

The snow was hard high up, too cold to have softened, but it felt great to be out. When I was outdoors skiing and hiking, I didn't think about a thing other than the beauty of being in the mountains and working my body. There was nothing in the world better than that, unless it was at the end of a day full of outdoor activity when that great sense of well-being nested in my chest. Let's hear it for endorphins.

I skied fast, hit the bottom, got in line again. After I warmed up on Apres Vous, I rode the tram to see how things looked on Rendezvous. With the inversion, it was warmer.

I'd kept my head down that morning to avoid eye contact, but Annie and I had lived here too long for me not to have run into a dozen people I knew in the first hour of skiing. Hey, Jess. Hi, Jess. How ya doin', Jess? I responded and moved right along. Not in the mood, sorry.

Annie went so far once as to call creativity a psychic orgasm. I mean, that girl left no area untouched by this philosophy.

When our sons were little, they used to plead, "Draw us a bunny, Momma" and Annie was stumped. Big circle, small circle, add ears. That was all the little guys wanted.

I'd say, "Ask for a snake, boys." Just joking, but Annie would shoot daggers at me, because—who'd believe it—she didn't know how to draw a snake. I'd do a wavy line in the air with my finger. She'd get a purposeful look on her face and carefully draw a squiggle. "Put a cat by it," Saddler would say and Annie was stumped again. Now wasn't this the perfect person to make a big to-do about the creative urge *and* be dismissive about its outcome?

After lunch at Casper Bowl, I decided to ski down to base and call her back. Apologize again for all my insults. The phone rang four times. Maybe she was thinking about whether to answer or not.

"Hello," she said formally.

"I said some nasty things. It's not true about your dancing like a wombat; I love dancing with you."

"Hmm," she said. And I supposed she was going to press for the "sorry" word. I was just getting ready to pull it out when she said, "I love dancing with you, too." She paused. "Though I might go ahead anyway and look for a new husband here in Florida."

I said, "Well, don't give me as a reference."

She started laughing quietly and ended up laughing hard. I could picture her head tipped back, hair falling between her shoulders. She'd probably gotten some sun streaks in her hair by now, and those shoulders were probably tanned.

Just to be a decent guy, I said, "I'm glad you like school. What kind of degree does a person get in . . . creativity?"

Annie said, "Art therapy." Musical notes rang out from her two words. She was hooked on something big. "I'd like to work with patients in hospitals."

I said again, "Well, don't use me as a reference."

No laughter this time.

I decided not to tell her about seeing Lola. I probably wouldn't go back. Lola already warned me that she'd want to talk about my *story* more. Sure. That would fix everything.

Twenty-five

Annie

As the sun set, the sky outside my screened porch duplicated the coals in my grill, gray with fiery coral on the edges. Behind me in the apartment, CNN evening news tacked me to the rest of humanity and the flow of earthly life. I spread the coals out from the pyramid I had piled them in and came inside to season the chicken. Bijou chewed on a pressed rawhide bone, and Kia flew to my shoulder, where she liked to tap her beak against my blue topaz ear studs.

The word "Miami" caught my attention on the news, and I paused to watch a story about a nursing home filled with pets. Birdcages housed singing canaries and clowning parakeets. Fish tanks sparkled with neon tetras, cats sat on windowsills and greyhounds laid their muzzles on frail laps in wheelchairs.

According to the reporter, statistics showed that around animals people lived longer, heart rates slowed, immune systems perked. And scientists had proven that bones knitted faster if you interacted with animals while you healed. They didn't mention hearts, but I was convinced. My pets had created a home for me and speeded my healing.

One Thanksgiving weekend a few years back, my dogs were the only creatures in the house that befriended me. The urge was strong to seek distraction from this memory. But it had been nipping at my heels long enough now, demanding acknowledgment of its presence. I turned off the TV, set Kia back in her cage, poured a glass of wine and took it to the porch to watch the final colors drain from the sky and the stars brighten.

That phone call with Jess. Even though it had occurred a couple days ago now, his dismissal of the enthusiasm I had expressed for my studies in creative energy provoked a range of emotions and the remembrance of one miserable night in particular.

That evening the dishes were cleared from our Thanksgiving dinner, and I worked on the dining room table, cutting pictures out of old *National Geographic* magazines for a collage I was putting together on card stock. Suddenly I looked up to see Jess, Cam and Saddler standing around the table like a posse, waiting for me to break my concentration and notice them.

I laughed out loud at how engrossed I'd been. Saddler was home on holiday from his second year in college and Cam, a senior in high school, was also on break for the long Thanksgiving weekend. Our store was closed until the beginning of ski season in December, so we'd all hung around the house that day, while snow accumulated outside the windows.

I stopped laughing when no one joined me. I waited, feeling puzzled, for someone to speak.

I remembered how all three of the dogs circled around my feet as Jess, Cam and Saddler pulled out chairs and sat at the dining table, facing me. They had turned off the television.

Jess spoke first. "We've been talking, and we've decided to tell you that we're having some trouble with you." Then all three of them talked on top of one another, volleying accusations at me. I spent too much time with my projects. Dad was trying to get along, but I was being selfish. Why did I go on weekend trips alone; why didn't I watch TV with everybody; why didn't I change back to how I used to be?

I didn't even hear all their words. I was overcome with the shock of their approach, the surprise of their attack. I was outnumbered and overwhelmed, and my first response was one of feeling I had transgressed somehow. That was followed within seconds by an avalanche of shame over my complete ignorance about how I was failing everyone.

I began crying. I lurched up from the table and went to our bedroom, wounded and confused. I asked myself if their accusations were true. Was I being selfish? Was I ignoring the family when I chose not to watch TV with them, but to read, knit, sew, work with paints and paste images, instead? Why were guilt and shame my first responses? Why was it anyone's first response when they were ganged up on? True, I wasn't following the conventional path anymore of going along with whatever the family wanted to do whether I wanted to or not, but rather trying to blaze a new one for myself. Alone I attended gallery openings, craft classes and lectures. Did that make me selfish? Or did it make me finally mature, a full person in my own right?

All that work, all that searching and pondering for the last couple of years, in the effort to make my marriage work. And the long search for meaning in my life, as I yearned to make my days satisfying, while I also stayed within the family framework and continued in the business. My struggle to maintain balance—be a loving wife, a good mother, while trying to keep alive an essential part of myself.

Was all of it a failure? Was I way off track?

I had to take seriously that the three people closest to me suggested I was abnormal and should "fix" it.

That Thanksgiving night I paced my bedroom while the TV droned downstairs with old holiday movie repeats. I curled into a ball on the carpet and held myself. I wept and whispered to myself. Hours later I heard my sons come upstairs to their bedrooms.

The house quieted.

Jess didn't come up.

That Thanksgiving night a couple hours before dawn, I sat

against pillows on my bed, lamplight casting a yellow circle around me, and the word "intervention" occurred to me. The label helped me sort out my bewilderment. An intervention was what you did when all else failed, when each person involved had attempted on three different occasions to introduce a private discussion with the one in denial of their problem—an addiction, usually. And when the attempts failed to advance the situation toward a solution, an intervention was arranged: the family gathered and confronted the troubled person.

Not one person—not my husband nor either son—had approached me even one time. In fact, Jess had turned away my attempts to discuss our relationship, sometimes with a joke, sometimes with impatience or anger. I realized then that Jess had used our sons' normal parental gripes—and perhaps their fears of their parents' growing detachment—to bolster his personal trouble with me.

That night I walked downstairs and woke Jess with bright lamplight in his face as he slept on the sofa.

"You are married to me. You dignify that from now on with the privacy and the honor that deserves. When you have problems with me, you talk to me directly. Never again bring our children into our marriage."

Jess apologized in today's politically correct way. He said, "If I did anything to hurt you, I'm sorry."

An apology weakened by the fact that I had to challenge him for it. He didn't come to me. He slept. I came to him. A pattern I was finally recognizing.

Going to a marriage counselor didn't come from him, either, but he agreed to accompany me. Maybe the sleep deprivation and bright light in the eyes played a part.

I used the same tactic on our sons. Went to each of their bedrooms, turned on the overhead light and announced the rules for an intervention: three private attempts before a group encounter. See me after breakfast.

Both boys showed sleepy but sincere contrition.

I became full of clarity and strength that dawn. I realized that I had never been so happy as I had during the past couple years of directing some of my energy and attention to myself. The search for a sense of personal identity was expressed by my craft projects. They connected me to an essential part of myself and gave me great pleasure. Yet my sons' father was having one hell of a hard time with that.

Even then, I recognized that the boys' concern was with their parents' relationship, not their personal trouble with me. Saddler was in college; Cam would soon follow. They joined Jess in his ambush on me because they were afraid for him, for what would happen when they were both gone from home. The boys were so busy with their own lives, they didn't notice their parents' lives, and that was exactly the way they wanted it: parents happy in the background; themselves happy in the foreground. Jess' trouble threatened that peace.

Yet for the sake of giving the marriage counseling my best shot, I cleaned my projects off the dining room table that next morning, put them away. The mistake I made was not getting them out again.

I rose from my chair and stirred the coals. Jess' continuing lack of support for my interest in creative work had showed its shadowed face once again during our last phone call. This time I wouldn't back down, wouldn't pack up my craft projects and try to renew my interest in the store. Finding work that gave me joy and knowing I could make my way toward it had lifted me these weeks in Florida. I had wanted to share this with Jess, but he hadn't wanted to hear it.

I brought the chicken breasts out to lay on the grill and returned to the kitchen to make a salad. I believed in art therapy; I was experiencing its success in my own life as I filled my lap with beautiful yarns and my worktable with card-making supplies, images, markers and paints. My marriage was going to be stronger because of it. This was work I loved; I could imagine succeeding at leading others toward the same happiness and satisfactions I was discovering. But Jess dismissed my interests and ridiculed my past creative attempts. What I tried to help him understand was that it didn't take an artist to enjoy creative energy or to awaken it in others. Just as it didn't take a mechanic to enjoy driving or to teach driving to others.

But what I had to understand myself was that my creative energy was my responsibility, and I must protect it.

Turning a chicken breast on the grill, I recalled my dream the night after my phone call with Jess. I dreamed that I carried a small pile of wood that held fire. I took this fire around with me, trying to keep it burning. I was looking for a place that was safe to set it. A place where the flame would continue to flare.

This love I held for creating wasn't about producing craft projects; it was about connecting to my inner life, about self-knowing and self-realization. It was about paying attention and coming awake to my own experience of living.

I spread a basil-and–pine nut pesto along the length of each chicken breast, let it heat through, then removed one breast to my plate for dinner and took the other in the kitchen to cool for another meal tomorrow. I brought out the salad I'd prepared along with sliced melon and freshly rinsed grapes.

As I sat out in the dark porch to eat with only a candle and the dim glow of the coals offering light, I realized that part of my need to distance myself from Jess was to protect something fiercely essential to my well-being. His disdain could be a powerful force to me, because I had always looked up to his opinions. I had buckled under his disapproval a dangerous number of times.

Oddly, I accused Jess of sheltering in innocence, of hiding in a state of not knowing, but my marital amnesia had served me in a similar way: I protected myself by forgetting the hard parts, the pieces of our love that sat jaggedly apart from the smooth, throbbing heart center. I must learn to stand by my own opinions and experiences. And I must kindle the flame of my dream and keep it safe.

I poured a half glass of wine and toasted that thought, just to mark it in my mind.

Twenty-six

Jess

My favorite memory happened at the Teagues' house one Easter when Annie and I were college students and going steady. The Skipper dragged out the family's old home movies of Annie and her sister, Daisy. In the movie I remembered best, the Teagues were hosting a small reunion for the Skipper's side of the family at a breakfast cookout on Hutchinson Island. Huge Australian pines shaded the picnic tables and sea grape wrapped the sand dunes. Annie was ten years old with a serious overbite and ears bigger than palmettos sticking through her thin hair, but she was so full of life she dimmed the sun.

I envied her clear sense of place in life. She looked so awake inside her skin that the people around her—her parents and aunts and uncles, the other little cousins—seemed to move like lizards in the cold. She showed off in front of the camera, dancing to some tune in her head, crowding the camera lens, grinning up close to her future husband. I remembered I had laughed and gotten teary in the gray movie light of the Teagues' fancy living room.

Later that night I sneaked out of the guest house, darted through the shadows cast by the lighted pool and slipped into the main house. Scents of Easter ham and sweet potato, laced with lemony coconut cake, still floated in the stairwell as I climbed to the second floor. My heart paddled double time like oars in a canoe race, flicking drops of sweat on my forehead when I walked past the bedroom where the Skipper and his wife slept. He rarely slept a full five hours, and that was often accomplished in shifts during the night. But the shock on Annie's face when I appeared in her bedroom was worth the gamble of being thrown out of the house for life. To her that night, I was the bravest male on earth. I would call it stupidity now, but I was happy to confuse it with courage then. I pushed the scene by crawling into bed with her.

I wanted that light, that beam of pure energy in my life. That night I wanted deep inside it. Annie and I made love. And I asked her to marry me.

I slipped out of Annie's bedroom with the same luck I had entered it, without encountering her father. The Skipper was big man on this campus. At any given moment all three female faces— Annie, Daisy and their mother, Carrie—were likely tipped his way. He demanded attention the way a squawking parrot did, flashing its brilliant feathers in the sun. He was fast-talking, fast-moving, rich and generous. The joke around the house was that he was the Big Typhoon, a play on Big Tycoon. He never minded the joke that he was a big wind instead of a big magnate, and even named his boat *The Big Typhoon*.

That night, after I left Annie's bed, I sat up on the veranda until dawn, then showered, walked to the closest busy road and hitched a ride into town. The Teagues lived in Palm Beach at the time, and like an idiot I had thought I could buy an engagement ring for the money in my pocket. After frustrating myself looking in the shop windows on Worth Street, I came to my senses and realized two hundred and eighty dollars wouldn't buy a bottle of wine in this town or a decent ring in any town. I had an image to uphold with Annie's family as the poor but artistic suitor. Even the Skipper liked the idea that my entire wardrobe fit into the small duffel bag I'd brought for my stay. I owned two pairs of khakis and two oxford cloth shirts, which I wore over and over, washed and pressed by my own hands. "Live simply. That's what I admire," he'd said, his emerald pinky ring flashing like the swimming pool in the sunshine.

So I dropped the idea of a small diamond and sat on a bench beneath a royal palm on Worth Street, elbows on knees, head down, staring at the sidewalk. A pearl? How much would that cost? I lifted my gaze and noticed a flyer tacked to the trunk of the palm. It advertised a flea market south on the highway, and I felt a prickle of hope. Hitched out, browsed the outdoor stalls just then setting up for the day beneath faded awnings. I found one selling jewelry. The fellow was hauling out fake-leather cases from his parked car and stacking them on a long table.

"What you looking for, bub?"

"I need a ring. Kind of fancy." My voice sounded forlorn to me, a bit hopeless.

"What size?"

The short of it was, this guy rooted around in the trunk of his car and came up with a ring that fit my beloved's image of me as quirky but tasteful. This was Annie's first blue topaz, had two tiny chips that looked like diamonds on each side of it, and the band was stamped fourteen-carat gold. The guy settled for two hundred and fifty dollars; I stuck the ring on my little finger and hitched back out to the Teagues' in time for brunch by the pool.

When I walked into the backyard that morning and approached the umbrella table with Annie's family sitting around it, I saw once again that show-offy ten-year-old grin of AnnieLaurie. For one long moment she and I stared at each other—me dopey with love and luck, Annie celebrating our audacious lovemaking and engagement the night before. The family—even the Skipper, even their dogs, a pair of chocolate Labs—fell silent and still as I stood beside the table, eyes locked on my future wife.

Annie sparkled. She flaunted our secret. Her eyes tangoed with mine and her smile—teeth aligned into precision, thanks to years of braces—dared me to flirt openly with her. I remembered halting there, stunned with the beauty of her. Her ears had been pinned during her preteens—with a few tiny stitches and excruciating pain, she'd told me. The thin hair of her girlhood had thickened into a spill of honey. And her vitality glowed through the pores of her skin. My eyes teared up and Annie's grin widened into a laugh of pure glee. I swear, we got married that instant. Something in us joined and exchanged vows.

One of those vows must have been to trade emotions with each other, because then Annie teared up and I laughed. And we have continued that throughout our lives, switching emotional sides even during arguments.

Our laughter and teariness spread to the others, at least to Mrs. Teague and Daisy, and though nothing had been said outright yet, we all seemed to agree on something that had especially to do with Annie and me.

I cleared my throat. "Mr. Teague, I'd like to marry her," I said, staring at Annie and not looking at the Skipper at all.

"Who? Carrie? She's my wife; she's already married."

"Skip, don't ruin things," Carrie warned.

"Daisy, here? I been hoping to get rid of Daisy before she costs me a bunch of money—four years of college and all the books and clothes that go with it. You can have her."

I realized he was going to force me to lay it all out, slowly and clearly. If I had known him to be a bigger man, I could have thought this was for Annie's sake. So she could have a long moment in the sun with a formal request for her hand. But it was the Skipper who liked to stretch his moments in the sun.

"AnnieLaurie. I'd like permission to marry AnnieLaurie."

"Now you ask? I've already paid for two years of college. Where were you at high school graduation?"

"Daddy," Annie said, shyness setting in with the significance of the occasion.

"God, Daddy," Daisy chimed in. "Just say yes like you're supposed to do."

"Do not take the Lord's name in vain, Daisy, until you're

twenty-one years or older," the Skipper said, disclosing one of his stranger parenting ideas. Then he gave in.

"Okay, yes, Jessup McFall. If my daughter agrees, and her smiling over here with teardrops sparkling on her cheeks suggests she does, then you may have the hand of my elder daughter, Annie-Laurie Teague." He paused and allowed us all to feel mushy a bit, then added, "But couldn't you chip in for some of the cosmetic work we had to do on her to catch one of you fellows?"

I considered telling the Skipper it was his daughter's Dumbo-eared, Thumper-toothed beauty I fell so hard for, that some of her purity had leaked into self-consciousness, thanks to him and his procurement of pinned ears and braced teeth, but there was never any use in competing with the Skipper. He insisted on winning, whether it was croquet on their rubbery Florida grass or holding the floor during his daughter's marriage proposal.

Finally we got the job done, the ring on Annie's finger, the brunch eaten.

I had rarely spotted that pure happy energy in Annie's face during the decades we were married, had our children, started our business, until a couple years ago when she was deep into her own thoughts and her creative crafts on the dining room table. And then it just made me mad.

Twenty-seven

Annie

"Good morning, Daniel."

"Good morning, Annie Teague." He squinted in the sunlight. "Your dad back in Stuart?"

"Left a few days ago." Asking after my father accomplished a sense of immediate familiarity. Here was the only person I had met in Hibiscus who had also met my dad. But I didn't want to make things that comfortable for him, so I said, "And *your* friend?" I tipped my head toward the park, where the same man with binoculars who had watched us before now leaned against a parking lot post and watched us again.

Daniel laughed. "I knew I'd like you."

I smiled at him. I liked him, too.

"Come aboard. I've made coffee." He nodded toward Bijou. "Bring your girlfriend." He held out a hand to help me onto the boat. I hesitated, then took his hand. "Come below and help me carry the mugs and coffee up." I had stooped down to pet his dog, who had already flopped belly up to make my job easier. "Or stay here and I'll bring it up."

"I'll stay here." Sending signals of distance in return to his signals of invitation.

This was a guy who knew what he wanted and how to get it. Refreshing after Jess, who seemed to live in a prolonged stall, engine sputtering since the kids left home. Yet I was a woman who knew what I wanted and was fast learning how to get it. Perhaps

Jess had flirted with the idea of an affair with whoever answered the store phone that day I called, but I'd had time to move beyond my early fears. What I knew about Jess—and didn't particularly admire—was that Jess flirted with lots of things—ideas, intentions, goals—and followed through on very few. This young girl that answered the phone, surprised that Jess had a "wi-ife," was a project of which, I knew, he would not follow through. Mostly because he loved me too much, and I knew that, too. Sorry, little girl.

I found a deck chair and swiveled around to find that Binocular Man trained his glasses on me, the new person on the boat, but now as I watched, he dropped his binoculars to hang around his neck and sat down on top of a picnic table, feet on the bench, leaning back against his hands. What a boring job . . . except when it got interesting.

Daniel came up with a coffeepot in one hand, two white crockery mugs in the other and a small carton of half and half pressed between his arm and his chest.

"Do you take sugar?" I shook my head no and helped him unload.

He said, "That's good. I don't have any."

He pulled out a striped awning overhead and we settled in the shade beneath it, poured our coffee, both of us adding cream, sat back and watched the water. Watching the water never got old. I could do it for hours, and did, sitting on the beach just staring at the water, the sky, where the two met. Even when nothing happened, the water was flat, the sky was gray, that "nothing" was a continually changing aliveness of light and color and rocking rhythm.

"I want to hear your story, Annie Teague."

"Are we going to trade stories, Daniel?" I let my eyes trail over to Binocular Man again.

Daniel laughed. "You know, I think I could do that with you."

"Then I'll tell you the most important thing about me right

now." A lump rose in my throat for a reason I could not at once label, and I cast my gaze far across the sea. Was I about to burn a bridge to something new, wonderful and exciting? What if this was the loving, attentive intelligence I longed to partner with in my life? The man who would look deeply into me and not be afraid of anything he saw there. I took a big breath, let myself regain balance; then I looked at Daniel.

"I'm married to a man I love and I'm down here in Florida for a while, but then I'm going home."

"Is he a bastard?"

"No. Actually not. I just need time to realign myself . . . whatever I mean by that." I took a sip of coffee. Daniel watched. "You know. Been a mother, wife, helpmate in all the typical ways. Now it's time I learn who I am aside from those definitions."

"Been a daughter."

"That, too."

"Skip said your mother died a few years back. Sounded tough. And your father . . . he hasn't come out of that too well, is my guess."

I felt my body come alert. "Why do you say that?"

"Something in his look; I've seen it before. I don't mean to alarm you. But his skin color or eyes—I don't know. Have him checked out." He looked at me with regret. "I'm sorry. I had no business saying that." He shook his head. "Damn, I don't know what I'm talking about. Ignore me."

Instantly the skin on my neck had heated at hearing Daniel's words, and my heart beat loud with fear. I felt an urge to jump up and phone Daisy. Cry. Then I realized that somewhere I kind of knew this. That Daniel was tolling a warning that I had heard before and not heeded, as if a far-off bell were ringing and not for the first time. And I said so to Daniel, thinking out loud to him about the mental muck I had been nearly smothered by since settling in Hibiscus. I had depended on Dad being a solid presence, quirky, annoying, but there for me, representing the familiar, my original self before Jess and the boys.

Daniel let me sit quietly a moment, while we both held our coffee mugs and gazed out toward the water. The two dogs had found their places beside us: Bijou delicately curled at my feet and Jeter, bones knocking on the wood deck while he'd found his position, sprawled like a five-point star in the sun. Daniel was easy to be with, and in the comfortable silence between us, I began thinking how I had spent much of my adult life reacting to others. Reacting to children, to Jess, to employees and customers. Reacting to family upsets, housekeeping crises, small business emergencies. That my first response to Daniel's words about Dad had triggered sensations I felt comfortable with—jump to, take care. I had lived my adult life as an EMT, on call for others' emergencies.

A kind of calm entered my inner scenery then, accompanied by the realization that I was a person unto myself. That I would always wish to help others, but that such help needed from now on to rise from this deeper sense of being I had lately been exploring within myself.

I took a big, full breath of the warm air and smelled salt, fish and fuel. I looked at Daniel. He poured more coffee into my mug and a dollop of cream. How come I wanted to know this man? What was it about him that attracted me? I enjoyed his male interest in me and his alive awareness, yet overriding that swam a sisterly sort of interest tinged with concern. And him? Were his words of warning about Dad contrived to create an immediate intimacy between us? Because it accomplished that and perhaps I should feel leery. My face easily transmitted my thoughts, I'd been told, and Daniel was watching me.

"You don't know me," he said.

"No." I set my mug down on the low table between us. "Are you dangerous?"

"I have been. I'm clean now. This bozo over here"—Daniel

cocked his head behind him—"just hasn't been assured yet." He added, "You're okay with me."

I asked, "Is it a long story?" Figured I'd give him an easy out, if he wanted it. I could just finish my coffee and mosey on down the dock.

Daniel said, "True stories can be pretty short." We watched a pelican fly to the pier, settle itself on top of a piling. "As a pilot, I flew drug interdiction for Customs, for the government, down along the Mexican border. Got into the department pretty young and was mentored by a man quite a few years older than me."

Daniel appeared conflicted at the memory of this man and those early times. His eyes softened a moment, but then he adjusted his body's relaxed position in the chair, switched his legs around, crossing his left ankle over his right knee.

"He taught me everything I needed to know to become a good pilot— I flew Black Hawk helicopters, the King Air, Citation jets— he sat second on all of them until I got as good as he was. He helped me get ahead in the office and eventually . . . he pulled me into his extra work on the side."

"You mean . . ."

"Drug agents make the best drug smugglers."

To sound polite and cover up my shock, I offered an excuse. "Did you need the money?" Not that an excuse would have absolved his actions for me.

"I didn't need the money, even though it could have helped to send my daughter through medical school. I did it because I couldn't say no. Because it was hard to refuse helping someone who had helped me so much."

"So you have a daughter in medical school?"

"Jamie." His smile was beatific. "She's finished with her schooling now. Works in a clinic in India. Bodhgaya, big Buddhist place. Tends to as many stray dogs, after hours, as she does people during her workday and doesn't know how she'll ever leave, because the work will never end. She loves it." He smiled at some inward images.

"Jamie's a great kid and I had nothing to do with it." He said, "Jamie's mother and I separated shortly after she was born."

"Are you still . . . um . . . smuggling or whatever?" This was not my language.

"Not for many years now. Got myself transferred off the border, cleaned myself up. Retired early, came down here, bought a boat."

"And now you're a fishing guide."

"Yes, it's good work."

"And your bozo? He's especially suspicious of fishing guides?" I was trying to sound offhand though I didn't feel that way. I wanted to know more and was afraid Daniel wouldn't continue if I sounded too affected by his story.

Daniel said, "Let me take you out. I mean now, on the boat. We'll just cruise around the inner waterway. And I'll tell you the rest."

"Daniel, I don't know you. You are being watched by someone who doesn't care that he's seen watching you, which suggests to me that he is on the side of the authorities and that you are not. I'm not going anywhere with you."

"Right, I understand. But there's no one you'd be safer with. Because Bozo is just one of the men watching." Daniel raised his eyebrows toward the water. "There's a guy on that small blue boat out there and a couple more on the go-fast boat sitting on the horizon. They'd be following, if that makes you feel better."

The ridiculousness of that reasoning struck us both at the same time, and we laughed together. Something about this guy. He was either genuine—if you could call a professed double-dealer genuine— or he knew just what buttons to push to make me feel that I shared something with him that did not measure up to the short time we had spent together so far.

He said, "Okay, then let's go below and scramble some eggs for lunch."

"Nope."

"Trust me, you'll be fine."

"Daniel, I'd be stupid to trust you. You lied to the United States government. Compared to them, I'm easy to fool."

"Actually, you are much more discerning than our government. But, okay, down to the Turtle Nest, then. End of the marina. Bozo will be happy; he's starving. I usually like to keep him waiting longer. If we went below, he'd be stuck on shore for hours. Here." Daniel handed me his binoculars. "Check these guys out. I'm going to get my wallet and change my shirt." Before he went belowdeck, he said, "Look at Bozo. It drives him crazy when you do that. Check out the blue boat; should be one guy on that in civies. The go-fast boat has two officers and they're in uniform."

"Really? 'Go-fast' boat? That's what you call it?" Sounded like something little boys would say.

"Right. They go really fast. I'll be back up in a few minutes."

I lifted the binoculars and sighted. It always takes me a while to fool around with the focus and figure out where I'm looking. Started with the go-fast boat way out there—blue water, blue sky, blue water. There it was. Long and narrow, a cigarette boat. Two men in uniforms, both standing toward me, couldn't see their faces. Then the blue boat—blue water, blue sky, blue water—got it. Could see the glint of sunlight off someone's binoculars, but no face. Then Bozo. His face would be clear, if he lowered his binoculars. I saw he'd wised up some. Was wearing shorts—Bermuda khakis—with his long-sleeved white shirt, dress shoes and black socks. Somebody ought to start a school for these guys.

He was twenty-some pounds overweight, and those dress shoes were wingtips. Bozo dropped his binoculars and let me look at him straight in the eyes. He had a round face with wire-rim glasses, pale blue eyes behind them, sparse eyebrows. Couldn't think of him as Bozo anymore and couldn't glass him without embarrassment. He was a human being, and I had been considering him as an object of derision, maybe even the enemy. Daniel traveled in a strange world.

Yet I found it briefly—and ridiculously—thrilling to stare at these people, who were staring at me. As if I were experiencing my fifteen minutes of fame. Though most likely I was an object of derision. Or the enemy.

"Daniel," I hollered, "now they know who I am."

"Yeah, but, Annie." He came up on deck, slipping his wallet in his back pants pocket and cell phone in his front pocket. "Now you know who they are, too."

"Do you know his name?"

"Who?"

I tipped my head over toward the park.

"Oh, sure. His name is Burl Stocker." Daniel looked at me mock-accusingly. "I shouldn't have let you look at him up close. Now you'll worry about him when it rains." I laughed. "Just seemed you should know what he looks like, since he knows what you look like."

"Have you incriminated me?"

"Possibly. That's why I'm going to tell you everything. Really, I'm straight now. These guys are just checking the truth of that."

"So they don't believe you, either."

Daniel laughed again; he had a good laugh, free and easy. "Come on, let's eat. My treat."

"No, I'll pay for my own lunch."

"I plan on doing all the talking; I'll pay." He took a look at me. "It's not a date, married lady."

We walked down the pier, both our dogs following; Daniel waved to Burl Stocker as we passed, and Stocker nodded back. We climbed steps to the restaurant hanging over the water and took a table out on the deck so the dogs could accompany us. We sat beneath a yellow-and-red umbrella. Daniel reached into his pants pocket and tossed his cell phone on the table. And that reminded me that I wanted to call Daisy. I told Daniel I was popping into the restroom. He said he'd order for me. There he was, again, with that natural intimacy. There I was, again, enjoying it.

Inside the restroom I phoned Daisy and told her what Daniel had said about Dad. Daisy said, "That's the thing. I can't decide whether Dad is acting as odd as always or whether he is too quirky for his own good and we should worry. Who's Daniel?"

"Just some guy Dad and I met at the marina while walking one day." Daisy was used to Dad engaging strangers in conversation.

"Oh, and then you saw him again?"

"Well, he and I are having lunch here at the pier." I gave her the old we're-just-friends line, then seriously assured her, before asking, "What happened with Candy/Brandy?"

"I was going to phone about that. Her name is Sherry and turns out she is not the one interested in Dad. She wanted to match him up with another one of her customers, an older woman, older than Dad even. And Dad is broken up about that, though he denies it. But clearly he has dropped into a very low place. He's eating a lot of potato chips and watching golf all day on TV."

I thought about how Dad had perked up over attracting a younger woman. Ready to use "scalping lotion" and take her to a restaurant that made his "wallet quiver." He didn't need this disappointment.

Daisy and I decided we probably should schedule a checkup sometime soon. We left it rather vague, since we couldn't face the struggle we'd have with Dad to get him there. After Mom died, he swore off doctors—"All they say is bad news and all their medicines kill you."

While Daisy and I wrapped up our conversation, I walked out to the entrance of the restrooms and watched Daniel order our food, pointing every once in a while to my chair. He was probably older than me by a few years, dark blond hair, curly like Art Garfunkel's of Simon and Garfunkel, fine features, hazel eyes, well muscled. If he lived in Jackson Hole, I'd assume he was a climber. He had a bit of nervous energy, as if at any moment he might jump up, dive into the water, kick around fast, climb back out, just so he could sit still and talk a little longer. And he was bored with his life and not used to that. Normally I don't like to be around bored people. Daniel, I liked to be around. I watched a waiter pour ice water into our two glasses at the table, and I said goodbye to Daisy.

"So what did you order for lunch?" I sat on the chair Daniel pulled out for me.

"Grilled mahi vera." He sat back down. "Made with garlic, onions, parsley, oregano, cumin, chopped tomatoes, lime juice and olive oil." He listed the ingredients as if counting on his fingers. "Got the recipe from the chef a while back. Keep meaning to fix it, but it's easier to order it here."

"That's dinner, not lunch."

"Next time I'll take you to the Cooler, up the beach, and order the taco tot special. For sure, that's lunch."

"Taco tot?"

"A platter of Tater Tots smothered with nacho cheese, topped with ground beef, picante sauce, lettuce, tomatoes, sour cream. Four seventy-nine and it includes a medium drink. Your kind of place?"

"My dad's kind of place. The price alone would win him over, though he'd haggle for a large drink, no extra charge." I still had my phone in my hand, so I set it on the table, telling Daniel that I'd told Daisy about his concerns.

"What did your sister say about Skip?"

"She's been uneasy, too, about some of his behavior; we thought it was depression." I was struck that Daniel and I sat here talking about a condition concerning my father, when I hadn't even mentioned it yet to Jess. Just to remind myself how much of a stranger this guy really was, I asked him to continue his story.

The waiter brought us a bottle of white wine. Daniel passed on the tasting and the waiter poured two glasses and left.

"So where was I?"

"Your mentor."

"Parson Fields. I never knew my dad. For many years Parson was a good step-in. Took care of me during my early years in the department. I got on the take because I felt I owed the guy. But no excuses. I did it. Became disgusted with myself over my lousy ethics and put in for a transfer to get out from under his control and cleaned up my act." Daniel turned his wineglass in a circle with his index finger and thumb. "I contributed to the misery in the world during my short time of running drugs. I've regretted that and worked at making amends."

When talking about his mentor, Daniel seemed less animated, and I imagined a certain amount of grieving was involved in this relationship. Then he mentioned that Parson had experienced a brain aneurism a while back, though he'd come through it. I wondered if that was what he'd meant earlier about having seen the look of Dad's eyes and skin color. I took a sip of wine.

"How do you smuggle drugs under the eyes of the governmental department in charge of catching smuggled drugs?"

"Easy enough, if you've got the right help. You catch eighty-nine percent of the drugs coming through and let the other eleven percent go by."

"Go by?"

"You arrange to be elsewhere the night the run is scheduled. It's a passive-aggressive crime. Offense through nonaction. Appeals to young, idealistic guys trying to please a superior, like I was."

"So you're saying these guys"—I gestured toward the go-fast boat—"are here from something that happened in the past?"

"Over a decade ago. But Parson is stirring things up again." Daniel took a sip of his wine. "Let me back up. I worked on the Mexican border for ten, twelve years before Parson needed my help one night and I incriminated myself. Fifteen months later, I was able to transfer to the Canadian border in Washington State;

shortly after that, Parson was promoted to a position in D.C. and life went on."

"You stopped working with him. How come?"

"You mean besides the repulsion of looking in the mirror every morning? That and disappointment in my mentor aside, the game lost its charm fast. What happens is that the smugglers begin to call the shots. Once you start to work with them, they own you." Daniel looked out over the white-painted railing of the deck toward the go-fast boat anchored on the horizon. "I don't like to be owned."

"Can't you quit whenever you want?"

"No, ma'am, you cannot. You quit when the smugglers say you can. 'Just one more time,' they tell you. Again and again. They begin to take over by telling you *which* eleven percent to let through. They run the show from then on. And they've got you. They can turn me in at any time." Daniel held his wineglass and wiped sweat off it with his thumb.

"Parson himself stopped playing games when marijuana smuggling switched to cocaine. A lot more money was at stake then. Things got nasty real fast. Contract killings, kidnapping." Daniel paused for a sip of wine. "Thirteen years go by and suddenly the activity moves into my territory on the Canadian border. Same players. It got dangerous for me. An Internal Affairs investigation was heating up. I wasn't sure how the probe would come out for me—I wasn't involved, but my old contacts were, including Parson. I'd just turned fifty. So I put in for early retirement and left for India to get to know my daughter and assist her in the clinic. I kept quiet about where I was headed, hoping Parson wouldn't attempt to contact me again."

"But you needed your pension checks, didn't you?"

"Right. I have direct deposit to a bank back in Washington State, a post office box in the Midwest and a forwarding system. Just covering my tracks. It was only a matter of time before the feds would find me. But they were not the problem—aside from Parson."

"What brought you back to the States?"

"After a year or so with Jamie, I'd gotten word that Parson was dying. I decided to move back to the States since the threat of his interference with my life appeared over. I trained for my captain's license down the coast in Stuart—Chapman School of Seamanship. Skip probably knows about it."

"Oh, sure," I said. "It's quite well-known."

"I bought my boat to start a guide business. Parson recovered. Next I hear from him, he wants to get back in the game. And wants me to partner with him. I turned him down flat, but Parson has sway with people on both sides, and it looks like he intends to pull in his credit with every one of them."

Daniel shook his head. "Enforced retirement is age fifty-seven, a bit young for men used to aeronautical acrobats as a regular diet. I've had my own trouble with adrenaline addiction; took it out on working around the clock, helping Jamie at her clinic. Parson didn't have another outlet. He stayed active for several years after his retirement, consulting, but was cut loose when he became ill. His whole life was his career. No family, no kids."

While Daniel took a sip of his wine, he glanced inside the restaurant. He set his glass down hard. "Son of a bitch."

My body straightened. "What? What's wrong?"

"Look what that guy's eating."

"Who?" I followed Daniel's stare through the double doors, toward the bar in the front of the restaurant.

"Stocker. He's got so damn much mayonnaise on that ham-and-cheese sandwich, it's dripping out the sides."

I was startled. "You watch what he eats?"

"Somebody has to. He sure as hell doesn't." Daniel glared at Stocker's image reflected in the mirror behind the bar. If somebody looked at me like that while I was eating, I couldn't have swal-lowed. Stocker just dropped his gaze and continued chewing.

Daniel turned back to me. "I like to run six or seven miles in the morning, but I'd kill the guy if he tried to follow, so I run around the park in stupid circles, so he can sit on a bench and watch me. You know what he did yesterday? Bought an ice-cream bar from the vendor when he peddled past. Sat there eating it while I was running."

Laughing didn't seem the thing to do, but the desire to do so rose strongly. I covered up my grin by sipping wine.

Daniel watched Stocker take another bite with a grim set to his lips. He sighed. "I've been trying to get him in better shape. Started fast-walking a mile down the road with him, then moved into a short jog, and planned to build from there. Last night I tossed some good running shoes in his open car window when he took a restroom break. Now look at him."

Daniel uncrossed his legs and positioned his body with his back to Burl Stocker, but before giving up the subject, he said, "He could have ordered soup."

Our salads were served. Daniel said, "I'm talking too much."

"No, it's interesting. Tell me more about Parson Fields."

"Well, Parson was a star pilot and despite the shadow of suspi-cion around him during the years he turned, he later became a very well-connected administrator working out of Washington, D.C. He's gambling with his life right now, but he seems to figure he has nothing to lose. He's pulling in all his favors and apparently thinks I owe him some."

"Do you?"

"Not by my mathematics. And though it doesn't whitewash my crimes, I sent every penny I acquired illegally back into Mexican housing projects around Juarez." Daniel took a couple bites of his salad. Then he added, as if thinking out loud, "Maybe he figures since he succeeded in pulling me in once, while we were both active, it should be easy to pull me in again, now that we're both retired." He looked up. "So that brings me to why I'm in hiding down here."

"Hiding?" I stilled my fork. "But, my God, they've found you."

Daniel smiled. "No, they haven't found me. These guys, like I told you, they're just watching to be sure I'm really out of the game, now that Parson is active again. Nobody ever had anything on me, other than my close relationship to Parson. I've done what I can in restitution. It's the Mennonites and their cartel that I'm in hiding from."

"The who?"

"Anglo-Mexicans, the Mennonites."

"Like the religious group?"

"One and the same."

"You can't mean. . . ."

"Back in the nineteen twenties, the Mexican president offered land to the Canadian Mennonites, because Canada was pressing them to join their army and conform to public schooling."

The waiter brought raw zucchini sticks and a tarragon dip, along with an apology for a delay with our lunches. I set my salad aside and tried the dip while Daniel gave a brief history of the Mennonites in Mexico. He said the Mennonites accepted the invitation to resettle in Mexico so they could continue to school their own children and stay out of the army. They farmed the land given to them, crafted the furniture they were known for in the Old Colony and followed their religious traditions. Eventually they farmed marijuana, then cocaine, and smuggled it across the border in their handcrafted furniture.

"Damn nice furniture, too," Daniel said. "Mission style. Quite the rage in Texas and New Mexico."

"But *Mennonites*?" I was picturing the darkly dressed men and the women with their bonnets and long skirts. "Mexican drug smugglers?"

"It's the strangest thing to see. They're white-skinned, blond and blue-eyed. Speak fluent Spanish as their first language, but teach their kids English in order to do business in the U.S.—"

"Their kids do business?"

"They bring along the whole blond, blue-eyed bunch—parents, grandparents, kids and babies. Load up their pickups and trailers with their handmade furniture, packed with drugs, cross the border, unload, collect their cash, get the kids ice cream and go home. Now they're working the Canadian border and even recruiting smugglers in Manitoba from the Old Colony, where some still have relatives."

During the story, the waiter had brought a basket of warm rolls covered with a napkin and another apology. I was getting hungry, wishing we'd ordered a sandwich dripping with mayonnaise like Burl Stocker. I reached into the basket for a roll. I said, "But Parson Fields is retired, so are you, and yet these officers are hanging around." I swung one palm out toward the water and then over to Burl Stocker at the bar, his back to us with his eyes watching us in the mirror, sandwich eaten, now sipping an iced drink. "You're in hiding, but not from them."

I waited until Daniel finished a bite of salad. I asked, "How are you in hiding, exactly?"

"Daniel is not my name."

I could tell that I looked stricken with this betrayal. I tried to smooth out my face. What difference did it make what his real name was? I'd known this guy for . . . well, clearly, I didn't know one thing about this guy.

We sat quietly as the waiter, at last, set plates of mahi vera before us, removed our salad plates, poured more wine into each of our glasses, wished us enjoyment, then left.

Daniel smiled softly. "I'm sorry, Annie Teague."

The use of a name that hadn't been mine legally for decades, and for which I had not corrected Daniel's use of, put the situation in perspective for me. I shrugged.

Daniel took a bite of his mahi, then acted as if he'd just had a bright idea.

"Go out with me some evening and I'll tell you my real name."

"I know your real name." His fork halted midway from his mouth to his plate for a half second. I said, "Rumpelstiltskin."

He laughed.

"And no more talk like that. I'll leave." I took a bite and added, "After I finish this."

Daniel said, "It's great, isn't it?"

"It's divine." The spectacular flavors of the mahi vera burst through even in the face of my fascination with this story of Daniel's . . . or whatever his name was. Each flavor stood out distinctly while somehow the background of cumin pulled it all together.

After a couple of bites, I invited Daniel to continue. I said, "The Mennonites are who you're hiding from."

"Right. They owned me once; it would take very little for them to own me again. But I knew they wouldn't find me—unless they got some help, which my old mentor is lately willing to supply. On their own, there is no real reason for the cartel or its enforcers to look for me. They have other pilots who are willing to turn. That doesn't mean I'm out of danger with them."

"Why a boat? Why down here?"

"Adventure, challenge, learning new skills. It's beautiful down here. And far from trouble—or so I had thought." He scoffed, "Retired. I'm fifty-two years old. An interdiction pilot, used to high stakes, risk, combat—those were the daily components of my life. None of that leads toward the rocking chair, and the guys who think it does, like Parson, get themselves sick or in trouble." He took a sip of his wine and I continued to eat, happy that I just had to ask the questions, not slow my lunch by answering them.

In the background Jimmy Buffet's song "A Pirate Looks at Forty" played through speakers mounted over the deck. I thought, looking at Daniel, that this could be his theme song. "The cannons don't thunder, there's nothing to plunder." Daniel seemed to feel out of time and place.

"When a lone guy with a boat hangs around the water much, word gets out and he's invited to do a little job here and there. If he's interested."

I was relaxed, relishing the tastes in my mouth. Then I sat up straight. "Daniel, you're not working with them?" I set my hands on either side of my chair, ready to push back and clear out.

"No, of course not. The damage to humanity is fierce." He was quick to reassure me. "But I was approached. I reported that to friends I'd made in the coast guard, while I trained at Chapman."

He took a bite. "That's how I learned the Mennonites have begun moving their product into the States through Florida. That explained the surveillance and Parson's approach. But now"—he opened his palms—"I'm on hold. Can't move in any direction. Need to stay put to convince the feds I'm straight, while sitting like a duck in water for Parson and his contacts to implicate me. Jeter and I just hang loose." He reached his hand down to his dog, lying between us on the floor, and rubbed his ears.

We were quiet for a moment. Burl Stocker, at the bar inside, was lifting a hip to pull out his wallet and pay his check.

Daniel's eyes cast out toward the go-fast boat. "Got to wait this out, but I'm getting restless."

Overhead Jimmy Buffet was winding down: "Mother, mother ocean . . . An occupational hazard being . . . no occupation around."

"You aren't guiding now?"

"Bit awkward taking out clients with an entourage following. I have only one client right now, a lawyer friend, who loves to fish and knows what's going on. He advises me."

Our plates were removed. We passed on dessert, and Daniel asked for the bill.

"That's my story, Annie Teague."

"So what now?"

"Like I said, I hang out, prove to these guys watching me that they don't need to watch me any longer. I'm clean and staying that way. And hope that Parson and the Mennonites leave me alone."

"And if they don't, then what?"

"Then I'll need to relocate again. And the need could come up rather suddenly." He tossed some bills on the small tray the waiter had left with the check.

Daniel drained his glass of wine. He nodded to the cell phones lying on the table. "Which one's yours?"

I flipped them both open. Different wallpaper. "This one."

Daniel said, "Same, same. That's what they say in India."

I took a final drink of ice water, and Daniel rose from his chair and waited as I scooted out of mine. "I watched a little boy come into Jamie's clinic with spots all over his arms and legs. He pointed to each one, trying to communicate with Jamie, saying, 'Same, same.'"

We headed for the steps down to the pier. "Your daughter sounds pretty special."

"She is. I admire the hell out of her."

Daniel waved to Stocker, who waited for us while propped against a piling on the pier.

Daniel continued. "I never lived with her and her mother, but the kid turned out to be this bighearted young woman, calm, sweet-natured. Doesn't seem to distinguish good from bad—and I don't mean the way I once didn't distinguish good from bad." He laughed and I joined him.

"Jamie makes no judgments. She doctors everyone—monks in their clean orange robes, beggars in their dirty tatters, tourists in their L. L. Bean travel wear, donkeys, dogs." He shook his head in admiration. "I watched her tenderly care for a woman beaten by her husband—broken arm and nose, bruises from being kicked—and just as tenderly care for the husband, who'd had his eye scratched in the battle."

We reached Daniel's boat.

"Thank you for lunch."

"Come back to visit, will you?"

"I'll be back."

And I would. I wanted to offer my companionship during his struggle, and I wanted to enjoy his company during my own.

Before boarding his boat, Daniel glanced down the pier toward Burl Stocker, who was using his cell phone. "If that guy calls for a take-out order of key lime pie again this afternoon, I'm walking right over there and dumping it in the trash."

I threw back my head and laughed.

Either Daniel's training as a pilot and Customs officer accounted for his vibrant alertness, or he was drawn to the field originally because of his desire and ability to be exceptionally present. I found his bright attentiveness to life around him refreshing. On the walk home I realized that being in his company awakened the memory of how I, too, was once considered by my friends and family to be especially lively. I used to take pleasure in every aspect of my life to a degree that others seemed unable to reach. Jess told me long ago that he had fallen in love with me for that exact reason. Always happiness had pulsed inside of me and made me vitally awake. Somehow, during the past few years, life seemed to have rolled me over often enough to have rounded off those ebullient spikes, subdued those effervescent peaks. That was another reason I would be back to see Daniel. I needed reminders of that enlivened person I hoped to become again.

Twenty-eight

Jess

*O*nce AnnieLaurie and I sat in the movies and watched a black actor up on the screen, his naked back rippling with muscles, his shoulders broad as a ridge beam. In the film his character was eating a piece of toast and rhapsodizing at length about the texture of the bread, the creaminess of the butter, the joyous complexity of the orange marmalade smeared on top, until the theater audience howled and understood this character was in the grip of an extraterrestrial force. With wonder, I turned to Annie and whispered, "Shit, you eat breakfast like that every day."

A bit of an exaggeration, yet Annie recognized what I was saying and laughed self-consciously. She took great pleasure in the small events of daily life. For me, "Nice toast" said it. For Annie, a soliloquy celebrating the toast wouldn't be unusual. But then, according to her, I flattened the highs in life and belittled the importance of the lows.

The thing was: she wasn't all that easy to be around in some ways. Maybe it was just in contrast to me, but she seemed excruciatingly exuberant at times, and I don't think I was the only person who found that uncomfortable. I mean, it was like living with a psychiatrist who could read deep meanings in each of your actions combined with a goddamn mystic in ecstatic relationship with unseen forces. She was so *there,* I needed to hide from her. It wasn't like I was one of the store employees who was buoyed up by her happy presence, then got to go home at the end of the day. There was no rest around that girl unless I created mini-spas by absorbing myself in TV shows, newspapers or just plain spacing out. Then she accused me, "You don't listen to me, and if you do listen, you misunderstand, and if you don't misunderstand, you forget what I've said. There's no pinning you down, is there, Jess?"

Not if I could help it.

Who wants to be pinned down by a psychic surgeon—no anesthesia?

But now without her, without the fear that she could overrun me, a big, empty ache sat beside my heart.

I'd always suspected I'd feel this way without her, but couldn't stand to think about it. How could I have acted like a man while confronted with this knowledge and her bright presence at the same time?

Before this, I had caught glimpses that sideswiped me with the full brunt of knowing how much I needed her in my life. I remembered stepping out of the shower one morning after we'd made love, and just as if the shower door itself had slammed into my body, I suddenly felt the impact of her effect on me. I loved her; I loved her with my whole being, and somehow that knowledge threatened me, as if she held some power over me that gave her too much control. I felt afraid, thinking, What if I lost her? And then I felt an unreasonable anger toward her, as if she had plotted to get me in this place of vulnerability. None of this came to my mind in words, just one wash of feeling after another.

Sometimes I felt the urge to punish her for making me feel this way.

That morning, without thinking, I flung my wet towel on Annie's white cashmere sweater that she'd hand-washed and laid to dry on her end of the bathroom counter. The towel was a red, beach-sized sample embroidered with JACKSON HOLE, which a salesman had left at the store and I'd brought home and used without laundering first. That morning I didn't pick up my dirty clothes from my side of the bedroom, and I ate Annie's piece of coffee cake along with my own before taking off for the store.

We'd begun a routine of me opening the store; then Annie came in an hour later and stayed an hour after me to close up. That morning, first thing after kicking the office door closed behind her, she upended a large canvas bag on top of my desk, inches beneath my nose. My dirty clothes, the red towel and the now pink-stained cashmere sweater. Not a word. Just walked back out of the store, and I didn't see her again until late that night.

I learned afterward that she'd spent the day at the movies, watching two in a row, then went out to dinner alone. When she got home I called a friendly greeting from the sofa like nothing had happened. When she answered back, I thought, Whew.

I never brought up the ruined sweater and waited and waited for her to indulge in her usual rant about my deficiencies, but it never happened. From then on I felt suspicious about what was going on with her—when I thought to think about it at all—because she stopped reacting in the expected ways. Sometimes I thought that was her insidious revenge, keeping me wondering like that.

I fixed her; I stopped wondering.

But now I had to realize that Annie had left me; these old methods weren't going to work anymore. Many times she had told me that insulating myself against my feelings was damaging our relationship. And during our counseling, Lola had backed her up. She had suggested that my philosophy of what you don't know can't hurt you worked for me as a child after my mother's death, but was working against me now.

I closed the office door at the store, sat at my desk and lifted the phone. It felt as heavy as a log. I gripped it with both hands and rested my forehead against it. If I started down that long road, I might never again return to being the innocent boy before the accident. I might find it harder and harder to escape in the outdoors, in front of the TV, in numbness.

But maybe one more appointment wouldn't kill me.

I dialed Lola's number.

Twenty-nine

*L*ucille made raspberry jam from tomatoes and strawberry jam from zucchini. She had told me this a few days ago, while we stood in her backyard and watched our puppies romping adorably. Today she huffed up the steps and handed me a jar of each. They sparkled in the sun like pink lamps as she held up a jar in each hand to announce her reason for visiting.

"I told you, dear, that I'd bring you some," she said, once she caught her breath. Lucille, who was seventy-six and had spent the past four decades teaching history—American, Florida State and European—at the college, had just this year retired. She was plainly delighted with her free time. She and Shank had met at the school. He had worked in janitorial services and had also just retired recently. They'd never had children and Mitzi was their first pet.

I hoped to keep suspicion clear from my expression, but I was expected to ask: "So . . . how do tomatoes turn into raspberries and zucchini turn into strawberries?" I held open the door for Lucille, inviting her in.

"Well, dear, here's the secret: Jell-O. I use flavored Jell-O and you don't even know that you're not eating what the name of it says."

Though that sounded like many items on a fast-food menu, I felt compelled to express my surprise at the ingenuity of her cooking. "I have toast for breakfast most mornings; I'll try some right away."

"If you like it, I'll bring you some pineapple jam made from yellow tomatoes."

I thought, Here's a no-win situation, but I said, "Yum." I took the small jars and we stepped into my kitchen. She and Shank had been stern about allowing me my privacy and hadn't been inside my apartment since I'd moved in. I, on the other hand, had visited downstairs several times—for lemonade in the late afternoons after I'd taken Mitzi along with Bijou for extended romps on the beach and a couple weeks ago with the boys for Sunday morning tea and muffins. Lucille's muffins were spectacular; I hated to think what this jam was going to do to them.

Lucille and I shared the recently found pleasure of pursuing personal goals. When I told her about the joyous frenzy in which I had gathered my household decor and showed her the variety of items on my worktable where I was putting together a collage for my textile class, she understood completely. I dragged out my knitting projects, holding back on the surprise I was working on for her pup, a collar Caridad had helped design with lacy petals. Mitzi could wear it for Shank and Lucille's Sunday teas.

I showed Lucille around, introduced her to Kia; then we sat on my screened porch with glasses of iced tea. "I've been experimenting a bit myself," I said. "I've mixed herbal iced tea with raspberry juice." And used not a single tomato or zucchini, I added to myself. Mixing juice with iced tea wasn't originally my idea; I had borrowed it from the Green Bottle Café.

I liked imagining Lucille's love affair with Shank. The elegant, heavy-chested Lucille always dressed in either all white or all black, with a colorful silk scarf. I pictured her in the classroom—graduate degrees and faculty position with tenure—punctuating her lectures with petitions sent downstairs to the Department of Maintenance for help with jammed windows or hanging posters. And then I liked to picture the strong, hefty Shank grabbing those requests to do first.

I started my inquiry into the romance by saying, "So you and Shank met at the college."

"Shank saved my life. Of course, that's not why I fell in love with him. That happened first."

"Then he saved your life." No questions. I didn't know her well enough, and she carried a strong sense of personal dignity about her—a shield I supposed she needed to erect, living in the public realm of teaching in a small community.

"I was a secret drinker, dear. Fooled everybody but the one who loved me."

"Oh, gosh . . . that's a hard one, drinking."

"Harder on the people who care about you. Not so hard on the drinker. As long as you keep on drinking, that is."

"I once heard about a woman who was an alcoholic and learned she was dying of cancer. She decided to quit drinking because she didn't want to die drunk." I heard awe in my voice.

"Well, I quit because I didn't want to be loved drunk."

I didn't quite follow that remark and tipped my head, puzzled.

Lucille said, "I loved Shank and I could see he loved me. However, he had grown up with an alcoholic mother, so, Annie dear, I felt like home to him. He knew just how to love a drinking woman. I wanted him to love me for my true self. I began my drinking about ten years or so before Shank came to the college. It was my first teaching job; I was the only black instructor there and one of only three women."

I thought about conditions for black women forty years ago in the Southern states and marveled at Lucille's courage.

"I was so scared," Lucille continued, "that my voice shook even greeting students in the hallway. I had intestinal problems throughout the day, most especially dramatic in the middle of my lectures. In the classroom there was so much I wanted to tell my students, yet I could barely glance at them."

She took a long look at the triangle of ocean between the roof-tops.

"I don't think they intended to let me stay past that first semester. I discovered that if I had a bit of vodka with my orange juice at breakfast, I was steadier. You know how that goes—more vodka, more steady. Me, orange juice and vodka created a fine career for the following decade. I was commended with teaching awards and was popular with the students. I have always loved my students."

Lucille sipped her tea. "One day Shank showed up to repair my desk chair. We recognized each other, like you often do when real love happens by. But I wouldn't marry him until I had been drink-free for one full year. By then, though I hadn't realized it, I didn't need to drink any longer to conduct a classroom. I needed it for itself."

"Well, congratulations. I admire your taking on the struggle."

"I loved Shank and I had always wanted to be married, though by my midforties I had given up on the idea."

"A fairy-tale ending," I said.

"Marriage, dear. No fairy tales involved."

I told Lucille something of what I was doing living on a six-month lease above her garage. No fairy tale there, either.

"You know, some of us learn the most about life and ourselves through relationship. That was what I wanted when I took my vows with Shank." She raised her eyebrows and took on a Southern black accent. "And class ain't over yet."

We laughed.

Lucille said, "Shank struggled with being married to someone in a higher position on campus and making more money. I offered wide berth for that and excused his need to be in control. Yet time passed and I soon realized that his upbringing had instilled in him a need to keep an upper hand, as he had been in charge of the home life as the oldest child for his first thirty years or so.

"Shank needed to learn some survival tools living with his alcoholic mother and no father on the premises, and he learned to survive well. Trouble with our marriage is that he can't move on now, give up those tools he no longer needs to survive. He is still living in an imagined household of a drunken mother and eight children he must get ready for school. And I live in it with him."

Jess, too, I realized, had brought to our marriage old survival skills from his childhood that he no longer needed, particularly an insulating emotional position. And they impeded his relationship in marriage in a different way from Shank's, though just as forcefully.

"How do you manage?" I asked Lucille, imagining Shank overwhelming her on a daily basis with his need for wielding power from big things—finances—to small things—where to place the sofa. "You've been together . . . what? Thirty years?"

"Spaces in that togetherness, that's how I manage. We have a wonderful home life and we enjoy each other, but we are not together all the time. I cannot change him or anyone else; I learned that in the twelve-step program. So I have adjusted my idea of marriage. We are together—even now during our retirement—only in the evenings and one day or so on the weekend. The rest of the time I go my way, he goes his. We have lovely dinner conversations, telling each other what we did during our time apart."

"So he agreed to this?" I tried imagining setting up such an arrangement with Jess, because I recognized that our marriage held a lot of togetherness and could also benefit from time apart.

"No." Lucille smiled. "I quietly took action on it, bit by bit creating a nice life for myself. And I've since learned, talking to other women, that this routine isn't all that rare."

I refilled our tea and refreshed our ice cubes, using the pause to absorb my surprise over how wrong I'd been to assume my neighbors' marriage was as conventional as cooked corn. Before I sat back down again, I wondered if my few lone getaways the past couple years had been my attempts at creating breaks in togetherness.

Lucille took a sip and replaced the glass smack in the original circle of sweat left on the table. "Where we got the idea that just because we are married we have to do everything together is beyond me. I met a married woman the other day who has her own house."

"Really?" That sounded rather nice.

"They have a little cottage out back of their main house, and one day she slept out there because her husband was snoring. She liked it so much, she moved in. She enjoyed her own company during the day and came in the main house to have dinner and spend evenings with her husband."

"That takes money."

"Maybe your own cottage, but not creating your own life. I have my good friends, events we attend together, and times I just prefer my solitude and spend the morning at the library and the afternoon in my sewing room. Every week I discover something new I enjoy doing. Like this jam. Why, I had a big day making that."

Lucille had also been gardening, so we walked downstairs together to admire her work. Along the side I had always considered their private yard, beside their screened Florida room, Lucille had created an area with flagstones, ground cover and accent plants. Fountain grass spouted along a short stone wall, dracaena plants sat in pots and flame vine climbed the porch pillars. It was lovely, cool and colorful. We said goodbye after that, and Bijou and I headed for our daily walk on the beach.

I strolled four blocks through our neighborhood of older Florida homes, originally small houses with added bedrooms, extended living rooms, newly built screened porches and decks.

Everything that had made life good for me during the past few weeks had risen in a pure, energetic way, as if there were a luminous cord that spun up my spine, holding my body straight and sizzling my mind with new vitality. But along with this I worried about Jess, as if the farther I traveled into my own life, the farther away

I traveled from him. It wasn't because of the three thousand miles between us, but because of this personal place I had created within myself. We had both become used to me carrying him and his life in my consciousness—remembering where he'd tossed his wallet, keeping him current with friends and family, scheduling his store meetings with product reps. Where he once resided, now my own life took up residence and this created a sense of distance from Jess that I wasn't used to feeling.

As I reached across that distance, my fear arose. I became afraid Jess would do something to harm himself. Not deliberately—he did very little deliberately—but rather act rashly and without paying attention. I worried about his going backcountry skiing alone. If he packed his survival gear as carelessly as he placed his car keys, I'd never see him again.

On the beach, I snapped off Bijou's leash and she began her romp toward the water's edge. She got distracted by a sand crab and chased it until it disappeared mysteriously on her. I watched her turn circles trying to surprise it with a pounce.

This separation anxiety was all in my mind, of course, not so different from the mental space that opened for me when the boys first attended grade school. I worried about them even as I learned to let them go. Now I had to let Jess go. In part, that was what Lucille was talking about. Letting go, moving on myself.

My heart cramped suddenly and I was overcome with a bleak realization: I was helpless to create the fully engaged relationship with Jess that I longed for. I couldn't accomplish it alone. And Jess didn't share my dreams of love and closeness. Maybe he never would. It was as much a fairy tale as a wedding at Cinderella's castle.

I sat on the sand in despair. I wrapped my arms around my knees and buried my face them. My greatest fear since leaving for my marriage sabbatical was that I would discover I could not return. Was that the truth I needed to face now?

I lifted my head. But maybe I didn't have to leave Jess.

Wasn't that what Lucille was telling me, too? Change yourself, not the other. I sniffed and let the wind blow my tears into my hair.

After a bit, I got up and began walking again. I watched a sailboat far out in the deep navy blue water, where the setting sun illuminated the triangle of white sail. Bijou darted after terns that rose as a single body and flew low over the waves, two dozen striped wing bodies all perfectly spaced. Then as one, they flipped their angle and the image turned to flying white breasts flashing against a blue sky.

My heart swelled at the sight and somehow I felt reassured that whatever force orchestrated that rhythm and beauty was available to lend rhythm and beauty to my life, too.

I had been trying so hard to produce something I'd imagined, molding myself and my mate into some fairy-tale image, resisting anything that didn't fit it. When all along, like the terns moving in response to the moment, I had needed to live in tune with reality. My confusion over my marriage came from the reality not matching the firm grip I held on the fairy tale.

Bijou discovered where crabs hid and began digging just above the waterline, yet lost confidence when she didn't find one. Her underbelly was caked with wet sand.

Then the good news hit me: I didn't have to leave Jess, just leave him alone.

Give him room to do and be whatever he chose, give myself room to do the same.

I took in a big, shaky breath. A smile spread across my face.

Thanks to Lucille, I had found MARRIAGE RULE #4: Allow Space.

Thirty

Jess

I slapped my hand on the newspaper spread out beside my breakfast and dug in my pocket for my phone. Annie-Laurie had to hear about this. When she answered, I said, "Annie, remember when I told you about Wolf No. 9? That she wasn't expected to live much longer now that she was driven out of her pack?"

"Jess, did she die?"

"Well, you're not going to believe this." I laughed and folded the newspaper.

"What? Tell me," Annie pleaded.

"No. 9 . . ."

"She's alive?"

"She's alive. She's been spotted and is doing well. Really well."

"Oh my gosh, that's so good to hear."

"There's more. She's found a new pack and . . . are you ready?"

"Ready."

"She is alpha!"

"No! This is great."

"No. 9 and the male are the pack's dominant pair. One of the females from her old Rose Creek pack joined her."

"I could cry, I'm so happy to hear that."

"Isn't she something? The *Jackson Hole News & Guide* said that out of the one hundred and nine wolves born in Yellowstone since the reintroduction, seventy-nine of the pups are descended from her, children and grandchildren. No other wolf comes close to her contribution."

"To think that earlier this winter they were expecting her to die alone in the snow. She is amazing."

"They've named her new pack the Valentine pack."

Annie sighed happily.

"So happy Valentine's Day, Annie."

"I just opened your gift. Jess, it's so beautiful. I'm wearing the pendant right now. Looks wonderful with my earrings. Same intense blue topaz. Did you know that I pierced my ears with another set of holes, so I could wear both pairs of blue topaz ear studs you gave me?"

"Oh, God, you're going to make me look at those the rest of my life, aren't you?"

"Did you receive my gift?"

"And eaten some. Stuck two Honeybells in my pocket before I went snowshoeing with the dogs early this morning, and ate them while sitting on a snowbank."

"They were late this season. Still, that's it for the Honeybells."

"I love you, AnnieLaurie."

"I love you, too, Jess."

I flipped the phone closed and grabbed my gear.

Valentine's Day was the first day of the year that the sun shined fully on Snow King Mountain, often referred to as the Town Hill and—my favorite part—called the "steepest little son of a bitch in the West." A north-facing mountain, it was cold and in shadow all day during the first half of the season, so I usually waited until mid-February to ski it.

Couldn't let a season go by without runs down the face of Snow King Mountain. On a clear day like today, the chairlift offered views all the way across the valley to Yellowstone, fifty miles away. I craned my neck around to admire the Grand Tetons and to imagine Wolf No. 9 and her new pack moving together across the snowfields farther north. I basked in the memory of this morning's phone call to Annie. When I'd read about No. 9 in the *Jackson Hole News & Guide* with my breakfast, I could hardly wait to tell her. I didn't mention that I was taking the day off from the store to ski.

This mountain, like the rest of Jackson Hole, had become busier over the twenty-five years since Annie and I first moved here. In fact, even a decade ago it was so quiet on this mountain that many days I was the only person on the chairlift until later in the day when school let out. Once in late March the only other rider was a robin who rode up the mountain perched on the chair ahead of me.

Our boys learned to ski as toddlers, but by the time Annie and I learned, we were in our twenties, our bodies rigid with the fear of falling. Annie still didn't ski fast enough to get her ears cold, but over the years I'd become fairly decent. I remembered, though, that first attempt.

Just to advertise our stupidity we drove to the mountain with our rented ski boots already locked into the bindings and the whole business—boots and skis—strapped to the top of our car. We looked ludicrous and arrived at the resort to find our boots had filled with snow. We skied that day with cold, wet feet.

We were dangerous that first time on the slopes and didn't realize it. We didn't know how to snowplow or traverse, just headed straight downhill. Annie described how she saw a wedge of people below her standing in line for the lift and could do nothing but plow right through the middle of them. When she finally managed to stop, no one was standing but her.

I looked like a big Hefty bag myself that first day, wearing a shiny black one-piece ski suit, also rented like the rest of the gear. I rode a chairlift to the top of a slope that didn't look too steep from below, but once I got up there, I realized I would be in big trouble if I skied it. Made me shake just to think about it. So I bent forward to take off my skis; my weight shifted and I started sliding downhill.

To this day I didn't know how it happened, but I unexpectedly came up behind a woman with one of my skis on either side of her, as she was skiing just ahead of me. Hard to say which one of us was more terrified. She had no idea who I was, other than the big lug who was gripping onto her for dear life from behind. Locked together like that, we tore down the mountain and the whole way, I kept panting in her ear, "I'm sorry. I'm sorry."

Eventually Annie and I learned a few skills. There were rules for idiots out there. The Rule of Three: most accidents happen on the third run, after three o'clock in the afternoon, and on the third day. All because of tiredness that leads to carelessness.

As bad as we were, Annie and I were bound to have accidents on all those Rule of Three occasions. And we did, but none of them serious. Still, the rule we needed the most we couldn't quite remember.

"RICE. That's what you do for injuries," Annie had said.

I had twisted my knee in a fall, but not seriously enough to see a doctor. "RICE," I said. "I've heard that."

"Let's see. R is for rest. I is for ice. What is the C for? And the E?"

"That's probably it. Rest and ice. R—ICE. Get it?"

"E could be for elevation."

I said, "Rest and ice. That's good enough for me." Then I added, "Put some Scotch on that ice."

That wasn't the only time we needed that rule and we eventually learned that RICE stood for the first-aid treatment of rest, ice, compresses and elevation.

Today, the snow lay soft and creamy, the sunshine toasted the air to temperatures in the low teens and the sky capped the Town Hill in a solid blue. It felt good to relax in the chair and enjoy the scenery.

I should have kept that appointment this morning with Lola

the therapist, but once I remembered it was February fourteenth—
sun on Snow King Mountain all day—I couldn't resist. I had tossed
my gear into the car and thought as I drove into town: Maybe I'll
see Lola. Maybe I'll ski.

I looked around. I sure wasn't the only one who couldn't resist
getting out. There wasn't a chair left empty; no free ride for a robin
today, though it was too early for their return anyhow. I slid off the
chair at the top, nodded to Judy in the booth—she had worked this
lift for decades—and turned left to ski toward Grizzly Run, which
would take me down through the mogul field in Kelly's Alley.

"Hey, Jess."

I looked over and spotted a woman so bundled in gear that I
saw no clue to her identity, but the voice was familiar. Very familiar. And before my brain formed her name, my body knew exactly
who she was and responded with a hot flush that crept up my neck
and into my face. Thankfully, I was as bundled as she was—face
mask, goggles, wool hat—and for a moment I was tempted to act
like that wasn't my name. Ski downhill fast, jump into my car.

"Thought I might run into you here," she said.

"Lola."

I knew she was grinning her head off behind her balaclava, and
now I knew she was silently laughing, because the frosted breath
that had flowed in a steady, narrow stream from her now ballooned
in puffy clouds.

I joined her out loud. "Now you know who you're dealing with,
Lola."

"I knew all along, Jess." She leaned on her poles and slid her
skis back and forth with her head down a moment. She looked up.
"No charge, but how about a session while we ride the chair after
this run? I'd like you to know something."

"Sounds fine. Go ahead. I'll follow you."

I nodded to the left of me at the cornice, a five-foot shelf of
ice and snow that wind had created to hang out over the slope.

I'd had no intention of tackling that challenge this morning, but had planned to ski past it to enter the slopes farther down the cat track. It wasn't nice of me. Cornices were dangerous. They could avalanche at any time, especially on a sunny morning like this one. Besides that, most skiers avoided them because they didn't know how to ride them or make the five-foot leap to the slope they hung over. My brash invitation to hotshot the run could severely injure Lola, if she didn't recognize what was required of her.

I guessed I was pissed at her for catching me out here, after I'd stood her up for our appointment.

Lola poled off without hesitation, angled across the cornice and jumped. For a second, in her red ski jacket and white bibs, she was silhouetted against the blue sky in a perfect tuck. Suddenly it struck me that nothing I did surprised this woman.

She was on to me.

I felt hot and itchy around the neckline; then I let those thoughts go and followed Lola across the cornice, leaped into the air and flew down the slope behind her. She skied fast and gracefully. We had a great run, and by the time we merged into the lift line at the base of the mountain, I was happy I'd met up with her, at least for the skiing.

First thing she said was, "We don't really have to do this, Jess. We can talk about the weather if you'd rather."

"No, no." I was feeling just an edge of shame for my bad behavior. "Let's go for it." We poled up the line farther; then it was our turn. We got positioned to catch the next chair, placing our skis on the marker. We switched our poles to our outside hands, turned slightly to watch the chair approach. It caught us behind our knees, we sat, lifted our skis and were off. Seconds later we dangled high over the valley.

"Therapy is hard work, Jess, really hard. I don't blame you for choosing to postpone it. But there is something I want you to know. Something that may help you hold the issues that arose during our last discussion while walking in Cache Creek." She took a big breath. "And I hoped we could talk a little about your future with Annie."

"Sounds like a good news–bad news joke."

She ignored my attempt at lightening the atmosphere. She looked straight ahead.

She said, "I'd left my response to your story, Jess, for our next meeting. I felt you needed to live with your own words and the acknowledgment of your feelings before hearing what I had to say." She took a long breath. "But when you didn't show for our appointment this morning, I felt something was left unfinished."

I nodded.

"I want to acknowledge your relationship to your mother's death." Lola pulled her face covering down to beneath her chin and lifted her goggles to rest on top of her hat so that her face was fully exposed, and she turned toward me as much as dangling skis and the narrow chair allowed. "I want to affirm that yes, you are connected to the events that led to your mother's death. The connection, however, is not one of blame. As a young child you carried no capacity for being responsible for another's life."

Lola rested a gloved hand on my arm. "Jess, the connection was a causal link. Do you understand? This link between your presence and your mother's dying was not one of behavior or choices. A causal link, Jess. Causes created events and you were present and part of that chain." She paused, watching me. "I needed you to know that."

Her words felt like the truth. It was not the evasion I had groped for all my life, twisting the story around to make it fit my innocence. It was not the accusation I alternately wrestled with or floundered beneath, with its burden of shame. It was somewhere in the middle of those two; it was just the plain truth. A causal link. It happened; I was there.

Lola could have been reading me poetry, the way my heart

warmed. The warmth spread all through my body. If we hadn't been moving, I would have melted the eight-foot snow accumulation on the slope that was so steep at this part of the mountain it lay directly in front of me on the chairlift, not below as would be expected traveling over land. I lifted my goggles, which had fogged, and I pulled my mask down. I turned to Lola, who saw my tears.

"Lola." I could barely speak. I was swept up into the waves and waves of ease inside me that released some hard, iced-over place.

I tried again. "Lola." Then I gave up and hung my head and cried. Silent heaves shook my shoulders. My tears plopped onto my waterproof ski bibs and beaded fully formed on my thighs, sparkling in the sunshine like glass.

Lola removed her glove and dug in her pocket for tissues. She handed a couple to me, used one herself. We sat silently on the chairlift. Lola watched me, and I watched something inside of me dissolve and seep away into the glittering air, where cold temperatures iced our breath into iridescent flakes that fluttered before our faces in the sunlight. This memory of my mother, this burden of her death, was such a part of me, it felt like another spine—the story that held me together, framed and described me. Yet it had also held me in place. I was going nowhere till this story unshackled me.

Abruptly we arrived at the summit, and I scrambled to pull myself together to get off the fast-moving chair. These damn things stopped for no one. You just had to glide right off as if you were snow on a warm fender and land on your feet, ready to ski out of the pathway of the others coming quickly behind you. Not a problem for me usually.

Now one hand held ski poles, the other wiped tears and my gloves were tucked under my arm. Lola held my elbow and tugged me off the chair and onto the side of the path before I created a pileup. She handed me a couple more tissues from the bulge of them in her pocket.

I got myself mopped up and I said, "Thank you, Lola. Thank you for this."

Lola seemed to know that I needed a reprieve from the intensity of emotion. She said, "You lead this time. I'll follow."

I poled off and took us straight down Amphitheater, which was almost a perpendicular run below the chairlift cable we had just ridden up. We used the chairlift towers as a slalom and coursed down in high speed. Near the base, exhausted and breathing heavily, I looked back and there was Lola right on my ski. I skied past the lift line, turned to a stop and faced the sun with a big grin on my face. Lola followed and we both leaned on our poles and laughed from the sheer exuberance of it all.

I said, "Only in Jackson Hole does a therapist have to be a skier to keep appointments with her clients. And you're an expert skier." She was really something.

Still winded, she said, "Being a skier came long before being a therapist. I raced in high school and college."

The lift lines were noticeably longer. Noon-break skiers from the offices in town.

"Lunch? My treat." Figured I should get sustenance for the bad news part of this session.

To get to the resort's restaurant the easy way, versus the hard way of walking up slope in our ski boots, we had to get in the lift line for the Cougar Run, ski across Old Man Flats, then down to Rafferty and on over to the hotel. Once there, we took off our boots and jackets before the lobby fireplace, warmed our hands; then I asked a friend I spotted working there to store our gear for us, and we went upstairs to the restaurant.

We ordered; then Lola said, "I don't necessarily believe in endless therapy sessions, Jess. After today, we can continue our work on an as-needed basis, but I did want to make sense of our earlier meeting, after you spent some time with your thoughts. I wanted you to have a realistic understanding of your role in your mother's death. That was good news I needed to pass on to you."

"And the bad news?"

"Not bad news, that's your term. But life goes on and the past contributes to the future. You are experiencing marital difficulties. This is not unrelated to your boyhood trauma." Lola put her napkin on her lap and realigned her silverware. She looked up and said, "You and Annie glow in my memory of being two people who deeply love each other."

"We do. We deeply love each other."

"Which doesn't always add up to being happily married."

"No, I guess not." If your wife abruptly leaves on a plane the night of your anniversary celebration, a guy's got to admit something's off. I drained my glass of ice water and nodded to the waiter for a refill. I was damn thirsty. The first glass, I bet, just replaced fluids I'd lost in tears. The second glass replaced sweat from our ski runs; I was soaked to the skin under my bibs. After I drank more, I said in my defense, "But I make her laugh. We have great sex. . . ."

"To use your reference then, the good news is that you are a great date, Jess. But the bad news is that I wouldn't want to be married to you." Lola chose a lemon tea bag from the small carved wooden chest and began to unwrap it. "And perhaps Annie feels similarly."

I didn't find that particularly an insult. I said, "Great dates don't grow on trees."

Lola smiled. "Actually, they do. Palm trees."

She was okay. Good skier, good therapist, a sense of humor. But all joking aside, Lola didn't find my casual perspective on being a better date than I was a husband admirable. We left it at that. I wasn't interested in pursuing it further. We talked casually about our dogs and skiing, ate our lunch, then layered our gear back on for a couple more runs on the mountain.

About three o'clock, I was sent off with a "Good luck" and a pat on my upper arm.

"Whatever you have to do to turn being a great date into a good husband, Jess, do it. You and Annie together are worth the effort it will take from you." She pushed off toward her car in the parking lot.

I followed her toward my own car. "You sound kind of hopeless." That struck me hard at the moment. The remark about great dates growing on palm trees—did she think Annie might stay in Florida?

Beside her car, Lola pressed her pole tips onto her bindings, released them and stepped out of her skis. She leaned her poles and skis against the car fender. "Not hopeless. Not hopeless at all, Jess. Though not hopeful, either." She opened the driver's-side door and tossed her goggles and balaclava across the front seat and began to pare down a layer, removing her bibs to drive home in jeans. She tossed the bibs over the seat to the back, then lifted her skis and poles to lock them into her cartop carrier. She turned to face me.

"I am sorry to say so, but you've worn her down. I spotted that two years ago. You have exhausted her great love for you, Jess Mc-Fall. Just *wrung* her dry." Lola let that sink in a moment and she watched my eyes. "If Annie is smart, she will take her time restoring herself. And *if* she returns home, I hope she comes armed with skills to protect herself from you."

"What the hell do you mean?"

"Perhaps it's a result of your boyhood experiences or perhaps it's a result of your own personal laziness, but you take advantage of people around you . . . in the nicest sort of way. A wife—in fact anyone involved with you—must protect herself from your mild-natured abuse."

"Abuse. That's damn strong language, Lola. I don't abuse anyone."

"There used to be a playground joke when I was a kid that went something like 'When they were passing out noses, you thought they said roses, and you asked for a big red one.' Well, Jess, when they were passing out 'accountability,' I don't know what you thought they said, but you seemed to think you could get by in life without *any*."

"Well, I don't know about that."

"That's how you protect yourself: you don't *know* about it. This appointment you had with me today? I suspect you chose not to *admit* to yourself that you were going skiing, instead." Lola spoke forcefully; I'd never heard her sound like this. "How come you think I knew it, when you didn't?"

"Our meeting wasn't an accident?"

"Not even a causal link, Jess."

I felt some surprise over that.

"It's called 'accountability.' I felt *accountable* for responding to the issues raised in our first appointment." She stared me in the eyes, not smiling. She said, "You use people up—that's abuse."

"You called me a 'cuddly predator' a couple years back. Now you make me sound like a goddamn vampire."

"A vampire." Lola seemed to be speaking to herself. She nodded studiously. Then she got in her car, started it, backed out and drove off, all without looking at me. I had the feeling she wouldn't mind if she never saw me again in this lifetime.

She couldn't hear me but I spoke to her image in the side-view mirror as she pulled away.

I said out loud, "Ditto, lady."

What the hell did she know? Maybe she touched something earlier with my mother stuff, but as far as Annie was concerned, Lola knew nothing. If Annie were *smart,* she said. As if Annie shouldn't come home.

What did Lola know about *smart?*

I skied across the lot to my own car, ripping off gloves, hat and goggles as I went. When they were passing out *smarts,* Lola thought they said . . . Found my car keys, after searching eight of the damn zippered pockets in my jacket.

When they were passing out *smarts,* Lola thought they said *farts* and she asked for big, smelly ones.

Thirty-one

Annie

*H*ours of bliss had passed. All the windows and doors were open to the sound of rain as I sat at my worktable immersed in color. Classes had intensified and midterm project deadlines loomed ahead. For the pretend business I was assigned to create for my contemporary craft class, I needed a salable craft item, with supporting lines to market and a business plan. I had chosen to create a line of knitted dog coats and accessories. With the help of Caridad and the employees at the yarn store, I'd made leaps in my knitting skills. I had advanced from square items to circular ones, learned to follow patterns, purl, make stripes, increase, decrease, even crochet. Bijou and Mitzi made good models. I'd also pulled in Daniel's dog, Jeter, for variety.

Daniel enjoyed photography—a skill he'd picked up from his interdiction work—so he helped by documenting the project, not to mention allowing Jeter to model knitted coats and fancy collars.

I'd become excited by my imaginary business. The dog coats were knitted with abundant color and a variety of textured yarns and wild buttons. I got the idea while wondering one day how Bijou was going to hold up in a Wyoming winter and started knitting a warm coat for her. I'd added collars, knitted leashes, toys, and booties—Daniel said the booties were going to embarrass Jeter, but he had photographed him wearing them, anyway.

In return I had taken Daniel out to dinner. We dined away

from the beach, at a restaurant in town, on a patio with a fountain and potted palms, guitar music instead of waves as our background sound. I asked Daniel to tell me about a time in his life he remembered feeling the happiest.

He thought for a moment. The fountain trickled soothingly, silverware and ice cubes jingled at tables around us; the guitarist played a slow, lingering tune.

"When I was fifteen, I was sent to my grandparents' home in Maine for the summer and ended up staying the following school year, because my mother had fallen ill. I helped my grandfather; he was a lobsterman."

"Tough work," I said.

"Granddad and I were out there every morning on the *Polly*— named after my grandmother—checking lobster traps Granddad staked out in coves around the island. Cranked up the traps, emptied them, rebaited, lowered them again. Trap after trap. Cold, fog, sleet like iced needles—nothing stopped us."

"You describe it with a smile on your face." I laughed.

"Yeah, I loved it. My grandfather made his living supplying lobster to the restaurants in Bar Harbor, the resort near their bungalow in Seal Cove. I missed my mother and worried about her, but I could have stayed in Maine for the rest of my life."

We watched the guitarist, sitting on a stool off to the side, and listened to the music for a moment. The melody wafted as softly as the evening's warm breezes across the patio to us.

"Fell in love with a girl there, too," Daniel said, as if just remembering. "Allison Waters."

"There's your answer, Daniel."

"Answer to what?"

"Where you go, what you do next." Daniel had mentioned more than once during our times together that he didn't know where to go once he was cleared, that he was looking for a place to call home. It wasn't safe for him in Florida, nor could he return to the places he'd left. "Start with the last time you felt good about yourself," I said. "Where you were happy and loved. That's your pattern to follow."

If I sounded more like a counselor than a dinner companion, the distance that created wasn't completely unintended. I felt a bit vulnerable, dining with this man while wearing my prettiest dress. And though I chose to look my best with him and even wanted Daniel to notice that, awareness of my femininity sizzled on my bare skin like a eucalyptus rub, both invigorating and unsettling.

Daniel rested his hand on the stem of his wineglass and stared at it, his facial muscles relaxing in a way I hadn't seen before. Then, to cover up the pause, he lifted his glass, grinned and said, "If it turns out like some of the patterns you've created and made poor Jeter wear, I don't know if that's good advice."

We laughed. But I could tell he was riding a swell of hope and I watched it lift him. I suspected he hadn't enjoyed the throb of optimism for some time.

My hand lay on the table between us, as if I were about to lift my own wineglass, yet I really wanted to touch him, place my hand over his. And I believed he knew this.

He tipped his wineglass to clink softly with mine and said, "Can't help it, Annie Teague. You knock me out." He looked me in the eyes. "You are wise as well as beautiful."

We ate quietly for a while after that. Then Daniel said, "She looked a little like you."

He sounded surprised, as if he'd just now figured something out, as if two dots of a mysterious outline were joined and created shape and meaning.

"Maine," he said, and smiled at me. "I think I'm going to be okay." He warned that we couldn't talk freely on his boat, since he was fairly certain it was wired now, so this subject would have to stay here.

"But . . . Annie, thank you."

We were just getting ready to leave when a friend and fishing client of Daniel's approached our table. Daniel made introductions and asked him to sit. Will Waggoner, a big, tanned, silver-haired man in his midsixties, pulled out a chair while nodding and waving to many of the diners around us. Even I recognized him from the Miami news channel as a well-known divorce lawyer, semiretired, who took on selected cases, based on women seeking divorce from powerful men.

After introductions, Will nodded to Daniel and said, "This guy helps me figure out where the husbands hide their money. With powerful men there is always hidden money." He sat back in his chair, cocked his leg with an ankle over his knee. "Daniel and I have fun with the treasure hunt."

Daniel said, "I've collected plenty of stories about hiding drug money from working in Customs. I'm happy to put the information to use."

I wondered how much Daniel had told Will about the shady side of his work and how many of the ideas that Daniel had given his friend he'd used himself, though I'd believed Daniel when he told me he'd funneled his illegal gains back into Mexican housing for the poor.

Will said, "A man that likes to control money often likes to control women, and the desire to do both usually escalates as time progresses. Your information is being put to good use."

I said, "Women in the hands of somebody like that haven't much of a chance on their own."

"That's where I come in," Will said.

We talked a bit longer. Then Will made a fishing date with Daniel, kissed my hand in a gracious old-world way and returned to his own table. Daniel and I left soon after.

Raindrops still splattered on palm fronds and drilled the roof. I knitted another row of blue worsted wool on my circular needles.

This coat would be trimmed in a fuzzy peach, with three lime-colored buttons on the side where the belly band attached.

I wanted Daniel to succeed in making a good life for himself. I tried not to feel invested in the decisions he was facing, yet I sensed in this man a deep untapped well of sensitivity, a whole side of himself that his work had demanded he shut off. His daughter, Jamie, had picked up on it and had made a life from it, as often happened with our children.

I set the dog coat aside. For my classes I also had papers to write. So I wrote, then knitted, wrote, then knitted. The rhythm worked for me. Bijou lapped rainwater from the screens on the porch, amazed that it kept dripping down to her. Kia flew freely and played with pieces of yarn I gave her. If I didn't keep her busy she chomped on the edges of my papers with her sharp little beak, plucking out triangles along their edges as fast as pinking shears. Kia's favorite toys were empty toilet paper rolls, and Bijou's favorites were empty water bottles with small shells in them, so between the two of them, the house looked like a trash heap, as I tried to keep them entertained while I worked.

As I fulfilled my assignments that morning, I realized that my classes were building confidence in me. I seemed to honor my experiences and thoughts in a new way. Prior to my sabbatical, I'd been known to disregard the evidence of my own eyes if Jess refused to confirm what I had witnessed. Often he put his own self-serving spin on an event, yet to save our sense of closeness—which meant that we shared an experience of reality by sharing our emotional reactions to it—I dismissed my own body's responses. When the other person one lived with refused to confirm a shared experience, it was crazy making. For me, it created doubt and uncertainty.

I paused with papers in hand, recalling a night Jess and I attended a photography show at a gallery opening. The photos were of Afghanistan villages, exposing extreme poverty and the cruelty that was created. As I took in the flat eyes of the children, their rib cages stretched tight under dusty skin, I had choked back tears.

Jess noticed and said, "Don't get taken in, AnnieLaurie. This is art, designed to shock. You think this guy would have a gallery opening in Jackson Hole if he wasn't an expert at manipulating emotions?"

The only reason this memory stood out for me was because a whole room of people shared my response. The confusion that typically set in when Jess belittled my reactions was absent. I saw that Jess often opposed my perspectives and took on the job of getting me to doubt myself. And I was a willing victim, as I sacrificed my own experience in order to share one with my husband.

The phone rang.

"We're going, anyway." I recognized Marcy's voice.

"In the rain?"

"It's raining bathwater," Marcy said. "Besides, there's a canopy on the boat. So get ready. We're picking you up in thirty minutes."

Instantly, the mood of the day changed from one in which I was considering a cup of tea and huddling indoors all day to one of adventure. I lured Kia into her cage with a spray of millet, shooed Bijou outdoors for a potty break and changed into a pair of fast-drying shorts and shirt. I stuffed a rain jacket and a water bottle in my bag. Sunglasses, just in case. Then nestled a container with a dozen deviled eggs on top. Marcy was taking Perry, Sara and me on a meandering boat ride through the Intracoastal Waterway, skirting the river swamps where once the Florida panther hunted and where we hoped to spot manatees lurking in the dark waters near the mangrove props.

With our lunches and gear loaded on the boat, Perry and Sara and I sat under the fiberglass canopy while Marcy went through her checklist. Marcy took the helm and, once under way, turned into the perfect tour guide. She knew the name of every kind of tree—

cabbage palm, wild lime, cocoaplum. She pointed to the eyes of an alligator barely above waterline, its body submerged.

"That's why we don't trail our fingers in the water."

I jerked my hand up. Though I knew better, I'd been wiggling my fingers in the water like live bait beside the boat. Marcy had spoken calmly as if unaware she was announcing the possible end of my newly found craft career. The water was as warm as the air, and the air was as wet as the water. Even though we were sheltered from the rain, my fingers stayed damp.

Passing a small island, we stirred up a wild pig and her five piglets and watched them dart out into an open meadow. Around us, the raindrops slicked the air, dimpled the dark silk surface of the river, glistened the palm fronds on shore and made the whole world—river, land, air—seem created of one substance. We rarely spoke, the motor purred quietly, and we took on the slow, silent ways of the narrow, curving waterway as it flowed through the mangroves.

The sky loomed as dark as the brackish water we floated on, a mixture of fresh and salt water, colored a reddish brown by the tannin of the shore plants. Lazy raindrops ticked the boat canopy and bobbed the fern fronds, and the air smelled of the nurturing decay of wet earth. We rounded a curve and were captured in the silver rays of light shining from a slice of blue sky, low on the horizon. We dropped anchor where the grace of watery sunlight had found us and pulled out our picnic supplies, opened wine, passed napkins and sat in silence, eating.

Soon the rain eased and we spread out from under the canopy and draped ourselves over the sides of the boat to watch the fish underwater and try to spot the shy manatees. As the sun broke out more strongly, the river swamp enlivened. Birds waded out and flew overhead—a great blue heron, an osprey. Mullet jumped, piercing the water surface suddenly, making our heads spin in the direction of the splash that indicated the event was already over.

We, ourselves, became talkative, when before we had only whispered or pointed fingers when spotting something interesting.

I crunched a carrot stick. "Yesterday in psychology class I learned that psychologists agree on what constitutes a healthy-minded person." I'd been thinking about this.

"Oh, gee," Sara said. "I'm afraid to hear it."

"That's how I felt. I've been worried ever since I did hear it."

"And now," Marcy said, "in the role of a loving friend, you are going to pass this worry on to us, aren't you?"

"I thought if all four of us discovered we were unhealthy together it would help."

"Okay." Perry tossed her bangs from her face, held a palm out in invitation, gold bangles clinking. "Go for it."

"Well, the professor said that a well-balanced person knows which responsibilities belong to her and which belong to others, and she only takes on her own."

Sara raised her hand, posing as a confident game show contestant answering a thousand-dollar question. "What . . . are . . . boundaries?"

"Somehow it was the way she said it. I didn't hear it as another reminder about setting firm boundaries, once marriage and motherhood has smashed them to mush. Yesterday, it felt different. As if this were a basic kindergarten first-day-at-school rule: 'This is yours. This is your neighbor's. Leave your neighbor's alone.' You know? I got it." I added, "And I am not healthy."

"I don't know which responsibilities are mine or which are Guy's, and when I do, I take his on anyway, just adding a huff and a sneer to let him know that I resent it," Marcy said.

"Exactly," Sara agreed.

Perry said, "Well, I can't do that with Alex. He has to maintain his area of capabilities or he loses ground. And he doesn't know how to take on mine. Which makes him a sweet person to live with, because he hasn't a judgmental bone in his body. Though, really, he is just sweet at heart."

"Perry is healthy," I announced. And I thought to myself that Jess lost ground every time I took on his stuff, too. Pick up his dirty socks once and I was assigned the job for life.

Perry stood up. "Did you see that?"

"What?"

Perry whispered, "It was a manatee. It just poked its nose up through the water right there and slipped back down." She pointed toward the shore a few feet away, and we all sat still and hoped for another sighting.

Marcy said, "I don't think my problems are about boundaries."

I poured her a bit more wine and said, "What's up?"

"It's just that when Guy and I got married our motto was: gather experiences, not things."

Marcy swirled the wine in her plastic cup and studied the effect.

"But now he wants two brand-new cars every year, plus talks about getting a bigger boat. And he gripes about me working in the college library instead of taking a higher-paying job to build our savings. I said to him, 'Guy, I thought we were always going to be grasshoppers. Now you want to be an ant. We could spend our whole life getting ready for winter.'" She swallowed back tears, set her wine down to pat her pockets for a tissue. "He's changed his goals, but I haven't changed mine."

Perry said, "He needed to be reminded of those early plans."

"He called me irresponsible. Which I am." She held up both arms in a hopeless surrender. "I thought that was the *plan*." Her voice cracked.

I passed her a tissue from my purse.

"How about some dessert?" Sara rifled through her bag and lifted out a covered container.

I said, "Funny, one of the recommended criteria for choosing a mate is shared values, yet it doesn't really make sense." I took a brownie from the plate Sara held, broke off a bit of walnut from the edge and ate it. "Values are personal and subject to change through our different experiences. Just because the person we live with changes his value system doesn't mean we should change ours to match." I thought a moment about people who don't change or grow, like Alex and perhaps Jess in some ways, and added, "Or vice versa. If our partner doesn't grow, that shouldn't mean we stop as well."

I remembered Daisy's explanation that Marcus frowned on her purchasing books because he wanted to support the library—a value of Marcus', not Daisy's. And I realized that though this problem of shared values seemed unrelated to the problem of honoring each other's personal boundaries, they were two parts of the balancing act required in a marriage.

Perry said, "Marcy, carry on with your life as a grasshopper."

"But I use the new cars he buys."

Sara said, "Get your own car. Whatever piece of junk you can afford."

Marcy's face opened at that thought. "I could do that. Or, considering my small salary at the library, I could at least start gathering parts." She laughed and blew her nose.

I said, "I turned in my rental and bought a used car. It's been freeing to drive without Jess' piles of junk rattling around."

We each took a second brownie and sat quietly eating with far-off looks across the water. Possibly each of us was imagining the ways in which we could keep both our integrity and our marriages, because that was the issue at stake for us.

Soon we tucked our picnic supplies away, pulled up the anchor and continued down the river.

Once again we settled into a silence, this time basking in the sun that steadily burned the clouds away to expose more and more blue sky.

When I had learned about the accident that had killed Jess' mother, I saw in tall, handsome Jess the little boy who woke from his sleep when help arrived and stood bewildered on the side of the road as all about him struggled to revive his mother. And I saw the little boy who stood alone in the graveyard, the adults of his family moaning and sobbing, occasionally patting his head, as if this child were too unaware to see and hear the death and the sorrow surrounding him. An aunt had handed him a small top to play with; an uncle pulled a quarter out of the little boy's ear; his own father handed him sugary treats all through the burial.

These were people who could barely contain their own loss and were blind to the loss of the small boy. That boy became invisible to them and even to himself. Feelings, left unacknowledged by the grown-ups around him, became nonexistent to the boy. The grief went on for years with this family, and the invisibility went on just as many years with the boy.

This was the man I had married. The man onto whom I projected my expectations and with whom I was to share values.

I didn't know whom to feel sorrier for: me or him.

But it occurred to me as I again recalled the scene in the photographic gallery that Jess had learned about manipulating emotions—his own—as that little boy at the funeral. And he had also learned to downplay or dismiss the emotional responses of those around him. I might remember that and not feel as if I had to bend my own personal values to match his perspective.

Each time I stumbled across a marriage rule it took me by surprise, despite the fact that it had usually made repeated appearances before I recognized it.

MARRIAGE RULE #5: Honor Your Values.

Thirty-two

Jess

J made the mistake of telling AnnieLaurie that I had met once with Lola and scheduled a second session. Annie phoned last night to see how my appointment went.

"Did you meet with Lola again?"

"Yeah, sure. I . . . I met with her. Valentine's Day." No need to mention I'd stood Lola up and she'd found me on the ski slope.

"Oh, we talked that morning, but you didn't mention it. So I was picturing you skiing the King that day."

"Well . . . I did both."

"You sound hesitant. I just realized, this is your business, not mine. I shouldn't be asking about it."

"No, it's okay. She said something pretty important. She used this term to describe my role in my mother's death: causal link. She just set me free with that."

"My gosh, that's so wonderful."

"Other than that, it wasn't a great session in some ways. I probably won't be seeing her again."

"No?"

"Remember when she called me a 'cuddly predator'?"

"I do."

"You say that rather cheerfully."

"Well . . . go on. What happened?"

"This time she called me a vampire."

"Uh-huh."

"What the hell do you mean 'uh-huh'? What kind of therapist calls her patient names?"

"What else did she say?"

"That I was a great date, but she'd hate to be married to me. As if I'd spend another minute of my life with her, anyway."

"Because . . . ?"

"Because she doesn't *like* me."

"No, I mean, she'd hate to be married to you because . . . ?"

"I don't know. I don't remember."

"You always say that. You 'don't know' or 'don't remember.'"

"Now you sound like Lola. What does it matter?. It wasn't a real appointment. She never even sent a bill."

"What's that about?"

"Annie, for God's sake, do you have to drill me? I thought you phoned to have a nice conversation. You haven't even asked how I am."

"That's what we're talking about: how you are."

"Well, forget it. As usual, talking to you just pisses a guy off. Goodbye."

"Bye, Jess."

This morning in the store, Hadley looked worn down. Made me think of Lola saying I used everybody up. Hope she didn't mean Hadley, too. Couldn't let that happen. If Hadley wasn't here, I'd have to work in the store every damn minute of every damn day. Forget my powder runs. I checked my watch; the lifts would open in half an hour and I planned to lay first tracks on that snowfall we got last night.

I hollered, "Hadley, could you pop in here when you get a chance?" A minute later she came into the office.

"What do you need, Jess?"

"Just checking on you. You look done in lately." I got up and closed the office door.

"Things aren't going so well at home. Nothing new, I guess, but I can't put off making some decisions."

"And you're losing sleep over it." I sat at my desk again.

"Losing sleep, losing weight." Here she pulled her waistband out to show a three-inch gap. "Losing sanity." She leaned against the edge of Annie's desk—now Hadley's—and folded her arms. "Don't know where to go with this problem, but it seems to be escalating."

I sat in my favorite position, swiveled sideways in my desk chair, feet resting on the overturned wastebasket. Shameful to say, but this might have been the first time in weeks that I really looked at this woman. I fiddled with a pen while I checked her out. She looked tired all right. There was a dark smudge high on her cheekbone beneath her left eye. Probably a shadow cast by the overhead lights, but it reminded me of a couple times earlier in the season when I thought she looked roughed up—a lip that sat lopsided, despite lipstick drawn outside the line, a row of small bruises around her wrist and lower arm. I hadn't really thought about what was going on with her.

I started to feel bad about that, but somebody was guiltier than me. I nodded to her face.

"Is that a bruise?"

"Not the first."

"That piece of shit." I dropped my feet, sat upright and slammed the pen on the desktop. "I'm calling the cops."

"It's two days old, Jess."

"Leave the bastard."

"Yeah?" Hadley raised her voice at me; she had never raised her voice at me in our long history together. "How am I going to do that, Jess?"

"What's holding you up?"

"A roof over my head." She put her forehead in her hand a moment, then looked up and spoke more quietly. "Leaving Paul means leaving the valley . . . my friends, my work." She gestured out the window, to me, to the office. "He's an attorney; he knows how to play it; he's warned me about that throughout our marriage. And besides, I couldn't find a lawyer to take my case in the state of Wyoming who didn't owe Paul a favor or hope to get one owed in the future. That's how it works, at least according to Paul."

Hadley moved around to the other side of her desk, tidied paper piles, keeping her head down. "Without my savings or the investment I made in our house, I couldn't begin to make it here. You know that. I'm looking into moving away, but . . . this is my *home*."

Hadley choked on that last word and suddenly "home" took on all the meanings I had always taken for granted and all the meanings I had longed for since Annie left. Home. "Home" meant more than shelter; it meant the place where we loved and were loved.

Teton County, the most expensive county in the United States, was not a place just anybody could afford to live. Half the service industry that supported the valley's resort businesses had to drive in from another state—Idaho. The other half from another country—Mexico. There were a lot of houses in our valley—the wealthy loved to buy land and build houses in the world's most beautiful places and spend a few weeks in each of them. But there were far fewer homes—places where people kept their hearts. Hadley's heart had been kept in this valley since the day she graduated from college, some thirty years ago.

"You can't leave the valley." I thought for a minute. "We'll get you a lawyer from out of state, someone who owes Paul nothing—past or future. We'll get one from . . . Florida."

Suddenly I recalled Annie telling me about meeting Daniel's fishing client, a lawyer who chose his cases based on a longtime grudge against wealthy, controlling men who abused their wives. Annie had reported that Daisy and Marcus knew this fellow by reputation; everyone in Florida did. He sounded like the Gerry

Spence of East Coast Florida, though he didn't dress in leather fringe and cowboy boots like Gerry; instead he wore brightly flow-ered Hawaiian shirts and huaraches and maintained a deep tan. He'd told Annie that in the beginning he was fueled by revenge for a past experience of his mother's, but now he worked out of sympa-thy for women who had few resources, emotionally or financially. Maybe he'd have sympathy for Hadley.

I got up from the desk. I put my arms around Hadley.

"You can't stay with a bastard for financial reasons. And I can't do without you. When Annie comes back, she isn't going to work in here much—I can lay money on that."

I hadn't actually thought that out before I said it, but I knew it was true. The days of Annie and me running the store on our own were over; the store was getting too big and Annie was losing inter-est. I patted Hadley, then picked up the phone and called Annie. She was out walking her dog, Bejewel or Bejesus or whatever the hell she named it. I put her on speaker phone.

The three of us talked for an hour. We sorted out problems, then assigned jobs. Annie's job was to track down the lawyer. Mine was to move Hadley out of her house and into a safe place im-mediately. Hadley's job was the hardest of all; she had to call the authorities.

The safe place turned out to be our house; I would sleep at the store. And Hadley learned from the authorities that two-day-old bruises or two-hour-old bruises all added up the same. Paul no longer held all the cards.

Hadley pressed charges against her husband of twenty years.

Paul learned from the police that Hadley had left him and was filing for divorce. He digested that news in the clinker while wait-ing for his lawyer to process him out. I was the only one on our team who took pleasure in that image. It saddened Annie and wor-ried Hadley. I never liked the guy once he told me his "humorous" story about setting the house thermometer fifteen degrees higher than its reading, just to knock his wife off-kilter. I should have slugged that jerk right then.

The next day, when Hadley came into the store, I apologized to her.

"I'm sorry I didn't see the bruises before."

"You weren't looking. You haven't been in the store much."

"I don't deserve an excuse."

"It wasn't an excuse, Jess. It was an accusation. You've been playing hooky like a tenth grader."

That took me back. I had slept on the office sofa inside a sleeping bag last night just for her. Showered in a cold, concrete stall in our employee restroom that morning. And it looked like I'd be doing both again for who knew how long.

"I'm not covering up for Paul any longer, and as long as I'm at it, I'm not covering up for you any longer, either." She looked severe. "I don't know how Annie manages, but I am about crazy dealing with you."

Hadley walked around her desk, picked up a stack of papers and dropped them back on her desktop. "Your crap." She kicked the wastepaper can, my footstool, out of her path. "Everywhere I turn: your crap." With her toe she nudged my ski boots, my snow boots, two other pairs of boots. "Your crap." She pointed to the heap of my coats on a chair. "You spread yourself and your crap all over everybody else's space. You seem to deliberately place your crap in another person's way, just so they have to bump up against it." She walked over to the windowsill, pointed to a pile of catalogs and books. "Your crap."

If she said those two words once more I was going to start yelling myself. But suddenly she deflated and dropped into her desk chair, the only place vacant for her to sit. Yesterday's clothes were flung over the back of my chair. Today I was wearing some of the store's inventory: fleece pants and a sweatshirt. I looked like I was going to yoga practice instead of work.

Hadley said, "This is a small town. This story is going to ruin Paul. His practice will flounder. I spent half the night struggling with that. The other half I spent struggling with my problems working with you."

"Hey, I hardly compare to some guy who beats you up."

"There are different ways to beat up someone, Jess. You've taken advantage of me. I'm here today because I care about you and because I believe Annie will return and I'll enjoy my work once again. If I didn't believe that, I'd have to—"

"Hold it. Don't even say it. Okay, I've been distracted. Annie *is* coming back. This has been tough for all of us. But . . . but—"

"You were 'distracted'—if that's the word—before Annie left. Distracted by new gear to test and customers and reps to entertain. You were distracted by fresh snow, sunshine, ski slopes, backcountry trails. . . ." Hadley got up, moving restlessly around the desks again. "I'm sorry, Jess. I'm sorry." She folded her arms and stood looking out the window, her back to me.

"A person starts to tell the truth and it's like a dam breaks; all the boundaries erected for love and money . . . crumble." She turned toward me. "I don't blame you if you fire me now. You've given me your home and helped me with my trouble. I love you and Annie; I'd like to continue here at TFS. But I cannot nor could I ever count on you . . . if the powder was especially good."

I guess she was thinking about yesterday when I left her and Annie to finish talking on the phone and I went out to ski.

"You have a good heart, but you do take care of yourself and your pleasures first." Hadley looked exhausted from her outburst.

"Oh, my." Hadley slumped into an extra desk chair, sitting on top of a couple jackets of mine. "Forgive me."

What the hell was this? Paul was the bastard we were talking about. Now suddenly it was me, too? What next? Every male on the planet? I paced around the textured concrete floor of the office in a big circle like some frustrated tiger at the zoo. Once around, twice around. Hadley just slumped there, drained of emotion, expression and—I should have been thankful—further accusations. At least for the moment. Though my experience with women and their accusations suggested that if I gave them a chance, they'd come up with more.

The solution: don't give them a chance.

With Annie, I walked away, moved right out of reach. When she started following me, I stopped listening to her. With Lola, I stopped showing up for appointments. That hadn't worked last time, but I thought she'd keep her distance now. With Hadley . . . I wasn't sure what to do. The thing with Hadley was: she didn't need me as a mate, like Annie did. Or as a client, like Lola did. I was Hadley's employer, and we both knew with her excellent reputation she could replace me anytime. But I couldn't replace her. Hell, I'd had other business owners approach her right in front of me.

I looked at my watch. The lifts had opened twenty minutes ago. I'd missed it again. Just like yesterday. By now all the fresh snow was skier tracked.

If my life was going to go well—with or without Annie—I needed Hadley working at the store.

"Got a deal for you, girl."

I didn't say one damn thing to Annie first. She left me in charge, so I took charge.

I offered Hadley part ownership of TFS.

Thirty-three

Annie

*L*ately getting sense out of my dad was like getting chewing gum out of a carpet. After a particularly irrational conversation on the phone with him, I decided to drive down and see him, instead of getting Daisy involved. She had enough going on with the twins and the store.

I set up Kia with extra seed and water in her cage, packed up the things Bijou and I would need for an overnight stay and hit the road. No Interstate 95 for me today, not in that big a hurry; I drove over to A1A so that I could catch glimpses of the ocean and dunes along the way.

It wasn't the phone call with Dad that captured my thoughts while driving though, but rather the last phone call with Jess— also confusing, but what was new there? Since I'd been away from home, I'd begun to realize that Jess typically spoke in ways that couldn't easily be tracked, as if he didn't want to be held responsible for anything he said. Reading between the lines of the conversation the other night offered far more information than Jess had meant for me to have. Just because he diminished Lola's words didn't mean I did. I found a wealth of support from Lola in the bare-bone pieces Jess set out for me, then quickly snatched away. And the fact that he was now soured on her just emphasized what she'd said. Wasn't it just like Jess to belittle her worth once she found the least fault with him? He was one of the most even-tempered people I knew, yet he could turn on a dime and expose a severely sharp, nasty edge. That was especially true when his defenses were challenged.

Clearly, Lola had challenged them.

Still an old two-lane, it was the A1A I remembered from years ago when I was a child and the family drove south from Ohio along this coast. I could remember the FREE ORANGE JUICE signs and the ALLIGATOR FARM signs. Not that Dad would pull over for anything. Daisy and I had to threaten to wet the backseat before he'd make a stop on those Cincinnati-to-Miami trips. Today, traffic was scarce and I returned to thoughts of my phone call with Jess.

His position of "I don't know, I forgot" had kept Jess safely out of the reach of responsibility, similar to the story Lucille had told about Shank and how he held to his old family patterns for his new relationship with her. In Jess' case his survival as a child depended on an innocence tightly gripped.

That dark-haired little boy at his mother's funeral, adults sobbing all around him, had maintained his staunch ignorance of what was taking place and his role in it. Perhaps this was the four-year-old boy's fear: that he would die of his own awareness.

I stopped at a deli near a public beach and picked up some lunch to eat while I drove. Before leaving, I let Bijou out and gave her water. While she drank, I leaned against the car and watched boys surf the whitecaps, balancing on their boards as gracefully as ballerinas on toe shoes. Then we got back into the car and continued on the road to Dad's.

While raising our sons, Jess had diminished the importance of near concussions, cuts and bruises. And I had accepted his view as the tough, fatherly position that balanced my own soft, feminine one. Today, I saw this was Jess' typical position of minimizing events as a form of survival. He was in constant danger of being overwhelmed, so like the surfers I'd been watching, he maintained vigilance against losing his balance and being dragged under.

Jess had two choices now: he could continue on the safe path of his childhood innocence or he could take further steps toward acknowledging and accepting his responsibilities in his mother's death as well as his life with me. He'd met with Lola, yet rejected her perspective. Was this a step forward or a step backward?

Either way, I faced our marital problems with clearer eyes and an acknowledgment that possibly I faced them alone. I must accept that and not expect more. The things I once expected from Jess—support of my choices, acknowledgment of my emotional responses—I was now learning to give myself. The good news was that this understanding offered me the independence that would allow to me have both my own life and a firmer relationship with my husband. And I wanted both. I loved Jess the way I loved my breath and blood, the way I loved the sky and water. Jess felt as integral to my heart as one of its chambers. He'd moved in long ago at my invitation, dragging his old baggage with him.

After I drove through dense wetlands for half an hour, the view opened and the coast lay exposed again. Pelicans flew low in formation over the shore. Gulls screamed at one another in competition for some scrap near the waterline. Since I was traveling the road alone, I slowed, set my arm on the open window and took in the air, soaked up the sounds of the birds, and marked the colors of the waves—white to palest green.

Then I couldn't stand it; I pulled the car over, got out and ran with Bijou through the beach grasses to the hard sand at the water's edge. Slipped off my sandals and waded in with my pup. I'd pay for this later with a wet and sandy dog in my car, but the pleasure of kicking up water and feeling my toes dig into the wet sand was worth it. We splashed and chased each other, me laughing, Bijou barking. I pretended to grab at her ears; she pretended to snap at my toes. Then we ran up the shore and back again, finally falling to the sand and breathing heavily. I stretched my legs out in front of me. I hadn't noticed before: my feet had become beautiful. During the weeks of walking the beach and wading, the sand and sea had smoothed them into silk and the sun had tanned my skin so that my toenails gleamed like pearls.

I lay back on the sand with my head on my arms to let the sun dry my legs and the hem of my skirt. I closed my eyes to the glare. A line from a lecture in psychology class earlier in the semester rose to mind. It had struck me as a piece to my puzzle and I had tucked it away. The instructor had said, "A facet of the innocent little boy was the scamp, the mischievous stinker who continued to slip out from beneath the consequences, and if caught had story after story to explain it all away."

I knew where that puzzle piece belonged now and I snapped it into place.

I had wanted to save Jess; he had wanted to be saved. We were a pair. We were still a pair, but the space between us now must become roomy enough for each of us to move in our own orbit, arms flung wide.

I rose and brushed sand from my clothes and legs. One look back at the ocean, and then I called to Bijou and climbed back into the car.

Soon I pulled off the coast road and joined the traffic in town. Stuart would be crowded with snowbirds for another month yet. Daisy claimed driving around elderly people was frustrating; they looked in their rearview mirrors more often than their windshields, afraid of what was coming up behind them. Daisy said, "Usually, it's me trying to pass."

Instead of scampering around the gerbil wheel of Jess' defense system in my thoughts, I should have been worrying about my dad and what would greet me there.

When I arrived at Dad's house, I found that his usually immaculate place was disturbingly out of order. Red wine stains on his pale blue dining room rug had been left unattended. His water glass, on the sink, looked as cloudy as the sky now did, portending a storm. Dad himself was unshaven, his shirt unclean and rumpled.

He wore a belt, but had failed to thread it through the loops on his pants, and it sat below his ribs, gripping his shirt to his chest.

"Dad, haven't the Ready-Maids been here lately?" His weekly crew of house cleaners kept up his laundry as well.

"I called them off. I been feeling kind of fluffy."

"Kind of 'fluffy'?"

"Yeah, you know . . . fluffy."

I surprised—and worried—myself by understanding what he probably meant. Unstable, maybe light-headed. I hated to get into this, but I asked anyway.

"What have you been eating?" I braced for his answer, expecting it to be the industrial-sized purchase of whatever was discounted at Publix this week, eaten down to its final spoonful.

"I go out now. Eat eggs and sausage in the morning, steak for dinner and in between potato chips while I watch golf on TV."

Maybe Andrew Weil wouldn't have approved, but for Dad that didn't sound too bad.

"Well, Dad." I walked toward the phone. "I'm making an appointment with Dr. Jack right now." Jack had been our family doctor for decades. I tuned out Dad's backpedaling about fluffy not being a bad feeling; we'd been putting off an appointment long enough. I proceeded to dial. Daniel's words of several weeks ago poured into my mind—"Something in his look . . . his skin color or eyes . . . Have him checked out." There was something in his look now all right—a grayness to his skin and a lack of presence in his eyes. While I waited for Jack's receptionist to answer, Dad began to whisper. I covered the phone. "What, Dad?"

"Not you." He made conversational gestures to someone invisible beside him and continued his whispering.

"Katherine, hello." I paused, watching Dad.

I walked into the other room away from him, and speaking softly identified myself. I said I thought I had an emergency occurring with my father at this very moment. Katherine said, "Bring him in."

So much for saving Daisy trouble. I phoned her in a panic while we drove to the doctor's office and she met us there. Dad slept the whole way.

Hours of waiting and testing, hours of wrestling Dad in and out of his clothes, and finally he was home again. Diagnosis: a form of dementia, probably set off by a series of small strokes called TIAs. Prognosis: will worsen, maybe sooner, maybe later. Treatment: none available, watch him.

Oh, and take away his car keys.

That was a rough one. He had taught us how to drive, for heaven's sake. But the idea of him out there on the road, having a stroke and possibly harming someone, prodded Daisy and me into action.

We blamed it on Dr. Jack (he said we could), and Daisy and I told Dad that for now, until he stopped feeling "fluffy," he shouldn't be driving. All this was eased somewhat by Dad having misplaced his car keys. He was looking for them in order to prove us wrong about driving under the influence of fluffiness. He was going to the store for potato chips. When Daisy found the keys before he did, she quietly pocketed them. I found a golf game in progress on TV and some corn chips in the cupboard, which distracted Dad from his search. Problem solved for the moment.

We fixed dinner for Dad and sat with him for a while. I remembered that I had brought him a gift, a Peter Gabriel CD. I played "Biko" for him three times. When Dad was ready to turn in for the night, Daisy and I went to her house. After we tucked the girls into bed and even after Marcus wandered upstairs with his mystery novel, Daisy and I stayed up, worrying and wondering about Dad. We created possible future scenarios and we tried to solve them or talk each other out of their possibilities. Should we get care in place? What kind? Should we look at assisted-living centers or nursing homes? When we wound down from that without finding solutions to any of it, we decided before things became any worse we should all take a trip together: Dad, Jess, our boys, Marcus and the girls. Create a family memory.

We decided on a houseboat trip through the Keys. We'd rent one on Islamorada, load it up with food and head out to fish, kayak the mangroves, swim on the sandy beaches of small islands in the Florida Bay, watch for dolphins, enjoy sunsets. There would be something to do for everyone.

We planned it for the boys' spring break later this month. Since Mountain Time was two hours earlier, I called Jess, then lined it up with Cam and Saddler. It was all set. What supplies would we need, what food should we take? With relief over these easier questions, Daisy and I began a list.

Boneless ham, chocolate, coffee, milk, red licorice, bagels, garbage bags, ziplock bags, toilet paper, paper towels, paper plates, paper cups . . .

And then, because I couldn't sleep and it wasn't yet late in Wyoming, I phoned Jess again, after Daisy went off to bed. Aside from tonight's call to arrange the trip, our last talk hadn't been very satisfying. In fact, Jess had hung up saying that "as usual talking to you just pisses a guy off"—speaking in his passive, generalizing way, not exactly mentioning any guy's name in particular. I was probably crazy, but suddenly that felt like home and I missed it.

When Jess answered the phone I said, "Do you suppose it ever happens that when a guy dials a nine hundred number for phone sex the woman says she has a headache or is too tired?"

Jess said, "Sure, probably. It could be some woman's specialty. You know, a guy misses his wife—not me, not you—and he likes to call this woman just to listen to the same old excuses he'd get if his wife were home."

I laughed. Then I indulged in telling Jess everything that had happened with my dad at the doctor's office, and when that was finished, I reached back to my boat trip with my friends before leaving Hibiscus, and when that was finished, I filled him in on Daniel. Then I checked to see if Jess was still awake.

He was. He said, "What happened to the subject of phone sex?"

I said, "I'm too tired."

Jess said, "Tell me more, baby." And he panted suggestively.

I laughed. "Wouldn't it be nice if someday there was a nine hundred number for comfort?"

"Comfort?"

"You know. 'Now, I'm rubbing your temples in gentle circles, now brushing my fingertips over your eyelids. Massaging your forehead.'"

"Watch out. I'm getting relaxed."

"Sir, do you have your credit card ready?"

The next morning I drove over to see Dad. Since he couldn't find his car keys earlier, he'd taken his golf cart up to the clubhouse for breakfast and planned to return for dinner—the perfect solution. Dad was happy and claimed his "fluffiness" had settled. He looked like his old self. I phoned Daisy with the good news and rescheduled the Ready-Maids for a housecleaning. He and I went to the grocery store and loaded up on supplies. While Dad pushed the grocery cart up and down the aisles, he hummed "Biko."

After lunch I headed back to Hibiscus.

Jess and I usually left it up to our boys to make contact while they were away at school. College kids had their own ever-expanding lives and spent very little time thinking about their parents. Until—as the old joke went—they needed money. Phoning them last night to line up spring break had allowed us to catch up, and the family trip had assured my sons that all was well on the home front.

Which, happily, it was. I was feeling strong and clear that afternoon, driving back to my apartment. I had acquired five new Marriage Rules and I looked forward to seeing my husband soon. To celebrate, I stopped in town before heading to the apartment and went shopping for a new bathing suit to take on the houseboat. And I kept my eye out for an alluring dress to wear when I picked up Jess at the airport.

In the store I shuttled hangers along the swimsuit rack, gathered a few possibilities and took them into the dressing room with me, wishing Daisy were here to give her vote.

I was pleased the boys sounded excited about the houseboat trip; I was afraid they'd made plans already to get in some spring skiing. Our sons had become excellent skiers growing up in Jackson Hole, fearless but not rash. And thank God they didn't get into the record-breaking fever that went on in a resort like our hometown. Kids took life-threatening risks just to get a name and a big gear company's backing so they could travel around the world for free, taking more life-threatening risks. The fame, money and travel could look pretty glamorous to a kid.

I found two swimsuits and bought them both, a two-piece coral and a one-piece black with lacy inserts. One for causal daytime wear, one for formal evenings, I joked to myself. On a houseboat for several days, I'd be glad to have a change. I left the store and walked to the yarn shop.

By now the saleswomen and I knew each other by name. The store had taken an interest in my class project and offered to display my dog sweaters and sell them after my class was over. My pretend craft business was materializing into a reality. It gave me ideas. If I could return home with the makings of a small business, it could only help me in strengthening my independence from the store.

Inside the yarn shop, I stood for a moment, imagining the upcoming time when I would be shopping in Jackson for my yarns at Knit on Pearl. There I'd find the warm wools that were scarce here. I browsed through the ribbon yarns. The young saleswoman working today, Amy, told a customer who was learning to knit socks, "Just be sure you knit the second sock. During my mother's whole life she only knitted one sock."

I chose a lacy ribbon yarn in shades of lavender with silver threads running through it to combine with a soft cashmere yarn of purple. I was aiming for a very high-end dog sweater. I pictured a Florida woman toting a tiny shih tzu, then picked out three sparkly rhinestone buttons.

Amy nodded approval of my choices when I approached the counter. She checked out the sock-knitting lady ahead of me, handed her the bag and said, "Just remember: there are a lot of lonely socks out there in the world."

As I was leaving the yarn shop, my cell rang and I tucked my bags under my arm and rummaged for my phone. It was Hadley.

Right then, on the sidewalk of downtown Hibiscus, my hard-won balance toppled in a heap at my feet. I stood against a storefront listening to Hadley relay the offer Jess had made to her: my husband had given away part ownership of the store. I felt breathless at Jess' betrayal.

According to Hadley, yesterday Jess had left the store to go skiing, but before leaving, while climbing into his ski pants and jacket, he had offered Hadley one-third ownership . . . without conferring with me.

Distance from Jess had allowed me to see things in our relationship that I had been too close to see before, but distance had also allowed me to indulge in certain forms of marital amnesia. And Jess' repeated assumption that he had total rights over the life that we shared was one of them. When I flipped my phone closed after hearing that news (which Hadley had reported as a warning, not as having accepted Jess' offer—"Fresh powder," she'd explained), I seethed inside. A scalding rage burned my chest and throat. The skin on my arms and face prickled as if my anger had erupted into a rash with the effort to contain it. I wanted to scream my fury.

Instead I ranted inside my head, while blindly pounding down the sidewalk toward my car. I feared my lips moved and sounds emitted from my mouth at times. And once I reached the privacy of home, I sobbed with pain, loud enough to bring Bijou to my side and Kia to her birdcage door.

From anger to bereft hopelessness back to anger. I fumed. I wept. I boiled with fury and a sense of helplessness. The arrogance and self-centeredness of this man were an outrage. I lay on the floor exhausted with emotion and feeling alone in the world. Jess could have told me what he'd done. He could have called me. I had phoned him myself twice last night and he hadn't said a word.

When Hadley phoned, she had suspected I was in the dark.

Then I recalled the rest of my conversation with Hadley about her concerns in leaving her husband, Paul, and I felt ashamed of myself for feeling so miserable. It wasn't as if Jess were trying to overpower me, defeat me as Paul had her.

Or was it?

And then I saw it.

This was the ticket to my new life.

And I didn't have to disrupt one thing. Jess had done it for me. Suddenly I realized I didn't have to work at introducing the idea of financial independence, or manufacturing that space between Jess and me, or finding excuses for personal friends or acting on my values. And if on this occasion I didn't claim my personal power, I never would. Jess, with his preemptive act of giving away a share of my ownership in the store, had introduced all these concepts into our marriage for me.

When life fell apart, I scrubbed bathrooms. So I rose from the floor, went to the bathroom, tied my hair back and sprinkled cleanser in the tub. I washed the tiled shower walls, sprayed disinfectant on the toilet and took a brush to it, mopped the floor, shined the mirror. Then I stripped, showered and shampooed.

Separate money? Jess had just made an independent financial

decision. And he had often done so in the past. He ordered fleece by the truckload without one mention to me in regard to our joint accounts, while I alerted him to my underwear purchases.

Separate friends? Jess had his own friends, always had. It was only my friends we shared, couples we socialized with.

Claim personal power? There was a joke. Jess hadn't ever recognized anyone else's power but his own.

He had created space automatically with his choices to put himself and his playtime first and by not addressing the emotions his actions created. I thought this would be the hardest of the rules, yet thinking back to the many occasions when Jess walked away from our discussions, it seemed space had been a part of our marriage for some time.

If doing what you wanted, when you wanted was a part of honoring personal values, Jess had been a master.

It was me. Me who had not wanted separate money, friends, power, space or values. I had resisted all separateness, had seen it as a barrier against union and intimacy.

I had created the need for a marriage sabbatical all by myself.

Since coming to Florida, I'd learned more tricks than scrubbing the bathroom to help myself regain balance during difficult times. I had learned that if I could touch base with those parts of my life I particularly treasured—my creative energy, being outdoors, remembering the wisdom of others—I recovered my center. And when things were particularly bad, as they felt now, I thought I'd better enact every one of them. So I wrote in my journal; I knitted; I took Bijou to the beach. And I recalled Lucille quoting Rainer Maria Rilke. She had said, "When times get hard with Shank, I repeat these lines to remind myself what matters: 'Love consists in this, that two solitudes protect and touch and greet each other.'"

Could I arrive at that place by spring break?

*   *   *

A good night's sleep, another round of journal writing, knitting, walking and eventually my thoughts spread beyond my fury and dismay with Jess. I recalled the rest of my life. I remembered the fun our family always had with Daisy and Marcus, knew we'd all have a good houseboat vacation together. I let myself hope Dad would somehow be restored to his old self, though Dr. Jack and the specialists suggested that was an unrealistic hope. Yet Dad seemed happy and content during my frequent calls. Daisy reported that he had shifted his box of Teague Family Sports caps to the back of his golf cart and was sailing them out to everyone he passed in the neighborhood.

That morning when I phoned him between classes, he said he was, "Getting up and taking nourishment," a line that came from his grandmother. Throughout the years, he had turned it into a family joke. I felt absurdly pleased he remembered that.

As my anger toward Jess lessened and my balance was restored, I realized Hadley *should* be part owner. Her contribution over the years had earned her that. In the past she hadn't expressed long-term interest in the business, and made frequent remarks that suggested she was uncertain about her future. I understood now that she had been referring to her unstable marriage and the future she'd imagined she'd have to spend in a more affordable part of the country. Teton County was no place for a single woman in her fifties without financial means.

When Hadley had called yesterday, she knew that Jess had betrayed my trust; and with her joke about the fresh powder on the slopes, she had let me know she understood his motivation as well as I did, and held his offer lightly. I did not hold Jess' offer lightly, but I knew part ownership was Hadley's solution . . . and mine. I wanted her to know as soon as I did. I phoned, trusting Jess was out skiing again.

"Hadley, I second Jess' offer of part ownership, and I hope you will accept it. I see it as the perfect answer for each of us."

I told her we'd have our lawyer draw up formal papers with an arrangement that worked for all three of us. When I hung up the phone, I decided that I would use this opportunity to take the separation of finances a step further than I had originally intended. I would legally separate my one-third ownership of the store from Jess' third, as well as separate the earnings from my share. Jess should realize he had instigated this as well with his rash offer to Hadley.

To be fair, Jess often acted rashly and just as often it turned out to be an intuitively genius resolution to a given situation. As this was. Still, did it excuse him? And what did he care? He was skiing.

There was another facet to his unthinking response: the passive-aggressive stinker was still angry at me for taking a marriage sabbatical.

One more thing I wanted to do today. I needed to thank Daniel for the favor he had done in contacting his lawyer friend on behalf of Hadley. Will Waggoner had accepted her case. I knew his friendship with Daniel fully accounted for that. I checked my watch: three o'clock. Daniel should be back at the pier if he'd taken the boat out, cleaned up from his day of fishing, ready to relax. As I gathered my things—money, cell, leash—Bijou leaped high in the air all around me, thrilled she was getting two outings in one day. Not as rare as her behavior suggested, but she always lent a festive air to our activities.

Daniel joked that Burl Stocker needed more exercise, so we walked with our dogs in the park. And he wanted to talk without worrying about listening devices. Ahead of us, Jeter ran from tree to tree, leaving his scent, and Bijou followed, pausing behind to watch the ritual. I understood something about the stress Daniel was under. While he was trying to convince the feds that he was clean, Parson Fields was pressuring him into one more job with the threat that he'd disclose his identity to the local drug cartel. And Daniel had suggested before that the cartel had ways of punishing uncooperative players from the past.

"I'm in a bad place and it's getting worse." Daniel walked beside me. "I'll have to make a move soon."

"But move where? There doesn't seem to be any safe direction for you."

"I have a couple options. I can return to India, spend another year or so helping Jamie in her clinic. Parson isn't strong enough to wait me out too long. But that's Jamie's life, not mine. I'd like to clean up this mess, make a home in the States, enjoy my work again. So I might just disappear for a few weeks, then relocate."

I stopped walking and turned to Daniel. "You're trying to save Parson Fields from himself, aren't you?" I railed at him like I would Jess. "That is stupid." I reminded myself that I was not married to Daniel and had no right to talk to him like that. I took a big breath. "Just alert everybody."

"There is nobody to alert, Annie. No illegal action has occurred yet. Parson did me no favors in the end, but . . . he's damn sick. I'd like to keep him out of prison for his final months of life, is all."

I heard Daniel's struggle and it was easier to respond with compassion. "I know this isn't the black-and-white issue it seems. But you've worked hard to restore your reputation and self-respect. Please don't jeopardize your life for this guy."

"No, I don't owe him that." He looked away, took a big breath.

"You don't owe him anything."

Daniel looked down at me. "You're right." We began walking again. "Tough world out there."

I stopped him, laid my hand on his arm. "Your world is tough, Daniel. Not all worlds. And with the act of removing yourself from this, you'll be inviting another, better set of circumstances to become your world."

We stood looking at each other. I dropped my hand from his arm.

He said, "That's why I fell for you, you know. I want that other world . . . with you in it." I thought he was going to kiss me; he wanted to. I wanted him to . . . but I couldn't sort out the reasons why. Out of fury against Jess? Because Daniel was opening his heart to me? Because he was a man consciously making his decisions and I longed for a man like that?

I couldn't draw Daniel into my confusion; he had enough of his own. But my eyes filled and I turned from him and began walking down the path. He joined me, and when the clenching in my throat cleared, I said, "I think I just represent that other, better set of circumstances to you." My eyes may still have been red, but I looked at him.

"Had a whole life I could see for us." His voice sounded husky.

We walked close beside each other, though not touching.

I said, "That tells me and should tell you what you really want, what you are capable of creating for yourself." My words might have sounded harsh to him, but I went on. "You knew all along I was unavailable."

He didn't respond and I didn't look at him. But I wanted to press home what I thought was the important part of what he had disclosed. I said, "Now that you can imagine this other way of living, and feel that it can bring you qualities you want in your life—fun, love, relationship, engagement with someone special to you—you know what to go for."

Daniel said, "I thought I'd sent out that invitation already with my move down here. And things are better; I'm not alone with this. Will Waggoner advises me and I have trusted friends in the coast guard who are aware of my circumstances."

I was relieved to hear that.

Daniel said, "I'll have to leave in the next few days or so." We'd both stopped walking. He looked off, then back at me for a long minute.

"First, let me meet that guy you've been so true to all these months. Bring him by before you head for the Keys, would you?"

I promised I would, told him Jess wanted to meet him, too.
Daniel grinned, said, "I bet."

I was exhausted. It seemed the past two days had been spent
wringing my heart and mind for drops of truth, finding that the
truth took strength to accept and act upon. The truth here was that
I cared so much for this man, but what I had said to him was the
reality, as far as my mind could foresee the path ahead. And before
I acted against that wisdom, succumbed to his vision of us, I knew
I needed to leave Daniel.

I said goodbye. I probably wouldn't see him alone again, and
we both knew it. I headed toward town with Bijou on the leash,
but before I crossed the parking lot, I thought: what about Jeter?
If Daniel needed to leave abruptly, temporarily or not, wouldn't he
need someone to care for his dog while he was gone?

I checked my watch—four thirty, two thirty in Wyoming; I
gave Jess a quick call on his cell. He was between runs, down at the
base, in line for the Bridger Gondola.

"So let's see, one small dog, one big dog, a bird . . . Annie, I'm
flattered. You keep missing me like this, we'll have to move to a
ranch when you and your menagerie return." His voice sounded
light and happy. No worry there about giving away part of my
ownership of the store.

But for me, in the background between us, was his undis-
closed offer to Hadley. I knew Jess; he would never bring it up
on his own, just let it seep into reality however it *accidentally*
occurred. I decided right then: I wouldn't bring it up, either.
Let him create his excuses, or work at forgetting, or minimizing,
whichever of his unconscious responses he chose to pull out of his
dark sack. It was no longer any of my business to call him on his
behavior, but to take care of myself the best I could in the face of
his unpredictability.

I had kept Jess filled in about Daniel all along, so he understood
that I wanted to help him, and Jess agreed about Jeter. Who knew

how much of that was guilt on his part for giving away a third of the store, or gratitude for Daniel's help with Hadley?

I walked back toward the marina, called to Daniel from the dock, not wanting to board his boat. He stuck his head up from below. I beckoned him off the boat so we could talk.

"Jeter," I said. "What about Jeter?"

I offered Daniel my plan to care for his dog. I'd take him whenever Daniel decided to leave and keep him for as long as needed.

I could tell it eased Daniel to have a plan for Jeter's care. To make that plan appear normal, and not a signal to Burl Stocker and the other watchers later when I took Jeter for Daniel's escape, we decided I'd pick up Jeter for occasional overnight visits, starting right then.

Thirty-four

Jess

I heard from our lawyer that Annie had asked for a formal agreement to be drawn not only to legally secure Hadley's share, but to legally secure her own share, apart from mine. And to separate out the income that was generated from her share.

I called her on the spot, mad as hell. When she answered, I said, "What the shit is this? You don't need a legal agreement with me. I'm your husband."

Annie let a long, long pause spread over the phone lines.

Finally I sighed and said, "Okay. But it's your fault. You weren't here—"

She finished the sentence. "To protect myself from you."

Another long pause.

"I called to tell you about today's headlines."

"No, you didn't, Jess. You called to complain about my legal action."

"Okay, maybe I shouldn't have given Hadley a share without talking to you about it. And you shouldn't have given those orders to our lawyer without talking to me about it."

"If that's your apology, it lacks quite a lot. Sincere regret, for one."

"Look, Annie, I'm sorry. But it's done now. And I think it's going to work out for all of us."

Another silence.

I felt like slamming the phone down, but I hoped to change her mood by telling the good news I'd been saving for her. "Wolf No. 9 has denned."

"Really?"

Normally Annie would have yelped with glee. "They can't tell yet whether she has a new litter of pups or not. And we won't know for a month or so, till the pups are allowed out. But she was spotted digging a den and may have given birth."

"Gosh." Her voice lifted. "That's pretty big news."

"This will be her sixth litter of pups. That's the most any wolf has had in Yellowstone."

No reaction. I gave up and said goodbye.

Hadley lived on the phone lately. In between talking to her two lawyers—Will down in Florida, who was handling her divorce, and our lawyer, Philip, here in the valley, who was drawing up the papers for TFS—she was calling in orders for next year's ski season and the coming summer season. My job was to scramble around, keeping the staff happy and the store managed. These final weeks of ski season our attention was geared toward unloading the inventory. Everything we couldn't carry over into summer was drastically discounted, since next year would bring a whole new line of equipment and clothing. We constantly rearranged to keep the store looking interesting as the stacks of goggles and skier fleece dwindled.

I looked forward to leaving for Florida in a few days, then closing for the off season a couple weeks after my return. Most of April through mid-May we shut the joint up and typically headed for warmer places with no mud. Around here everything dripped, snow turned to slush, icicles dropped off roofs, creeks broke up and the shelves of ice, piled along the banks like shards of crockery, loosened and ran fast and dangerously downstream. We called it mud season, and this year I'd be sloshing through it, instead of escaping it. I might work on a project I had in mind, a big present for Annie.

A customer pushed through the door of TFS, greeted me in a foreign accent I couldn't place. I smiled back and shuffled through the remaining face masks, grouping them by size; we wouldn't be selling many more of these this year. We were into spring skiing now, with temperatures in the low thirties most days, threatening our snowpack. I called to Saundra to mark the masks half price when she got a chance. Right now she was twisting her hair and staring out the window; every once in a while she dipped for candy stored in one of her vast pockets.

Lizette and Todd pretended it took two to fold T-shirts, and Casey was online planning his off-season trip to Costa Rica. Hard to keep energy and interest high at the end of the season. They'd all be out of here if we didn't offer a big bonus for staying to the very last day. Time to lift spirits. I pulled out the sign and hung it behind the counter where only the employees could see it. It said:

WHY IS IT CALLED TOURIST SEASON
IF WE CAN'T SHOOT THEM?

I nodded to the foreign fellow again just to let him know someone was awake and available, in case he needed anything.

He nodded back to me and said, "I'm just watching." Guessed he meant he was just looking. Saundra and I exchanged amused glances. Then she went back to staring out the window. We all wanted to be outside. The air was soft; the sky was blue. When I'd driven to the village that morning, untracked snow in the fields on either side of the road had sparkled like a tray of jewels. This valley held extraordinary beauty cupped within its circle of mountains. There was no place like it on earth.

Now more customers wandered into TFS. It was nearing time for the lifts to close that afternoon, when it always became busy in the store. I moved to the fog cloths, another thing that wouldn't sell well the rest of the season. "Saundra, mark these half off, too." I added again, "If you get a chance."

Might do some fishing during off season. Time to get out my pale morning duns and blue-winged olives. Might try my hand at making some dry flies of my own. I'd lost interest in working with fleece; Malden Mills was selling out anyway and good quality stuff was harder to come by. Besides, my present for Annie entailed giving up a good share of my workspace. I'd need it to store all the gear I now had in that little cabin in the backyard.

I stuck the marking pen in Saundra's pocket so that the next time she dipped in for M&Ms she'd grab hold of it instead. That girl had a big fantasy life and I hated to intrude. I checked the stack of mail. There was an envelope typed on a typewriter. Didn't see that anymore. Opened it and found a letter written by a woman describing a product she made by hand. *I crochet small ducks in all colors. A tie beneath the chin allows it to be filled with M&Ms* (Saundra might like this). *Then with a squeeze in the middle of the duck, the candy will come out from a hole beneath the tail.*

I should take this letter with me to Florida to show Annie. She would howl. I lifted my head and savored how good it felt to know that I'd be with her soon. But I worried, too. Annie used to make what I called State of the Union addresses. And she made them far more often than our president did. The union, of course, was the two of us. What would she have to say now?

Thirty-five

Annie

J drove to the Orlando airport to pick up Jess and the boys. We would spend a night together in my apartment before meeting the rest of the family in the Keys. My feelings about seeing my husband after more than two months were conflicted: part anticipated pleasure, part protective self-armoring. As I drove across inland Florida against the slant of late-afternoon sunshine, I realized the patterns of my marriage had risen into high relief against this background of time and distance. That was my purpose in taking a marriage sabbatical, so I drove to this meeting with Jess, feeling confident about the necessity of leaving my marriage in order to save it.

Still I grieved.

I would not be returning to the same sanctuary I had entered twenty-six years ago. Never again would I live in such sweet, destructive union. I had left that dark womb, emerged from the sea of marital soup, and from now on, though we were mated in love and faithfulness, our lives would be furnished with more than "his" and "hers" towels. There would be "his" and "hers" money, friends, space, power, values.

I came to Florida feeling that Jess had become a pebble in my shoe, a splinter in my thumb, a continual drain on my energy. My frustration at the end of a day had often broken into wordless sobs that jarred my body with their rough passage. Jess would hold me, smooth my hair, murmur, "There, there," into my ear and take on the preparations for dinner himself.

Caring behavior? Yes. Also an arrogant response that came from a sense of disengagement: too bad I was experiencing problems; he wasn't.

I could never have figured out the trouble I felt while living within this mixed stew of covert abuse and overt affection.

I was happy to hear the news about Wolf No. 9. For me she symbolized what could happen in wild places, and I felt I had been in a wild place for the past months. If No. 9 could give birth under those tough circumstances, any female could do anything. I, for one, could solve my life and my marriage.

I was driving through a dense forest of pine scrub, the land flat as the back of my hand, resting on the steering wheel. Bijou rose from her nest in the fuchsia-colored fleece blanket tossed in the backseat for her and came to brace her front paws on the center consol and rest her chin on my shoulder. I tipped my face to hers to acknowledge her presence and hoped she wouldn't mind sharing me with Jess.

Nobody liked change. And, I knew, Jess would not like the upcoming changes one bit, as his response to the new financial setup at the store had demonstrated. In fact, Jess' fear of such changes, I realized now, was what had prompted him to instigate the boys' challenge that Thanksgiving evening a couple years back, when the three of them attacked my lack of interest in working at the store with Jess and watching TV with the family. Jess mixed it up, figuring that if I left our lifestyle, I'd leave our life . . . and him. He was working from fear and resistance. Didn't he know that what you actively feared and resisted usually became reality?

I had seen couples greet each other at airports like this before, people who I knew had been married for years. I had always wondered how you could stand face-to-face with a mate you'd been separated from and not mash your bodies, your breath, your mouths together in relief that the parting was over. But there we stood, Jess and I, separate, smiling, though not rushing into each other's arms. Jess, I saw, was attempting to mask the uncertainty of his standing with me. I did nothing to smooth his unease and, for once, did not take it upon myself to feel responsible for it.

I just stood there, looking at the man I loved, would always love, but seeing in him, too, the man who gave me the same gift of blue topaz ear studs for our anniversary that he had given me for Valentine's Day, who gave away a share of my store ownership, who derided my passion for creating, along with the man who loved me, who was a good father, who had shared life with me for twenty-six years. I saw it all.

Then I went to hug him.

If our sons had accompanied Jess on the flight, I would have wanted to put on a good show for them. Their plane was due a few hours later, and by then I hoped Jess and I would have had time to relax with each other.

Dinner together that night in an Orlando restaurant, the first since our anniversary dinner atop Gros Ventre Butte, didn't begin with champagne or gift giving, but rather quiet talk about our lives and our children. I didn't buy a special dress after all. My heart wasn't in it. But later, after picking up our sons, driving to Hibiscus, and settling the family in my small apartment, Jess and I retired to my bedroom and made love, sweet, slow love, devoid of urgency or lavish expressions of arousal.

Afterward, I lay beside Jess as he slept and remembered that woman who meshed herself so tightly into her husband—his body, his life, his awareness—that she pumped her own life force into his until she could not tell herself apart from him, his actions, his thoughts. His thoughtlessness.

And then I smiled to myself, because I recalled showing more enthusiasm when Jess' luggage arrived at the same time and place as he did, earlier at the airport, than I had in bed with him just now. This, too, would heal, I thought, and went to sleep myself.

*   *   *

Though I had brought Jeter back to the boat after a couple of his overnights, making the visits look routine for the watchers, I had let Jeter board by himself and only waved to Daniel before walking or driving away. Today, bringing Jess to meet Daniel at the Turtle Nest, was the first time I'd spent with Daniel in a week. After introductions, we settled at a table on the deck.

"You notice anything different?" Daniel asked me.

I looked around. As usual Daniel's cell phone had been tossed on the table; as usual the dogs had scooted beneath our chairs. The umbrellas were open, the sun shined and the staff inside was gearing up for the lunchtime rush.

"It all looks the same to me."

"No Stocker." Daniel tipped his head toward the inside, then toward the water. "No go-fast boats." He raised his eyebrows. "Been like that all morning."

"Well, that's good, isn't it?" Jess asked, though I knew he had been curious about go-fast boats and how it felt to be under surveillance. Even the boys had planned to stop by, after they fished with Shank, to meet Daniel and see a go-fast boat.

"Not good. My old partner's nearby, is my guess. He has a long arm and he's reaching for his IOUs."

Daniel was restless, shifting position, sitting where he could watch inside the restaurant, instead of in view of the water. He didn't eat much. I wondered what Jess was making of him. Daniel was not his typically cool self.

"What does this mean?" I asked.

"Have to leave."

"When?"

"In the next hour or so. I put my boat in the hands of a broker this morning when I got cued from one of the go-fast officers. Then everybody took off."

"Cued?" Jess said.

"One of the guys and I went to flight school together in Palm Beach years back. He let me know." Daniel demonstrated with his fist and a thumb slicing across his neck.

Daniel said, "Whatever's up is not standard operating procedure." He took a swig of his iced tea and added, "I don't plan to be one of those federal retirees collecting my pension in prison, which is where my old boss may be heading."

"I'll be damned; the government will still pay a pension to a prisoner." Jess enjoyed this talk, I could tell, but I could see now that he was leery of Daniel. Yet he'd been hearing his story as a kind of serial during our phone talks over the winter months. Each call, Jess would ask, "So what's up with Daniel?"

Daniel said now, "Most likely the officers didn't get much warning themselves. Probably an early-morning phone call to look scarce for the next couple days. I was just waiting for the two of you to show before I took off."

Daniel's phone blinked a red light from the table, and he excused himself. "Sorry. Go ahead and eat." He stood up, reached for his phone and walked around to the other side of the deck.

The second Daniel was out of earshot, Jess dropped his sandwich on his plate. It landed with a thud, and I looked up at him in surprise. He leaned across the table to me, hands braced on the edge, eyebrows raised.

"Hey! You told me Daniel was retired. I thought he was some old guy."

"He is retired." I hadn't thought before about whom Jess had imagined I was spending time with.

"Damn it, Annie. I've been picturing some bent-over, gray-haired senior citizen." Jess looked toward the direction Daniel had disappeared, then back to me. "What are you doing, hanging out with him? He's built like our neighbor, what's-his-name."

"Who?"

"You know, the guy who tells his wife he's going out for a run and then sprints up the Grand Teton and down before lunch."

"Oh, Richard." Jess was jealous. A first for us. There had never been an occasion for jealousy before; I didn't especially like the complication it brought to our reunion. It felt like a diversion from the real issues. I said, "Believe me, we've both had our minds on other problems down here."

"I know what his problem is. What's yours?" He sounded angry and challenging.

I was incredulous. "You," I practically shouted.

"Oh, great," he mumbled. Jess became very still and he stared into my eyes, looking grim and sad. I let him see the truth in my gaze: nothing had happened between me and Daniel.

"I love you, Jess." I hadn't said it last night, not even when he had said those words to me. But it was true: I loved him. And I wanted him to know.

He nodded his head once.

Our sons appeared then, thudding up the stairway and making the wooden-deck floor vibrate; they noisily pulled out chairs around the table and announced how ravenous they were.

"Where is he?" Saddler said. I had filled in the guys about Daniel last night during our long drive home from the airport.

Before I could answer, Daniel rejoined us. I introduced Cam and Saddler to him, and he waved the waitress over to get their orders, tossed his cell phone back on the table and sat down. We all talked for a while; then Daniel checked his watch and mentioned that he needed to meet his broker on the pier briefly to sign some papers. It would only take a minute. He invited Jess to walk down with him and see his boat. The boys' food was just being served, so I stayed at the table with them.

I reached out my hand to Jess as he was leaving. He took hold of it and came to my side. We looked into each other's eyes. After a moment he leaned down and kissed me. Jess had a generous heart; I felt glad of that.

He was both right and wrong in perceiving Daniel as a threat. The threat had been a reality from my first meeting with Daniel, but then so had the firm position I took in response to it. I hadn't come to Hibiscus to escape anything in my marriage; I had come to face it full-on. I hoped Jess knew that now.

After Jess and Daniel left, I asked the guys about their fishing trip with Shank.

Cam said, "We caught a ton of fish. Shank knows his stuff. We cleaned them, and Shank is packing them in ice for the houseboat. Sadd and I will grill fish for dinner tonight."

Saddler nodded to the cell phone lying on the table. "They've got trackers in these things. Since Daniel's old partner has access to governmental data, he probably has access to the data from the tracking device in the phone."

"Really?"

"We could buy your friend some extra time," Cam said and took a big bite of his roast beef panini.

I liked that he referred to Daniel as my friend and wanted to help him.

When Cam stopped chewing, he explained, "Your phone looks just like his."

"Oh, I know. He knows, too. He flips his open before pocketing it to check that it's his." I knew what Cam was thinking—switch phones and Parson would follow me, not Daniel. "That won't work."

Saddler said, "Remember when we were in high school and you and Dad warned us that if we broke our cell phones, you wouldn't replace them?"

I remembered that well. I should have made the same rule for Jess; he broke his regularly—dropping it in the snow, the creek, the toilet.

Cam said, "You never had to buy new phones for us, because we just removed our SIM card. It's a little plastic-and-metal card less than a square inch inside the phone. We stuck it in a friend's phone or any other old phone we found lying around." He grinned at me. "Sometimes yours."

Saddler said, "The SIM card holds all our information."

"What are you thinking?" I asked.

"If we stuck your SIM card in his cell, Daniel would still have his phone."

Saddler added, "But they couldn't trace him."

I said, "Well . . . sure. If that'll help." I handed him my phone. A misty fog seeped into my mind during technical talk. When machines—computers, cash registers, even vacuum cleaners— didn't turn on and operate the way I expected them to, it was as if I was injected with an anesthetic that turned me stupid. A kind of ennui flooded my normal curiosity at such times. I bent to pet Bijou and rub Jeter's tummy. He and I had bonded closely since he'd begun coming home with me most evenings.

"We better hurry." Saddler dug into his pocket for the Swiss Army pocketknife he always carried and handed it to Cam. "Use this to lift off the back of her phone; I'll use the table knife on his."

They began working with the phones in their laps, their backs to Jess and Daniel's approach. Cam said, "This will help because the SIM card carries not only a person's identification and phone contacts, but also has LAI—location area identity. You make a call and that information is sent to a mobile operator network."

I glanced up from the dogs. Saddler got the back off Daniel's phone, lifted out a tiny card, then reached for my phone from Cam. My heart pumped uncomfortably; I wasn't cut out to be in crime. My sons, however, worked with ease and efficiency. I leaned sideways in my chair to pet the dogs again and pictured Daniel's tiny card floating in the ocean below us. I wondered briefly what

Gina would think if she called me and Daniel answered. Was that how it worked?

Saddler handed me Daniel's phone and my own. "See? They both look like they always did."

Jess and Daniel returned up the steps just as I was placing Daniel's phone back on the table.

I looked up. "It's yours." I held my own phone in the folds of my skirt, then rustled a hand in my pocket, pretending to find my phone there. "Checking for messages." Opened it, closed it. I flicked a glance toward my sons, and they both looked at me the way they did when I skied an especially skinny, steep path through trees without wiping out. But I was sticky with nervousness and breathing funny, too.

Daniel sat on the edge of his chair and said, "I'm going to have to take you up on that offer with Jeter." The dog rose from beside the chair at the sound of his name. Jeter pressed his forehead against Daniel's knees, and Daniel laid both hands on Jeter's ebony head, then rubbed his neck. He bent to whisper a few words in his dog's ear.

Tears filled my eyes.

Jess said, "We'll take good care of him, Daniel. You can count on it."

"Thanks, Jess." Daniel nodded to him. "Thank you."

We set up a plan for getting Jeter back to Daniel, if at all possible while I was still in Florida.

"I won't put Annie in any danger, trying to get Jeter back, Jess. Hope you know that." Daniel looked down at Jeter, then back up. "And I appreciate your coming today; I wanted us to meet. You guys, too." Daniel included my sons, then scanned the water.

Jess asked, "See anything?"

"Not yet. But Parson is persistent." Daniel reached for his iced tea, keeping one hand on Jeter's head. "He's got all the cards for a showdown. Parson realizes now I won't be partnering with him. I can see he isn't accepting that." Daniel finished his drink. He set his glass down. "I didn't think he would."

He stood, pocketed his phone. He tossed some money on the table for the bill, insisting this was his treat. He shook hands with Jess, Cam and Saddler. He nodded to me, and I felt just like Jeter did. I wanted to press my forehead against Daniel in a long good-bye. Likely, neither Jeter nor I would see Daniel again.

Daniel walked away. I held on to Jeter's collar, soothing him— and myself—as we watched Daniel disappear down the steps.

During the drive back to my apartment to pick up our suitcases and the supplies I'd packed for the houseboat, I worked on the lump in my throat. Already I missed Daniel. Even in the presence of Jess and my sons, something about him stirred me. And I was worried about his safety.

Jess, the boys and I drove down to the Keys straightaway. Daisy and Marcus were bringing Dad. They would arrive on Islamorada a couple hours before us in order for Marcus to check out the boat and fill out the paperwork for the rental and insurance.

"Just enough time," Jess said, driving down US-1, "to completely destroy order on the houseboat. If I find your brother-in-law's wet bathing suit on my pillow or the twins' sandals on the breakfast table, I'm jumping overboard."

Like he was Mr. Tidy. He'd already started collecting pamphlets, brochures and free magazines about every tourist attraction on the Gulf of Mexico, and they were all flung across the back window ledge of my car. Next they'd be lying atop every horizontal surface of the boat. I wanted to enjoy my family, so I'd lowered my expectations for this trip to merely hoping that my dad acted halfway sane and the sugar ants weren't packed in Daisy's luggage.

We arrived at the pier in Islamorada and greeted Marcus, then toured the boat. We found Dad checking the view from the upper deck. He greeted each of us with hearty thumps on the back that made us look like bobble heads as we absorbed his affectionate pounding. Daisy and the girls were out looking for a store; she'd forgotten something. Jess and Saddler left to unpack the car, while Cam and I put away supplies in the tiny kitchen. I still thought about Daniel.

"Do you think the phone thing will work?" I asked Cam. My voice sounded raw and I cleared my throat to cover up. I handed him a six-pack of yogurt to set in the refrigerator.

Cam said, "One catch. I know there's an FCC regulation that you have to be within twenty miles of a cell tower for a nine-one-one call to be traced, so same deal for any call. Mr. Fields might have connections, but he still needs cell towers to trace location." He checked his watch. "We don't have time to move out of range tonight. Houseboats are slow. So that's no problem."

"What do you mean?"

His father called him to help carry Shank's cooler of fish, and before Cam ran off, he said, "Houseboats only go a few miles an hour." I knew that. I had meant, what did our houseboat trip have to do with cell-phone towers? I followed him down the pier to the parking lot to find out and saw that Daisy had just returned. Nell and Libby came running toward Cam and Saddler, flying across the final couple feet, both angled to leap into a cousin's arms.

After the hugs and greetings, Libby said, "Mommy forgot to pack our wonderwear."

Cam held her on his hip. "Wonderwear?"

Saddler held Nell.

"Underwear," I explained. "Their panties have Wonder Woman on them."

Nell said, "So we have to wear our baby suits."

Jess joined us, after having hugged Daisy. He said, "Are those kind of like birthday suits?" His question set off extended giggling from the twins, heads tossed back, their moon faces catching the sunlight.

That one I couldn't translate. Jess made another stab at it. "Bathing suits?"

We finished unloading supplies, stretched sheets on beds, gassed up, filled water tanks. And were off. Our destination was a small island on a map dotted with small islands. Our plan was to anchor there before dark. Marcus, our designated captain, said, "No problem."

Jess and I sat up on the top deck and watched the scenery glide by, a big blue platter of sky above us with a gathering of clouds toward the west. The water was smooth and glossy, the breeze surprisingly stiff on the upper deck. Cam climbed up and asked to borrow my cell phone and sat with it on the other side of the deck. He'd borrowed it earlier to make calls on our way down the coast.

I said, "Cam, where is your own phone?"

"Guess."

"You've broken it again?" I asked.

My dad followed his grandson up the steps. He called over to Cam, "If you're ordering pizza delivery, no anchovies or black olives for me." It was becoming more difficult to know when Dad was joking and when he wasn't. So I offered a grin that would serve in either case.

The houseboat moved slowly into the gulf. As nervous as I'd been while doing the switch with Daniel's phone, it seemed a rather silly prank to me now, a mild response to a situation my family and I only vaguely understood. Parson Fields probably had more to go on than some tiny card location. Then again, my sons might be right in thinking that their trick would slow and confuse Fields enough to give Daniel extra time. Out here on the quiet blue water with the family, it felt more like an unnecessary inconvenience to me, and probably also to Daniel, to be without our contact numbers.

I asked Cam, "So are you putting your tiny card thing in my cell?"

"No, I'm making calls with Daniel's SIM card in case anyone is tracking."

Jess said, "What's he talking about?"

"I don't know."

Dad said, "That's just how I feel sometimes. I don't know what the heck anybody is talking about." He didn't seem to mind; he leaned over the railing and hummed "Biko."

I was reminded of my earlier question. "Cam, what did you mean about cell towers and all that? And tell your father what you and your brother did with Daniel's phone."

When Jess heard, he leaned over the upper deck railing and called, "Saddler, get your ass up here."

I said to Cam, "You guys dropped that little card in the water at the Turtle Nest, right?"

"No, we got it."

Jess said, "You idiots. Where the hell is it?"

"In Mom's phone."

Dad broke into full voice. He stood at the front of the upper deck, the wind blowing back his thick silver hair, and sang loudly, "Biko, Bi-ko-oo-oo, Biko."

Saddler came up the steps, fully aware of the tension in the air and his likely role in it. To blunt the force of the coming confrontation and to divert attention from himself, he said, "Grandpa, did you know you're singing about a famous black man from Africa?" Saddler grinned. His grandfather's bigotry was an old family fact.

Dad paused, looked stumped for a moment, then said, "I'm singing about a famous game. Bingo." He turned his back to us, faced out toward the wind and water again and picked up his song.

Jess was angry. "What the hell were you two thinking? Whoever might be tracking Daniel is now tracking us. You've put your whole family in danger. Do you realize that?" He glared at his sons. "What made you two do such a stupid, damn-ass thing? Afraid you'd be bored hanging out with your relatives?"

That remark summed it up, I realized, as my sons confessed. They had expected to be bored out of their minds. Cam had wanted to spend spring break back home with his friends who were also returning home from colleges across the country to ski for a week. Saddler had wanted to spend it with Ella in Telluride. But they were worried about how the first meeting would go between their father and me. They had sacrificed their plans, believing that Jess and I needed them more. I was dismayed that they were so careless as to endanger others in their pursuit of excitement, but also touched that they had given up their vacations for the family. How could I have thought the company of adult relatives and four-year-old twin cousins was a match for anything else they could have planned? Maybe I had needed our sons present for this reunion with Jess more than I had acknowledged to myself.

Cam handed me my phone as if he were separating himself from the evidence.

Jess herded us all down below and told his sons to explain to the family what they'd done and the danger they had put them in.

It was hard to break the holiday spirit. Marcus and Daisy made jokes about being arrested, and the twins picked up on it. Nell cocked a hip, pointed a finger at her father, and said, "Stick-ed your hands up."

And Libby did the same. "You're under arrested."

Daisy said, "We're not feeding any pirates."

Marcus said, "We have plenty of food. Just don't give them our beer."

The boys were relieved by the reaction and practiced dueling with the barbecue forks. It went on like that until we all relaxed and even I began to believe nothing would come of the prank.

We pulled out drinks and snacks. Cam and Saddler argued over how to season the fish fillets for grilling. We reached our tiny island, dropped anchor in time to gather on the back deck and watch the sun set. Bands of juicy colors were shelved for the night, one on top of the other, in the western sky. Swathes of glitter spread across the water. As we all stood there together, silently awed by the beauty, I looked at my family's faces aglow in the golden light of the evening and the silvery glimmer reflected off the water. I felt grateful and full of love for each of them: Jess, my sons, Dad, Daisy, Marcus and the little girls.

Suddenly my eye caught something unusual.

I pointed off starboard. Dolphins. Eight of them broke through the glittering water, arced in the sunlight, seemingly smiled at us, nosed back into the water. We all laughed right out loud with the marvel of it. And again the dolphins surfaced, performing for us over and over. The sun fell below the watery horizon, the light faded quickly to deep gray and the dolphins swam out of sight. Then we wandered back through the hallway of the sleeping rooms to the front deck and gave our attention to dinner preparations.

We heard them before we saw them.

Abruptly chilled, I shuddered at the muted sounds of approaching boat motors and wondered how many there were and what would happen next. Somehow I'd only pictured a single boat with a wan and aged-looking man asking for Daniel. Except that wasn't his name, was it? I didn't know his real name. And not even knowing that, what made me think I could know what to expect?

Right then my cell phone rang—or was it really Daniel's cell phone? For a moment that ring unnerved me completely. Then I answered.

"Annie, you dope. What the hell did you do?"

"Just bought you a little time, Daniel. And it wasn't my idea; it was my sons'." I made eye contact with Jess and he moved closer while watching the darkness in the direction of the motor sounds. Were there two boats, three? Would people have guns?

"Well, drop the son-of-a-bitching phone in the drink, then get the hell out of there. Where are you?"

"On the houseboat off Islamorada a couple hours." I'd never heard Daniel sound angry before. "What . . . what do you think will happen?"

"I think, like I told you, that Parson will pull in all his favors and they probably include the FCC and the go-fast officers. Even I don't know how far his reach extends. Annie . . . My God, I hate having you involved in this."

"We hear them coming, Daniel."

"Remember one thing, Annie. They are acting illegally. They have no jurisdiction over you, despite what they say and how official they look."

"Okay, okay. That's good."

"Let me talk to somebody who knows exactly where you lie. I'm calling the MEOs, in case things get nasty."

As I walked toward Marcus, I asked, "MEOs?"

"Marine enforcement officers."

I handed the phone to Marcus.

"Yeah, Daniel." Marcus gave Daniel the proper information, then asked, "We're not in any danger out here, are we?"

I looked out into the deep blackness of sky and water and denser black of the tiny island our houseboat huddled beside. Everybody had stopped dinner preparations and stood on the deck, listening. From the muffled sound of the motors, I suspected the boats were approaching the other side of the hummock we were anchored near. In contrast to the motors, the slap of water against the hull of the houseboat had a steady, soothing beat.

Marcus said, "Okay, we'll stall them then." And he handed the phone back to me.

Daniel had hung up. Making his call, I supposed, to the MEOs. I had already forgotten what that stood for, aside from help for us. Then the phone rang again and I answered.

Daniel said, "MEOs on their way. Until then, I told your brother-in-law that there'll be threats nobody can carry out. But there will be threats. Stand firm. Give them my phone if they ask for it. And remember what I told you about Jeter."

I said I remembered what he'd told me. Then I asked if he was safe.

Daniel said, "I'm not in danger at the moment; don't put yourself in any. Tell them whatever they want to know. Take no chances." Quietly, he said my name: "Annie." Then the line went dead.

I passed on Daniel's information to the others.

I looked up into the black sky, blacker even than in Jackson Hole. In my valley the high altitude snowfields and glaciers always reflected light, no matter how little came from the moon and stars at night. Here, no moonlight, no shore lights, no lights from anywhere but the dim battery-run lamp inside our kitchen and the running lights around the hull of our boat. It was as if the thick mangroves soaked up all available illumination.

Then suddenly light was everywhere. From each side of the small island strong spotlights appeared and moved directly toward us. As one, we all raised hands to shield our eyes.

Libby said, "Daddy, now we can swim, 'cause we got lights." Except that she said "smim" with her sweet mouth twisting around the word. Nobody laughed. The family's joking had halted.

Marcus lifted both girls into his arms and Daisy stood beside him, holding Bijou, as they waited like the rest of us to see what would happen next.

Moments ago there was our boisterous family, living proof that nothing unpleasant could interrupt our fun, the twins "accidently" dropping chips in the water to feed the fish, my sons and my husband and I enjoying our first reunion since the New Year, and Jeter and Bijou—as Jess had so crudely put it to the boys—getting more petting than a cashmere sweater on date night. Spread around the deck were open sodas and bags of snacks. All this in celebration of Dad out for a final adventure with his family.

Then all hell broke loose as the loud boats sped in close, attaching themselves to us like tacks to a magnetic. In seconds, five men boarded the houseboat with commands to stay put, keep our hands in view.

"You are boarded by officers of the U.S. government."

Four men were in uniform. One older man in plain clothes gave the orders to us. No one flashed badges or ID.

I was shaken. Filled with horror at what my family had been drawn into. I had trusted and befriended a man I didn't know well, and dragged everybody I loved into this with me. Then, in the midst of the self-attack inside my head and the racket outside of it, I heard Jeter's low hum of a growl and saw him crouch beside me. I realized at the same moment that I did trust Daniel, had from day one. I was about to reprimand Jeter when Daniel's reminder on the phone recalled what he'd told me before handing his dog into my care a week ago.

"Always friendly. The only exception is Parson Fields. I took Jeter to the hospital grounds for a couple walks with Parson while he was recovering. Something happened behind my back. Jeter turned on that guy and Parson got rigid with fear."

"We're looking for Nickerson Addis. Tell him to come forward and we'll be on our way."

Dad spoke right up. "Here's your man, boys." He walked directly to Jess, gripped his shoulder, gave it a little shake. "Sorry, son, but you've been caught."

"Dad," I said.

"Dad," Daisy said.

The twins laughed. "Pop-pop's acting silly."

Marcus quieted his daughters, one on each arm, their bare knees clinging to their father's middle.

Jess stepped forward. "Officers, we'll cooperate. Tell us what you need."

The other officers maintained their silence, as their leader spoke for them. He needed Nickerson Addis, aka Daniel Taylor, recently of Hibiscus, Florida. Last address: Hibiscus Marina. He was wanted for a federal offense, and anyone who obstructed the law would also be considered a federal offender.

Jess asked, "Do you have a search warrant?"

"The marina," Dad said. "This is your guy. Don't take my daughter Annie. She didn't know. I saw one of you fellas; I knew something was up." Dad gestured. "Well, here he is."

"Dad, this is my husband, not the man you met at the marina."

Jeter began creeping his way across the deck, lips pulled back, rumbling louder, and I admonished myself for paying attention to my father instead of the threat at hand. I stepped toward the dog and laid my hand on his head to halt him.

Jess said, "I see no legal search warrant. None of you has any business being here."

Cam warned, "Dad, better cool it."

Both sons stepped up closer to their father.

Jess said, "Mr. Fields, leave right now and take these men with you."

Jess kept his eyes on Parson while he checked in quietly with me. "Are you sure?" Like me, Jess suddenly questioned his knowledge about Daniel.

"I'm sure." I spoke loudly to overcome the threatening sounds emitting now from Jeter, whose low, menacing rumble had escalated into a loud, aggressive growl.

Parson's eyes started shifting from Jess' face to the dog.

"Uh, better grab the dog, lady."

Jess said, "Mr. Fields, you need to leave our boat now."

I added, "I can't control this dog. Only Daniel can do that and he isn't here." I lifted my hand from Jeter's head, and he began to inch his way toward Parson. Parson backed up, one step, two, and the four officers separated themselves from their leader. Jeter bellied across the floor after Parson, growling louder.

"Would never bite anybody, even Parson," Daniel had said. I hoped he was right. I didn't want Jeter to hurt anyone. The dog was frightening when he showed his teeth and glared fiery-eyed. Still, I didn't call Jeter to me.

It was a standoff in slow motion between Jeter and Parson Fields, with incremental moves on both sides. As alarmed as I was, everything else faded to these two forces. Time became a taut line, and I hung on to it. I hoped help would come soon. The four officers stepped back onto their go-fast boats.

Saddler said, "Mom, better call off the dog."

Jess said, "Parson Fields, leave our boat."

"Mom," said Saddler. "The dog."

"Mah-om," Cam repeated.

"Mom, these . . . are . . . officers . . . of . . . the . . . law." Saddler spoke with his eyes on Parson Fields and the four uniformed men.

And Cam repeated, "Officers of the law, Mom." Both boys sounded afraid.

I had no intention of calling off Jeter.

"Men, that's Nick's dog." Parson kept his eyes on Jeter. "Nick is on board this boat."

The four officers were talking quietly together with their heads cocked back, looking upward as a sound came from above.

"Call the dog off, ma'am." Parson took another two steps backward. "Now," he commanded. No guns. I was watching that closely; I didn't want Jeter hurt.

Now the family, too, looked skyward.

"What your men are hearing, Mr. Fields, is response to our call for help."

Was Jess bluffing? Marine . . . something officers, Daniel had said. Help should arrive from the water, shouldn't it? Why was everyone looking up?

Then our attention was brought down to the deck with a loud bark from the dog. Jeter had backed Parson Fields to the very edge of the deck. Parson held his own for a moment, then fell overboard backward, arms waving in the air, legs kicking, mouth shouting garbled threats.

Maybe I'd watched too many Wile E. Coyote cartoons with the boys when they were little, but I'd have sworn that Parson spent a long moment paddling the air before the big splash came. Silence then, until his head surfaced and we heard sounds of gasping for breath and floundering beats on the water.

Nell's surprised laughter curled into the quiet; Libby joined her. "That man forgot to put on his baby suit before he smimmed."

Our anxiety eased, and we all laughed a bit. Even the go-fast officers.

That was when I remembered this man had recently experienced an aneurism.

I ran to get the lifesaver that hung on the outside cabin wall, but two of the four officers, standing in their own boat, which sat lower in the water, reached down, gripped Parson beneath the arms and pulled him in.

Then the air and water churned wildly. I looked up to see a helicopter hover over the water beside the mangrove hummock. My hair slashed my face, my skirt strangled my knees and all our bags of chips and boxes of crackers flew off tables and whipped around the floor of the deck. From the helicopter a bright circle of light shone down on us. I let go of the lifesaver and went to the edge of the deck to hold Jeter.

"You folks okay down there?" boomed a hearty-sounding voice over a loudspeaker.

Jess signaled that we were fine.

"Nick Addis sends his greetings and his gratitude." The voice was disembodied in the bright light and whirring racket of helicopter blades, but had a Southern lazy, good tone that comforted me.

The family cheered.

"He sends his greetings to you, too, Mr. Fields. And your friends. No gratitude, though. Hurry on back to Key Largo now, boys. We got some talkin' to do. You all been misbehavin' something awful."

This guy was having as much fun as my family was having once again.

Jeter kept his hackles raised and his stance stiffly on guard facing the dripping Parson Fields in the go-fast boat. I knelt down and calmed Jeter with long strokes down his back. Parson wiped his face and head on a balled-up jacket, then shouted toward the hovering helicopter, "Who's up there?"

"No friends of yours. Get goin' now."

The man in the helicopter had said "friends," and I wondered suddenly if Daniel—or rather Nickerson Addis, or Nick—was in the helicopter himself. Who knew what was possible? Though I had a strong feeling . . . and so did Jeter. Kneeling beside him with an arm hooked around him, we both stretched our necks upward. The feeling became stronger. I made a fist with my right hand and knocked it lightly against my heart, two times. My family would assume it was a gesture of gratitude to the pilot, and maybe that was all it was.

Then, amazingly, the helicopter wagged its tail, side to side, and so did Jeter. He relaxed against me, and we looked up toward the great friendly bird, its windows shining like onyx against the night, no faces visible. But perhaps Daniel—or Nick—was up there looking down at us.

Next the helicopter followed the go-fast boats around the hummock, then out of sight, toward the Keys.

We all stood with our arms wrapped around ourselves from the wind stirred by the chopper blades and listened to the motors of the go-fast boats and the helicopter fade, as the mangrove hummock absorbed the sounds and the air settled into stillness again. My eyes adjusted to the dim light. I petted Jeter and wondered if I would learn someday whether Daniel had been in the helicopter.

Dad said to Jess, "Well, son, you got away with it again." He shook his head at the trickery as he checked the water and sky, then looked around at the mess on deck, bent and picked up a bag of chips from the floor, reached in and ate one.

Thirty-six

Jess

I did something rash. As soon as I got home from Florida, I signed up for a ten-day silent-meditation retreat. Should have tried ten minutes first. Ten minutes of being silent . . . or meditating . . . or retreating. I felt like an impostor here, and I was.

When I first heard about it, I thought, There's my answer. I'd been feeling desperate to come up with something to help me absorb the past sessions with Lola and a way to figure everything out before Annie got home. Because after returning from Florida, I knew that if I didn't make a damn big turn-around—and quickly—our marriage would develop a slow leak that I would hear hissing in the background all of our days and nights until our love lay as flat and lifeless as an old rubber raft with too many patches.

At the Orlando airport Annie and I had sent the boys off, then waited for my flight to board. We stood together near the security gates, faces close, holding hands. People swarmed around us. Announcements droned overhead.

I said, "Annie, I'll do anything—*anything*—you need to make us work."

How she responded scared me so badly, I still felt my heart crumble into freeze-dried little bits when I thought of it.

She said, "Jess, I don't need you to do anything at all. I'm fine."

To me that felt like a loosening in my belay rope—whatever safety I had in this marriage had just given out. Something had finished, something else had started. And I didn't know what the goddamn something was.

If I went back to see Lola—and maybe she wouldn't even take me back as a client—I'd need to report some progress, and I had nothing to offer her.

Besides that, I'd gotten tired of going home to a cold, lonely house every night. I heard about this getaway in a nice lodge, with people to keep me company and three meals a day cooked by a chef, plus a bedtime snack. Since the store was closed now for off season, it seemed the perfect thing to do. So I arrived at the lodge in Granite Creek Friday evening, got settled in my small room, went to the dining room for dinner.

Vegetarian.

Worry number one.

But the food was delicious. Next we sat in meditation for *forty-five minutes.*

Worry number two.

The first twelve minutes I felt all smoothed out, and my legs were comfortably curled into themselves. I sat there feeling like a real meditator, a real spiritual dude. I was calm and happy and content, all at one time. Then my toes fell asleep. Then my whole foot turned numb and next the deadness moved on up to my calves, to my knees, to my thighs. Next—this, I'd never heard of—half my crotch lost sensation.

I was sure this was not a good thing, and I spent the rest of the meditation in fear that gangrene would set in. Would Annie be sorry then that she'd left? In my mind, I composed my end of the telephone call in which I'd report to Annie that I had gangrene in my testicles.

Was this possible? Should I scream for help? I opened my eyes a bit and every single person sat still as stone in the circle. Must have been twenty-five of us. A pillar candle was set in the center of the circle and another just in front of our teacher. Behind the sitters, small altars stationed here and there held Buddha statues and little brass cups filled with water, vases of flowers and more candles. The room was a hunting lodge normally, but the local group, the Teton Sangha, had turned it into a serene meditation hall. I lifted my eyes to stuffed heads of elk, pronghorn antelope, deer—white-tail and mule—mounted on the walls. Buddhists don't believe in killing animals, not even for their meat, so it was pretty funny to have the retreat in a hunting lodge. Candlelight glittered in the glass eyes of the animals, and the sangha had draped each one with a white silk scarf around its neck—a kata, I learned it was called. Meant to express honor.

Finally, our teacher hit the singing bowl with his wooden gong three times, ending the sit, and announced that we would do a short walking meditation before meeting back here for the dharma talk.

Walk, ha.

I was locked into position on the floor, a long way from even rising from the cushion. I used both hands to lift my right foot, then slowly laid my leg out straight. It buzzed and sizzled, and while I waited to see whether I'd need hospitalization, I slid the other leg straight and waited for it to come more alive. With both legs stretched before me, I looked around; I wasn't the only one taking my time getting up. Also I noticed some of the guys sat on two cushions, which raised them higher, giving their legs more room. I'd try that next time, because I had to come up with something; there were nine of these sits each day. But I couldn't think about that right now.

While I limped over to get another cushion, I noticed a stack of back jacks, little floor cushions with back rests attached. Took one of those. I could sit with my back against this and my legs straight out if I needed to. Maybe this was going to be okay. At least it would give me time to figure out my escape.

During the first dharma talk, we took the Buddhist vows to

honor the five precepts for the duration of the retreat. No killing (that referred to animals for meat, not each other); no sex (this definitely referred to each other); no stimulants such as alcohol and drugs; no unnecessary talking; no stealing. Suddenly I wanted it all: meat, alcohol, drugs, talk, sex, even things I never cared for like cigars, pornography, heroin—urges just rose up one after the other. So what was it like to shoot up heroin? I should find out.

I fell into bed that first night, thinking that I didn't really like anybody there, and I'd made a major error in signing up. I was probably just showing off for Annie, which was pointless because there were no phones, e-mail; even cell phones didn't work down that canyon, so I couldn't call and find out how impressed she might be.

That night at dinner we'd been told to select a tea mug and write our name on masking tape and stick it on. Our job was to take care of that mug, use it, wash it, keep track of it throughout the retreat. Easy. I had nothing else to do. Chimes rang to signal waking up, meditations, dharma talks . . . didn't even need to keep track of time, only a tea mug.

I lost three mugs by the following afternoon. Three mugs floated around the lodge with my name on them in bold Magic Marker. The place was not that big, but I couldn't find them and I was thirsty. Couldn't get a drink of water without my tea mug. This mug deal was sort of an exercise in mindfulness—we walked and ate in mindfulness, which meant we were paying attention, aware of our actions. Mindful people did not lose their tea mugs, much less three of them.

I headed back toward the dining room for my fourth tea mug, deciding this time I was not putting my name on it, only an initial. I walked in and there on the windowsill, beside the tea station, were my three mugs, all with my name on them: JESS, JESS, JESS. Somebody had found them, when I had failed to, and set them there. The whole damn place couldn't miss the message in that.

Quickly I ripped the tape off two of the mugs, and from then on I found myself snapping my head around to be sure my one and only mug didn't travel off without me.

Today, Sunday, some lucky ducks went home. They only signed up for the weekend. I spent every meditation session this morning, starting at five forty-five, trying to figure out how I, too, could casually pick up my zafu (took me a while to catch on that was the cushion I sat on) and my zabuton (the pad the zafu sits on) and scuttle the hell out of here. Forget the money I paid. Shit, forget the zafu and zabuton. Get out, I shouted in my head. Get out now.

But then, during a walking meditation, I realized that if I left, I'd feel like I did about the rest of my life: a dropout. Not exactly a failure, rather someone who left the scene one way or another before anyone could attach the label of failure to me, including myself (and highlighting Annie—who never actually used the nasty word). And, of course, my history, that backward glance that showed the path behind me strewn with unfinished projects, unmet promises, intentions that once throbbed with pink-cheeked enthusiasm, then paled from lack of nourishment, like a young boy starved of milk . . . or meat. My God, I'd give anything for a steak. A steak, onion rings, a baked potato, a bottle of beer.

But I was supposed to be meditating, not planning menus.

Walking meditation was the strangest of all the activities I'd engaged in during this retreat. It was a slow motion of lifting the heel, lifting the ball of the foot, lifting the toes. Move the foot forward; shift weight. Do the same with the other foot. All for only ten to twenty feet before turning around and going in the other direction. Back and forth.

Sometimes a force just rose up inside my chest, and I took off at a rowdy clip down the dirt road, walking as fast as I could before breaking into a jog, running until I exhausted myself.

This time, I tried to stick to the program. I staked out a stretch of snow-free ground beneath a big spruce, walked from a mushroom that had popped up overnight, moist dirt still stuck to it, to a dark stone a dozen feet away. Turned. Headed out on the long, tedious journey with eyes on the mushroom. Soon I was getting into the rhythm and it felt good.

Walking meditation was not what I expected would be the strangest thing about this retreat. I thought the strangest thing— aside from me in attendance—would be the silence.

Turn at the mushroom, head for the rock.

Everyone I told about this retreat said the same thing: *Silence? You mean like no talking?* But that part was the easiest. No talking felt completely natural. The underlying idea was that there was no talking even with your eyes. No need to look at anyone, nod or smile when passing on the steps or when eating at the same table. Do you know what a relief that was? Usually you only get to do that at home when you're mad at everyone.

Turn at the rock, head back toward the mushroom.

Still, this was no picnic. Walking meditation was followed by sitting meditation, followed by . . . you got it . . . walking meditation. All day long, interrupted only by meals. With my eyes on the mushroom, I wondered why I had chosen something so hard for myself.

Right then, a squirrel scampered out of the tree above me, ran over, snatched my mushroom and tore off. I stopped in my tracks. My eyes had been *glued* on that damn mushroom; I felt jarred to my bones by its sudden disappearance. And mad as hell. The little shit. Who did he think he was, taking my mushroom?

Then I remembered my new training: cling to nothing, everything changes, all living things suffer, have compassion. I looked up, and the stinker was watching me from a branch with his little seed-shaped eyes, my mushroom in his paws.

"Hell, you can have it. Don't want you to starve." Then I quickly glanced around to see if anyone caught me breaking silence. With a squirrel.

The bell rang for sitting meditation and I sent the squirrel *metta,* which is Pali for "loving kindness," and headed for the lodge. Back on my cushion, I thought of how this began. Three weeks ago I overheard some people in the store talking about a Vipassana retreat and it actually rang my bells—to make a bad retreat pun. This is it, I said to myself. Ten days of being alone, in silence, no distractions, getting it all figured out, just thinking about my life.

First thing I learned was that we were not supposed to be thinking at all. That was not meditation. If I'd gotten it right, meditation was sitting in stillness, as if "beside a river," Luke told us. "A river of thought, sensation, emotion." Focus on the breath, let the river flow by, do not engage in it. Vipassana, another Pali word meaning "insight meditation," was a form of Buddhism that emphasized a kind of intuitive knowing, a thing I could find handy right now. So here I was: knees kinked, feet tucked into my crotch, back ramrod straight, hands curled on my thighs, head racing with menus, conversations with Annie, stories from my past that ran on circular tapes, just repeating themselves over and over. Little things surfaced and I got pissed off at total strangers from the past; somebody who boisterously called for their money back at the end of their vacation after skiing in our brand-new gear, bought when they first arrived. Then I got furious at the credit card companies that backed up bums like that, plus charged *our store* extra when their own cheap cards wore out and *we* had to manually punch the numbers in. I sat here on my cushion, my zafu, steamed at these people. I got hot and antsy, and everything itched as I argued in my head, knowing I was right, and they were wrong.

Breathe, for God's sake. Shut up and breathe. Just let it all go: the cheap bum, the credit card company. Let it go.

I shocked myself during my personal interview with Luke Trapper, our teacher. I told him about letting my mom die when I was a kid. I choked up, too. And this, after he told the whole circle that others were trained to help with our stories; he could help us with our meditation.

Luke and I were alone in the small library of the hunting club, each on straight chairs angled toward each other. Beside us on a round table sat a lit candle, a box of tissues and a clock. Luke scheduled individual time with each participant. He listened to my story with soft eyes.

"Stuff like this comes up when we sit with ourselves. It's important work. Let it come," he said.

"My wife left," I blurted. Geez, was I going to tell him the size of my underwear? "She loves me, but she left. I don't know how this is connected, but I think it is."

Luke said, "Your story is more than a difficult memory; the enormity of the grief impressed you as a young four-year-old boy with such force that the pattern of behavior—falling asleep in one form or another—likely has formed a template for your life."

Luke checked my eyes with this comment and saw the affirmation in them. It was true. In fact, right then, instead of talking about this more, I felt a strong urge to space out.

Luke went on. "Notice this desire to disconnect. Acknowledge it. And when the memory of your mother's death arises, accept the emotions that arise with it. Be aware of how your body feels and give attention to the desire to escape the feelings. If you'd like to stop this memory from chasing you, this is a good, safe place to let it catch you."

I said, "For a guy who claims not to know how to work with our stories, you're sure working with mine."

"There are many ways we fall asleep," Luke said. "We over-schedule, watch a lot of TV, play computer games, read spy novels—my personal favorite," he said, and laughed. "Some eat too much, drink too much. You could say our culture more than any other excels in offering a vast array of avenues to avoid waking up. None of these things are bad or wrong, but the use of them in order to avoid life is damaging."

He suggested, since I had acknowledged this pattern in my life, that I give it a little bow of honor and return to just sitting with the awareness of it. Any other kind of work was for later, for inquiry, for the inner work of getting to know myself. A retreat was for gaining intuitive insight from the quiet mind.

"Just sit with this," Luke said again.

So I sat with it.

Did I mention that we sat nine times a day? Annie would not believe this.

Things went pretty well the second half of the retreat. Except one morning I woke with the old song "Delta Dawn" in my head and couldn't get rid of it all day: "Del-ta-ah Dawn, what's that—hum-hum—you got on?"

I didn't even know the words, but I started making some up during the day. Hour after hour, singing in my head and making rhymes. Finally, I remembered to notice my breathing and the tune passed on.

Hard to describe but the last couple days of the retreat something inside me felt more . . . maybe the word was "organized." That was the only label that explained the calmness and orderliness inside my mind. It was as if a landslide had occurred years ago, early in my life, blocking the path ahead. During the retreat, boulders and stones, sand and dirt, broken trees and bruised plants incrementally moved on down the mountainside, eventually rolling into the river I sat beside, watching. A narrow path at my feet was cleared. The ease in my mind and body brought relief and gratitude.

Most of all I moved through my days with a new spaciousness in my head. My chest felt full, in a nice way, a soft swirl of feeling. Didn't know what that was about.

So head empty, heart full, I was still pretty sure I was the over-grown ski bum I had always been. Yet by the end of the retreat, I'd come a long way from that first weekend. The last day I teared up like every other person when my turn came to hold the talking stick, actually an elk antler, decorated with a turquoise stone, feathers and wrapped with rawhide. This was Jackson Hole, after all—got to get the cowboy-and-Indian thing in. That was closing council and we were to pass the talking stick and say a few things, if we liked, about our experience.

One guy said he was going to pay for two spots next time so he could eat twice as much food; he thought it was so delicious. Another said he kept expecting our teacher Luke to detach, create some distance between himself and the rest of us, but—here the fellow choked up and had to regain his voice—Luke never did, was always right there, available. I choked up then, too. That was a typical guy's experience with other men, especially leaders of any kind, including fathers—detachment. The Kleenex box got passed around the circle on that one.

I was relieved to hear one woman talk about how much she sometimes wanted to jump up halfway through a sit and snatch the gong to end it. I was embarrassed to confess how much of my own time was spent imagining the same thing.

But for me—and I said this out loud—it was being left on my own with people all around but no one to impress, no reason to act in any special way, no approval to seek, no need to make a story to explain anything. Me. Without a story. Now that was a new experience.

One more thing left to do. Call Lola, and make another damn appointment.

Thirty-seven

Annie

"Jess, you're finally back. Your phone message said you'd be gone on a retreat for a while. It was a *long* while." Not that it mattered. The store was closed now in mid-April until summer season began in mid-May, and Jess had warned me that he might go out of town.

"I know. Should have signed up for a weekend, but I signed up for two weekends . . . including the week in between them."

"You were on a retreat for ten days?"

"And nights."

"What kind of retreat? A ski retreat?"

"This is what helped me stay there the whole time, looking forward to telling you this—wish I could see your face. It was a Buddhist retreat."

I was aghast. "Buddhist?" I said it again, louder: "Buddhist? What made you do such a thing?"

"I thought they said 'nudist'—ten days, no clothes, naked women, sign me up."

I laughed. "You did not. Tell me."

"Hard to explain. Somebody came into the store—you know, like they always do—wanting to tack up posters. I read it, told the woman I'd sign up. A whim. I don't know what the hell got into me. Thought it'd be good. You know, a pretty place, somebody else cooks. There are talks in the evening, company around."

"And?"

"It was all that. It was held in Granite Creek Canyon, in the lodge near the hot springs. The food was great, the talks were exceptional . . . but it was a silent retreat for all-day meditation."

"You meditated?"

"For ten days."

He sounded proud and . . . forlorn. I got the giggles. Jess joined me, and the laughter accelerated as we both held the image of Jess sitting in meditation day after long day.

I said, "But now how do you feel about having done that?" Instantly I regretted the question. This was the kind of thing Jess hated—*How do you feel?* I started to rephrase it.

Jess butted in, "I feel good. I don't know why, but I feel good."

"Oh, gosh."

"And I'm making an appointment with Lola."

"Oh, gosh."

"You're a college student now. Expand your vocabulary."

"But . . . Jess. Gosh."

"I know."

A Buddhist retreat. An appointment with Lola. I was spinning. I alternately swooned at this news of Jess grabbing hold of his life and addressing his problems, and laughed when picturing him sitting on a cushion on the floor with his legs curled.

I asked, "What was it like?"

"Meditation is all about awareness, paying attention to your mind. And my mind is like a new puppy sometimes, got to watch it every second. Or the puppy will pee on the carpet, chew the cherrywood table leg or hide my boot. Busy scampering all over, then suddenly it falls asleep. That's me in meditation."

I laughed. But clearly something else had also happened for Jess. He was present with me; his defenses seemed at rest. We talked about the boys, the business and my classes. Seemed Jess was full of talk, as if having stored it up for ten days made it multiply and burst forth. Perfect for seeing Lola.

I mustn't expect anything, I kept reminding myself after we hung up. Yet I had reason to hope. Jess was trying to make changes. Not just talking about them, but taking action toward them. I warned myself not to alter my path because of his. If changes occurred, great. Whether they did or they didn't, I must live my life. And allow Jess to live his.

Then, as Lucille said, we could get together for dinner and have lovely conversations.

I arranged with several of my professors to work toward my degree in art therapy back home in Jackson Hole, online and during short campus sessions here in Hibiscus throughout the next school year. The college was making every effort to enable my independent study.

In Jackson Hole the main project for my art therapy degree was a program I had already begun to set up with St. John's Hospital. I had gained approval to offer art supplies and journals to patients, along with guidance from me during hospital room visits. First step was to set up a wheeled cart like the one they already used for offering patients DVDs and library books. My cart would hold sketchbooks, journals, watercolors, clay, yarn, card-making supplies. Besides earning me college credits, this project allowed me to begin my intended work of enhancing the healing process through creative energy. The hospital in Jackson Hole was supportive, and I looked forward to the work and imagined eventually pulling in artists and writers to volunteer their talents.

My creative toolbox had become more fully equipped with each skill I had been taught: encaustic, pastels, sand play. And in the next year or so of schooling, it would become fuller yet. Already I had begun picturing my life back in Jackson Hole after my final classes this spring. I intended to work part-time at TFS, and if my other two partners agreed, I'd stock a pet corner. Carry a line of collars and leashes, dog backpacks and especially my knitted sweaters.

Customers had always spent time with our dogs, since they missed their own left at home. I thought those customers might like to take back a souvenir for their pets.

I walked Jeter and Bijou to the marina during the times Daniel—or, rather, Nick—and I had agreed upon for the possibility of returning Jeter, lunchtimes on Tuesdays and Thursdays. It had been a month since our houseboat trip, and I no longer expected to see Daniel whenever I approached the pier where he had moored his boat. Still, I leashed Jeter, because the boat sat unsold and I was afraid the dog would try to board it. Today I intended to say goodbye to this place, as I was doing with all my favorite spots. Soon I would be returning home, and it looked like I'd be taking Jeter with me.

Stocker no longer sat on a picnic table wearing his wingtips and shorts, binoculars around his neck. The go-fast boat no longer sat riding the waves on the horizon. It was my habit to walk the length of the pier, past Nick's boat, to the Turtle Nest, where we had lunched together so often, then down onto the boardwalk and across the wide stretch of grassy park, dotted with Australian pines. As the dogs and I stepped off the boardwalk onto the grass, Jeter pricked up his ears, looked across the stretch of grass and trees to the parking lot, then looked pleadingly at me. I followed Jeter's look, my own heart pumping in rhythm to his excited tail wagging.

A maroon SUV was angled against the curb, wavy air emitting from its tailpipe. A man stepped out of the driver's side, leaving the car door open, and I saw it was Nick. Still not out of the woods, I guessed by his careful actions. So I didn't wave. Jeter pranced in place. I bent down and unleashed him and watched as the dog raced, ears back, teeth exposed as if in a smile, across the grassy park toward Nick, who had squatted down to catch his dog's headlong run. Nick greeted Jeter, enfolding him head to toe; then he held my eyes for a long moment.

A sob gathered in my throat.

Nick stood and motioned for Jeter to jump into the opened car door; then he turned to me. We stared at each other another long moment. Nick made a fist. He knocked it against his heart, once, twice.

I answered. I knocked my fist against my heart, once, twice.

He got in the car, pulled off and was gone.

My shoulders heaved and I swallowed hard to hold my sob, put sunglasses on and walked away, down the boardwalk.

It was difficult to concentrate on wrapping up my school semester, while saying goodbye to people I cared about, and at the same time preparing to meet my life in Wyoming. Underlying all that, worry continually churned over Dad—were we doing enough, had we thought of every possible solution, could we have prevented his strokes? All concerns Daisy and I bounced back and forth between us, while lobbing questions to every medical authority we could find. Meanwhile, we followed Dr. Jack's advice to prepare for the future.

Today I was in Stuart for my last visit before leaving Florida. Daisy and I needed to sign legal papers giving us power of attorney. We picked up Dad on our way to the lawyers. We all felt uneasy. I sat in the backseat of Daisy's van, and as often happened to people during stressful occasions, my attention latched on to the mundane. I made a mental list of the array of items strewn on the floor and seats of my sister's vehicle—a curled-up bathing suit looking as if someone had just rolled it wet off their body, crayons, photos, candy wrappers, straws, beach umbrella, boxer shorts, a stuffed monkey, sandals, hairbrush. There were nail clippings in a cup holder, fishing hooks stuck in the sandy carpet and pairs and pairs of dirty socks. I recalled having heard one of the twins say, "Mommy, we need to go shopping. We don't have any socks."

Gratitude rose whenever I thought about the success of our

trip on the houseboat. Dad had seemed to remember his best self around the family, corny jokes and all. He'd played his old tricks on the boys, despite their being college students.

"Grandpa cheats at rummy," Cam complained. "He makes me look at something, and when I do he takes an extra card off the deck."

"He pulled that on you when you were eight, pointing out the window, then stealing a bite of your dessert. Time to catch on, sweetie. Don't look."

"He told me there was a naked girl on the beach."

Those memories of our houseboat vacation, that final family trip, both cheered and saddened me. When I had decided to spend the winter in Florida last January, I had never suspected how meaningful it would be.

After the lawyer's appointment, back at Daisy's house, I set out ingredients for making soto ayam, or at least my version of the Asian chicken soup. I began to poach the chicken breasts.

"Well, hell," I said.

From the dining table, where she was reading the newspaper, Daisy asked, "What?"

I wailed, "The sugar ants are on the stove now."

"Just turn on a burner. Heats up their tiny feet and they leave."

I glared at her. She turned a page of the newspaper and continued to read. I stood before the stove for a moment, ready to give up and take everybody out to dinner. Then I turned on the burner beneath my chicken broth, and in seconds the sugar ants evacuated the stove top. I glared at her again.

Daisy laid her arm across the paper to hold it down as a breeze from the deck blossomed a page up from the dining table.

"I have a confession to make," I said to her, keeping my head lowered to chop vegetables. "There's something I want to do before leaving here, at least something I want to say."

Daisy said, "Forget it. I'm not getting rid of the sugar ants. They're part of the family."

I tossed the diced onions and sliced carrots and celery into the chicken broth, then turned to her.

"It's just . . . well, I want Dad to know that it's okay for him to talk about dying."

Daisy's eyes teared. "You think he's worried?"

"I don't know." In Dad's presence, Daisy and I had taken on the cheery position that all would be well soon, but I was feeling more and more uncomfortable with that falseness. Somewhere inside, our father may be feeling uncomfortable with that fiction, too. And if so, he was aware of the truth and facing it all alone. Dad, despite being the Big Typhoon, held some fundamental ideas that he'd left unexamined during his life.

I began to chop the cilantro. I was considering teaching Dad how to make clouds disappear. Since that morning years ago when the family sat on the beach together and made clouds disappear by following the directions in a book Cam read to us, I had held a different view of life and death. I carried the realization that nothing died; everything just changed. Clouds didn't actually disappear. They changed into another form of moistness—dew, rain, mist, another cloud.

Our family had shared the experience with Daisy and Marcus one day while on their boat, so I bounced the idea off her.

"The experience might inspire Dad and give him comfort," I said.

Daisy said, "You thought he'd be inspired by seeing the Hale-Bopp Comet, too. Remember? You took him to the beach one night to view it. Then those thirty-nine people committed suicide, and for years afterward Dad called it 'your killer comet.'"

I'd completely forgotten how he used to refer to my "sentimental crap."

Daisy said, "I don't think he'd be comforted. He'd just blame you for every drought on the planet."

Daisy and I decided we'd stop our positive talk about the future and watch more carefully for Dad's need to know the truth.

When I returned to Hibiscus, I invited Sara, Perry and Marcy to a picnic on the beach for our final gathering. Trip after trip, I carried food, wine and blankets from my car up and over the dune bridge. I had collected driftwood during the week and cached it in the sea grape for a fire tonight after the sun went down. After carrying over my last load, I pulled out the firewood and stacked it. One by one my friends appeared over the dune and walked barefoot, sandals swinging from their hands, to where I waved.

We walked along the shore before eating, stopping now and then to examine special shells, though most often we stood ankle deep in the warm salt water, waves occasionally wetting the hems of our shorts, caught up in talk. For each one of us, school had become a lively focus and had changed every part of our lives. We loved to talk about how that was going.

Perry had settled her sights on becoming a decorator; next semester she'd be taking the textiles class I had taken. Sara wanted to teach middle school. That career excited her much more than being a paralegal, which her husband had been promoting; Sara loved the energy and possibilities of preteen kids. Marcy hoped she'd discover a direction for her studies soon. She said Guy was pressuring her to choose a major and she couldn't decide on one.

I asked Marcy, "What do you want to do?"

"Thanks. I thought you were on my side."

"Sorry. I should know better. That's how I felt every time someone asked me exactly why *did* I leave on a marriage sabbatical."

"Yeah, why did you?" Marcy said.

"Okay, we're even."

"So it's the same deal," Perry said. "You had to leave Jess and create the time and space to figure out why you left, and, Marcy, you have to take some classes to figure out what you're interested in besides new cookie recipes, after all those years of being a mother and housewife."

We stayed on the beach long after dark, talking around the bonfire, hating to say goodbye. Eventually we gave in to the reality of final hugs.

Tonight I was spending the last night in my apartment. Tomorrow after packing the car and having breakfast downstairs with Shank and Lucille, I would hit the road for the long drive to Wyoming with my bird, Kia, and my pup, Bijou, in the backseat.

I had come to love so many things in Florida that I was going to miss. Hidden courtyards in Old Town Stuart with twisted ancient vines holding up the walls and stone fountains with algae-covered grout and mossy corners. The sound of raindrops on tile. Small stretches of exposed creeks between town buildings in Hibiscus surrounded by patches of dense growth. Tiny frogs leaping from trees. Blossoms wafting heated fragrance.

In Jackson Hole, extreme skiers called the response to facing something difficult "flashing the crux." When the sudden appearance of an exposed boulder looms while skiing the narrowest part of a couloir, a skier must blow through it without hesitation, just make the jump to fresh snow. That's how I'd have to leave Florida, blow through the severing without hesitation, flashing the crux.

As I completed my packing, I found Jess' note to me.

I love you for a hundred raisins.

I held the card to my heart and suddenly experienced a burst of awe over the force that had kept us together during our long history and that even now pulsed with new life and promise. I realized Jess may go only as far as he needed to in order to keep peace between us, and then backslide as usual, but we were surely more related to each other than to anyone else. Though science claimed that siblings were the closest biological relationship, Jess and I had breathed each other's moist night breath for twenty-six years, those exhalations that carry the tastes of the same foods eaten and the fragrances of each other's dreams.

Jess resided within my body. I resided within his.

Jess was a different man today from the thirty-year-old of two decades back, dressed in layers of rugged outdoor wear, coddling an infant in the crook of one arm, while promoting the merits of a Rossingnal ski held in the other. Or later when he put our toddler sons in adult-sized ski boots at the store to keep them from walking too far, too fast. Or later yet, when the four of us together skied the slopes of every mountain that circled Jackson Hole. I loved Jess then; I loved Jess now.

I pulled into my driveway, exhausted from the five-day drive across the country and exhilarated to finally be home. I sat for a moment filling my eyes with the sight of my house, its old log porch with the uneven chinking, the hundred-year-old Engelmann spruce rising beside it. I knew that any moment Jess would burst through the front door, and my heart beat fast in anticipation of seeing his face. I opened my car door and slammed it loudly. Still no Jess.

Suddenly our three dogs rounded the corner of the house, spotted me and seemed to sprout wings as they flew toward me. I bent down and held all three in my arms.

"Oh, girls, I missed you."

Tails flung themselves side to side and noses pushed into my neck, while soft, almost human sounds rumbled in their throats.

I said, "Take me to Jess."

Off they trotted, swinging their heads behind them to be sure I followed, around the side of the house where they'd come from, all the way to the small cabin in the backyard, where Jess stored his snowmobile, kayaks, fishing rods and other gear.

The cabin door hung wide-open and I stepped in.

I stood there stunned at the transformation.

Once, this cabin was piled nearly to the log rafters with Jess' junk. The floor, in the few places it had been visible, was covered with patchy old linoleum; cobwebs had draped the windows and the logs had been dull with dust. Now it was cleared of gear and boxes, carpeted, filled with sunlight, and the logs shined and smelled of Murphy's Oil Soap. The windows had been replaced, the old stove reblacked and a beautiful stone pad sat beneath it. The walls were lined with new carpentry work. Below a counter that stretched along one wall, a pair of familiar denim-clad legs protruded.

The dogs each gave a sharp bark.

Startled, Jess jerked upright and whacked his head on the ledge.

"Shit."

"Jess!"

"Annie!"

He flung aside a screwdriver he'd been holding, scrambled up and wrapped his arms around me. It felt so good to be home and held by Jess. I breathed in the fragrance of laundry soap from his shirt, cupped his warm neck in the palms of my hands and felt the length of my whole body melt into his.

"Hey," he said, pulling his face back to look at me. "How do you like your new studio?" He stepped aside, keeping one arm around my shoulder so that I could get the whole view.

"Really? For me?" My smile spread wider and wider as I took it all in—the long expanse of countertop, the shelves and cupboards. I moved around the cabin, my hands touching the smooth, clean wood. "Oh," I breathed. "My very own work space."

"I put in lighting, baseboard heat, insulated windows, and I'm just screwing the plates on the electrical outlets to finish it off."

I looked at my husband. Was this the same guy who had given me the gift of blue topaz ear studs twice in a row?

I said, "This is the best gift I have ever received."

Once, I had thought love would transform me. To me, love had that power. I had the romantic notions of a naive girl, yet I hadn't been proven entirely wrong. I looked at Jess now through different eyes from those of the girl who married him, eyes surely transformed.

So it didn't happen the way I imagined it: love through its ecstacy soaring me into magical kingdoms, inflating my world. It happened like this instead: love through its unrelenting demands pushed me farther and farther into new territory that enlarged me.

Finally I had grown from the woman who abandoned herself for the sake of others into a woman who loved herself enough to include all others.

That was how it began and now I stood on my log porch, once again watching the tulips scoop wind and the aspens sway on the slopes of Snow King Mountain, newly sprouted into pale green gauze that barely hid their limbs, reminding me as it did every year of flirtatious women wearing see-through dresses.

And beside me, Jess.

Tina Welling lives and writes in Jackson Hole, Wyoming, with her husband, John, and four-legged family members Zoë and Miko. You can reach her at www.tinawelling.com

TINA WELLING

This Conversation Guide is intended to enrich the
individual reading experience, as well as encourage us
to explore these topics together—because books,
and life, are meant for sharing.

A CONVERSATION
WITH TINA WELLING

Q. What gave you the idea to write about a marriage sabbatical?

A. Marriage can be absorbing and isolating. There are just the two of you tussling over a range of issues from the most intimate to the most mundane. Marriage partners can lose perspective after many years of closeness. Privacy within the relationship can become insulating and we can get locked into certain views.

I've been invited to attend writers' residencies that have taken me away from my everyday life for extended periods. The solitude and the absence of responsibilities that defined me at home offered new perspectives.

That's when I thought: what if a woman decided to leave temporarily to deepen a relationship with herself? In my case, there was a legitimate work reason for leaving home, but I wondered what it would take for a woman to go against the cultural grain and spend time on her own away from her marriage.

Q. You suggest in the novel that marriage is currently evolving as each generation finds new ways to address its rewards and limitations. Do you think we'll ever get it right?

A. I think we've always got it right. My grandmother Margaret's marriage was perfect for her and her times, so was my mother,

Alice's, and so is mine and my children's. Marriage presents challenges that are mirrors of our society. Yet typically each generation evolves the concept of partnering to a new level.

I like watching how emotional and physical intimacy that once was considered the wife's domain has also become the responsibility of the husband. Don't you love seeing those men with diaper bags over their shoulders? And I love how a strong sense of self, which was once the husband's domain—remember dens, those special rooms designed for a man to get away from the family and pursue his own interests?—is now also an honored pursuit of a wife.

I've witnessed among my friends the imbalances that can occur with such growth, and one of them is men holding back on the provider end, as I suggest Jess does in the sports business that he and Annie share, and the women taking charge of everything inside the home and out, as Annie did. Confusion can slip in when we share life and authority. There are few guides for evolving partnerships.

So there is no right way or wrong way. Many of us come into our marriages hoping to acquire all the love and acceptance and understanding we felt we didn't receive from our parents—plus the sizzle of sex and romance. It's a setup for all kinds of challenges.

Q. *In the conversation guide of your previous novel,* Crybaby Ranch, *you describe how that novel grew out of the exciting intersection of your own experience and your creative imagination. Was that true for* Fairy Tale Blues *as well?*

A. Definitely. For me, that's how the creative process works. The two—reality and imagination (which is to say the range of possibility I can conjure)—join and produce stories. Yet the end result is always fiction. There is nothing of the memoir in my novels. For example, the longtime love my husband and I share opens my vision to the many possibilities partnering can take and aids me in expressing the experience of deep intimacy and caring, but the result on the page does not in any way resemble my personal actions or those of anyone I know.

It's a creative process that is a microcosm of the natural world of birthing—how could it be otherwise?—in that male and female mate and the result is a whole new being. Not one or the other, but an original creation unto itself. So it is with story. Reality and imagination (or possibility) mate and the result is a unique story.

Q. Many writers say that their final work never quite lives up to their intention, never quite says all that they meant to say. What did you want to say in Fairy Tale Blues *that might not have gotten said?*

A. I wanted to say so much that I had difficulty in choosing my issues. Many issues I touched on, but wished to say more about. For example, I wanted to say, "Look what else you can do besides divorce." There are a dozen steps of separation that couples can take in response to unresolved issues, while saving the valuable parts of the relationship. I wanted to say, "Create your own form of partnering."

Q. How did the experience of writing this novel differ from your experience writing Crybaby Ranch?

A. I wrote *Crybaby Ranch* over a long period of time while I also owned a resort business in Jackson Hole, Wyoming. It's hard to write seriously while working in the business world, and I have a lot of sympathy for those who face this struggle. I've since let go of my shop. With *Fairy Tale Blues* I was able to write full-time, which was wonderful. It seemed an entirely different process. More concentrated. I loved it. The lifestyle that writing a novel demands matches me perfectly. It's easy for me to be self-disciplined. In fact, I don't even call it that. It feels more like freedom—oh good, I get to wake up and write all day again tomorrow.

Q. Do you continue to read avidly, even when you're deeply engaged in writing? Are there writers you've particularly enjoyed who have influenced your work?

A. I love to read and wouldn't stop for anything. Some writers say they can't read while writing because they find themselves aping another writer's style. I don't have that experience. Yet, in another way, everything I read influences or inspires my work. I especially love beautiful language. I become entranced by it and find that even though I am reading in bed with only the pleasure of the story in mind, I am still studying where the author placed the commas, pondering the sentence structure and word choices. I admire Barbara Kingsolver very much, her wisdom and humor. I don't know that I am particularly influenced by her, but I aspire to her vision and her skill in relating that to her readers. I am especially interested in reading poets who write novels, because of the careful language and the deep awareness for which poets are noted.

I read both fiction and nonfiction. And though I will have several nonfiction books going at once, I will usually read only one novel at a time.

Q. What do you hope to accomplish during the rest of your writing life? Do you have a long view with several projects in mind, or do you take it project by project?

A. What I love best about reading a novel is when the characters' realizations within the story clarify personal issues for me. To have a writer put words to a troublesome concern of mine is a wonderful experience that grounds me and allows me to move forward. A similar thing occurs when a writer finds the language to express beauty and insight. I glow with the celebration of it. I hope to give that to readers myself.

So perhaps I aspire to a little of both: a long view of continuing to write and offer readers the gifts I love to receive, yet the subjects are still to be discovered.

Q. You came to writing novels later in life, having accumulated much experience from which to draw inspiration. How crucial was that timing in contributing to your success? And what advice would you give other writers, both older and younger?

A. Timing is mysterious. For years I felt that my true self was a writer, yet few people acknowledged me as one, so I felt as though I lived a secret life. Perhaps the most comforting aspect about being published is that my inner and outer lives have been united.

Yet I know that if my work had been published earlier I would have given it more weight in my life than would have been well balanced for me. By the time my first novel was published, my work had been rejected by publishers for many years. I had to learn not to take that personally, or I wouldn't have been strong enough to continue to write and to fully experience the immense joy I receive from it.

Now I don't take my current success personally either. I enjoy it very much. I love the opportunities that are available to me now and the wider acquaintanceship of people with whom I interact. But being published doesn't have much to do with how I see myself, just as I had learned not to let being unpublished affect my self-image.

I think writing is like every other creative pursuit: we must do it for itself and not for any result we imagine it may bring us. Writing is our concern; what happens to it after it leaves our hands is no longer our business. For me writing is an act of unconditional love. I do it for reasons that have nothing to do with what it may bring—money, acceptance, self-esteem. As soon as I stepped onto that path of thought, something was released in me. I continued to send my work out, but I wasn't attached to it as I had been before.

I would give the advice to writers that the poet William Stafford offers in his book *Crossing Unmarked Snow* (University of Michigan, 1998): "Make writing a way of life, a practice that can lead to self-realization, to a fuller involvement in one's own experience." What could be better?

QUESTIONS FOR DISCUSSION

1. Annie realizes she has had expectations about marriage that weren't realistic. Are there fairy tales about marriage that you've believed? Has that changed over the years? How does your experience compare to Annie's?

2. Tina Welling provides snapshots of several other marriages besides Annie and Jess'. Did anything about them particularly surprise you? Appeal to you? Appall you?

3. Annie is energized and inspired by the creative projects she undertakes, but Jess disdains the high value she places on Creativity with a capital C, distinguishing between "art" and "crap." Where does your opinion fall in this age-old argument?

4. Jess is described as a "cuddly predator." Have you known any cuddly predators, male or female?

5. Annie is drawn to Daniel, a reformed drug smuggler. What is he able to provide for her that Jess can't, or won't?

6. What is the Skipper's role in the novel? How does he compare to the senior citizens you know?

7. Annie's sons help her see her marriage from a new perspective, and suggest that their own experience of marriage will be different from hers. How are the young marriages you know different from older ones? Do you see those differences as healthy and encouraging, or not?

8. Describe the role of the natural world in the lives of Annie and Jess. How important is the natural world in your life?

9. In your opinion, does Annie do the right thing in leaving Jess? Does she do the right thing at the end? What kind of future do you see for them?

10. Has there been a time in your life when you sought solitude in order to make a major decision or achieve a new understanding? What was that experience like for you, and what changes occurred as a result?

11. Annie comments at one point that many people come to know themselves through their relationships with other people. Are you that kind of person?

12. If you left your spouse temporarily, where would you go? What would you do?